PRAISE FOR *WALKING IN THE LIGHT*

"Readers will fall in love with Theodore Pitsios's Greek merchant seaman, Kostas Karaoglou, who jumps ship in New Jersey and travels to Miami's Little Havana as an illegal immigrant in pursuit of the 'Good Life.' Kostas's new friends come alive in Technicolor on every page as he explores relationships with Cuban and Haitian immigrants at the 'greasy spoon' diner where he gets his start in America and dreams of owning his own restaurant. His adventures include a racy romp across the beaches and nightclubs of Nassau, where he travels during a mandatory waiting period for his green card. A platonic marriage of convenience with a Cuban refugee who waitresses at the restaurant—the first step towards his green card and citizenship—shows hope for Kostas to find true love, and what he calls 'the desperate desire for respect and acceptance in the new environment.' Pitsios gives us all the feels, all the dreams, and even all the tastes and smells of the dishes he cooks up in the first year of his life in America."

—Susan Cushman, author of *John and Mary Margaret*, *Friends of the Library*, and *Cherry Bomb*

Walking in the Light
by Theodore Pitsios

ISBN 978-1-64663-417-0

Published by

3705 Shore Drive
Virginia Beach, VA 23455
800-435-4811
www.koehlerbooks.com

Dedicated to the memory of

Marigoula, my mother, and Brenda, my wife.

WALKING
IN THE
LIGHT

A NOVEL

THEODORE PITSIOS

VIRGINIA BEACH
CAPE CHARLES

He who walks in the darkness does not know where he goes. While you have the light believe in the light, that you may become sons of light.

—The Gospel of John (Chap. 12: 35-36)

CHAPTER ONE

My Break

Ordinary people seem to think a man has to have luck on his side to make it big in life. That's the ordinary people. I believe a man has to have the balls to go looking for his luck instead of sitting, waiting for luck to find him and pull him by the hand. And most important, a man has to have enough sense to recognize when he's getting a lucky break and jump on it.

I shifted on the mattress, trying to get away from a broken spring, and once again told myself, *It was a damn lucky break I got, no matter how bleak things seem to be right now.* I adjusted my head on the pillow and resumed staring at the ceiling. I had taken a long time to fall asleep last night, my mind reliving everything that happened the last three days on the road from Hoboken to Miami. I should have been dead tired, but instead the first light of day found me wide awake, staring at the ceiling, creating imaginary shapes out of the water stains. *That dark one, the one over the door, looks like a loaded mule. This long one right over me looks like three naked women line dancing. And the rust-colored one near the window, that could be my old ship, the* Aegean Sea.

It could be the new environment—I was used to the ship's gentle rolling and the rhythmic sound of the sea splashing against the sides—or it could be that I was too excited. After all, this was not going to be an ordinary day. This Friday, the first day of October of 1965, I would be starting my first job in America, my first step toward making it big in life.

I stretched again, then continued studying the ceiling stains floodlit by the early sunrays filtering through the newspaper taped over the window. *That big brown one definitely looks like my old ship.* Only seventy-two hours had passed since I'd left her, but already it seemed like something that had happened a long time ago. Right now the old rust bucket should be somewhere in the Atlantic, pounding the waves on her way to Aruba. The two deckhands filling in for me would probably be having a snack in the crew's lounge, griping about what crumbs they were getting paid for their overtime. And with their engine room watch over, Anastasis and Liapouras would be there too, playing backgammon for one cigarette a game.

Liapouras, who had lived a few months in Boston and knew everything about everything, would be repeating in his squeaky voice for the umpteenth time, "I knew Kostas Karaoglou would jump ship as soon as we got to America. He didn't fool me, not for one minute, he didn't." A typical ship's crew, all of them. Ordinary people with small dreams and short horizons, happy in their own little world, boasting of their petty triumphs, trying to outwit and out-insult each other, completely oblivious when a life-changing break hit them right in their face.

I spotted my lucky break the day I signed on the *Aegean Sea* and the steward put me in the same cabin with Telemahos. It took just a few minutes of talking with him to sense that he and I thought the same way. He had worked in Savannah, in America, for over a year, he told me, until a bastard squealed to immigration and they shipped him back to Greece. He was going to try it again, he said, and after he beat the daylights out of that squealer shit-pot in Savannah, he would go to work in Miami.

"There is a man in Miami who owns a fancy restaurant and a luxury-apartment rental business. His family owes my family big favors, and he told my folks he'll give me a job there anytime I want," Telemahos told me.

I convinced him that for an undertaking like this, an extra pair of eyes would be an advantage, so we made the ship-jumping plans together.

We worked out every detail of the operation with more attention and more thoroughness than the landing in Normandy. All that was left was for the ship to call on an American port.

Then Telemahos got a telegram from Greece saying his father had fallen and broken his hip and he had to dash back from Bermuda two weeks before the *Aegean Sea* docked in Hoboken.

Before disembarking, he wrote for me an introductory letter to the man in Miami. He let me read it before sealing it. *The man bringing this letter*, it started, *is Kostas Karaoglou. His father, like yours, came as a refugee from Asia Minor. He is a family relative and an honest and hard worker*. There was a line mentioning the owed favors and promises their families had made to each other, and the letter ended by saying, *Anything you do for Kostas is the same as doing it for me.*

"Thank you; that's sure to get me the job," I said, handing it back.

"He got his name Americanized," Telemahos said while writing the address on the envelope. "His real name is Stavros Allimeroglou, but now he calls himself Steve Allen. I hear he isn't the type who burdens himself with scruples, so don't expect too much. Then again, it's the same everywhere: when they know you're illegal, they'll squeeze as much as they can out of you. But any job will be okay for a start. Even Onassis started at the bottom."

"Maybe I'll get lucky," I said.

I snuck off the *Aegean Sea* half an hour before she departed Hoboken, took a bus to Pittsburgh, then headed south. Telemahos had said there was less chance of running into immigration inspectors if I took the inland route. As soon as the bus arrived in Miami, I dashed out and caught a taxi. Keeping a tight grip on Telemahos's letter, I showed the driver the address on the back of the envelope.

"Eighth Street," he read. "That's *Calle Ocho*, that's Cuban Town. You Cuban?"

I made a move with my head that could be taken for either yes or no and put the letter back in my pocket and kept my hand over the envelope. It was my ticket to the Good Life.

Twenty minutes later, the driver pulled into a parking lot. "Here you are," he said. He pointed to the Parthenon restaurant, set amid a group of one-story brick buildings that made up a small shopping center. On one side of the restaurant was a shoe store, and on the other a Western Auto.

Before going in, I sat on the bench next to the door and ran through what I would tell Steve. It was not the fancy place I had pictured, but there was no going back now. Two cigarettes later I followed a Cuban-looking couple inside. I told the waitress at the counter I wanted to speak to Mr. Steve Allen, and she went to the serving window and shouted his name. A couple of minutes later, a man appeared at the kitchen door.

"What you want?" he growled at the waitress.

"Steven, this man asked for you," she said, nodding toward me.

Steve was short, seemed to be around fifty, bald, with a thick mustache and a large, round belly. He wore a sweaty white undershirt and white pants held up by a pair of blue suspenders, and kept wiping the sweat from his head with a baseball cap that had a dolphin on the front.

"*Giasou*," he said when he got near.

How does he know I'm Greek? I handed him the letter from Telemahos, and he put it in his back pocket without looking at it.

"Come back tomorrow. I'm busy now," he said, adding to my nervousness.

"I will wait," I said and lit a cigarette.

"*Opos théleis*—as you wish," he said.

A long hour later, I was still sitting at the counter smoking cigarettes. The kitchen help and the waitresses had already left. Through the serving window I saw Steve doing the closing chores—turning off the grill and the fryer, putting the covers on the trays of the cold table. Then he emerged from the kitchen and trudged over to the cash register. He spent ages counting the money and comparing the cash register tape with the green order slips. I kept looking at him, hoping to see even a trace of something cheerful.

Finally, he slammed the drawer shut and, mumbling curses, motioned me to follow him outside. I got off the stool slowly, afraid he would notice my legs shaking. In the parking lot, he unlocked the passenger side of a white Cadillac and gestured for me to get in, then went around and flopped behind the wheel with a long sigh. He cranked the engine and we drove off.

A few minutes later he stopped at the parking lot of a pinkish building, turned the engine off, and smoked while looking at a photograph of a horse in the newspaper next to him. I pretended to study the building while watching him from the corner of my eye.

"Look," he said finally, "I read your letter, but right now I don't need anybody."

"Telemahos said you promised his family he could have a job anytime he came to you."

"That was long time ago. Things have changed since then." He wiped his forehead with his baseball cap.

"His father had an accident, otherwise he would have come too," I said. I expected Steve to ask me what kind of an accident, but he didn't. He kept looking at the paper and smoking until the cigarette was finished and he flicked it away.

"Well, since you're here, I could let you do something at the restaurant and something over here to earn your keep." He nodded toward the building in front of us. "What do you think?"

I didn't say anything.

"I'll pay you twenty dollars a week and let you stay in there for free." He lit another Pall Mall.

I took a Winston out of my pack and, while I smoked, took stock of the fix I was in. My hopes for quick riches in America had just taken a nosedive. Although twenty dollars a week was more than I had been getting on the ship, it didn't come close to the big money I had heard the Americans were making. Even the stevedores—the unskilled laborers unloading the ships—were making ten dollars for every hour they worked, I'd been told. I stared at the hood ornament, a silver statue of a curvy Greek goddess with outstretched arms and a clinging robe.

"I worked at a restaurant in Volos for a year," I said half a cigarette later. Steve didn't answer. "And I was assistant cook on the ships before I changed to deckhand."

He wiped his forehead again with the baseball cap. "Look at it this way. I'm only doing this as a favor to Telemahos's family. You'll be paying no rent, and you'll be eating free. What else is there—pussy? That's also free in this country."

I pretended to consider. "I got an old mother and a crippled brother to support back home," I said. I was sure God would forgive a small lie.

Steve seemed to be studying two women across the street. "I'll tell you what," he said. "I'll make it twenty-five dollars a week. That's as high as I'm going to go. And for that you'll have to cut the grass too." He took a deep drag on the cigarette and blew out the smoke with force. "And you better do some good work or I'm sending you back where you came from in a *jiffy*, as the Americans say. It's bad enough I'll have to worry about the fucking immigration." He put his arm on the door handle to get out.

I stared at the Greek goddess for a while longer. In my predicament, there weren't many options. I mumbled agreement and opened my door. *I'm starting at the bottom. Did Onassis start from this far down?*

"The restaurant is open only five days, Monday through Friday," Steve said when I was out of the car. "On Saturdays and Sundays, and in the mornings before you come to the restaurant, I want you to paint and do the outside chores here." He motioned for me to follow him. "Come, I'll show you where you'll stay. Is that all you got?" He pointed at the Sears & Roebuck shopping bag I carried, and I nodded.

Inside the building, Steve attempted to open the first door in a long corridor. He tried different keys from a thick cluster attached to his pants by a chain and cursed each one that didn't work. A young woman came down the hall, hugging a plastic basket overflowing with pink towels and sheets with tiny red roses on them. She paused and watched Steve for a moment. She seemed to be between twenty and thirty years old, short and curvy, with a pretty face and short blond hair, wearing a tiny top and minuscule, tight shorts.

"Excuse me," she said and tried to get around us. "Who's your good-looking friend, Steve?" she added while sliding by.

"Kostas," Steve growled as he fought with the lock.

"Oh, how nice. I'm Karen, Kostas. Sorry I can't shake," she giggled and nodded toward the basket. "I was at the laundromat." When she squeezed by me, her breasts and thighs rubbed against my back.

"Nice neighbor," I whispered when she was gone.

"She is *off limits*," Steve snapped back, the last two words in English.

"What does that mean?"

"It means stay away from her. She's the daughter of a friend. I catch you messing with her and I'll have the immigration send your ass back to your goats before you know it."

"She lives here?"

"I let her stay here to keep an eye on her kid."

I vaguely recalled that there had been a child holding on to her belt, but I couldn't remember what it looked like or if it had two heads or three legs.

"You sleep here," Steve said. He had finally found the right key.

He shoved the door open and turned on the light. I looked over the room, full of old appliances and broken furniture, and smelling of stale food.

"Pick out what you need," he said, gesturing toward a junk pile. "Some of this stuff is almost brand new. Damn pigs, they destroy everything."

I leaned against the wall and breathed in the young woman's gardenia-blossom perfume, relishing the tingle I'd felt when her body rubbed against mine. I was sure she had done it on purpose; there was plenty of room in the corridor.

"I'm going to get you some sheets and a towel." Steve snapped me out of my dream and left.

"Okay," I mumbled. I would sleep on a bed of nails just to be that woman's neighbor. I dug in the pile of broken furniture and pulled out the mattress with the fewest stains on it, then looked for a usable bed frame. Not finding one, I wrestled with the appliances until I cleared enough floor space to set the mattress on the floor, against the wall opposite a window. I put a short, doorless refrigerator next to it as a night table and stored the socks and underwear from my Sears bag in one of the stoves, draping my pants over a two-legged table and hanging my shirts from a nail behind the door.

Steve came back about an hour later, looking drained and disheveled and smelling like a gardenia blossom. He gave me a pink towel with blue seashells on it, two pink sheets, and a pillow in a pink pillowcase with red roses on it.

"You're all set for now," he said, acting as if he was in a hurry. "You can keep the pillow and the sheets. If you need any more, there is a store down the street. I'll come in the morning to show you what to do here." Before he went out the door, he turned. "Be sure to write Telemahos that I gave you a good job and a place to stay."

⁂

The light was coming in through the window stronger now, and I gave the room another look. Until I was legal, this would be my home. If I got rid of some of the junk, it would be as big as the biggest room at my mother's house. I could put a closet in the far corner and a table with a chair by the window, to sit and look out. *The hard part is almost over. All I have to do now is lie low and stay out of trouble. The good life will be here soon. Not bad for a start—better than lots of other people.*

Pavlos, my older brother by ten years, used to tell a story about a young couple from our village who migrated to Australia. When they wrote back, they said that the first few months they couldn't afford a place to stay, so they slept outdoors. They had to sleep in shifts so one of them could watch out for the snakes.

"They thought they would find it better than our Taxiarhes," Pavlos would say. Always the same words, always the same chuckle.

I looked at my watch—6:30. In Greece it was 1:30 in the afternoon. In the village at this hour, Pavlos and his mules would probably be hauling olives from somebody's grove to Gourgiotis's olive press. Unless it was raining; then he would be sleeping in the upstairs bedroom, snoring like a rock crusher. Before I got drafted into the navy, I used to help him with the hauling. He was a hard boss to please. My loading and unloading of the mules never met his approval—the flagstone loads were always unbalanced, the firewood bundles always fell too close to the mules' legs, and the chestnut sacks were always too high on the saddle.

"You never do it right," he complained. "You carry half the load and you work the beasts twice as hard. Poor things, they break into a sweat every time they see you coming." That last part always brought laughter from everyone close enough to hear it.

Funny how different some siblings could be. If it weren't for the sameness of our looks, I would wonder if we were really brothers. On the inside, our heads are completely different. I used to tease him that he got the brains of a sheep. He has not a hint of ambition and no trace of curiosity as to what the rest of the world looks like, content to spend his days in the village, right where providence dumped him. When I pointed out that Mr. Kartalis and Mr. Stakos and all the other great benefactors of our village hadn't spent their lives holding on to the tail of a mule but had gone abroad where the opportunities were, and made tons of money, Pavlos's answer was always the same. "It's all in your head."

I reached for the pack on top of the small refrigerator and took out a cigarette. Only eight left in the pack, and this was my last one from the ship. The night before, I noticed the price was fifty cents a pack at the cigarette machine in the restaurant, a huge jump from the dollar a carton I'd been paying on the ship.

I took a deep puff and exhaled. If a man hasn't traveled, he hasn't lived; that's the way I see it. And during my years as a merchant seaman, I had done quite a bit of traveling. I was only twenty-five and had already been around the globe three times. "You've gallivanted all over God's creation," my mother used to say. I had already seen and done more than the men in the village experienced their whole lives. Most of them have never ventured one kilometer beyond the mountain ridge.

Oh yes, I'd have some stories to tell my grandchildren for sure. The way I sneaked by the immigration guards at the docks in Hoboken alone was worthy of a Hollywood movie. Then the odyssey of getting from the docks to the bus stop and the zigzagging all over the country before ending up in Miami was worthy of another. All the false alarms about immigration inspections at the bus stops that afterward made me burst out laughing, and the close calls that almost gave me a heart attack, could fill a book. And God only knew how many more stories I would accumulate before children and grandchildren came along.

I took another puff of the cigarette and watched the smoke rise toward the ceiling. Yep, that stain definitely looked like three naked women line dancing—three naked women with big boobs. That ushered the Karen meeting into my mind. Had she really meant it when she called me Steve's "good-looking friend," or had it just been American politeness? I was sure she had winked at me as she went by. I would definitely try to get to know her better, and soon.

I stopped what I had been rubbing and jumped out of bed before it was too late. This would be a good time to take a shower.

Trying to force my bare feet into the shoes made me wish I hadn't left behind the *sayonares* I had bought in Yokohama. Those slippers would be handy right now. But I hadn't been able to stuff anything else into my coat pockets. I almost left behind the English-Greek dictionary, and I had worn three of everything I owned—underwear, socks, pants, and shirts, and on top of all that the winter overcoat I'd bought in Rotterdam. At the Hoboken bus station, I went to the bathroom and took off all the extra clothes and stuffed them into the Sears & Roebuck shopping bag Telemahos had given me when we were making our ship-jumping preparations.

"Always remember," Telemahos had said, "merchant seamen returning on board with bags is a normal sight, but seamen leaving a ship with bags gets people asking questions. When you're jumping ship you don't pack your bags and walk down the gangway; you wear as much as you can so you won't be buying new clothes right away, and pretend you're going to the seamen's bar or for a good-bye visit to the girls."

I drowned the cigarette in the Coca-Cola bottle I'd found half-empty in one of the refrigerators. Then I wrapped a towel around my waist, got the soap I'd brought from the ship, and headed for the shower that Steve had said was at the end of the hall. I was halfway down the corridor when I remembered that I was not on the ship anymore. I couldn't go walking down the corridors with only a towel wrapped around me. I dashed back to the room and put on a shirt and pants. When I was almost at the door, I turned back and took my wallet from under the pillow and put it in my pocket. Better be safe.

The corridor smelled musty, was cluttered with tricycles and toy wagons, and half of the ceiling lights were out. The bathroom was also stuffed—with mops, buckets, and rakes, miles of garden hose woven through them. Of the mirror over the sink, all that was left was a triangular piece and some brown tape that sometime in the past must have held the rest of the pieces together. A spiderweb extended from the showerhead to the water handles. On the walls, English and Spanish cuss words and crayon drawings of naked people could be seen through patches of thin paint. I turned the water handles, half expecting it to be a wasted effort, and got startled when hot and cold water came gushing out.

I showered, shaved, and went back to the room to pick out clothes to wear. Everything was wrinkled and smelled of sweat. Too bad I hadn't thought to lay the pants under the mattress before I slept, like I used to do on the ship. Maybe I could ask Karen to loan me her iron. Maybe if I asked her the right way, she would offer to iron them for me or even wash them. Greek and Latin American women always do that for "their man." My mother used to say that when I put my mind to it, I could talk the devil into taking communion. Hopefully she was right; today I was going to ask Steve for a fifty-dollar loan to buy some new clothes and suggest that he take the repayment out of my pay at five dollars every week. That way I'd be sure he would keep me at least ten weeks.

I settled on the shirt I'd worn on the bus, the red flannel one with the black checks. It would be all right for one more day. Besides, it was my lucky shirt. I'd bought it and the yellow hat with the word *Caterpillar* on the front in Aruba when Telemahos and I were preparing our ship-jumping. "Lots of Americans wear these goofy hats," Telemahos had said. "They call them *bez-ball-kap*."

I tucked my shirt into the pants, put on the hat, and searched for a mirror but had to settle for the glass door of a stove. I made sure the cap sat right on my head.

"*Bezballkap*," I said aloud and almost laughed at the funny sound of it. Oh yes, I was going to keep this goofy hat and the checkered shirt. And years from now, I would show them to my children and say, "That's what I wore when I came to America. I was dressed like an American, so I fooled them all."

I took out all the dollar bills from my wallet and from the secret pocket of the coat and the rolled-up socks in the stove. I counted them and the total came to $145—my entire earthly wealth. I rolled some of the bills tight and scanned the room for a crack or a crevice. After some searching, I stood on a stove and unscrewed the brass-looking cover of the ceiling light. I put the money inside the cover and screwed it back. That last hundred was going to be my extreme emergency fund. I put one of the twenties inside the mattress through a hole in the bottom and the other in the stove beneath the underwear. As soon as I got my papers, I was putting my money in the bank. Stashing money in underwear and under mattresses was old fashioned.

Gradually the building seemed to be awakening. I heard doors slamming, people yelling, things banging into the corridor walls, and kids and women shouting at each other in Spanish and in English. Outside, cars were starting up, one after the other. When Steve drove me here the night before, I'd noticed the parking lot was full of cars of every shape and every color. Everybody in this building must own a car. And if they lived in this building, they were not rich, that was for sure.

Liapouras, the oiler on the *Aegean Sea*, had said during one of his storytelling sessions in the crew's lounge that when he'd stayed at his cousin's apartment in Astoria, New York, he used to see about a hundred cars parked in front of the building across the street. "I thought it was a car factory until my cousin told me they were making furniture. 'The cars you see belong to the people working there,' he said."

Anastasis, the fireman who never missed a chance to bug Liapouras, had said, "That's the fairiest of all the fairytales you have told us, old man. How could people polishing furniture and sweeping sawdust make enough money to buy their own cars?"

"You know nothing about America," Liapouras scoffed, waving his hand as if Anastasis's opinion didn't count. "My cousin told me that if you put a hundred dollars down, you can buy any car you want in America. He got his big *Shievroletta* that way. You can even buy a house with just crumbs up front, he told me. And if you have served in the military, you don't even have to do that. The government will loan you the down payment, he told me. They'll even pay for you to go to the university if you want."

Anastasis pretended to ignore him, concentrating instead on rearranging the backgammon pieces.

"All *I* got after serving twenty-four miserable months in *our* infantry," Liapouras went on with a raised voice, "was a piece of paper with a bureaucrat's signature. I didn't even get the bus fare back to the village. I'm telling you, I curse the stork every day for dropping me in the wrong country."

I walked to the window and peeled back a corner of the newspaper taped on it. Looking out at the parking lot, I thought the old windbag might have been right. The two cars closest to me looked new. One was bright red, low, and stretched, with two doors. It had a black canvas top and a galloping silver stallion on the grill. The other was dark blue with long, raised fins in the back, like a swan. I cocked my head sideways and read the letters on the side: *Impala*.

A man about forty years old holding a coffee mug came from the building and went over to the car with the stallion. He looked up at the clear sky for a few seconds, then got in and cranked the engine. Soon the black canvas top folded neatly back, revealing a shiny dashboard and light-brown leather seats. The man raised his right hand and waved to somebody in the building before driving out of the parking lot with one hand on the wheel, the other resting on the stick shift. I watched him slowly drive down the street until he was out of sight. I pictured myself in a car like that, gliding down a stretch of a smooth American road with the top down, steering with one hand and shifting gears with the other, and for an instant, I was the happiest man on the planet.

A minute or so later, a heavyset woman pulling two fat children loaded with school bags walked with quick steps to a yellowish station wagon. She shoved the children in and made the tires squeal as she darted out of the parking lot. Then a middle-aged man carrying a lunch box and wearing green coveralls drove off in a white Volkswagen. Every one of these car owners seemed to be ordinary, working-class people.

That's the great thing about living in this country, I thought optimistically. *Everybody has a chance to live "the Good Life." And you can do it while living in peace. The wars, revolutions, and invasions are happening somewhere else, far away.*

I'm going to get my share of the Good Life no matter how hard the immigration guys are looking for me.

CHAPTER TWO

A Refugee's Lament

While I surveyed the parking lot, waiting for Steve, a white van with dents and scratches on all sides and ladders and paint rollers on the top drove into the lot and parked under the banyan tree at the far end. Two tall, skinny men wearing white caps and white, paint-stained overalls, one of them limping slightly, picked up one of the long ladders from the top. With each man shouldering one end of the ladder and carrying a paint can each, they trampled over the bushes separating the two buildings and went out of sight next door. One man came back a few minutes later and, moving quickly, connected an old garden hose with lots of splices on it to the faucet below my window, then trotted back to where he came from.

The Americans were going to work, and soon I would be among them. Steve should be coming any minute now. I readjusted my *bezballcap* and went outside for a quick survey of the area. After walking to the far end of the parking lot, I turned and looked at the place where I was staying. The building that would be my home—and prison, until I got my green card—was a long, two-story structure with a red-tiled roof and stucco walls painted a color too dark to be called pink and too light to be red. The doors, windows, and all the wooden trim were a light greenish.

Walking at a steady pace, trying to look as if I were going to my car, I reached the other end of the parking lot and scanned the area. Across the street was a two-story, Mediterranean-style house painted yellowish orange. Next to it was a squat wooden bungalow painted dark purple with a tin roof. The houses, trees, and flowers of the neighborhood reminded me of a Latin-American city. People were walking and riding bicycles, greeting each other in Spanish when they passed, and for a moment I felt like I was in Balboa, returning to the ship after spending the night ashore.

An elderly American woman holding a long leash with a small shaggy dog at the end walked toward me along the sidewalk. The dog stopped constantly to sniff the hedges, and the elderly woman seemed to be addressing a steady, soft, scolding monologue toward that end of the leash.

When she drew close to me, she smiled and said, "Good morning."

I smiled back and said, "Good morning" also.

By 9:30, I had examined half the cars in the parking lot and rehearsed a thousand times in my head what I was going to tell Karen the next time I saw her. I was looking over a Ford Falcon next to the painters' van when I saw Steve park his convertible Cadillac in front of my window. He must not have seen me because he stormed out of the car and marched into the building, mumbling curses as if looking for a fight. I caught up with him and tapped him on the shoulder while he was knocking on my door.

"Ah, the devil take you! You spooked me," he snapped. "Come on, we're late." He kicked a child's wagon out of his way. "Damn accountant took all day. Fucking tax collectors. They expect me to support every bum and whore in Miami."

As he got in the car, he noticed the garden hose hooked up to the faucet and stopped to trace it with his eyes.

"What the hell is going on here?" He plowed through the hedge separating the two parking lots, and a moment later I heard him calling somebody a crook.

"You *más grande* crook!" somebody yelled back.

Steve came trampling through the boxwood hedge with one painter following behind, shaking a fist at him, and the limping one behind him.

"I want my money now, *cabrón*!" the painter shouted.

"You never fixed the window," answered Steve. "*To gamises kai psófise, maláka.*" He stopped, apparently realizing he was talking to him in Greek, and searched for the right word. "*You* fucked up everything and I had to pay to put in a new window." He grabbed the hose. "And now you're stealing my water, you *sanavabitch.*" He yanked at the hose, and one of its many splices snapped out, shooting a stream of water straight at the painters' faces. "*Sanavabitch,* that will fix you!" Steve burst out laughing. To me he said, "Get in the car. We're already late."

"I will get even with you, *cabrón*!" shouted the painter while trying to shut off the water. "You will see!"

"I will see nothing, you fucking good-for-nothing moocher!" Steve got in the car and slammed the door.

As we pulled away, I took another look at the building. "Which one is your apartment?" I asked.

"I don't live here," he said. "I've got a place in Miami Beach. This used to be a damn good neighborhood, ten times better than Coral Gables over there." He gestured ahead and to the left. "Fucking Cubans. They turned it to shit. You know what they call it now? Little Havana. Fucking freeloaders."

Soon after, Steve parked in front of the Parthenon restaurant, and we got out of the car.

"Did you see how far I drove? Only two blocks straight down

from your room." He pointed toward the apartment building. "You can walk it in five minutes. I want you here at 9:30. That's when the others come in."

He looked around as if expecting someone to be waiting there, then pulled the overloaded keychain from his sagging pants and unlocked the glass door while mumbling curses about some *sanavabitch*. I followed him inside. He walked over to the coffeemaker, checked to see if it was filled, and pressed the *ON* button.

A few minutes later there was a knock on the door. Steve muttered more curses as he walked over, let in an old man, and locked the door behind him. The man was medium height and thin, wore a blue bow tie, and had his white hair combed back. He said, "*Buenos dias, señores*," nodding, and went into the kitchen.

"*Buenos dias, señor*," I replied. Steve said nothing. He poured himself a cup of coffee and sat on the stool by the register. I asked if I could have some coffee, and he made a gesture that could be interpreted as a yes.

I filled my cup and walked behind the counter, looking over the dining area. I was a member of the workforce now, and, unlike last night's visit, I saw the place with the eye of someone from the inside. The counter situated across from the entrance door had twelve stools in front of it. That was good arrangement; it made it easy to see who was coming in. At the end of the counter nearest the door was the cash register, and next to that an empty pie case.

The dining room had six booths along the walls and ten square tables in the middle, each with four chairs around them. A large, round table with eight chairs stood in the far corner. All the tables were covered with plastic, blue-and-white, checkered tablecloths. On the white stucco walls, held up with brown tape diagonally at the four corners, were posters of Greek island scenes. The cement floor had been painted blue some time ago but was now peeling in many places. A pay phone hung on the wall by the entrance.

The man with the bow tie returned from the kitchen, pushing

a mop in a galvanized bucket on wheels. He wore a yellow plastic apron, and his eyes expressed tiredness and resignation.

"That's Julio," Steve said, nodding toward the old man. "He cleans before I open up. If you listen to him, he'll tell you he was some big lord in Cuba, a real aristocrat with a name two meters long." He took a sip of coffee and cleared his throat. "Look here, I'll tell everybody you're my nephew. It's none of their business, but that way they'll think you're here legal. These moochers talk a lot."

"Shall I call you Uncle Steven then?"

He shrugged. "No, no need to."

There was another knock on the glass door. Steve shouted to Julio and motioned with his head toward the door. Julio opened it and let in the frail black man I had seen cleaning the tables the previous evening. Julio locked the door and, walking backward, ran the mop over their footprints.

"Pascal, you are late, again," said Steve.

The clock in the Coca-Cola sign over the counter showed fifteen minutes to ten. Pascal glanced at it and walked into the kitchen without answering.

"Unlock the back door, Pascal," Steve shouted after him.

A few minutes later, the waitress I had spoken to the previous night came in through the back door. "*Buenos dias, señores,*" she said as she went by and stored her straw purse under the counter.

Pascal came in with a loaded tray of clean coffee cups and started putting them under the counter.

Steve cleared his throat again and spoke to Pascal. "Hey, you. Come here." He turned on his stool and motioned for the waitress and Julio. "You too, come closer." Then he pointed at me and said, "This here is my . . . my . . . *anepsios.*" He thought for a moment, then started again. "This here is Kostas, my sister son. He work here now." Then, as an afterthought, he turned to me. "This is Pascal, that's Julio, and she's Carmen." He pointed toward each of them.

"Hi, Kostas. Welcome to the group," said Carmen. She put on a white apron and got busy refilling the napkin holders. I thought there was a trace of a smile when our eyes met. The night before when Steve had tried to get rid of me and I said I would wait until closing, she had put a cup of coffee in front of me. When she came to refill it, she had smiled with a hint of sympathy in her large, dark eyes.

I watched her now going from table to table, a certain grace in her moves. She was medium height, almost as tall as I was, no more than thirty years old, with athletic hips, small breasts, and light-brown skin, like a Scandinavian after two weeks on a Greek beach. I looked for a wedding ring, but her fingers were hidden.

A few minutes later, her voice rang out from the far end of the dining room. "Need to change this tablecloth over here, Steven. It has cigarette burns in the middle."

"Put the napkin holder over them," Steve said. "Damn pigs don't deserve any better."

"Bad night at the track, Steven?" she chided. "Your dog stopped to piss again?"

"Fuck you, slut," said Steve in Greek. He got off the stool and walked into the kitchen. "Time to start getting ready."

I followed behind, eager to take a look at the place that would be my stepping stone to the Good Life. The kitchen was small, and everything in it looked old and neglected. Pascal sat on a Coca-Cola crate, peeling potatoes and tossing them into a pot while humming a tune.

Steve went over to the grill and turned on the gas. Then he took out an apple pie and a key lime pie from the walk-in cooler and handed them to me. "Put them in the case out front."

The apple pie was uncut, but only two old-looking, shriveled pieces of the key lime remained in the tray. I put the pies in the case next to the cash register, then went in the kitchen and checked on the grill. It had already gotten hot, and the area filled with the smell of charred meat, the remnants of last night's work; somebody hadn't cleaned it right.

Steve stood over Pascal's shoulder for a moment. "You're peeling them too thick! You throw half the potato away. Next time I'll pay you with potato peels."

"I should use frozen fries," he said to me in Greek. "The pigs out there wouldn't know the difference, but I don't have any freezer space."

"They have machines now that peel the potatoes," I said.

"Yeah, but those who have them don't give them away. Besides, I don't have the room in here for that either." He made a sweeping gesture with his cigarette-holding hand to emphasize the smallness of the space.

"How many people work here?" I asked.

"They come and go all the time," he answered, walking over to the fryer. "*Sanavabitch,* he forgot to change it! Pascal, why no change the oil, *vre*?" He turned to me. "Right now, I got this Haitian here"—he nodded toward Pascal—"and Milio, the *sanavabitch* over there, for a cook." He gestured to a spot by the grill where the cook should have been standing. "He's been missing a lot of time lately and I'm about to kick his ass."

He held his palm over the grill to check the temperature. "I got Isabella for waitressing during lunch and dinner, and I got Carmen working behind the counter. She's been here the longest. Oh, and I got Julio, the Cuban aristocrat out there. The Haitian could be doing the cleaning, but Carmen talked me into giving his lordship the job. I think he's fucking her."

He noticed Pascal trying to shove the empty lard can under the fryer drain. "Watch out, *vre,*" he yelled at him. "No spill grease all over the floor. And put the can out the back door, for Pepe to pick up." He turned back to me. "Some Italian Jew comes and picks up the old grease. He doesn't pay me anything, but the city won't let you pour it down the drain anymore."

He handed me the pumice stone: "Here, start scraping the grill. Where the hell is Milio? If he doesn't show up again, I'll fry his ass."

Then, as if he'd just remembered, he added, "I've got to go pick up something from the apartment. Here's a five to pay the lord in case I'm not back by the time he's done mopping. Make sure he mops everything. I'll be back soon." He handed me the five-dollar bill and went out. In the dining room I heard him shout at Julio, "You no mop bathroom yesterday! I pay you for whole shop, Julio. I no sucker."

"Yes, Mr. Steven," the old man said.

I finished cleaning the grill, refilled my coffee, and for a while watched the old man working. He moved the mop over the floor with gentle, measured strokes, as if conducting an invisible orchestra. Without the mop and the apron, he could pass for a banker or a professor.

"How's everybody at home, Señor Julio?" Carmen asked from behind the counter.

"Difficult, Señora Carmen. My sister cannot get work anywhere, so she looks after the baby."

"How old is your granddaughter now?"

"She became four last month, señora." He stopped mopping and straightened to rub his back with his right hand. "She's becoming a beautiful young lady. It is sad her mother cannot see her. Today is exactly three years from the day of the disaster," he said with a sigh.

"It seems like yesterday," said Carmen. "At least she has the two of you to raise her."

"My sister does the raising. I can contribute very little. And how is Señor Simon? Any improvement?"

"No, Grandfather is the same as when you came to see him last week. Nothing changed."

I went back in the kitchen. A few minutes later, Julio came in pushing the mop bucket.

"I finished," he said. He stopped and stood holding the mop handle with both hands, breathing hard.

"*El baño, está limpio*?" I asked him.

"*Sí, sí, todo limpio, señor.*"

"*Gracias*," I said.

"Did they teach Spanish at your school?" he asked.

"No, but I have been to places where they speak Spanish when I worked on ships. I like to listen and try to remember the words."

"It is good to learn things," he said. "Knowledge is good."

"What did you do in Cuba, Señor Julio?" I asked.

"I was director of the customs office in Havana." He let out a sigh. "I had big house in the city and a plantation by the sea."

His voice had the same pained, nostalgic tone I had heard from the refugees in Greece when they described what they had left behind in Asia Minor.

"Many people work in my plantation," the old man continued while staring into the mop bucket as if he could see beyond the muddy water. "I have beautiful horses, beautiful friends, and beautiful life. Every weekend have big parties at my plantation and many important people come—*profesores, artistas, oficiales* from the government and from the university." He let out another sigh and raised his head to look at me. "Now I have nothing. Castro take everything. Over here, nobody will give an old man a job." He started toward the storage area with slow, defeated steps, pushing the mop bucket ahead of him.

All the refugees of the world must be thinking the same. When the Turks kicked the Greeks out of Asia Minor, the Greek government had settled those who washed up on its shores in places shunned by even the most destitute of the locals. And although the shantytowns and desolate villages where they settled did not even remotely resemble the places they'd had before, they gave their new towns the names of the ones they had left behind: New Smyrna, New Moudania, New Ionia, New . . . whatever. And for the rest of their lives, as they struggled to scrape by, every one of them would lament the loss of the riches they'd left behind. The anger and the pain of having something cherished taken away and the desperate desire for respect and acceptance in the new environment magnified and gave brilliance to everything they'd had before. Every hovel became a mansion; every thorn-congested piece of scrubland was a plantation.

In Taxiarhes, at the outskirts of the village in a one-room stone cottage, lived Nickolas Paneroglou. He and my father were among the masses of refugees who managed to get out of Smyrna. He married a woman with no dowry, and for the rest of his life he struggled to raise crops among the rocks of an almost vertical mountain plot. The more the locals snubbed him, the bigger became the mansion and the wheat fields and the olive groves he had left behind.

I guess my father was like the other refugees too, but I was only two years old when the Nazis killed him, so I didn't remember much of him. I asked my mother once about it, and she said that Father did not like to talk about what he had left behind. "Too painful," he told her.

Señor Julio took off the yellow plastic apron and hung it on a nail. He washed his hands, combed his wavy white hair, and came back to the kitchen. I handed him the five dollars.

"*Muchas gracias, patrón*," he said, bowing. He put the money in his pocket and started to walk out. "*Hasta mañana*."

A moment later, a thought came to me and I called out to him before he got to the door. "*Uno momento,* Señor Julio." I went to the display case, got the two slices of key lime pie, put them in a box, and handed it to him. "For the granddaughter," I said. Carmen was cleaning the counter at the far end. I wondered if she would tell Steve.

"*Muchas gracias, patrón,*" he said. "*Muchas gracias*." He held the box with both hands and slowly walked out.

Through the glass door, I watched him shuffle across the parking lot. A Cuban Nickolas Paneroglou.

⁂

Steve was gone for half an hour. When he came back, he went to the cash register, put the opening money in the drawer, then slammed it shut. As he turned, he glanced inside the pie case. "Sold the key lime pie before we opened?"

"I gave it to the old man," I said. "It didn't look good. I dropped it putting it in the case and didn't think it would sell."

"These pigs will eat anything you put in front of them."

"I heard Carmen say the old man is raising a granddaughter. I think her family drowned coming over."

"I like to know how generous you'd be if this was your business," said Steve. "Not even a whole hour on the job and already you know everything. Well, let me set you straight on how things are here. You do *nothing* without asking me. Got that?"

"Yes sir," I said.

"Did you know that every one of these moochers is on welfare?" Steve went on. "As soon as they get off the boat, they get a fat check from the government. Then once a month all they got to do is show up to collect another one. The rest of the time they sit around, drink, and make babies, like the blacks. And *my* taxes are paying for it." He poured a cup of coffee and dumped spoonfuls of sugar in it. "And another thing, if word gets around we're giving away food, you'll have every Cuban in Miami lined up at the door. It'll scare away the paying customers."

"Take it out of my pay then," I said. "I didn't think it would matter that much."

I went in the kitchen. Steve came in behind me and started taking the covers off the cold table. A few minutes later, a man who looked to be around fifty-five came through the back door. He was bald, fair-skinned, short, and muscular.

"*Buenos dias*," he muttered and, looking straight ahead, walked to the back wall of the kitchen. He got an apron from a nail, then dragged a cardboard box full of chickens out of the cooler. He pulled a cleaver from a drawer, put a chicken on the block, and started cutting it up and throwing the pieces into a twenty-four-quart pot. His arms were massive, his strikes firm and sure of their target, and his face had the look of one who was pissed off at the world.

Steve took a few steps toward him, then stopped and cleared his throat. "*Emilio, qué pasa* yesterday, *vre? Por qué* no come to *trabajo*?"

Emilio didn't answer. He flung the chicken pieces into the pot with force, as if trying to hurt someone hiding in the bottom of it.

"Eh, *vre*?" repeated Steve.

"*Calabozo,*" growled Emilio. And as if it were the chicken he was settling the score with, he started whacking it even harder. "*Hijo de puta*," he muttered as the cleaver landed on the villain. "*Cabrón*!" The cleaver got stuck in the wood, and as he yanked it loose, the counter where the block was secured shook, and everything on top rattled and jumped.

Steve seemed to soften. He reached and grabbed my shirt and pulled me toward Emilio. "*Vre, sí,* this *aquí está* Kostas," he told the cook. "Kostas *trabajo* here now. Kostas *está* you helper. *Comprende*?"

Emilio turned two bloodshot eyes toward me for a moment, then resumed killing whomever the chicken represented.

Steve walked out of the kitchen and motioned for me to follow. "Don't think that *sanavabitch* will stay out of jail long. He's another one of those Cuban lords. Says he was some kind of big chef in a fancy hotel over there. They're all like that. They bellyache about the greatness they left behind, and when they talk to folks back home, they brag about what big shots they are here."

Sounds like you. Luckily, I bit off the words before they came out. "How long Emilio been working here?"

"About a year. His daughter goes to the university and she's running around with a black from Jamaica. Milio's chasing him off all the time. Sometimes the neighbors call the cops and he gets locked up. You learn to do the cooking in case they don't let him out next time."

"What kind of dishes you cook here?"

"Cheap and fast. These pigs will eat anything."

By eleven o'clock when Carmen unlocked the front door for the customers, the mutilated chicken had been transformed into a huge pot of *arroz con pollo* with tomato sauce. Plates were piled high and served with green beans out of a size-ten can, perked up with sautéed onions and diced tomatoes. Most of the customers seemed to be Spanish-speaking people from the neighborhood who joked and carried on brief conversations with the waitresses.

Around 12:30, Karen walked in and went straight to the cash register to speak with Steve in a low whisper. I was loading the coffee cup station at the time and stopped to look. She wore a thin, loose-fitting dress kept in place with an elastic band just above her breasts. Under it I could see the outline of a two-piece bathing suit. A cloth bag with a sailing ship embroidered on it hung from her shoulder.

Whatever she told Steve in her sexy, cuddly way resulted in Steve handing her a twenty-dollar bill out of the register. She turned to leave, then stopped. "Oh, Steven, I'd like something to drink," she said.

Steve turned to me. "Hey," he said in English, "give her a Coke." Then in Greek, as if bragging: "And close your mouth."

I took a bottle of Coca-Cola from the cooler and handed it to her after opening it.

"Thank you," she said, reaching for it. "You . . ." She dragged out the *you* for a moment. "You're Kostas, right? See, I remembered." She gave me a triumphant smile and headed out the door, leaving a cloud of gardenia-scented perfume in her wake.

During lunch and dinner, the waitresses darted between tables, shouted orders, and hooked green order slips on the wire above the serving window. The slips seemed impossible to read, the writing even more confusing than Arabic, but Emilio would glance at that scribble, and a few minutes later he'd set the loaded plates on the serving window and ring the bell.

Steve sat on a tall chair by the cash register. He took the money from the customers, gave change, and nailed the order slips on a spike. Every so often he growled and jerked his head to remind the waitress that her order was waiting at the window or that a customer was ready for his check. I offered to do the dishwashing so Pascal could do the table cleaning, and Steve shrugged in agreement. That way I wouldn't have to go out to the dining room. The fewer people I was seen by, the better.

Carmen attended the customers sitting at the counter and the three tables closest to it. Her movements were like a ballet dancer performing onstage: she cleared the empty plates, wrote down orders, poured coffee, clipped the green order slips on the wire, transported the loaded plates, and refilled the water glasses, all with synchronized moves that seemed effortless, while asking one customer how his wife was and another if his brother got the job at the shipyard. As customers left, she almost always asked them to give her regards to somebody, then cleared the vacated spot and put the tip in a plastic margarine jar under the counter.

Isabella took care of the dining room area, gliding from table to table, chatting and refilling just as effortlessly as Carmen. She kept her tips in her apron pocket.

Around two o'clock, while I was putting clean cups by the coffee maker, two policemen came in and sat at the counter across from Steve and ordered coffee. I finished stacking the cups as calmly as I could and, trying hard not to look alarmed, walked into the kitchen, grabbed a broom, and started sweeping behind the freezer. From that spot I could see them through the serving window, and the short distance to the back door would come in handy if I had to bolt.

One of the policemen pointed to Steve's cap with the blue dolphin on the front and said something about "cowboys" and "Texas." It must have been funny because he and his partner both laughed. Steve didn't laugh. He grumbled something, but all I understood was "*sanavabitch* quarter" and "back."

About that time, the two painters who'd argued with Steve in the morning burst through the door and headed toward the cash register at "full speed ahead"—until they saw the two policemen sitting at the counter. They shifted to "full astern" and left as fast as they had come in.

I stayed in the kitchen until the end of the day. After the last customer left, I stepped out and went to refill the soft-drink cooler behind the counter. Carmen had folded her apron and was counting her tips in the margarine jar.

"Better than last night," she muttered and put some of the money in a Styrofoam cup by the register.

Isabella emptied her apron pocket on a table and counted her tips. "Your nephew brought us good luck, Mr. Steve," she said as she put some money in the cup also. "This was one of our busiest Fridays. Is he going to share tips with Pascal?"

"Don't care," said Steve. He rattled the change cup in my direction. "Hey, this here is the tips they've been sharing with the Haitian. She's asking if you want to split it with him."

I thought about it for a second. "No, I no want," I answered and kept spreading the ice in the cooler. I wanted to make money—lots of money—but taking a few pennies away from somebody who probably needed it more than I did was only good for making enemies.

Steve ran the tape of the cash register and started counting the money in the drawer, scribbling the amounts on a brown takeout bag. The waitresses picked up their purses and started toward the door.

"Good night, Steven," Carmen said when she walked by. "Don't bet it all on the first race."

"Fuck you, lesbian bitch. You made me lose my place," Steve muttered in Greek and started the counting all over again. When finished, he put some small bills and all the coins in a blue bank pouch and set it on the counter. He put the rest of the money in a brown cloth bag with strings, stashed it inside his pants, and tied it to his belt.

"Don't keep more than a ten in the wallet," he said when he saw me staring.

I finished spreading the ice in the drink cooler and dried my hands on the apron before taking it off and throwing it in the dirty-laundry box.

Steve turned out the lights, and we started to leave; then he turned back and picked up the bag on the counter. "That's the opening money," he said. "I used to hide it in here, but since I started closing on the weekends, I don't leave anything. Not in this shitty neighborhood. Little Havana my ass."

He double-locked the front door and started toward his car with me walking beside him.

"Now, you remember how to get to the room?" he asked.

"Yes."

"I'll come in the morning to show you what to paint." He opened the car door. "Be careful in this shitty neighborhood. You're not in Volos."

I headed toward my room with sure, purposeful strides, like a local returning from work, pretending not to notice the houses lining both sides of the street—all of them with green lawns and flowering vines of red, pink, and purple cascading over their stucco courtyard walls.

A pleasant breeze blew against my face as I walked, and I wondered how cold it was in Taxiarhes right now. In my next letter to Mother, I would write that the weather here was always nice. "Even now at the beginning of October," I'd tell her, "I'm walking around in a short-sleeved shirt."

My watch showed 10:30, which meant it was 5:30 in the morning in Taxiarhes. My brother would be getting the mules saddled. He was probably all bundled up with everything he owned, trying to keep warm, but he wouldn't complain. He never did. My brother has always believed there's a reason and a purpose for everything, even cold, miserable weather.

At the corner of Eighth Street and Twentieth Avenue, I waited for the light to change. A car with the top down and the radio blaring pulled up at the intersection. Two blonde girls in the front seat were singing and gyrating along with the song "Stop in the Name of Love." I smiled at them and they smiled back. The light changed and they drove off, waving at me as they went.

Oh, yes, I am going to like it here. No doubt about it.

CHAPTER THREE

Meeting Karen

On my second morning in Miami, I woke as the first sunrays strained through the newspaper covering the window. This time I got right out of bed, got dressed, and went outside to have another look at the cars before Steve came with the painting supplies.

The balmy, sunny morning felt nice, and I spent a lot of time studying each car in the parking lot. It wouldn't be long now before I was zooming on the highways. Liapouras had said that in America a man could buy any car he wanted with only a hundred-dollar down payment. The burden of selection already weighed on me.

Steve pulled up at nine o'clock, cutting short my appraisal of a blue Dodge. He had the top of his Cadillac down, and the radio blared an American rock-and-roll tune.

"Get in," he said. "We're running late. Need to get the stuff and get you started."

On the way to the store, I constantly twisted in my seat, scrutinizing every house we passed as if I were in the market for one. *That's a nice one; it has tall palm trees and a blooming flower garden in the front. Or that one on the corner that has a swimming pool. Or the pink one . . . Maybe by next winter I could get a bigger place and ask Mother to come and spend the winter here to get away from the snow and cold weather of the village. Wouldn't it be something if Mother said to go ahead and send the ticket?*

She had crossed the county line only once, to visit her uncle in Larisa, a town about seventy kilometers from our village. From then on, she dated everything in her life by that event: "This happened one year before my trip to Larisa," or "That happened two years after I came back from Larisa," the same way other women in our area used their pregnancies and childbirths to mark the passage of time. What would she think of this huge city with buildings taller than the tallest cedars in the village, cars running back and forth like ants in an upturned ant bed, and supermarkets where you could find anything you could think of and where you could walk around for hours without anybody hovering over you?

And when Mother got back to Greece, wouldn't Pavlos's jaw drop to his knees when she told him what a nice, comfortable house I lived in and what a big, modern city Miami is and how the weather is always perfect? I needed to find out how much a ticket from Greece to Miami would be. Maybe if my mother came and visited for a while, she wouldn't be too upset with me for staying in America.

"God has His reasons for putting people where He did," she'd said the first time I hinted that I would like to try my luck in another country. "And going against His will is asking for trouble."

Before I could say anything, my brother butted in: "Those who have it in them," he said, "do well wherever they are instead of going to some faraway place where nobody knows them. It's like trying to hide your ineptitude among the strangers."

Won't he eat his words when Mother gets back from America and tells him what she's seen?

My brother seemed to be satisfied with the crumbs life handed to him, content to spend his evenings at the coffeehouse playing cards and retelling stories from the few months he had spent beyond the mountain ridge, when he was in the army. He farmed a tiny plot of land in which nothing thrived but stones and thorns. For added income, like most men in the village, he hauled loads with his three mules—olives, chestnuts, firewood, or building material if somebody was building something. During the summer months, he hauled fat tourists to the Milopotamos beach. For a whole day's back-wrenching loading and unloading and prodding the mules up and down the steep mountain paths, he didn't earn any more than people in the city spend for one evening's dinner at a restaurant. But my brother thought God was splurging on him.

The rest of the villagers were like that too. When they tried to outboast each other, their bragging consisted of who had been the most resourceful at finding ways to load the huge flagstones or the huge bureaus and headboards onto his mule saddles a couple of years back, when a movie star from Athens had built her vacation cottage on the Filaretou Overlook. In my opinion, that was the sorriest of ways for a man to spend his life—holding on to the tail of a mule, counting farts.

I didn't know what reasons God had for planting me in Taxiarhes, but I didn't think He would hold it against me for jumping ship in America. I had gotten a job that paid more in a month than my brother made in half a year, I had a place to live, and after I got my papers and learned my way around, I could look for a location to open my own restaurant and start making the really "big money." And then there was Karen, the young, sexy thing oozing lust from every pore of her body who lived in the same building and had the hots for me. What better proof did I need that God was on my side?

When we arrived at the Lainhart & Potter Building Supply, a tall, muscular black man stepped away from the counter and greeted us as soon as we were inside the door.

"Good morning, gentlemen."

"I want paint," Steve said, not bothering to answer the salesman. "I want the kind that dries like plastic, so can clean with wet cloth." He looked the salesman straight in the face and mimicked the cleaning with a circular motion of his hand.

The salesman smiled. "I have exactly what you want—water-based latex." He gestured toward a wall of paint cans. "When it dries, it's as hard as plastic. You can wash it with soap and water."

"That's the kind I want, water basis. That is the kind I mix with water, right? How much water I put in it?"

The salesman studied Steve for a moment, and it seemed that his smile got bigger. "If you are going to paint with a roller or a brush, you don't need to thin it. Just clean up your rollers and your brushes with water."

"You say before I can mix with water. How much water?" Steve gave the black guy a suspicious look.

"Only if you want to make the paint thinner," the salesman said. "Like if you were to run it through a spray gun or you wanted to cover a bigger area with a thinner coat, then you add some water into the can." He described the "bigger area" by moving both hands, like a pelican taking off.

He talked more about paint colors and paint durability, then told Steve that for the area he was trying to paint, he would be saving money and time if he bought a five-gallon can. Steve bought two gallons instead. "To see how it is," he said. He also bought an all-purpose paint roller, a paint pan, and two paintbrushes, one wide and one narrow.

"You'll need a pole too," the salesman said. "Makes it easier to reach the high places. We have them in aluminum or wood." He held out one of each.

Steve picked the cheapest one. "Bet you a broomstick would be just as good," he muttered as he handed it to me. Then he turned to his side so the black man behind the cash register wouldn't see the wad of bills he pulled out of his pocket.

Back at the apartment building, Steve pointed out the places that needed mending and painting.

"Look at that," he said, gesturing down the corridor. "They write on the walls, they scratch the doors, they ride their bicycles up and down inside here. They destroy everything."

The walls, ceilings, floors, and everything in between were in desperate need of nailing, caulking, and painting. I walked next to Steve, nodding to show that I understood. He'd said he didn't need anybody and was only hiring me as a favor to Telemahos's family. The way I saw it, there was enough work here to last a couple of lifetimes.

"Start here." Steve pointed at a spot on the wall to his left. "Let's see how it goes inside, and later you'll paint the wood outside. The stucco is all right—stucco lasts a long time. I'm not too crazy about that stupid color, but I'm not changing it." He kicked a tricycle down the corridor. "Fucking pigs."

He leaned against the wall and seemed to be thinking while scratching his testicles. "Look," he said finally. "I figured out how you'll do this. Painting is the biggest job in here. Everything else is small stuff—sometimes a leaky toilet and maybe a few holes in the walls. You'll get started at six in the morning and work inside, then work outside when it gets light. By 9:30 you can get plenty done. You've been in the navy, right? All it takes is a plan and discipline. Okay?"

I nodded.

"Good. You do what you're supposed to do and I won't bother the immigration. Now get started." He walked away, but at the door he turned. "Don't forget to thin the paint with water. I don't care what that black at the store said."

I moved my head in agreement again. I opened the can and stirred the paint with the stick the store guy had put in the bag. As it was, it didn't look like it could stand any more thinning. It would take at least two coats to cover the scratches and the crayon drawings. I poured some of the paint into the pan and got started. First with the small brush, carefully along the edges of the wall, then with the roller

I screwed on at the end of the pole. I moved up and down in even strokes, and for a moment, I was standing on the dock, painting the hull of the *Aegean Sea*.

Soon I started sweating and took off my shirt and wiped my chest with it. There was some of the Caribbean tan still left on me. I hummed a song—an old Greek folk song with a slow tune—to go with the rhythmic up-and-down moves of the roller. After a few bars I substituted the song's lyrics with my own words:

> *Kostas my lad, la la la la,*
> *be patient 'til you get the green card, la la la lalum,*
> *and learn your way around this country, lum la la lalum,*
> *and learn the language, la la lalum,*
> *and then you can get even with the fucking cheap bastard,*
> *trala la la lalum.*

I had been painting for almost an hour when, out of one of the doors at the far end of the hallway, who should appear in the corridor but Karen, coming slowly toward me. *Yes, indeed! God is on my side!*

A small boy followed behind her, whining and trying to find a spot on her tight shorts to grip. She stopped and said, "Hi, Kostas," in what I thought was a deliberately sexy kind of way. I stopped painting and stared at her while she considered the wall. "The gray is too dark," she said. "It needs something brighter, to bring more light in here."

I didn't answer. I couldn't think what to say. I smiled and started painting again. I moved in slow, measured strokes, pressing the roller against the wall as I moved it up and down.

"Pink or a light-cream color would look pretty," she added and stepped closer.

"Steve say put this paint." I had to say something. I wanted to tell her that the cheapskate, saint-robber Steve had wanted a dark-brown color so the dirt wouldn't show and wouldn't have to be painted so often, which would have made the place look like a cave, but the salesman talked him out of it. Unfortunately, all the words I had rehearsed earlier seemed to have left my head.

I picked up my shirt and dried the sweat from my chest, then took a deep breath and tried to remember the words for washing shirts, since it seemed like a good time to ask her.

"Nice tan," she said before I could speak. "Do you work out?"

"Steve say work here now. Finish here and paint out after." Too bad she didn't speak Greek or Spanish. How could I convince the devil to take communion if I couldn't talk to him?

"You speak American like Steve." She giggled and moved closer. She had on the same kind of tight denim shorts she'd worn the first time I saw her, with a top made out of less cloth than a handkerchief. The child climbed on a tricycle and tried to get it moving.

I turned to face her, determined to try some kind of conversation even if it was sign language, but just then the little boy fell off the tricycle and let out a cry.

"Joey, I told you this is too big for you, didn't I?" She bent to pick him up at the same time I reached to right the tricycle, and we almost bumped heads. In that move I discovered that the handkerchief-sized halter top didn't cover anything, and a wave of hot blood rushed to my head. It seemed like eons since I had been with Consuela at the "love palace" in Aruba.

"He's only two and a half, but he thinks he can do everything," Karen said, setting the boy back on the tricycle. "Are you a relative of Steve's?"

I started to say I was Steve's *anepsios* but couldn't think of the English word for it, so I said, "No, I no relative with Steve."

"Oh, he said you were his nephew. He came in the other night all flustered and got some sheets and a pillow. He said you just got off the boat and you were going to be staying here."

Ah, yes. That first night when Karen went by us in the hall. Steve had told me then that she was *off limits* and he had made sure I understood what *off limits* meant. Then later, when he came back with the sheets smelling of gardenia perfume, he had said those were his own. So now I began to understand the situation.

"No, I am no relative with Steve," I repeated and gave her my best movie star smile.

Halfway down the corridor, Joey fell off the tricycle again and started crying.

"I got to go," Karen said. "I was taking him to the playground. I'll talk to you later." She collected the child and set him on her right hip as she walked away. Before she went through the door she turned and said bye in the same erotic kind of way she had said hi earlier.

Could Steve be Joey's father? I would look at the boy closer the next time. I started painting again, moving the roller up and down with slow, firm strokes, replaying the encounter in my mind.

So Steve says she is "off limits," eh? Oh yes, Master Steven, I'm going to find a way to bed your Miss Off-limits. Just give me a couple of days, no more. And I'm going to enjoy it like no other lay. It will be my revenge, slow and sweet. You can count on that, Master Steven.

⁜ ⁜ ⁜

On Monday morning, just as I prepared to walk to the restaurant, it started raining. Not a downpour, but neither was it a light drizzle I could run through. I hadn't found any umbrellas among the junk stored in my room, so for a while I stood at the front door, looking at the sky and waiting for it to stop.

Then the idea came to me. This was a God-sent message, the perfect opportunity to get to know Karen. Ever since our short conversation about the wall paint on Saturday, I had been rehearsing the opening sentences that would make our acquaintance blossom into a warm and passionate "friendship." But despite my vigilant corridor watching, I hadn't seen her again.

Now I had a perfectly good excuse to knock on her door and ask if she had an umbrella I could borrow. Even if I had gotten her signals wrong and all her smiling and coyness were just American friendliness, she wouldn't have reason to get angry since I was only trying to get to her boyfriend's place of business. It was a perfectly believable excuse, even if Steve happened to be with her. Yes, it was a God-sent signal for sure.

I hurried to my room and looked for a piece of paper. All I found was the brown bag the man at the paint store had put the brushes in. I smoothed it out and wrote two sentences in Greek. Then I leafed through the Greek-English dictionary I had smuggled from the ship and wrote the corresponding English word under each Greek one.

I read it aloud and tried to memorize it: "Perhaps you have one umbrella to borrow me to go to shop of Steve? Will her bring back the evening." And in the evening when I returned it, I could bring some kind of pie from the restaurant as a thank-you. If she really wanted me, she would ask me in to share it. Brilliant! I repeated the sentences, but I forgot some of the words, so I took the paper with me.

I kept glancing at the brown paper and repeating the words as I knocked at her door. I knocked several times, but there was no answer. After a while, I went back to my room, disappointed my surefire "get acquainted" plan had been wasted. Frustrated, I looked out the window and noticed the rain had stopped. I put the dictionary in my back pocket and headed for the restaurant.

While walking, I tried to think of another plan to get better acquainted with Karen. Maybe I could try to borrow something else, like the iron or the electric broom. Or maybe I could ask her for directions to a cinema and then ask if she would like to join me. But then, how would I say all those things in her language? I could almost hear my brother laughing his head off at my predicament.

I passed the Woolworth's store and saw my reflection in the window glass—a handsome man, possibly Cuban, walking with slow, heavy steps, his head down, hands deep in his pockets. Somebody looking at him would probably think, *There goes a serious man with all of the world's cares on his shoulders.*

Despite all the strenuous thinking, by the time I got to the

Parthenon restaurant, I still hadn't come up with any satisfactory answer to the Karen conundrum.

Carmen had told me that most of the customers were regulars—utility drivers killing time, construction workers grabbing a quick lunch, and, in the evenings, a few pensioners on their night out. Carmen seemed to know the names and eating habits of every one of them and had their drinks in front of them the moment they sat down.

I did most of my dining room observations through the serving window, avoiding being seen by the customers as much as I could. Even in this neighborhood, you never knew what kind of bureaucrat might come in for a cup of coffee. Only the few times that Pascal couldn't take out the clean coffee cups or refill the soft-drink cooler would I venture out. I would hurry to get the chore done quickly, then retreat to my shelter behind the pots and pans. From the kitchen, the back door was a short dash if I had to run.

If other illegals got caught by immigration, they got a couple of free meals and a free ticket back to where they came from to rest and try it again. But if a Greek merchant seaman was sent back to Greece, it was almost impossible to get a job on another ship. Shipping companies don't hire those who have jumped ship because they might do it again, and American immigration slaps hefty fines every time one of their crew goes missing.

When Telemahos, my old cabinmate, got caught in Savannah and was shipped to Greece, he had to spend a small fortune in bribes to crewing agents and personnel managers to get the job on the *Aegean Sea*. "It was a good thing I had put aside most of what I'd made," he'd said.

But I was just starting out. I couldn't bribe anybody, and I would end up working in some tavern in Volos, or worse, work with my brother in Taxiarhes and be the subject of the sarcastic jokes that seem to be the penance for those who society considers failures.

Today the Parthenon was busy during the lunch hour. For almost three hours, everything in the kitchen was going "full speed ahead."

The pace didn't slow until after 2:30. The last lunch plate went out of the serving window sometime around 3:30.

Steve counted the money in the cash register, muttering his usual complaints. "Lousy business. I hate Mondays." Then he left to pick up Karen from the bus stop.

I finished scraping the grill with the pumice stone and sat down to leaf through the dictionary. Usually when I got caught up with the kitchen chores, I looked up the names of the dishes in the menu or words I'd heard from the customers. This afternoon I was trying to find the word *wetback*. Steve had been muttering it all morning.

Emilio was cutting a chunk of ham on the slicer that would become item four on the dinner menu: ham steak with pineapple. Pascal scrubbed the rice stuck in the bottom of the twenty-four-quart pot, humming a Haitian tune. The two waitresses sat at the counter, Carmen listening to Isabella's man problems while sipping Coca-Cola with a straw. Everywhere in the world, the time between three and four seems to be the slowest hour for restaurants. That's when the kitchen cleans up from the lunch rush and prepares for the dinner crowd, the waitresses get a quick count of their tips, and the bosses take off for a nap or a quickie at their girlfriend's.

The only customers in the place were an old man with a big cowboy hat and an old woman eating slowly and talking in low voices at the corner booth. Those two, Carmen had said, ate only one meal a day, always at 3:30.

When the old couple shuffled out, Isabella called toward the kitchen, "Pascal, number five is ready for cleaning."

He started to rinse his hands, but I stopped him. "I will clean number five," I said and put out my cigarette. The poor fellow had been lugging loaded tubs all morning. Besides, it was safe now; the dining room was empty.

I had put the plates and glasses in the plastic tub and started wiping the tablecloth with the wet towel in slow, overlapping strokes, my mind occupied with Karen, when suddenly the door slammed open. Out of the blast of blinding sunlight emerged the tall painter I had seen arguing with Steve last Friday at the parking lot. He walked with long strides toward the counter where the two waitresses were sitting.

"*Dónde está el patrón*?" he shouted. "I want to speak to him!"

"Steve is not here," Carmen said.

"I want my money! He never paid me for the window." He kept shouting, "What, he thinks I am somebody stupid?"

"I will tell Steve when he gets here," Carmen said.

"He said the job was no good. Bullshit! I'm not stupid. The job is very good, but *he* is a crook. I want my money!"

"I told you," Carmen said, raising her voice now, "I will tell Steve when he gets here."

"You tell that *mama pinga* I want my money." He moved closer to Carmen, and I saw him raise his right arm as if he were going to hit her.

I dashed over and yelled, "Éla tóra stamatá tis malakies!" I shoved him aside. "Stop foolishness," I repeated, realizing I had spoken to him in Greek the first time.

He grabbed my shoulders with both hands and held me against the counter. His face was red and his eyes had the shine of a madman.

"Look, Greek," he said, shaking me. "You understand Spanish?" And without waiting for the answer, he went on, "I bet you're one of his relatives he brought here to work for nothing. I bet you got no papers, no work permit, no nothing. If I don't get my money, I'll go to the police and get both your asses kicked out of here!"

He let go of me and turned again to Carmen. "You make sure and tell that *mama pinga* that I want my money or I come here and break the place up!" His right hand was raised again.

I reared back and landed my right fist on his face. Immediately he let out a curse and grabbed his nose. I was going to hit him again when Emilio grabbed my arm.

"No necessary to do that," he said, then turned to the painter.

"Jose, you're drunk again. Go home. I speak with Señor Steven when he comes." Emilio pushed him toward the door, and the painter reluctantly obliged.

Before going out, he turned and shook his fist at me. "I am not finished with you. I'll get even, you'll see." With his other hand he held a paint rag to his bleeding nose.

As I headed back into the kitchen, Carmen said, "Gracias, Kostas."

I didn't know why she said it, so I didn't answer.

On my way home that evening, I replayed the painter episode in my head. A fine mess I had gotten myself into. Now I had one more person to look out for. I shouldn't have been so quick to react. Maybe he was not going to hit Carmen. Maybe he had just raised his hand to make a point. The Latinos are like Greeks—they talk with their hands. I kept looking over my shoulder and into doorways and alleyways, expecting the angry painter to leap at me at any moment.

I did not sleep well that night. I dreamed that the immigration people, with the Cuban painter in the lead, raided the restaurant and arrested me. I tried to run away and rolled off the mattress for a rude awakening. When I managed to get back to sleep, I dreamed I was in the "love palace" in Aruba, rubbing one of Consuela's boobs with both hands. When I woke up it was too late to prevent the damage. While changing underwear, anger and pride and prudence battled it out in my head. I had been unable to solve one of the most basic problems for men my age. It would be my luck to get caught and sent back home without even one story to tell about bedding an American woman.

Liapouras, the oiler on the *Aegean Sea*, had said that after he and his cousin, Fanouris, jumped ship in New York, they started going to the Greek church in Astoria.

"Hell, between me and Fanouris, we couldn't say ten words in American. Where else could we go to meet women? Paying five dollars for *short time* ate up everything we made. The second Sunday there, I met a woman," he told us. "She was young and wild and married to an old goofball. The fancy restaurant I was washing dishes for opened only for supper, so I had most of the day free. She talked her husband into hiring me to paint the garage 'so the neighbors won't get suspicious,' she said, and every day I'd show up with my brushes and paint cans, but always before we took off our clothes, she would call his office. 'Sometimes he forgets some important paper and comes back,' she told me. 'I heard on the radio there was an accident on the freeway, darling,' she'd say on the phone. 'I'm worried about you driving in that awful traffic, darling. Be careful on your way home, darling.' Then we would jump in the bed and get to planting the horns on the *darling*."

To a group of seamen cooped up on a slow-moving tanker on a month-long passage from Mina Al Ahmadi to Yokohama, Liapouras's recollections sounded like those of men adrift in a lifeboat, reminiscing about steak dinners and cool mountain streams.

"It was great," Liapouras would continue with a sigh. "But it didn't last long. You see, where there are immigrants, there's always a father who dreams of his daughter marrying a young man from *the old country*. In Astoria, there was this fellow who had two marriable-age daughters. Both with mustaches thicker than mine and noses that stuck out like shark fins. The matchmaker fellow told me that if I didn't marry one of them, their father might go to the immigration. I told him it was too high a price to pay for a green card and shipped out on the first ship I could get. Fanouris agreed to do it, and now he's short-order cook at his father-in-law's greasy spoon. He has the old man and the wife bossing him around. The way I see it, a bear dancing in the county fair with a chain through his nose has it better than him."

Telemahos told me something similar. He'd turned down a matchmaking proposition with the daughter of a big-shot Greek in Savannah, and later that same day the immigration had him on the plane to Greece.

Even in my dire predicament, I agreed with Liapouras, but then, celibacy was getting painful.

CHAPTER FOUR

Meeting a Philosopher

Maybe it was because I had been in the military or because I had spent time on board merchant ships, but after a few days in Miami I had worked out a routine as automatic as if I were an AB, an able-bodied seaman, again. I pretended I was on the eight-to-twelve watch on my first ship, the *Poseidon*, an old Liberty-type freighter owned by a company famous for its cheapskatedness.

On a ship, the AB spends half of his watch doing ship's maintenance—cleaning, painting, and repairing. He spends the other half at the helm and on lookout. On Steve's ship, I started work at six o'clock. First, I did the inside chores like patching holes in the sheetrock and painting the walls; later, when there was enough light, I did the painting of the wooden trim outside. At 9:30, I cleaned up and walked to the restaurant and worked till closing at 10 that night.

On my third Sunday in Miami, I convinced myself to write a letter to Mother. I had put it off long enough. From the Woolworth's on the next block, I bought a box of airmail envelopes, the kind with the red-and-blue stripes around the edges, and Steve let me have one of the notepads from Eli-Witt Food Supply, so I couldn't think of anything keeping me from getting started. I folded back the newspaper covering the window, put a salvaged table and a crippled chair by it, then sat down determined to get the writing chore over with.

After the customary opening formalities, I got to the part I had been rehearsing in my head for days—how to explain to Mother why I wanted to stay in America. I eased into it by writing how big and how modern Miami was and what great opportunities for making money were here.

> *Here, you are the master of your own destiny instead of having a bunch of crooked politicians or some egomaniac dictator telling you how to live your life. Here, you can earn what you are worth and you can get as high as you deserve, even if you don't have royal ancestors or relatives in high places.*

For added convincingness I included the Alexander Vournaris story I had heard on the ship, substituting Miami for Mobile.

> *Vournaris jumped ship in Miami and made millions selling sausages from a pushcart. Now he owns ships and movie theaters and God knows what else.*

I saved the part with what I thought had the most redeeming value for last.

> *In Taxiarhes right now, you're probably bundled up with layer after layer of clothes, but over here I'm walking around wearing only a short-sleeved shirt. The weather is always mild in Miami. Next fall, I'm going to send you the ticket to Miami. After the olive harvest is finished, you can come and spend the winter*

here, to rest and get away from the cold weather. There is a nice neighborhood not too far from where I work where the houses look a lot like the ones in our part of the world. You can plant flowers and vegetables in the backyard to keep from getting bored. Beans and tomatoes grow the whole year over here.

The nice neighborhood I was referring to was Coral Gables. Steve had told me the first day that his neighborhood used to be ten times better than Coral Gables until "the damn Cubans turned it to shit," and the previous Sunday, I had taken a walk over there to see for myself. Most of the houses were Mediterranean style, with trimmed lawns and wide sidewalks under tall, flowering trees. I wished I had a camera so I could take pictures and send them to my brother and tell him that's where I lived. My brother lived in the stone house our father built when he got married. The sheep and the goats were on the ground floor, the people on the second, and the mules in the lean-to. Wouldn't it be something to see the expression on his face? I bet it would turn red enough to spot from across the ocean, like another sunrise.

I ended the letter by saying that the twenty-dollar money order I was enclosing would soon be doubled, because there was no limit to how much money a man could make in this country.

✣✣✣

One evening while slicing a chunk of roast beef in the kitchen, I heard Steve talking with someone in Greek in the dining room. I had been working at the restaurant for over three weeks, and this was the first time I'd heard someone speaking Greek. I turned off the slicer and rushed over to my observation post by the serving window. Peeking from behind the stack of plates, I saw a white-haired man between sixty and seventy strolling toward the corner table. He had a thick white mustache, a Greek peasant's cap slightly crooked to the right, and a brown jacket draped over his shoulders. His right-hand fingers were busy twirling a string of amber worry beads. For an instant, I was in Taxiarhes watching one of the villagers walk into Fatolias's coffeehouse.

After the man sat, Isabella rushed over to him. "The usual, Mr. Pete?"

"*Sí, linda,*" he answered. "Too old to change now."

Isabella clipped his order on the clothespin over the serving window.

Steve read the green slip, then called to the kitchen, "Milio, this is for Mr. Pete." He added in a sarcastic tone, "Remember, he has delicate stomach." Turning back to the customer, he said, "I thought you went to Greece, Diogenes. Haven't seen you for a while."

"I was in Nassau," the old man replied. "I did some fishing with the nephews."

Emilio prepared his sandwich—thinly-sliced roast beef on toasted dark bread with melted Swiss cheese—and put it on the serving window. "Tomorrow I'm making *ropa vieja,* Señor Pete," he said through the serving window.

"Thanks, Emilio. I will remember it."

I didn't speak to Pete until Friday, two days later. Emilio hadn't come to work that day, and Carmen had to rush home when somebody called and said her grandfather had slipped in the bathroom. I prepared Pete's "usual" roast beef sandwich, doctored the way I had seen Emilio do it. Then I got creative and trimmed off the crusty ends of the bread and cut the sandwich diagonally in four pieces and garnished it with sliced radishes and thin celery sticks. Since Isabella was stuck with a fussy customer, I took the sandwich out to Pete myself. I put the plate in front of him without saying anything and turned to leave. I was choosy about whom I spoke to, and when I did speak I was very frugal with my words. Most people seemed to have trouble understanding me anyway.

"Fancy," exclaimed Pete, looking at his plate. "Did you work on the passenger ships?" he asked in Greek.

"In the navy," I answered.

"I heard you talk with Carmen. You speak Spanish pretty good. Learned it at school?"

"Latin America," I said.

"Were you on a ship?"

"On a tanker. We ran Maracaibo–Cartagena a lot." *What's with the interrogation?*

"Bravo," said Pete. "Most seamen, all they get for their money is the clap. It's good to see one of ours with brains once in a while. There is a great future in this country for a man willing to learn new things."

"I got a pot on the stove," I said and walked away. *I bet he has a daughter looking for a husband from the old country.*

Later, when Isabella was busy and Carmen hadn't come back yet, Steve called me and nodded in Pete's direction. "Get him a refill."

I refilled his coffee cup, and since my cover was blown anyway, I asked him how long he had lived in Miami.

"Quite a few years," he said.

"Are you retired?" My turn to interrogate.

"You can say I am. I was a merchant seaman like you," he said. "Now I work two days a week, as an air-conditioning maintenance man at the dog track, just to stay in shape. At my age I don't need much. As long as I have a good drink and a good book, I'm happy. I have time to do a little fishing and a little reading."

"What did you sail as?" I asked.

"I was an engine-room worker—a donkey man," he said. "When the opportunity came, I jumped ship, got the green card, and sailed on American tankers as a wiper." I asked him what part of Greece he came from, and he told me about his village on the island of Paros. He spoke in the soft, confident tone of a man who knew what he wanted and wanted what he got out of life. He seemed to have done with his life exactly what I wanted to do with mine, except that when *I* retired, I would have my pension sent to the village, convert the dollars into drachmas, and live like a pasha.

The next Friday, Pete was again the last customer in the

restaurant. When he got up to leave, I was stowing the water glasses under the counter and Steve was at his post, reading the newspaper a customer had left on the counter.

"Any predictions about tonight's races, Steve?" Pete asked when he stopped by the cash register.

"I'm not reading the race column, Diogenes," Steve answered. "It says here there is a storm coming from the west." He tapped the paper with his finger. "I'm going to Tampa in the morning to spend the weekend with a sweet young thing and don't need the weather spoiling it." He rang up Pete's ticket. "I'm looking forward to this trip. She's really something, this one. She could be Lolita's younger sister." As he handed Pete his change, he said in a teasing tone, "You seem to know everything. You think the storm is coming this way?"

"They told you wrong, Steve," Pete replied. "I don't know everything, but I do know that it doesn't do any good to worry about things you have no control over. If it's meant to happen, it will happen. You only need to worry about things you do have control over, like messing up the life of a naïve young girl."

"Don't start preaching again, Diogenes," Steve muttered and turned to face me. "Listen, *if it is meant to happen* and it does rain tomorrow, work on patching those holes in the corridor I saw yesterday. They're about a meter down from your door. And *if it is meant to happen* and I find out who made those fucking holes, I'm going to kick his fucking ass all the way back to Cuba." He mimicked Pete's voice every time he said "If it is meant to happen."

"Good night, Steven," said Pete. When he got to the door he called back, "Be careful with the young thing. Some mother somewhere probably has high hopes for her."

"You're full of it tonight, Diogenes." Steve slammed the cash register drawer shut and glanced at Pete's order slip before nailing it on the spike. "Every night the same," he muttered. "Four seventy-five. The old goat is richer than Croesus. What the fuck is he going to do with all his money?"

"Is he really rich?" I asked.

"Damn right he is. You know a wiper in an American ship makes more than a chief engineer in the Greek merchant marine? Damn Diogenes is loaded, but you can't pry a penny out of him with a crowbar. He puts all his pay in big stocks like Coca-Cola and General Motors."

"Why you call him Diogenes?" I asked. "I thought his name was Pete."

"Because he has lopsided ideas about life, and because he's always philosophizing."

I pondered his answer for a while and concluded that Steve had the name wrong. Solomon was a more suitable nickname. Maybe, after I got to know him better, I could ask him for help in getting the green card.

Just as the weatherman predicted, it *did* happen to rain. Not the big storm the newspaper was talking about, but a slow, steady rain. Enough to keep me from doing outside work.

On the *Poseidon* in weather like this, the ABs would be painting the passageways. On Steve's ship, I got busy repairing the holes on the sheetrock in the corridor. I hadn't bothered putting on a shirt—no need dirtying clothes if I didn't have to. Besides, lots of people walked around like that in Miami.

I was almost finished with two of the three holes when Karen walked down the corridor, hugging a laundry basket, as I stepped out of my room where I had gone for more sandpaper.

"Good morning," I said. "You look very pretty today."

"Good morning, Kostas," she said. Her voice sounded extra-cheerful this morning.

"I no see you for many time."

"I went to my sister's for a few days."

"No baby boy with you? He sleeping yet?"

She giggled. "I like the way you talk. It's cute. No, baby boy stay with sister. Her youngest is the same age and they play well together."

I had exhausted my prepared speech, so I stood staring at her. She wore short pants and a halter, fluffy and loose. Craning her neck, she peeked behind me into my room. "You fixed up the room real nice. This used to be a dump." She put down the laundry basket and stepped inside. "You put the mattress on the floor?"

"I am Japanese," I said.

"I don't believe that. I know you're from Steve's hometown." She walked over to the window and touched the newspaper. "You need some curtains here. You shouldn't cover it with newspaper, even if it's the Sunday funnies." She giggled again. "I think I have some that will fit here just right." She started measuring with the width with her palm. "One, two, three, four, and a half. Yeah, they'll fit. I'll bring them later." She turned to walk out. "Where are you going to hang this?"

She pointed to the 1966 calendar lying on top of the bedside refrigerator. A salesman for Cheney Brothers Food Distributors had left it at the Parthenon yesterday. When Steve saw me leafing through, he said I could have it. "I've got enough stuff stuck on the walls."

It was one of those large landscape calendars. When I was on the *Poseidon,* the salesman for Marlboro cigarettes in Cape Town had brought one about the same size and hung it in the crew's lounge. Cowboys galloped through wide-open plains on every page, and I used to stare at it for hours, wondering if such places existed. This calendar had photographs of seashores and white sailboats, mountain ranges, and green valleys with clear streams running through them. The kind of eye-soothing pictures that let one's imagination run unbridled.

"I want put it there." I pointed to a spot on the wall. "Because I like look from bed."

She looked up. "There's already a nail there. I'll hang it and you see if it's right." She picked up the calendar and stretched toward the nail. "I need to step on something to reach it." She moved the one-gallon paint can with her foot. "You lay down and tell me if it's at the right spot."

"Okay," I said and assumed my relaxing position.

A half hour later, as I lay in bed puffing on a cigarette and staring at an orange sunset on the wall calendar, I went over what had just happened. After Karen hung the calendar, she must have tripped while stepping down from the paint can. In trying to keep her balance, she must have stumbled backward a few steps, slammed the door shut, then spun around and landed right on top of me. The flimsy halter outfit had come loose, uncovering what little it had been covering.

After that it was like a tornado, an earthquake, and a volcano eruption all happening at the same time. When it was over, Karen jumped up. "I left my laundry basket in the corridor! It's probably gone by now!" she cried and ran out.

I rose and retrieved my shorts from where they had landed on top of a stove. Old Pete was right when he'd said that if providence wanted it to happen, it would happen. All of my hard thinking trying to find ways to get acquainted with Karen had been unnecessary.

Could providence have something in store that would get me the green card?

CHAPTER FIVE

Exploring the Surroundings

Every other Saturday, I cut the grass around the apartment building—the chore Steve had added when I tried to squeeze a few more dollars' pay out of him. He'd agreed to pay me twenty-five dollars instead of twenty, but I had to cut the grass too. I found out later from Karen that he'd been paying a landscape company fifteen dollars for the same work.

Fortunately, the grass around Steve's parking lot was a strip about two meters wide instead of the meadow-sized lawns in front of some buildings. The lawnmower was a strange, clanking machine with a missing muffler and an even stranger contraption attached to its side for collecting the clippings. I pushed it back and forth, making sure I cut straight, slightly overlapping rows and occasionally making a run to the dumpster to empty the grass catcher.

While doing that, I pondered the weirdness that existed in the world. Would anyone believe me if I told the men at the Fatoliases' coffeehouse in Taxiarhes how much effort and money the Americans spent on taking care of the grass around their houses? They watered it, fertilized it, sprayed it with all kinds of chemicals to kill any bugs that might hurt it, then watched it grow strong and healthy just so they could pay somebody to cut it back every other week and then pay the trash man to haul the clippings to the dump.

I could almost hear Old Man Fatolias chuckling and saying, "Next thing, you'll be telling us they tie up the dogs with sausages over there."

It would be impossible for their minds to grasp that anyone would throw good, healthy, livestock's-dream kind of grass away. The biggest arguments among the villagers happened when somebody's sheep trampled somebody's grass before scything or when a farmer tethered his donkey with too long a line and it ate from the neighbor's field.

This Saturday, after I finished with the mowing, I got the urge to do something different. It was the middle of November, and it occurred to me that although I had lived in Miami for over a month, I hadn't seen much of the city. I hadn't dared to venture much farther than the restaurant and the Woolworth's store at the end of the block.

The sun was shining and the temperature was just right, so I thought it would be a good day to get a closer look at the famous Miami Beach—the "Jewish Colony," as Liolios, the deckhand on the *Aegean Sea*, used to call it. I could ride the city bus from the corner of Calle Ocho and Twentieth Avenue, have a beer at some safe place by the beach, then come back the same way. If that trip went well, maybe the next weekend I could ride a bus to the end of another route and back, just to see how big Miami was.

I practiced that routine during my years in the merchant marine. Whenever my ship was in port, after the obligatory visits to the love palaces, I would spend my nonworking hours riding the public transportation through the city: watching the locals go about their daily chores, getting on and off the bus with their shopping bags and satchels; eavesdropping on their gossip and talks about sports and politics. It gave me a native's view of the place while maintaining the loftiness of the visitor. I got to see places that most of the old salts didn't know existed. Not many seamen could say they had walked on top of *las murallas* in the walled city of Cartagena, from which Spanish guards scanned the horizon for approaching English men-of-war a few hundred years earlier, or that they had been to Fort Hamilton in Bermuda and seen the wax figures of the pirates. So lifelike and so fierce looking that the first time I saw them, I had jumped back and bumped into an elderly lady behind me. It was embarrassing.

For today's exploration, I put on my lucky flannel shirt with the red-and-black checks and the "bezballkap" with the word *Caterpillar* on the front. I bought a copy of the *Miami Herald* from the corner newsstand and stood among a group at the bus stop. I was pleased to see lots of people waiting; I always felt safer in a crowd. Some were in maids' uniforms, some in hospital workers' clothes, and others in colorful, touristy clothes.

When the bus came, I let the others get on ahead of me, trying to see how many coins they put in the fare box. By the time my turn came, I still hadn't figured it out; to avoid asking how much it was, I handed the driver a five-dollar bill, indicating with a shrug that I didn't have anything smaller. I got a seat by a window, then opened the newspaper and tried to look relaxed, comfortable, and slightly bored, as if I did this all the time.

A moment before the door closed, a man came on board and after scanning the interior came and sat next to me. He was around fifty and wore a light-brown suit and tie. Immediately, I regretted my stupid sightseeing idea.

He must be a government inspector, I thought in a panic. *Who else dresses like that in this weather?* When the bus started rolling, I concentrated on the sights outside to calm my thumping heart. Then the stranger turned his focus to the window as well, so I opened the paper and pretended to read the news to keep him from asking me about the sights we were passing.

In one of these make-believe news-readings, a photograph of a fishing vessel unloading a group of people onto a wooden pier caught my eye. From the words I understood, I learned they were refugees from Camarioca, Cuba, landing in Key West—a mixed group of about fifty people: men and women, some very old and frail, some very young, all haggard and weary and clutching clothes bundles. Everyone was looking up at the camera flash. Their faces were pale and their eyes extra large and scared, like the photographs of Greek refugees from Asia Minor disembarking in Piraeus. I think the paper said that this boatlift would end in two days, and the people were rushing to get out of Cuba. The man sitting next to me cleared his throat as if to say something, so I turned the page and brought it closer to my face to show I was absorbed in reading.

The entire lower half of that page was packed with photographs of passenger ships and advertisements for cruises.

Sail with us to the Bahamas, said one advertisement. *Have a dream weekend in Nassau and Freeport for only fifty-nine dollars on the fun ship* Bahama Star.

Explore the Caribbean with us on a seven-day cruise for only one hundred and sixty dollars on the SS Ariadne, said one that took half a page.

Two men got off at the stop by the Miami Dry Dock Company. The bus driver waited for a while with the door open, but nobody got on board. I supposed no shipyard workers lived in Miami Beach.

In front of the Miami Port Authority on Flagler Avenue, the bus stayed longer than at any of the other stops. Four large women with overstuffed bags squeezed off, and a frail old man struggled to lug his suitcase toward the exit, making very little progress. The man sitting next to me rose and picked it up. "*Con permiso,*" he said to the old man and walked out with him. From my window I watched them walk toward the dock, the old man pointing to one of the passenger ships. I took a deep breath and my heart returned to normal.

The four passenger ships I saw from my window were the same

ones whose advertisements I had seen in the paper. Docked one behind the other on a long pier not far from the bus, they seemed to be taking on provisions. The smallest of the four was the *Ariadne,* and I wondered if the ship was Greek. The one ahead of her was the *Bahama Star,* the biggest one. The one nearest to the bus seemed to be the oldest. When I read the name, I quickly repositioned myself for a better look. She was the SS *Florida.*

Four months earlier, when I was on the *Aegean Sea,* a deckhand named Simple had fallen inside a cargo tank and broken everything breakable in him. Our ship was sailing west of Grand Bahama at the time, and the captain had called for medical help from any ship in the area. The SS *Florida* had responded and sent a lifeboat with a doctor around midnight. And while the doctor was doing his examining, the ship had stayed some distance away, all lit up like some huge chandelier, continuously bombarding us with the mute artillery of camera flashes. I had read the name *Florida* on the bow of the lifeboat and on the sailors' crisp khaki uniforms and wondered aloud what it would be like to work on a ship like that. The third mate, who had been standing next to me, said that it was like being in paradise.

"Good-looking women running around practically naked, trying to get laid by any crewmember who can get it up. And the food—fancy meats and pastries and cakes piled on the tables as high as the crow's nest, free to everybody."

"How do you know all that?" I asked.

"I cruised in the Caribbean for six months on the *Evangeline* some years back."

I asked him why he'd left, and he said his mother got sick and he had to rush home, but a deckhand from the same village whispered to me later that his mother had died in childbirth.

The doctor from the *Florida* said Simple had to go to the hospital, so they took him to the cruise ship for transport to Miami. Our captain sent the chief mate along as interpreter.

"Fucking captain," the third mate cursed when he saw them

leaving. “He knew I speak better English than anyone on this ship. He should’ve sent me.”

Our chief mate was a stout man around forty, with simple tastes and few words. He always carried in his shirt pocket a picture of his wife and baby daughter. He rejoined us in Aruba three days later, and all those who had heard the third mate’s tales swarmed around him.

“Were naked women running around? How many did you bed?”

“I didn’t see any. I stayed with Simple all the time.”

“How about eating? Did you try any of their fancy dishes?”

“I asked the steward to bring me a plate in the cabin. I ate some spaghetti and some fish with rice. They were good.”

“How about their cakes and their fancy pastries?”

“I got some peaches. They were good too.”

On the bus, I got up and moved farther back for a better look of the ships.

The most elegant looking of the four was the *Yarmouth Castle*. She looked like something out of an old postcard. Her mahogany decks, bronze portholes, and varnished handrails gleamed in the afternoon sun. She seemed like one of those ships you read about in novels, where a blue-blooded heiress to a shipping fortune is taking a cruise to cure her melancholy and falls in love with the young and handsome helmsman.

On the starboard bow, two deckhands sitting on a scaffold were touching up the name, one the golden letters of the word *Yarmouth*, and the other *Castle*. A pang of longing ran through me. *I had lots of good times when I was a deckhand*. The two men on the scaffold didn’t have to worry about anyone turning them in to the immigration or about getting the green or the purple card.

I got off in Miami Beach and walked slowly along the boardwalk, appraising the holding capacity of the bathing suits worn by the women lying on the sand to my right and marveling at the tall buildings and fancy hotels on my left.

Many of the women lay facedown on their blankets with the tops of their bathing suits untied in what must be a universal custom. One summer when I was in the navy, I and a couple of my navy friends gave a boy two drachmas to walk along the beach, pulling a plastic mouse on a thin fishing line behind him. We stood a few meters away, laughing our heads off as, one after another, the terrified women let out bloodcurdling screams and jumped up, forgetting to retie their bathing suit tops. Ah, carefree youth.

At a coffee shop by the street, I zigzagged through the tables to a spot with the best view of the beach and the ocean beyond. The waiter was at my side before my back touched the canvas chair.

"Bring me one Budweiser," I ordered. "In bottle, no can." I had heard some of the expert beer drinkers say that Budweiser was starting to sell beer in cans now and it didn't taste half as good as the bottled stuff.

"Can I see some ID?"

I looked at him. The waiter was short and middle aged with dark hair. His eyes had the tired, bored look of having to repeat a bothersome task and had his hand extended as if to receive something.

"*Qué*?" I always switched to Spanish when I felt insecure, and the waiter looked Cuban anyway.

"An ID—passport, driver's license, anything." The waiter's voice confirmed the boredom of his eyes.

"Oh, *sí, sí*," I answered, and my heart sped up. "*Un momento*." I pretended to feel my back pockets, then emptied them on the table, making sure the waiter saw the folded dollars under my lighter.

"*Cabrón*," I said after a while. "*Olvidar la cartera en el cuarto*." I made a vague gesture toward the beachfront hotels to my left.

"I don't speak any Spanish. You got an ID or not?"

"I said I forget my wallet in room." I made a faint arc with my arm again.

"Can't serve you beer without an ID." Same why-always-me tone of voice.

"*No problema*," I said quickly. "*Una* Coca-Cola."

"Pepsi okay?"

"*Sí, sí*. Pepsi okay."

Must be the only one in Miami who doesn't speak any Spanish. Could he be a government spy? I wondered.

"Want a menu?" asked the waiter half-heartedly, as if he were sure it was a wasted effort. He extended a plastic-covered page to me.

"Yes, yes, I have dinner." Maybe if I had a big meal and left him a good tip, he wouldn't think I was some deadbeat illegal.

"I'll be back," he said.

I looked at the menu and immediately rejected the "big meal" idea. Everything was priced almost three times higher than at the Parthenon. *Must be lots of rich people in the Jewish Colony.* When the waiter came back with my drink, I ordered a "ham-boorger de-looxe" and fried potatoes.

I looked around the dining area while I waited for my food and counted 16 four-chair tables. At the prices he charged, the owner of this place must be making millions. I lit a cigarette, sipped on the drink, and let my gaze run over the beach. Almost the middle of November, and people were swimming and sunbathing. A warm, gentle breeze from the ocean brought a faint scent of iodine. Yes sir, this was the life. I bet in Taxiarhes, Pavlos was shoveling snow—could be waist-high right now.

In the distance, a ship—a tanker or maybe a bulk carrier, too far to tell for sure—was heading south. For a moment, I felt sorry for my old shipmates. A few months back, on an afternoon like this, one day before we got to Surabaya, a group of us sat at the stern of the *Aegean Sea*, talking about what we were going to do when we got into port. We were carrying a load of crude oil from the Persian Gulf where there was no female entertainment, so the conversation was about women.

Liolios the deckhand was reminiscing about his conquests in Cuba when he was with the *Olympic Flame* of Onassis.

"We were running between Havana, Jacksonville, and sometimes Miami. Beautiful life, really beautiful life." His voice almost cracked with emotion. "One time, when we were passing Florida a couple of miles east of the Jewish Colony, heading south toward Havana, two boats a bit smaller than those two"—he pointed at two fishing boats in the distance—"came within fifty yards of our starboard. Both boats, loaded with wild women, sailed alongside us for over three miles, all the time flirting and teasing us. Some took off their bathing suit tops and waved them at us. Even the engine-room watch got on deck. Everybody was hanging over the rails, drooling like hound dogs."

"Where is this Jewish Colony?" a fireman asked.

"It's Miami Beach, my boy," said Liolios, his tone implying that he forgave the fireman's ignorance. "They call it that because so many Jews live there."

"Only there? There are Jews everywhere," said the fireman. "Even in my village we have two families. When one of their sons married my cousin who had no dowry, both Jewish families put up the money to buy a barn and make it into sawmill for him."

"That's how they are," Liolios said. "The Jews help their own. There used to be a sign at a hotel in Miami Beach that said, 'Admittance not allowed to dogs and Jews.' The Jews collected money, bought the hotel, and took the sign down. The Greeks, *ph*, would still be arguing about how they were going to beat up the guy who hung the sign."

I kept watching the faraway ship. Wouldn't it be something if she was the *Aegean Sea*? I took another puff on the cigarette and pondered the turns a person's life takes through the years. When Liolios was doing the storytelling about the Jewish Colony, we were at the other end of the globe. I had no idea where Miami Beach was, nor had I any plans of ever visiting there. Now I was sitting right in the middle of it, enjoying an evening by the sea as if I were one of its upstanding citizens.

Maybe this would be a good place to meet a Jewish woman, and maybe her people would help me buy my own restaurant. I had it from a reliable source that Jewish women were the best in bed, too. Telemahos was bedding the barmaid at Lum's Restaurant, where he worked before he got caught, and told me he had never met another woman like Myra. She could make his legs feel like rubber.

It would be nice to meet a woman who could help make up for my shortcomings in the language, in the business connections, and the social graces. When you grew up surrounded by livestock and peasants in a tiny village tucked away on a remote mountainside, it was hard to learn how to behave among people with money and class. The fact that the Jews supported each other was known everywhere, but it was also a universal truth that "money goes to money." Who would marry a penniless dishwasher?

And how could I meet a woman of that kind when I was afraid to go anywhere and got scared to death every time somebody in a clean shirt looked my way? Also, I didn't have a car or even the license to drive one. Those were serious problems all right, and I had to be careful about how I tried to get around them.

Maybe Pete Papas had some good ideas. I could trust Pete to give me useful advice. He didn't seem the gossipy type, didn't have any daughters looking for a husband, and lately it seemed that he lingered a bit longer after finishing his meal, always coming up with new things to talk about. Most recently he'd asked me if I had ever seen an American football game.

"I saw some games on the television in my room," I said. "It didn't make any sense. It's not like our football."

"It's different when you watch it on the field," Pete said. "I'll take you to a game sometime and explain it to you."

After a while, the table next to mine became occupied by two women. Both were brunettes around thirty, with looks that could be Latin American or Mediterranean, or maybe Jewish. I kept glancing over at them, wondering how I could get to know them better. Both seemed absorbed in sipping their bright-colored concoctions out of tall glasses and laughing at each other's jokes.

An annoying little voice inside pointed out that when all you knew of a language was a handful of words, it was hard to charm anybody with your conversation. Maybe I could speak to them in Spanish. I could tell them I was from Argentina—that had an exotic ring to it. One by one, the persuasive points were stacking up.

I could say I was from Buenos Aires.

I could say I was into breeding racehorses.

I could say I was visiting the area for a horse show.

I put a cigarette in my mouth, turned off the gas of the butane lighter, and clicked it conspicuously a couple times so others would notice it wouldn't light. With cigarette in hand, I rose and started to ask for a light. Both women had just lit up.

I was about to open my mouth when the one closest to me said to the other, "Look at the balls on that guy." She nodded toward the counter a couple of meters away where a man in a tight, European-style bathing suit was standing, sipping on a drink. She had spoken in clear Greek without hesitation, with the accent of someone who had grown up in Athens.

"Yeah, he's a stud all right," said the other woman. Just as clear, just as Greek.

Quickly I sat back down and lit my cigarette, pretending to gaze at a sailboat far away.

The women concentrated on sipping their drinks for a while. Then the one farthest from me said, "How's everything at home, Elli? George doing okay?"

"Everything's the same," said the one who had spotted the man with the balls. "The doctor changed George's blood pressure medicine, and I think this one keeps him from getting it up. Not that we were doing much fucking before. He always had trouble with his little worm. Thank God for Charlie."

"The bug man from Nozzle Nolan?"

"No, Charlie is Jamaican. He's the night clerk at the Castaways Inn. He's got a tool bigger than an English cucumber," said Elli.

"I tried it a few times with a black just to have a primitive lay, but I liked it better with Ramon. He knows how to use his tongue. I get hot just thinking about it," said the other, and they both giggled.

A car stopped at the no-parking area in front of the place and a bald, stubby man rushed toward the two women.

"Hurry up, ladies. We're running late."

"Can't we stay a little longer, George? It's nice over here," said Elli.

"We'll do this some other time, darling, I promise."

"That's my George," Elli sighed. "Always promises, promises."

They paid their bill and left. I watched them get into their car. They never considered there might be somebody around who could understand them.

After spending a whole day locked up in a stinking jail in Colombia, I'd learned to speak like everybody around me was listening. I and three of my shipmates from the *Aegean Sea* were in a dentist's waiting room in Cartagena, and while waiting, three of us were critiquing the anatomy of the two young women across from us. Anastasis said he would like to do it with the skinny one, and Liolios said he would like to play with the boobs of the fat one. And so on and so on, a normal conversation among normal young seamen on their first trip ashore after a month at sea. The two little tarts probably knew they were being talked about because they giggled and acted coy.

About ten minutes into our erotic appraisal, Mihalis, who was the oldest man on the ship, said, "Better watch it, fellows. You never know if somebody understands what you're saying."

"*Orthós emílisas.*" (You spoke correctly.) An old matron startled us, and my face got hot. All that time, she had been reading a book and acting as chaperone to the two girls. She closed her book and in accented Greek she repeated that Mihalis was correct. "You are a disgrace to your country and your civilization, and I shall teach you a lesson."

She had the dentist's receptionist call the police, and when they came, she told them, "These three repugnant persons insulted my granddaughters with vulgar and obscene talk. I demand you do something about it!"

It turned out that she was the wife of the German consul in Cartagena, who had been in Greece on his previous assignment. The old woman was nuts about Homer and Aristotle and understood enough Greek to get us locked up. It took the shipping agent a whole day to bail us out, and we were not allowed to go ashore the rest of the time the ship was in port. For the next three weeks, I had to endure the torture of my shipmates describing in vivid detail the orgies in which they claimed they were participating every night ashore.

I had finished my ham-boorger and Pepsi long ago, and it was getting late. I thought it best to leave before the waiter got a notion to start a conversation. I paid and left a whole dollar for the tip. As I walked away, two beautiful women in shorts and tight blouses came jogging from the opposite direction. They smiled as they passed by, their perfume following close behind. I turned and watched them bouncing down the sidewalk until they turned the corner.

Yes, Miami Beach was a nice place. And there must be lots of nice places around, but without the damn green card, I was scared to set foot out of my room and in no shape to enjoy any of them.

CHAPTER SIX

A Ship on Fire

At the bus stop I sat on a bench next to an old man wearing a hotel worker's uniform. I opened my newspaper to discourage conversation and, peeking around it, watched the street traffic. A delicate-looking woman jogged across the street holding a leash with a hairy dog almost as big as she was, gasping alongside her. Soon after, a wrestler-looking man with a gray, pointy beard and straw hat marched by as if he were in a parade, holding a leash with a small, sausage-like dog at the other end. The legs of the little thing were in overdrive as it struggled to keep up, looking like a centipede chasing an ox. I wished my brother could see that.

When I boarded the bus, I put the thirty cents in the fare box like a frequent commuter, then sat by a window on the left side, in front of a middle-aged couple. At the stop by the port entrance, two of the cruise ships were leaving. The *Ariadne* and the *Bahama Star* slowly glided through the channel toward the Atlantic. On their decks, a colorful crowd of passengers lined the rails, waving and pointing to things ashore.

The *Yarmouth Castle* was also just getting underway. The line handlers cast off the ropes, and from the decks the passengers threw confetti and streamers and blew kisses to those on the dock. Somewhere on the ship a band was playing a fast, cheery tune.

"Listen, Howard," said the woman behind me to the man next to her. "They're playing 'Anchors Away.'" The man didn't answer. "It would be nice to go on a cruise," she said with a sigh. "Lucky people. We never do anything like that, Howard."

"They're rich, Eugenia," Howard said. "We can't afford it."

"You always say that." She let out another sigh.

"Because it's the truth," said Howard; then, as if he were talking to the bus, he urged, "C'mon, get going! I'm missing *Bonanza*."

"Look at them," Eugenia said, almost in a whisper. "They look so happy. Lucky people."

Moments later the bus started rolling and Howard muttered, "'Bout time." Two blocks farther up, the bus stopped again. "Now what the hell is the matter?" Howard growled.

"There's something going on at the Freedom Tower, Howard," Eugenia said.

I poked my head out the window. There seemed to be at least three hundred people packed in the square and on the streets around a peach-colored building with a tower that looked like a belfry in the center. Many of the people held signs that said something about Cuba and America. They marched back and forth, shouting and waving their arms.

"Damn Cubans," Howard said. "That's all they're good for."

"Howard, somebody might hear you," whispered Eugenia.

"Don't care if they do. I'm missing *Bonanza*. Lazy moochers."

The driver said the police had closed the street and he'd have to go a different route. He named the streets we'd be going through and the new places where he would stop, and those who knew what he was talking about grumbled that it was out of their way. Eugenia suggested they get off now.

"Damn lazy moochers," muttered Howard, getting out of his seat. "Making me walk three full blocks to get to my house."

I thought it couldn't be too far to my room—not more than a few minutes walking anyway. I started to follow the older couple off the bus but quickly returned to my seat. If the cops rounded up the "lazy moochers," I would be in a hell of a fix when they found me among them.

Three stops later, I felt sure I recognized my neighborhood—the purple house and the Sinclair gas station on the opposite corner. I got off and walked with brisk steps toward what looked like the back of the Woolworth's store near my apartment. It turned out to be the back of a department store I had never heard of, so I kept on walking.

I didn't dare ask anybody for directions because I knew my English sounded neither Floridian nor New Yorkish, and I didn't want to ask in Spanish because they might start a conversation, asking me where I was from and how long I'd been here, and they might get suspicious. A flunky working for a shipping agent had told me once that in America, the immigration paid fifty dollars a person to anybody turning in illegals.

I didn't want to take a taxi because I kept thinking that I was only one block away from my room. Besides, everybody knew that taxi drivers, when they sensed that you didn't know your way around, would zigzag back and forth and drive you all over town just to raise the fare. Wouldn't that be ridiculous? And I couldn't even complain to the cops.

So I kept walking, pretending to be in a hurry so I wouldn't seem lost. With every step I repeated to myself that I needed to get my green card problem resolved soon. This was not the way for a man like me—young, healthy, and handsome—to live his life. I could make a lot of money in this country and have lots of fun while doing it if only I were legal.

But the only ones who got to be legal over here were the political refugees, those trying to get away from the communists, like the Cubans. If you were a young Greek escaping the mules and the goats, you were out of luck. When I was on the ship, I had heard that sometimes big businesses brought into America foreigners with skills that were in short supply. Unfortunately, no one seemed desperate for dishwashers and hamburger flippers.

Of course, another way to stay here was by marrying somebody. Karen would probably jump at the chance, but then she would spend every penny I made and cuckold me while I wasn't looking with anybody who could get it up. Every crew member on the ships had a large collection of horror stories about shipmates who'd paid one thousand dollars to some hooker to marry her. Then, as soon as the money was gone, the hooker went to the cops and said he was beating her up. The immigration had the poor sucker on the plane to Greece before he knew what happened.

Five blocks after I got off the bus, again I was sure again I'd spotted the Woolworth's store near my apartment, only to find out that it was the back of the Food Fair building.

I knew the Parthenon restaurant was almost on the corner of Eighth Street and Twentieth Avenue. I got angry at myself for not paying attention to whether the numbers went up or down while I was walking. The barely readable sign on the light pole said *SW 103rd Street*, and across the corner, going the other way, another sign said *NW Seventh Avenue*. I turned right and walked along the avenue, watching for the next street number. When I got to the corner, there was no number anywhere, so I kept on walking.

At the next corner, I read the street number and cursed my stupidity: the number was 105th. I had been walking in the wrong direction all this time. I turned and started back with renewed confidence. I walked by a coffee shop where two people played dominoes on a table on the sidewalk. A group of spectators clustered around, critiquing each move and bombarding the players with advice. Almost like a Greek coffeehouse.

I was on Seventeenth Avenue, and the street numbers got lower every block. I was on the right path now. I eased up my pace a bit, my head buzzing with unanswered questions about my green card predicament. Suddenly an unpleasant but familiar-sounding voice interrupted my thinking. I turned and saw the painters' van parked a few yards ahead. Jose, the painter I'd punched in the nose, stood next to it, shouting to someone on a second-floor balcony above. I took a fast sidestep and hid behind the furniture being unloaded from a Sears truck.

Why the devil did he have to be here? I wasn't afraid of meeting up with him—I wouldn't have any trouble breaking his face up some more; but if there were a disturbance and the police came, it would be goodbye Miami and goodbye America for me. I peeked over a dresser, and when he was looking the other way, I put my hands in my pockets and walked in the opposite direction, trying to look as if I were out for an evening stroll.

Had the son of a bitch seen me? He knew where I lived and he had a car, so he could be waiting for me at the parking lot.

When I got to my building, I scanned the lot from across the street for signs of the painters' truck. I didn't see it, so I dashed to my room and locked the door. Kicking off my shoes, I turned on the television and collapsed in bed. I had walked for almost two hours.

The screen on the little television set lit up just in time to see three cowboys galloping over a hill in the fading daylight. Immediately after followed an advertisement for Marlboro cigarettes, and after that an advertisement for a Ford car, the kind with the galloping stallion on the grill. Painted some shiny color, it had the top down, and was driven by a curvy blonde on a straight country road. The blonde waved at the camera, and I almost waved back.

I had dug up the black-and-white set from the junk pile that used to be in my room. Barely bigger than a shoebox, it had pink plastic casing and two chrome-plated wires sticking from the top for antennas. The only television station I could get was ten. I watched anything that came on, and I graded myself on how many words I understood.

After the advertisements, a lot of drum beating and cymbal clanging and a voice announced that it was time for *The Tonight Show with Johnny Carson.* A big fellow sitting on a couch next to the desk said, "Heeeere's Johnny!" making the *here* last a whole breath's worth, as if this Johnny person didn't want to come out, was holding on to something behind the curtain, and the big man was dragging him onstage.

Johnny came out to thunderous applause, grinning and wide-eyed, looking left and right with short, quick turns of his head as if he were spooked by something. He started talking to the audience and to the big fellow on the couch, whose name I surmised was Ed, and every time he stopped talking, the audience burst out laughing. Johnny used a lot of fancy words, and I couldn't understand any of his jokes. A few minutes into the show, I dozed off.

When I opened my eyes, the television was showing a ship in flames. Sometimes they showed old movies with pirate ships battling in the high seas, and I liked to watch them, but tonight I wanted to continue my sleep. I staggered up and reached for the knob, but just as I touched the set, the announcer mentioned the ship's name and my hand froze. I looked closer and there she was—the *Yarmouth Castle* turned into a huge fireball. Instantly all sleepiness went away. I turned up the volume and watched dumbfounded as dazed passengers in their pajamas plunged into the sea.

Every so often the television would show the passenger ship *Bahama Star*, and a freighter standing farther away, surrounded by lifeboats. I lit a cigarette and stared at the images in awe. Only hours earlier, those same people now getting fished out of the water, singed and half-drowned, had been throwing streamers, blowing kisses, and dancing on the deck.

From time to time, I saw one helicopter with Coast Guard markings hovering over the ships, and part of another one, probably from the television station. I tried to get a clearer picture by moving the antenna wires to different positions, then sat cross-legged on the mattress as near to the television set as possible.

I had heard many stories of shipwrecks and of ships torpedoed and sunk by the Germans. Every old-timer in the merchant marine had an inventory of disaster stories, all of which—appropriately embellished when recounted in mess halls and poop decks during calm, long passages—happened in stormy seas where they had to swim in frigid waters, battle lifeboat-swallowing waves and starving sharks, and drifted in the ocean for days before they got rescued. But this was my first time witnessing a real ship disaster happening practically in front of me, and to people I had almost met only hours earlier.

I watched the disaster unfold for the rest of the night. At first light I rushed to the corner newsstand and bought the *Miami Herald.* The Sunday edition always weighed a ton, filled with advertisements and movie star magazines that made it hard to find what I was looking for.

I kept the news section and handed the bundles of glossy pages and grocery store coupons back to the guy at the newsstand. "Take this back," I said. "Too much paper."

"For you, probably *is* too much paper," answered the guy, and for an instant I wanted to punch him.

I found a two-page section that seemed to have been added at the last minute. Lots of photographs showed people in orange lifejackets bobbing in the water, their hands raised and their mouths open; others recorded people crowding the ship's deck as it listed, about to roll over any moment. Flames flickered out of every porthole.

The name of the captain seemed to be Greek. I couldn't understand many of the words in the article, but the person who wrote it didn't have any good things to say about the captain. I wondered if there were other Greeks in the ship's crew. The men on the *Florida* lifeboat, when they came to pick up Simple on the *Aegean Sea* four months earlier, had said most deckhands on their ship were from Spain.

Too bad the Greek captain had turned out to be a disgrace. I would ask Pete Papas what he knew about the ship and the captain when he came for supper on Monday. Pete would give me an accurate account of what happened. He was a retired seaman himself and saw things from the inside. To the blabbermouth reporters sitting warm and rested in an office, telling everybody what the captain should or shouldn't have done at that moment of crisis came easy.

⁜ ⁜ ⁜

But Pete Papas didn't come in at all on Monday.

"Probably some goofy old woman snared him to her house for a home-cooked dinner," said Steve. "The old goat might be able to get it up still."

Monday mornings were when most salespeople called at the Parthenon to get their orders for the week: the vegetables, the frozen items, the paper goods, and everything else a restaurant needs to operate. Most of them would order a cup of coffee while waiting to talk to Steve. They'd tell the waitress to keep the change from the dollar; then, innocently, they'd query her for some inside information, like whether the lunch hour had picked up or the cook was using margarine or real butter. Only Bill from Quality Meats came shortly before closing on Fridays. He called Steve "buddy," dropped useless tidbits of business gossip while writing down the orders, and laughed his head off at every one of Steve's corny jokes before it even got to the punch line.

This week, Pete came in late on Friday. Since his usual table was occupied, he sat by the counter on the stool closest to the cash register.

"I'll keep an eye on your tricks when you're giving the change," he teased Steve.

"Have you seen me milk quarters out of my nose?" said Steve.

"No, but I know you're good at making dollar bills disappear."

Carmen picked up a paper someone had left on a table and read some names of the officers on the *Yarmouth Castle*. "Did you know any of these people, Steven?"

"Hell yah, I knew them all," Steve said. "A bunch of losers and suckers. I could sell seaweed for silk ribbons to every one of them, as we say in Greece." He cranked up his usual sarcastic laughter.

"You are *muy alegre* today, Steven," Carmen said. "Must have hit the trifecta last night."

"Damn right I hit it. They were giving ten-to-one odds, but I watched those dogs when they walked them out and I knew the goofball making the odds didn't know what he was talking about."

"It never fails, Steven," Pete said. "It reminds me of an old Chinese proverb."

"Oh yeah? What?"

"I'll simplify it for you. It goes something like this: 'When it comes to something we feel strongly about, even a small success in it can make us feel important and smarter than the rest.'"

"Diogenes, your philosophizing is getting harder and harder to understand." Steve laughed again. "I thought you kicked the bucket; haven't seen you for a whole week."

"We went on a little cruise. It was the lady's birthday."

"Taking care of that pussy, eh?" Steve said. "Smart old man."

Bill from Quality Meats burst through the door, holding a bottle of Coca-Cola. "How've you been doing, buddy?" He slapped Steve's back and set his order book on the counter to open it. "Same as last week, buddy? Two boxes of rib eyes, two T-bones, and a box of cube steaks?"

"Yeah, the same," said Steve.

Bill started scribbling. "I'm perfectly honest with you, Steve. You know a good deal when you see it. By the way, I hear the county hired a new health inspector. He's one of those *minority* persons, but they tell me he's all right."

"I met him already," Steve said. "And listen what I did to him."

Bill had already started chortling, as if to warm up his laugh machine.

"He comes here the other day, this inspector," Steve said. "A little black guy about this high." He gestured the height of the counter. "He comes in, shows me his card and says he's the health inspector. I said okay. He pokes his nose in the bathrooms and in every corner in the kitchen. Then he asks me to show him the dishwasher. He wants to check the temperature, he says. So, I call Pascal over and say, 'Hey, Pascal. I didn't know you were running a fever; this man here wants to take your temperature.' You should see the look on the little guy's face." Steve burst out laughing.

Bill had already bent over and was holding his stomach. "I swear, Steve, I'm perfectly honest with you, buddy. I don't know how you think of these things. How did you do at the track last night?"

"I hit the trifecta, with ten-to-one odds."

"I'm perfectly honest with you, Steve, you know how to pick 'em. They can't fool you. No siree, that's for sure." Bill closed his order book. "Well, Steve, old buddy, I always enjoy talking with you and always hate to leave your place, but I got to run. I got a mean boss. Your crew is lucky. They got the nicest boss in the county." At the door he called back, "Good luck tonight, my friend."

Pete Papas followed him with his gaze. After he was gone, Pete handed Steve his meal check and a ten-dollar bill.

"Steve," he said while waiting for his change, "salesmen are as good a material for friends as bartenders. I think Mister Perfectly Honest Bill here is playing you for a sucker. I would check prices and quality with the other meat suppliers if I were you."

"Well, you are not me, so don't worry about it," Steve snapped. "You stick to your philosophizing."

Pete nodded like he'd expected that response. "Good night, everybody," he said.

I followed him to the door. "I wanted to ask you about the fire on the *Yarmouth Castle*," I said. "Do you know anything about it?"

"I know plenty about it," he replied. "I'll tell you all you want to know tomorrow. I'm off for a few days, so I'll take you to the dog track, and you can see how some Americans try to get rich the fast way. I'll pick you up around six."

"I'll be ready," I said.

CHAPTER SEVEN

The Legend of Alexander Vournaris

I was outside my room soon after five o'clock the next day, just in case Pete showed up early, and occupied myself, as usual, by looking at other people's cars. Pete pulled up a minute before six.

"Shall we ride in yours?" he teased, nodding toward the Chevy Impala whose interior I had been scrutinizing.

"We go in yours. I only drive mine on Sundays." I got in and he drove off. "Nice car," I said, admiring the dashboard. "What brand is it?"

"It's Oldsmobile Super 88," answered Pete.

"Did you just buy it?" I asked.

"No, I had it for a while."

"Looks brand new. How old is it?"

"It was new when I bought it back in 1960."

"Five years old yet looks brand new." I took out my pack of cigarettes and got ready to light.

Pete extended his hand to stop me. "I prefer for people not smoke in the car. Makes it smell bad."

I put the cigarette back in the pack.

Pete said he needed to make a quick stop to give some keys to a guy from work. "It's not too far out of our way," he added, as if apologizing.

A few minutes later, we stopped at what looked like a playfield. At the center of it, two teams of young boys were involved in some kind of a game.

"Jack is coaching Little League baseball," Pete said. He must have sensed I didn't understand, because he quickly added, "Little League is what they call the children's teams over here. That's Jack over there." He pointed toward a burly man with a beet-red face. "It won't take me long."

Pete got out and headed over. The man was delivering a fierce sermon to a group of boys no more than seven years old standing in a half-circle around him. Their uniforms were brown shirts and white pants, the white barely discernible under the grass and dirt stains. The shirts had a number on the back and the words *Integrity Plumbing* above it. And in the front, in big letters, the word *Lions*.

The burly man held a bat, which in his hands looked like a popsicle stick, and he was swinging it with enough force to send the imaginary ball to the ends of the earth. Some of the boys closest to him stared in bewilderment, others scratched the ground with their shoes, and a couple farthest from the center were busy shoving each other.

I climbed out of the car and walked closer to the play area. The ball field had stands on two sides where a few people, probably the boys' parents, were sitting. A few older couples sat in front of the stands on folding chairs.

Across from the Lions' den was the other team's camp. The players wore yellow shirts that had black numbers with the words *Mario's Pizza* and *Hornets*. Their coach was a tall, thin man who must have been telling them a joke, because I could hear the chirpy laughter of the boys from way over where I was standing.

The smell of grilled meat drew my attention, and at the other side of the field I spotted a man cooking hamburgers on a grill. Kids and grownups holding dollar bills stood in line behind the small kitchen on wheels.

Maybe after I get the green card, I could do something like that if I can't raise enough money to buy my own restaurant.

On the *Aegean Sea,* some of the crew had talked of a Greek who jumped ship and made a fortune selling hot dogs out of a pushcart. I went in for a better look. The cart seemed simple and inexpensive. All the man had was a small grill, a kettle for boiling hot dogs, and a propane tank under them. The only supplies were some boxes with the special buns and plastic packages with the relish, ketchup, and mustard. It shouldn't take too much money to get in that kind of business.

"Jack is the Lions' coach," Pete said, startling me. "They are getting stung by the Hornets, so he's all worked up. Let's watch for a while."

Soon the teams took their places. The Lions were spread out over the field, and one of them, dressed like a fencer, squatted at one corner of the play area.

"He's the catcher," explained Pete. "He's supposed to catch the ball thrown by that kid in the middle."

A Hornets player holding a bat almost as tall as he was got in front of the squatting kid. Every person on the stands and on the ground seemed to be shouting instructions. Some were telling the kids out in the field to come closer and some to go farther out. A group of parents from the Lions side shouted, "Take your time! Don't rush it!" to the kid who was throwing the ball to the one with the funny chest armor. And the parents of the Hornets shouted, "Make him pitch to you! Don't swing at balls!" to the kid waving the bat.

It didn't look to me like any of the boys were paying attention to this bombardment of instructions. Most of them seemed preoccupied with shoving each other, searching for things on the ground, or kicking the things they found.

The kid in the middle threw the ball a few times, and the kid from the Hornets swung the bat but missed every time. With his head down, he walked to the fenced area and joined his teammates. Another child, punier than the first, came and stood in front of the catcher. He swung the bat over his head a couple of times, looking like he was going to tip over at any moment. At the first throw, he hit the ball and sent it into a slow, lazy loop toward the spot where two Lions were examining something in the dirt. The people on the stands next to the Lions' den sprang to their feet and, waving their arms, yelled, "Get the ball! Throw to first! Throw to second!" until they were hoarse.

The kid who'd hit the ball started running, which got the fans of the Hornets shouting, "Run to first! Run to second! Go home!" and waving their arms in the direction they wanted the kid to go, as if to create a favorable draft or give the bewildered child an imaginary push.

The two Lions out in the field looked up. When they saw the ball coming toward them, they moved over and watched it plop to the ground and roll for a couple of yards while one of them picked his nose and the other looked toward the stands. Then both of them decided to go after the ball, only to collide with each other and fall down just as they were reaching for it. The people in the stands were delirious, and I was surprised and confused. The only time I had seen a grown-up so excited was when my goats got into Mr. Psirakis's bean garden and destroyed a whole year's planting.

Americans might seem crazy, I thought, *but maybe they have figured out the right way to bring up a child—to look at their kid as an extension of their own selves, a friend and comrade instead of free labor.* If I had a son, I would bring him up as my friend, give him pointers on fishing and on European football. Hell, I'd do that even if I had a girl.

"Let's go." Pete jolted me out of my thoughts. "I don't want to be around when Jack has a heart attack."

When we arrived at the dog track, Pete greeted every usher and floor sweeper with their first names and asked them about their health and about their children. Some workers teased him about being unable to stay away from the place even on his days off, and Pete said he missed them too much. He said he needed to see somebody in the storeroom, and I waited for him in the main lobby.

I leaned against a column, lit a cigarette, and looked around. So, this was the dog track. I had heard stories from those who had been to America, about fortunes being made and lost "at the dogs." When told, the winning was usually in first person and the losses happened to someone else. "I made a killing every time I went to the track," or "He inherited a fortune but lost it all to the dogs, damn fool."

The place was built like a stadium where runners competed, only instead of stands all around the track, only one section stood in about a quarter of it. That section was enclosed and air-conditioned, and the wall facing the track was made out of glass. Electronic boards hung from the ceiling, as tall as a man and just as wide, listing the names of the dogs, their odds, and the results of the previous race. Men and women of all shapes and races holding programs in their hands studied the electronic boards or stood in line at the ticket windows.

A trumpet sounded, and everybody turned their attention to the front. Eight young men, each with a dog on a short leash, walked by the glass wall. All the dogs looked alike, slim and long-legged, like the one painted on the sides of the buses I'd ridden from New Jersey to Miami. They were all muzzled, and each dog wore a different-colored jacket-like thing on its back with a large number on it, from one to eight.

The dog parade paused at the middle of the stands, and a man's voice over the loudspeaker introduced each dog by number and name and said a few things about each animal. Lots of people seemed to be paying attention, some even jotting notes on their programs. I guessed they showed off the dogs so people like Steve, who thought they knew what to look for, could take a closer look and figure the odds themselves.

Soon after, the young men led the dogs to the starting point, and people rushed to the ticket windows. The odds on the electric boards kept changing, some going higher and others lower. Those who'd bought their tickets edged closer to the front and craned toward the starting point, muttering things like "C'mon, get started. What're you waiting for?"

A few minutes later, the trumpet sounded again, and a man with an authoritative voice announced through the loudspeaker, "Here comes Rusty!" A hairy toy rabbit darted out of a box and ran along a steel track. An instant later, the doors of the dog pens opened, and the dogs leaped out to chase the fake rabbit.

Just as fast, all those holding tickets erupted, shouting encouragement to their number. Some leaned against the chain-link fence and urged the dogs on. The pack zoomed by a yard or so behind the toy rabbit, with the lead changing as the dogs negotiated the turns or bumped into each other. After making a complete circle of the track, they crossed the finish line in front of the stands.

Immediately there was a roar of curses and tossing of torn tickets into the air, the shredded paper raining back down in a downpour. A few people quickstepped it to the cashier's window, holding their un-torn tickets.

At the far end of the lobby a neon sign said *Joe's Café,* and I walked toward it for a closer look. On a chalkboard by the serving window, a handwritten menu in shaky capital letters listed hamburgers, hot dogs, French fries, and grilled cheese sandwiches, all at double the prices of the Parthenon. Some people placed an order, paid, then munched on whatever was handed to them without taking their gaze from the field or the overhead boards.

A place like this could be a gold mine. These people would chew on old shoes and couldn't tell the difference.

Pete tapped me on the shoulder. "Come, we'll eat at the restaurant upstairs. It's much nicer." We took the elevator to the restaurant one floor above, and a man in a black suit and bow tie showed us to a table near the glass wall.

"So this is where Steve spends his time," I said when we sat down.

"Yep, this is where he makes most of his deposits. Here and at the Jai Alai. I'll take you there too someday." He fanned his face with the menu. "I'm going to tell Steve to come here more often. They need a new air-conditioning unit."

He looked at the crowd gathered around the fence below and seemed to recognize some among those eagerly looking toward the starting gate.

"Quite a few Greeks come to this place," he said. "Gambling is in the Greek blood, I guess."

"That reminds me," I said. "What do you know about the *Yarmouth Castle*? I heard she had a Greek captain, and from what I could understand in the news, they blame him for the fire."

"There is enough blame to pass around to lots of people," said Pete. "The captain, the chief engineer, the owners, the big shots at the office, and everybody in between. Last I heard, it was about seventy people dead or lost."

"Did you know anybody on the ship?"

"I knew all the Greeks—the captain, the chief mate, and the officers of the engine crew."

"They say some of the fire hoses were rotted, and those that weren't didn't have enough water pressure."

"They'll say a lot of things now." Pete sighed. "The fact is there is a whole fleet of cruise ships competing for the business, and the only places they can cut costs is in places the passengers don't see—the ships' maintenance. Have you seen any of the advertisements? Seven-day cruises on the *Ariadne* for one hundred sixty dollars, cruises to Nassau and Freeport on the *Yarmouth Castle* for fifty-nine dollars. That's not even as much as three meals like this." He pointed at the price column of the menu. "And you should see all the food they put out. I'm telling you, those passengers eat well, and boy, some of them can do some eating."

The waiter came to our table and Pete ordered for both of us. "T-bone steak, cooked well, with baked potato and salad."

"Will you have some of your wine, Mr. Pete?" asked the waiter.

"Yes, of course. Bring us a carafe," said Pete.

I pulled a cigarette halfway out of my pack and held it out to Pete.

He shook his head. "No, I gave it up years ago. It's a stupid habit. You should give it up too."

I lit one up without saying anything. I was planning to quit after I got my green card. The waiter brought the wine and poured for us.

Pete and I toasted. "To health!"

"Good wine," I said after taking a sip.

Pete nodded. "Homemade. I have a friend who is chief engineer with Karras Shipping Lines. They come to Miami every third month, and he always brings me a demijohn of wine and a bottle of *tsipouro*. I keep some of the wine in the back for when I eat here. A glass of wine goes good with the meal."

The place was almost full. The waiters buzzed around the tables, constantly bringing beer bottles or mixed drinks and refilling the water and iced tea glasses. Most people had their attention on the track and seemed oblivious to what the waiter put in front of them.

When our food came, Pete asked the waiter if he'd had a good week—and about his wife's arthritis, how his son was doing in college, and whether his daughter has decided which school she would be going to. The waiter, a tall black man around fifty whom Pete called Ernie, said they were all doing fine. The son might get drafted into the Air Force after he graduated, and the daughter was offered a scholarship at Florida State.

"And the job here has been real, real good, Mr. Pete," Ernie said. "Thanks again for putting in the word. I had a real good week this week. Yesterday, two of my tables hit the quinella three times in the row, and another hit the exacta. They said I brought them luck. I told them I always bring good luck to my big tippers."

A little later, Ernie came around holding a pitcher of tea in each hand. With a big smile he asked the two plump women at the table next to ours if they cared for a refill.

"Yeah, yeah," said one of them without turning her head from the dogs.

"Sweet or unsweetened, ma'am?" asked Ernie.

"It doesn't matter, whatever. C'mon, seven! I don't care. Move up, seven, move up! Oh, shoot."

"Who owns this restaurant?" I asked.

"The New York corporation that owns the dog track. They have a manager running it." Pete gestured behind him toward an enclosure that could be an office. "This one has been running it for about a year. Nice lady."

"They brought a woman all the way from New York?"

"She was already here. After her husband died, she moved to Miami to be close to the grandkids."

"Oh, I guess it's cheaper to hire an old woman," I mused.

"She's not that old. She turned sixty last week. Do you want to bet on any of the races?" The way he asked about the betting sounded to me like he wanted to cut the lady-manager talk short.

"No, I don't bet," I answered. "Don't even play cards on New Year's Eve."

"Well, now, for someone in your place," Pete said in a confiding kind of voice, "getting ten, twenty dollars out of the Parthenon cash register every now and then wouldn't be that hard. You hit a couple of good ones here, you're all set. Steve would never miss it. It's not as if he's got a family. He'll squander it on some young slut or the dogs anyway."

From his tone, I wasn't sure if he was joking or serious. Was he spying for Steve?

"That's stealing," I said. "Makes no difference if you do it to a saint or to an ass. Stealing is stealing. Anyway, Steve might not be the kind of man I would want my sister to marry if I had one, but he gave me a job and I owe him. He isn't any worse of a boss than some other bosses I've worked for."

I stopped to swallow a piece of steak. "Stolen money is cursed, and to steal from somebody to bet on a skinny dog running after a fake rabbit is also stupid. That's not the way to get rich. That Joe who has the café downstairs, *he* has the right idea. And this restaurant, I bet you this *nice manager lady*"—I gestured toward the direction Pete had indicated earlier, "is making some good money too if she was smart enough to negotiate a percentage of the profits."

"She was." Pete grinned and concentrated on cutting his steak with slow, thoughtful strokes.

While we ate, I scanned the tables and tried to compute the tab per table. At some of them, each person had two, even three bar drinks and desserts. I figured it must be at least fifty dollars per table.

Pete ate his salad, half the baked potato, and only a small part of the thick T-bone steak. He pushed away his plate. "Ate too much again," he said, patting his stomach. "I'll have to walk an extra turn around the block to burn it off."

"You don't look like you need any exercise," I said.

"Need it to keep the heart going," said Pete. "You know, man is the only critter in God's earth who will make work for himself when he doesn't need to, like eating too much, then exercising to burn it off."

Maybe Diogenes wasn't too far off for a name. Only, why would he suggest taking a few dollars from Steve's cash register? That wasn't like the character of a man who took the high road in life. Was he up to something? I finished the rest of my meal in silence, eating the steak and the potato but only half the salad. It had too much lettuce and not enough onions and tomatoes.

Pete watched the people gathered by the fence, then seemed to follow with his eyes a very fat man struggling to climb the few steps from the ground level to the ticket booth. The man held on to the rail with both hands, trying to heave his massive body up, then stopped to rest for almost a minute before trying the next step.

"Yep," Pete said finally, as if continuing our earlier talk, "the doc says I got to cut down on meat and dairy. Cholesterol is too high."

Because of old superstitions, Greeks usually only divulge their medical problems to the most intimate of friends. To everyone else, when asked about their health, they give vague, all-purpose answers. I took Pete's disclosure of his cholesterol problem as a sign he was beginning to consider me a close friend.

Emboldened by that thought, I asked, "How did you get your papers, Mr. Pete? You said you worked on American ships. How did you do it?"

"It's a long and boring story," he said and got up. "Bathroom visit."

When he got back I asked, "Did you have to marry somebody to get your papers?"

"I didn't have to. It was different with me. It's not an interesting story."

"To me, anything that'll get me the green card is more than interesting."

"When the time is right, something will come up," he said. "Don't worry."

When I first met Pete, I told him I was Steve's nephew, the same thing we told the help and everyone else who asked. Pete had nodded and left it at that, but now that I knew him better, I was sure he saw right through the smokescreen, so I gave up pretending. Finishing up a nice meal in comfortable surroundings like these was a good time to get Pete to tell me how he got his green card. After all, he had confided his cholesterol problem to me. I decided to push a little more for an answer.

"I hope the time gets right before the immigration comes looking for me," I said. "If you didn't have to marry, how did you do it?"

Right then the trumpet sounded, and Pete turned toward the track without answering me. The previous cycle was repeated—Rusty running for his life, followed by the barking dogs and the bettors' shouting, urging, and curses, until it disappeared down the hole, the worthless tickets tossed in the air.

"Lots of paychecks being swept up down there," mused Pete, nodding toward the man pushing a broom on the lower floor.

"In my way of thinking, it's the wrong way to go about making the big money," I said.

"That's right," said Pete. "This should be considered entertainment. Never take it seriously. In this country, if a man has it in him and works hard, the *big money*, as you call it, will come to him."

"But a man needs to have a foundation," I said. "A stepping stone, something to get him started."

Pete's lips stretched to form a faint smile. He took a sip of coffee and wiped his mouth with his napkin. "Maybe now is a good time to tell you the story of somebody I know," he said.

I repositioned myself on the seat.

"When you were sailing, did you hear of the Vournaris Shipping Corporation?" Pete asked.

"Yes, I did," I answered. "They say it's a small company; three or four ships, I think. I hear they're one of the best to work for, but I'm not planning on going back to sea. If I don't make it here, I'll go someplace where nobody knows me. I'd rather have the people back home think I'm dead than a failure."

Pete laughed. It was spontaneous, hearty laughter, which puzzled me because I considered what I'd just said to be serious.

"That's exactly what Alexis told me," Pete said when he stopped.

"Who's Alexis?"

"Alexandros Vournaris."

"Did you know him?"

"I was one of the pallbearers at his funeral last year. We sailed together for a while."

"You did? Isn't that something." I put down my fork. "When I was in the navy, I was stationed in Paros. There was a tavern there that most of us navy guys used to frequent. Every night, when the owner of the place—an old man with a limp—flicked the switch to turn the lights on, he shouted, 'God Bless Alexandros!' I asked him who was Alexandros, and he said he was the ship owner who paid to build the power plant on the island. 'If we waited for the damn politicians, we would still be in the dark. God bless Alexandros,' he said.

"The man with the limp was Barba Gerasimos," Pete said. "He was the bosun on the *Agios Nikolaos* the time Alexis jumped ship." He took a sip of his water and adjusted his body in the chair. "I better start from the top. Alexis lived in a dirt-floor lean-to behind my parents' house on the island. It was him, his crippled mother, a brother seven years younger, two goats, and a donkey. His father, like mine, had been killed in the war of Asia Minor. They were poor as poor can get. Hell, everybody was poor back then. We grew up together, running around all over the island barefoot and snot nosed. As soon as they would have us, we signed on with a freighter from Hios—Alexis as a mess boy and I as an engine wiper. We had been around the world a couple of times before we got fuzz on our cheeks. Then, the first time we got to America, Alexis jumped ship."

"Lots of people have done that," I said.

Pete cracked a loaded smile. "But Alexis didn't just get off the ship and disappear like anybody else. Oh, no. Alexis didn't do things the ordinary-people way."

The waiter came by and, with a gesture, asked if he could take the plates.

"You can take mine," Pete said. "The young man is still working on his. And bring me a coffee, please." When the waiter was gone, Pete went on. "That ship, the *Agios Nikolaos,* was one of those English-built jobs that have the crew's quarters aft, over the steering gear, and the officers' accommodations amidships. We were underway on ballast from Galveston to Mobile to load wheat. That afternoon, about three hours before we were to pick up the pilot in Mobile, Alexis came in the mess hall, singing and dancing and talking like a crazy man. He was blind drunk, and it shocked the hell out of me because I had never seen him like that. He was the kind of person who ran the words twice through his brain before he spat them out, as they say.

"Well, that day he was staggering and tripping and telling everybody that in Galveston, he got a letter from his mother saying that his sister was engaged to a rich fellow on the island and that after the wedding, his new brother-in-law promised to give him a foreman's job in his factory, so he wouldn't have to sail on the stinking ships ever again. You see, nobody on the ship but me knew that the only females in his household were his mother and the two Maltese goats. Anyway, Alexis was drinking the whiskey like it is lemonade and jumping around wearing a goofy Chinese hat he had bought in Shanghai, singing and acting like an out-of-his-head drunk."

The waiter brought the coffee. Pete took a sip and went on: "Then Alexis says he's going to tell the captain to send him home from Mobile and staggers out the door to go amidships. Half a minute later, we hear a bloodcurdling scream and run out on deck, just in time to see his goofy hat going by on the starboard side. We threw a couple life rings in the water, and I ran up to the bridge yelling, 'Man overboard! Man overboard!' I grabbed the third mate on watch by the shoulders, telling him to turn the damn ship around and shaking him so hard that his head almost fell off. The captain gave the order to turn, called the American Coast Guard and reported it, and everybody went through the motions of searching and calling his name, but we all knew it was hopeless. We were empty, and the way the propeller—half out of the water—was chopping the waves, crazy Alexis was shark food the minute he hit the water."

"So, what happened to him?" I asked.

"Remember I told you, Alexis didn't do things like other people. We didn't find out until three weeks later, when we loaded and the bosun went to seal the vents, that Alexis had hid inside the vent cowl of the number-four cargo hold. He made a floor inside the vent with scrap lumber and stored food and water and even a blanket in there. He didn't come out until one day after we docked in Mobile."

"That was pretty smart all right."

"I saw him a few years later when I went to Mobile with another ship. 'Your poor mother must have gotten a hell of a scare,' I told him. He said he'd told his mother about his plans and not to believe anything she heard. As for the rest of us, he said what you just said a few minutes ago—if he couldn't make it big, he would rather have us believe he was dead."

"How did he make his money?" I asked. "I heard he started by selling hot dogs."

"In a way," said Pete, shifting on the chair again. "First he went to work for somebody in the painting business. Painting and restaurants was what most Greeks did back then. Alexis worked long hours, saving as much as he could from the crumbs they were paying him, and as soon as he had enough, he bought a pushcart. Like the ice-cream carts back home, only his had a little kettle and a stove, and he started selling hot dogs. That's all, hot dogs with grilled onions and popcorn. He pushed that cart all over town: to parks, games, parades; everywhere there was a gathering of people, he was there."

"Sounds like he had a good head for business," I said.

"Oh, he did." Pete nodded. "In the evenings he would go to a city park in Mobile. People used to go and promenade on a long pier there, and Alexis would set up under a big oak tree at the foot of the pier. He was afraid that if he called out to sell his stuff, people would make fun of the way he spoke, so what do you think tricky Alexis did? He got an old movie projector, hung a bedsheet from the oak tree, and started showing movies with the two funny guys, Laurel and Hardy. 'The Fat and the Skinny,' we called them back home. Back then they were very popular. You would piss yourself laughing even if you didn't understand a word they were saying. Alexis would have the sausages cooking and the popcorn popping and the onions simmering in the frying pan. The people promenading would pause to look at the movie and the smell would remind them they were hungry. Alexis was selling his stuff like crazy. Pretty tricky, ha?" Pete paused and noted that I had finished eating. "Do you want any dessert? They have good apple pie here."

I was still chewing, so I shook my head no.

"Anyway," Pete went on, "that sausage cart was his stepping stone, as they say. After that, he bought a restaurant, two movie houses in Mobile, a big house by the square on the island for his mother, and paid for his brother to go to a fancy university in England. Some years back, he bought at half price two freighters that an American shipyard built for somebody who couldn't pay for them and put his brother in charge of the office in New York. That was the beginning of the Vournaris Shipping Corporation. Before he had the heart attack, he bought another freighter at an auction in Mobile."

Pete finished his coffee and wiped his lips with the napkin before continuing.

"But unlike other people who came to America and made their fortunes but forgot where they were born, Alexis helped everybody who went to his door. He built that power plant in Paros, set up trust funds to pay for children's schooling, for medical relief of old folks, for dowries for orphan girls, and all kinds of other help. They loved him in Paros. They would ring the church bells every time he visited the island."

For a few moments, neither of us spoke. Then I said, "All of that starting with a pushcart."

Pete nodded. "I told you his story to show you that in this country, anybody willing to work hard can make your *big money*."

"A whole shipping corporation started from a hot dog cart," I repeated, almost to myself.

"Yes, nothing shameful about the lowly hot dog cart. I read in the paper the other day where another Greek, I don't remember his name, had one of those carts across from the Guggenheim Museum in New York. When he died, he left over a million dollars to that museum."

"How come you didn't ask your friend Alexis for an office job?" I said.

Pete cracked one of his loaded-with-meaning smiles. "I like it better this way. But we used to get together every once in a while in Nassau and go fishing. He had a house in Lyford Cay."

We left soon after that. When Pete dropped me off at my building, he said he would take me to a ball game soon. "There is a good game next week. You'll see how Americans play football."

"Thanks, I would like to see that," I said, and with a springy stride, I walked to my room. I was becoming an American. Soon, when I heard the customers at the restaurant saying that the Dolphins stunk and the Braves had slaughtered the Giants, I would know what they were talking about.

CHAPTER EIGHT

A Promotion

The football stadium Pete took me to a week later had enough seats to fit all the people of the city of Volos and a village or two more. Pete said they called the stadium the Orange Bowl. Americans had strange taste when it came to naming things. Why would they name a playing field after a dish for storing fruit? Maybe they didn't have enough famous people to name things for. After all, America isn't that old of a country.

Pete said one of the teams playing was the University of Alabama, and the other was the University of Texas, both very good teams. Another American strangeness. I'd had the impression that universities were for schooling people. In Greece, those who were smart enough and rich enough with the right connections and the good fortune to be accepted in the only university in the country had their noses permanently buried in their books. Becoming an engineer, a doctor, or a teacher took an awful lot of studying.

"How often they have a game?" I asked while looking over the army of food and drink vendors at the parking lot.

"This is what they call a 'bowl game,'" said Pete. "It's like the final for the 'cup' back home. But they have regular games every week."

"And every week there are this many people and this many food peddlers," I said in awe.

Pete read the seat numbers on the tickets, and we weaved halfway up the stands. Soon after, two groups of players dressed in shiny helmets and thick shoulder pads like gladiators of some kind trotted out from opposite sides of the field. A young woman sang the American national anthem, and after that a referee tossed a coin, and the teams took their places.

A few minutes into the game, I decided that American football was boring. Most of the play time consisted of the men clustering together in a circle, then lining up and facing their opponents for a few seconds before crashing into them and spending a lot of time getting themselves untangled while the referee searched for the egg-shaped ball at the bottom of the pile.

I spent most of the time studying the spectators, surprised to see they got just as excited as the spectators in Greece watching a real football game. Only, the excitement here seemed to come in spurts, like waves. When a man tucked the ball under his arm and started running, they would spring up and shout, "Go, man, go! Go! Touchdown!" Then, a few seconds later when that poor fellow got bulldozed by someone from the other team, they would utter, "Oh, shit" and sit down like punctured blowups.

In the end, the team with the orange shirts won the game twenty-one to seventeen. As we drifted toward the exit, people were having a lot of heated discussions about whether a fellow named Pear or Bear Brant should've had "Joe Nay-math," who had been playing a "quarter in the back," pass the ball to somebody that was wide and open instead of having a slow-moving somebody else try to "run it up the middle."

When Pete dropped me off, I told him I had enjoyed the game

and was grateful for an interesting evening. Although I didn't think I would ever become a big fan of American football, I had discovered another place where I could take my sausage pushcart when I owned one.

"Sometime in the spring, I'll take you to see *professional* baseball," Pete said. "They're practicing not far from here."

"That will be nice," I said. A chance to see another crowd-gathering place.

⁜ ⁜ ⁜

I got the first letter from Mother three months after I jumped ship. I had given her the mailing address of the Parthenon restaurant, and the letter came together with the bills and the junk mail. Fortunately, Steve spotted it as he was about to throw the bundle in the trash. When he handed it to me, he asked if I had written to Telemahos about Steve giving me the job.

"I sent him a *card-postal* the first day I started here," I answered.

"Hope he tells my folks," said Steve. "They expect me to be telling his old man thank you for the rest of my life."

"Why is that?" I asked.

"They feel obligated to Telemahos's family for something."

He walked away as if he didn't want to talk about it, but I already knew. Telemahos told me that his parents had let Steve's family stay in their house for free for more than a year when they got kicked out of Asia Minor in 1922.

"All they brought from Smyrna were the shirts on their backs and baby Stavros on their lap. My folks helped them get a new start, and they never forgot it. His mother still brings us *couloures*—the round cakes my mother likes—every Easter and New Year," Telemahos had said.

As soon as the lunch rush was over, I found a quiet spot at the far side of the kitchen. Sitting on a five-gallon lard can, I read the letter from Mother.

> *I wish you didn't choose living among strangers in a strange place, away from those who know you and care for you and who have watched you grow up. Many people have done well where the Good Lord saw fit to put them. Now-days, it seems that the tourists have discovered our part of the world. They come by the busloads and spread like goatherds up and down the mountainside, taking photographs of every old church and hovel. A tavern at the square serving that fancy food you've learned to cook would be a gold mine.*

After that followed some village news before she got to my offer of a ticket.

> *As for me coming over there, I believe old women like me should sit on their eggs, as they say, and not go gallivanting to the other end of the world. The Good Lord has seen me through all the winters up to now, so I'm sure He will keep me a few more. But since you went ahead with that cockamamie idea of yours and stayed in that country, may God guide you and keep you out of harm's way. Be careful whom you choose for your friends and whom you keep company with, and like the Gospel says, "Walk while you have the light and God will protect you."*

I repositioned myself on the seat and lit a cigarette and read the letter again, this time at a slower pace. When I finished, I stared at it for a while. She didn't sound as hurt as I was afraid she might be. And with that line from the Gospel, it was as if she was giving me her blessings.

I put the letter in my pocket and went to refill the soft-drink cooler. Maybe next Sunday I would write to her again. I'd think of what I was going to say by then. I could tell her that as soon as I got my papers straight, I'd visit her often so she wouldn't feel like I had disappeared from the face of the—

"Going to the bank. Keep an eye on the front." Steve's voice snapped me out of my thoughts.

I nodded and continued putting ice in the cooler. Steve had started "going to the bank" more often lately, and it wasn't because the cash register was overflowing.

And Karen told me he'd started coming in the middle of the day and only a few times during the night. "He's either getting jealous or thinks I'm cheating," she said.

She'd sounded worried, which got me worried. Right now, it was a perfect arrangement. A couple of times during the weekend, I'd go to Karen's room when I was sure Steve was at the dog track or the Jai Alai. We did all our loving while little Joey slept in the other room, and then I would leave, always ahead of the closing time of Steve's "banking" places. Since Steve had a key to the apartment, we always slid the dresser behind the door. If he happened to come while I was there, I could go out the window, and Karen could say she had barricaded herself because she was afraid. But he never came early. Sometimes, way after I had gone to my room, I could hear him kicking a tricycle in the corridor or mumbling curses at Karen's lock as he looked for the right key.

It's like they say, I thought while leveling the ice in the cooler, *nothing lasts forever.* If Steve got it in his head to make a change, it would screw up the whole setup. I'd have to learn how to wash my clothes in those machines at the laundromat and spend money to buy an iron.

Later that day, while walking home, again I pondered my predicament. *What could have made Steve suspicious?* But no matter how many times I repeated the question, I couldn't come up with an answer.

Next day I was up and working much earlier than usual. As soon as it was light enough, I dragged the shaky ladder from storage and started painting the northwest corner of the trim, under the roof. It was the hardest part of the job, and I had left it for last. Fifteen minutes into the painting operation, I saw through the window the newlyweds in apartment 2A going hard at it, and that got me all worked up. I splashed some paint on the trim so that it looked painted from a distance and declared the job finished.

I marched into Karen's apartment and grabbed her as she was picking up toys from the floor. We did it on her hard floor, on her soft bed, on her kitchen counter, and on her every piece of furniture in between. Now and then we would stop to catch our breath, then attack each other again.

"You damn fool," Karen said during one of our mini pauses. "Marching in here like this is a sure way to get me kicked out."

"What you mean?"

"I mean Steve could've been in bed sleeping," she said. "He sleeps late when he comes back from the track. If he catches us, I'll be back to dancing in the clubs. Good thing he didn't come last night. He must have lost again. When he wins, he comes all happy and slobbery and wants to fuck. When he loses, he goes straight to his house and leaves me alone."

I raised my hands. "Sorry, couldn't help it."

We lay in a tight tangle of body and limbs, our sweat mixing with her gardenia body lotion until we heard Joey waking up in the next room. I looked at the clock and sprang out of bed.

"Damn, Steve will come looking for me," I said and darted off.

I walked at a quick but casual pace so I would not attract attention. In that neighborhood, if somebody was running, it meant somebody was chasing him.

At the restaurant, Señor Julio was mopping the dining room floor. He saw me through the glass door and started toward it, but I signaled him I would go around the back, through the kitchen door. I went directly to the sink and washed my hands with a lot of the lemony-smelling soap and rubbed a soap-soaked washcloth on my chest and around my neck.

While putting on my apron, I sniffed my arms again for traces of gardenia-blossom smell, and again I resolved to tell Karen to take it easy with the stuff. Steve was buying it by the gallon, and she practically marinated herself in it.

When I was sure all traces of the perfume were gone, I walked out of the kitchen and went to get a cup of coffee. Steve was putting the opening money in the cash register. I reached for a coffee cup under the counter and saw two five-dollar bills on the floor near the register, about one meter away from Steve's chair. I handed them to Steve.

"The money box is running over," I said.

"Must've fell out last night," he said. "That's why the register was ten short." As he smoothed the corners of the bills, I noticed that both had a red mark on them.

I filled my cup and was walking toward the kitchen when Carmen rushed through the back door, all flustered and ruffled as if she had been in a fight. She collapsed on the first chair she came to and crossed herself.

"*Madre de Dios*!"

"Have fight with boyfriend, Carmen?" asked Steve.

"I almost got killed crossing the Twenty Avenue," she answered.

I carried a glass of water to her. "What happened?"

"Gracias." Carmen drank some water. "For three days now," she said in Spanish, "a big cement truck parks at the corner of Ninth and Twentieth Avenue. It's impossible to see the other side when crossing. I did not see the bus coming and, thanks to God, a man pulled me back before I got hit. One moment later, I would be dead. Mother of God." She crossed herself again.

"Yes, yes. I know the place," said Julio. "They make a big building at that corner. Cement trucks come all the time. I think the city should have policeman at that corner. Very dangerous."

"Never liked that damn language," Steve muttered to me. "What are they yapping about? Did she get slapped by her pimp?"

"She almost got run over by the city bus," I said. "Good thing somebody pulled her back."

"I bet she was *trying* to get hit," Steve said in Greek. "Then she would sue the city for a fortune. They do it all the time, you know." The second part was in English, as if he was trying to tell Julio and Carmen he was aware of their Cuban tricks.

"Would not be good for *her* if the bus killed her," I said in English also.

"No, they try to get bruised a little, that's all," Steve said. "So they can collect disability for the rest of their lives. And if the injury is serious, their relatives get rich also. Insurance pays lots of money, especially when it's the city's fault. I know."

"Steven, you crazy." Carmen rose and went to the bathroom.

When she got back, she put her purse under the counter, got two bundles of napkins, and started refilling the napkin holders. The old man finished mopping and rolled his bucket into the kitchen. I followed behind him.

"Your Spanish getting better every day," said the old man, probably alluding to my translation of the bus incident to Steve.

"It's not doing me much good here," I said.

"It is doing you plenty good with Carmelita." He nodded toward the end of the counter where Carmen was filling the napkin holders.

"With women it's different," I said with a chuckle.

I meant it as a joke, but it was true in Carmen's case. She seemed to be able to understand what I was trying to say without even hearing the words. I was sure I could communicate with her even if I were deaf and mute. I asked Pete in a roundabout way, so he wouldn't suspect anything, what kind of family she had, but all he said was that in life, some people get more than their share of misfortune.

Steve left to "go to the bank" soon after the lunch hour rush. He came back around four o'clock, looking refreshed and cheerful.

"I stopped by the apartment to check on the kid," he said. "The paint outside looks all right."

My plan had been to wait a few days before I told him I had finished the painting. I'd been looking forward to a work-free Saturday.

"I could have been done sooner, but it took a lot of scraping and caulking," I said.

"Did you have any paint left?"

"For the outside? Only half a gallon."

"Save it. Use it for touchups. The store had a hell of a time matching the color," said Steve. He poured a cup of coffee while humming a peppy tune, then perched on the high chair by the cash register and lit a cigarette.

"The kid's mother must've treated you to a cake," I said.

"Both ugly colors—the stucco and the trim," said Steve, ignoring my joke. "But the wife liked it. Stupid woman."

"The walls are the color of the *orquidea* flower, Steven," Carmen called from the far corner of the dining room. "Here, they call it orchid tree. The wood is the green of the tree leaves. Your wife had a big orchid tree in the garden of her vacation home in Camarioca."

Steve said nothing. After a moment, Carmen went on.

"No forget, Steven. I knew your wife before *you* knew her. She was very smart and a very good woman." She sounded miffed.

"Yeah, yeah, I know," muttered Steve. "I still would like to paint the whole building white with blue trim, but it'll take a thousand gallons to do it." He looked at me while blowing a smoke stream, then turned toward Carmen. "You look sexy today. Have a new boyfriend perhaps?"

"Perhaps," she answered.

"I keep telling you, you need to get a Greek boyfriend, like me or Kostas here, eh?" Steve gestured toward me and laughed.

"Perhaps," she said again, and for an instant I thought I spotted the traces of a smile, or maybe it was my imagination.

"I think something is not right with her," Steve said in Greek. "I don't think she likes men, but I like to tease her."

"She's too old for you anyway," I said. "I thought you liked them young."

Karen must have faked a damn good orgasm, because the goofball was trying to get on everybody's good side.

"Yes, because it keeps *me* young. You go with old women, pretty soon you start feeling old."

Through the serving window, Pascal could be seen peeling the potatoes and humming a song.

"Not peel so thick, *vre*!" Steve scolded him. "You must have been a rich man in Haiti, you throw half away." He sighed. "No way around it. I've got to make room for a peeling machine." Then he chuckled as if he'd just remembered something funny. "When I was with the passenger ship, I run into a Greek that lived in Haiti. He—"

The telephone rang and Steve stopped short.

"I'll tell you when I come back." He walked over to the pay phone by the door. A couple of minutes later, he was back. "Carmen! Isabella is going to be late. She have to go see the kids' teacher." He settled on the stool and added in a lower tone, "She probably got her tits caught in a door. Damn Cubans."

He took a sip of his coffee and called me over.

"Look," he said, "you have been here two months now. You know how everything works, and you are done with the painting. That was the biggest job in the building." He readjusted his load on the stool. "I've got some other things to take care of and need to be coming late, but I don't trust any of those *sanavabitches* with the keys. I want you to start opening up in the mornings and get everything ready for the lunch hour. I think you can handle it. Even Diogenes seems to think so."

Getting up early must be interfering with his night life. I lit a cigarette and tried to look like I was thinking. "How about that raise you said would be coming my way?"

"It will happen, trust me. And if this works out, you can run the place for me in the summer. Maybe I'll go to Greece. Haven't been there for a while."

The way I saw it, I didn't have too many options, but I asked anyway, "How much of a raise?"

"Five dollars a week," said Steve.

I thought for a moment. "That's how much you're taking out for the fifty I borrowed. I'm almost paid off. You had said would be fifteen-dollar-a-week raise. My heart won't be in it otherwise."

"I'll think about it," said Steve. Then he got off the stool and went into the kitchen. I heard him shouting to Pascal, "If any of the Health Department faggots comes in here, they'll cut my ass to pieces. I speak to you all the time—no let dirty pots pile in the sink."

A few minutes later, he came back to the counter.

"Okay," he said. "I'll make it ten a week, but I want your heart and your brain and your ass to be in it. If you do okay, you'll get the other five in a month."

"Okay," I said, barely suppressing a shout. "When do I start?"

"You can start Monday. Here—I got a set of keys made for you." He handed me three keys on a chain. "The small one is for the cash register. Make sure it's locked anytime you're away from it, even going to piss."

"Don't worry about a thing, boss."

"Don't forget, I'll be watching you," said Steve.

CHAPTER NINE

Avoiding Limpets

I hustled to the restaurant one hour earlier than usual on Monday morning.

When Señor Julio came I told him to mop behind the counter first, then the dining room. I turned on the burners for the grill and the fryer and got busy filling the trays of the cold table. When the others came in, I put the opening money in the cash register. I sensed someone's presence behind me and turned.

"I finished," said Señor Julio.

"*Uno momento*." I pulled a five-dollar bill from the drawer. "Here." He said *gracias* and started to leave. "Wait," I called after him, "I have something else for you." I reached over the pie case and took the tray of pumpkin pie with two pieces left. I put it in a to-go box and handed it to him. "For my little friend."

"You are spoiling her, Señor Kostas."

"She's worth it. *Hasta mañana.*"

"*Hasta mañana*," echoed the old man.

He left and I resumed counting the change in the cash register. Carmen came to refill her cup from the coffee pot next to me.

"He thinks you are God-sent," she said.

I shrugged. "It was old. Couldn't sell it anyway."

"Steve would. He never gives anything away. And if he couldn't sell it, he would throw it away. He gives nothing for free."

"I know, he told me the first day I started here, but that's Steve. Not everybody is the same. Besides, the old man's granddaughter likes sweets. I saw them at the Woolworth's last Saturday. She was pulling him with both hands to the table with the candy. I bought her a small chocolate, and she gave me a hug and said she wanted to marry me. Sweet little thing."

"Yes, her mother was a sweet woman also," said Carmen.

I closed the drawer and got a cup of coffee. "Carmen," I asked after my first sip, "how long have you been in America?"

"A long time."

"How did you get here?"

"It's not a cheerful story." She sounded as if she wasn't planning to elaborate. She took a bundle of napkins and walked to the farthest table to refill the napkin holder.

I studied her while she worked. I'd caught myself doing that quite often, lately. She didn't have a wedding ring on her finger, but that didn't mean she was not married. Maybe she was divorced. She had the look of someone with many cares, but I hadn't heard her, even once, talk about her problems or her family or what she did after work. She was not like Isabella, who talked constantly about her rebellious daughters, her lazy husband, and her trashy neighbors.

Carmen would be a good prospect for a fake marriage if she was not already married. She seemed serious and kind, and if she put up with Steve's attitude, she must need the money. The solution to my problem could be right in front of me. She never asked me any personal questions and seemed to have accepted the explanation that I was Steve's nephew who was here legally. I resolved to figure out whether Carmen was married and, if she was not, how to proposition her. But I had to find the right time and suggest it in the right way; otherwise it would be a disaster.

Steve got to the restaurant around eleven and went through the ritual of counting the order slips on the spike, then the contents of the cash register.

"Slow Monday again," he said. "The damn moochers are either broke or hungover."

The only customers in the place were two telephone company workers sitting at the far end of the counter, each nursing a cup of coffee and talking about the Dolphins beating the Cowboys.

"It's early," I said. "The lunch hour hasn't started yet." I was filling a plastic bucket from the icemaker.

Steve poured a cup of coffee. "I'm telling you the fucking Cubans are taking over Miami. I pull in for gas and tell the man to check the oil too and he talks back to me in Cuban. 'You no speak Spanish?' he says and acts surprised. They've got some nerve I tell you." He lit a cigarette. "They even have their own radio station now. Have you heard it? '*Aquí ejército rebelde*.'" He tried to imitate the announcer's voice.

"Yes, it's the revolutionary army station," I said.

"Revolution? Bullshit," snapped Steve. "They're probably broadcasting from some pool hall—the only thing the men are good for, hustlers and pimps. And the women, good for bed ornaments, that's all."

"It's the same all over, Steve," I said. "If you remember, they said the same things back home about your folks and mine when they got kicked out of Turkey and washed up in Greece. People called them *refugees* and screwed up their noses as if the word stunk."

"That was different," said Steve.

"Was it? Remember what Pete said the other day when you were griping about the Cubans?"

"No, what did he say?"

"He said the first one to shout that the lifeboat is full is the one who got in last."

"Never understood any of that windbag's philosophizing. What's that got to do with the Cubans? Now, let *me* tell you something. I don't—"

"Need to order napkins, Steven," Carmen said. "This one is the last." She waved a bundle of napkins in his direction from the far end of the counter.

"Got a case last week. I put it in the closet, if you bother to look." Steve craned his neck to look at Carmen's behind when she bent over to put the last napkin bundle under the counter. Turning to me, he spoke in the tone of someone who'd just had his theory confirmed. "Like I said, the only thing they are good for is bed ornaments. Don't have brains for anything else."

I emptied the ice bucket into the drink cooler. "Up to now, we've been storing the napkins under the counter," I said. "*Your* wife, was she one of those bed ornaments?" I nodded in Carmen's direction.

"No, she was American," said Steve. "From an old Miami family. She inherited the restaurant, the apartments, and a bunch of other property from her first husband. She had a big country home in Cuba and more money than she had sense." He took a drag off his cigarette. "I met her when I was third mate on the *Holiday Voyager*. We were sailing out of Miami then—all cruise ships were sailing out of here then. Now most of them moved to Port Everglades. They are talking of making Dodge Island into a cruise terminal, but it'll never happen. Fucking politicians. They're all crooks." He ground out the cigarette in the ashtray.

After a while, the two coffee-drinking customers got up to leave. One of them handed Steve a five-dollar bill. Steve gave him the change, then stared into the drawer before closing it with a sigh. He took another cigarette out of his pack and tapped the filter end on the counter before lighting it. He took a deep drag and tapped on his coffee cup with the spoon, and when Carmen turned her head he indicated with his finger that he wanted a refill.

"That ship, the *Holiday Voyager,* I mean," he said, "seemed to draw all the rich goofballs. Old women mostly. I guess they figured instead of staying home grandmothering they'd have one last fling. Quite a few guys from the crew caught themselves a prize and got settled for life. I caught mine six months after I signed on."

I finished loading the drink cooler and carried the empty crates out. Steve started humming an American song about a pretty woman.

"I wish I could find an old woman with money," I said. "It would solve all my problems."

"It's better to marry a young woman," said Steve. "Young American women marry for love, then after a while they get bored and ask for divorce. An old woman will stick to you like a limpet on a rock."

"Oh, I hadn't thought of that. What happened to *your* limpet?"

"I got lucky," he said. "Four months after we got married, she had a heart attack. She dropped dead at a place where they do exercises. They said it was all the diet pills she was taking." He sipped more coffee. "It was a shame because she was not that old—only fifty-five. And now that I think of it, she wasn't a bad woman either." That last part seemed an afterthought. "Find yourself some crazy young thing. You will be better off," he concluded and got off the stool.

At the moment, the only crazy young thing I could think of was Karen, but marrying her was out of the question. She *would* stick to me like a limpet. Carmen, on the other hand, would be perfect for a temporary wife. Hell, even for a permanent one. But I had to find the right way to present the deal to her.

"I'll start practicing," I said with a chuckle. I walked toward the kitchen and started singing, "No step my bloo skoosh shooz, ya ya ya!" flinging my arms and legs like a drunken gorilla.

⁘ ⁘ ⁘

The next morning, as I trotted down Ninth Street, trying not to look like I was running, I cursed myself with every step. It was damn stupid of me to stay up so late to see the ending of that goofy movie. It made me oversleep, and now I was late opening. Only the second day after Steve trusted me with the keys, and I was already screwing up.

I could picture Pascal sitting on an empty crate by the back door, humming a tune, and Señor Julio pacing nearby with his hands behind his back and his head bowed. Both would smile and meekly say, "Good morning, Mister Kostas," when I showed up, but I knew they would think I was a slacker and they could start slacking off too.

When I crossed Seventh Street, I saw at the corner of Twentieth Avenue, just one block before the restaurant, three police cars with their red-and-blue lights flashing at full speed. A mass of people were gathered around something lying on the ground, all of them shouting and gesturing, just like in Greece after an accident. I started in that direction for a closer look, but a few steps later I made a sharp left turn and went around the block, on Seventh Street. I should stay away from crowds, especially if there were policemen in them. As I turned the corner, an ambulance with sirens blaring and lights flashing sped by.

When I got to the restaurant, neither Pascal nor Señor Julio were waiting. I checked my watch; it was fifteen minutes past their usual time. *Must be something in the air. Everybody is oversleeping today.*

I put the opening money in the cash register, turned on the coffeemaker, and made sure the soft-drink cooler was full while rehearsing in my head the lecture I would give Pascal and the old man. True, those two hadn't been late before, but if I let them get away with it once, they would do it again. They were probably testing me, so I had to be firm and allow no excuses.

I was loading the cold-table trays when Pascal rushed in through the back door and collapsed on a sack of potatoes. He looked like he had run a marathon.

"It is terrible, Mister Boss," he uttered, almost out of breath. "It is terrible bad catastrophe. Very bad."

"What's the matter, Pascal?" I asked calmly. He wouldn't escape the ass-chewing that easy.

"Mister Boss, *Monsieur* Julio is dead."

I dashed closer. "What happened?"

"The big bus—it start to move and hit Monsieur Julio."

"When this happened, Pascal? How it happened?"

"Every day I go on city bus and come out same place, the place where is big construction. Every day same time, I come out same bus and walk here."

"Yes, Pascal, you said that. What happened today? What happened to Señor Julio?"

"Today when I come out of bus, I see the big cement truck take out cement same as other time. Then I see Monsieur Julio walk in front of truck the same moment the city bus begin to go. It was terrible. I run and see Monsieur Julio under the bus. The police come and the ambulance come, and the doctor examine and say, 'This man is dead.' They put Monsieur Julio in ambulance and take away. It is very tragic, Monsieur Kostas. Very tragic."

"Yes, it is very tragic," I said and went into the kitchen. I knew it sounded hollow, but the word *tragic* seemed to cover the old man's ending. When a man lived in a place of his own choosing, content and happy and on top of the world, and then suddenly some hothead, egomaniac punk preaching a lopsided idea of fairness and justice took everything away and the once happy man ended up cleaning toilets and depending on handouts, what else but *tragic* could it be called?

Carmen came in half an hour later, her eyes red as if she had been crying. "You heard about Señor Julio?" she asked me.

"Yes," I said. "I'm very sorry."

For the rest of the day, all of us went about our chores silently, each wrapped in our own thoughts. Steve came in around eleven, whistling a peppy tune. He saw Carmen's sullen face and said, "What happen, Carmen? You boyfriend leave you?"

She told him about the old man's accident.

"Bet you he did it on purpose," said Steve. "Bet you he only want a small scratch so he collect a bunch of money."

"You don't know anything about Señor Julio, Steven," Carmen said, sounding vexed. "He would never do anything that made his granddaughter unhappy. He worshipped her."

Steve shrugged. "Now she get a ton of money from the city."

"Pascal said there was a lot of wet cement where he was," Carmen said. "Possibly he slip and no have time to get up."

"Yeah, sure," said Steve.

While I scraped the grill, I ran through every conversation I'd had with Señor Julio, searching for a clue about the old man's actions. Had he really slipped on the spilled cement? Had the old man's mind wandered off to his plantation in Cuba, and he didn't watch where he stepped? Or could it be that he couldn't take it anymore and decided to end it all? Could it be that he'd sacrificed himself so his granddaughter would have a better life?

Either way, it was still a tragic ending for an old man.

CHAPTER TEN

Mister Citizen

The next day, Peter Papas came into the restaurant unusually late, just a few minutes before closing. Isabella and Emilio had already left. I was spreading the ice in the drink cooler, the last chore of the day, and Steve counted the money in the cash register, scribbling the totals on a paper bag and mumbling his usual curses about lousy business and lazy Cubans. He lifted his head and scrutinized Pete as he walked in.

Pete wore a blue suit that looked brand new, with a red-and-blue tie with white stripes and a white silk handkerchief in his left pocket. On his left lapel was a pin of the American flag.

"Diogenes, you're decked out like a groom," Steve said. "Must be going to some fancy ball."

"I'm just coming back from one," said Pete.

Steve closed the register. "That's good, because the kitchen is closed."

"I'm fine," said Pete. "I'll prepare some appetizers for us so we can have a drink."

He put two brown bags on the round table by the corner, then approached Carmen and asked for some small plates and silverware. He busied himself setting up the table for a few minutes, then turned toward the counter.

"When you guys finish, come over here and try some of this," he called.

We walked over a few minutes later with me two steps behind Steve.

"What have you got here, Diogenes? Moonshine?" Steve was looking over a clear two-liter glass bottle full of liquid.

"It is ouzo," Pete said. "Homemade from Andros. And this is pickled octopus, also homemade."

"Where did you get this stuff?" asked Steve.

"A chief engineer with Karras Shipping brings it to me."

"A relative of yours?"

"No, we sailed together some years ago," said Pete. "I was the engine room foreman on the *Ocean Trader,* and he was an engine cadet, fresh out of the academy. I got his ass out of trouble a few times and he never forgot it. His ship comes to Miami every three months, and he always brings me a demijohn of wine, a bottle of ouzo, and a supply of appetizers from the island. His brother-in-law in Andros makes them."

Steve reached for a piece of octopus but stopped halfway to turn toward the kitchen.

"Pascal!" he shouted. "No forget to change the grease in the fryer. And put the cans outside for Pepe." He turned back and said to no one in particular, "I'm gonna ask that Italian Jew to start paying me for it. I bet you the fucking weasel is making a killing selling my grease. He's probably the one who told the Jews in the city council to make the stupid law."

"What law is that?" asked Pete.

"The one that says you can't pour the grease down the drain

anymore," said Steve in a bothersome tone that implied everyone had heard of the "stupid law."

He looked over the octopus pieces Pete had arranged on the plate. "Now, let's see what we have here." He sounded like a doctor about to examine a patient. He put one piece in his mouth and worked it with his jaws, his lips, and his tongue, in slow, accentuated, circular moves, like a food critic judging a new dish.

"Good stuff," he finally decreed. He took another piece and repeated the process, then washed it down with a sip of ouzo. "Huh-huh, it *is* good stuff."

Just then Pepe stuck his head through the kitchen door. "I'm emptying the grease cans. Didn't want you to wonder what all the banging was back here."

"You got perfect timing, Pepino," said Pete. "Come, have a drink with us."

"I wouldn't want to intrude," said Pepe.

"Oh, come on now, Pepe," Steve said. "You would join the Foreign Legion if they were giving something for free."

Pete called out to Carmen, "Carmelita, come join us. And, Kostas, could you please ask Pascal to join us also?"

I went to the kitchen door and called Pascal. A few minutes later, he came out drying his hands on his apron and approached the table with short, timid steps, as if he were expecting to be chastised.

"Here, Pascal, try some of these," urged Steve. He put a large piece of octopus in his own mouth and chewed it with exaggerated delight, the way one does when trying to convince a child that something is safe. "Mmmm, good stuff."

Pepe and Pascal took the glasses and the loaded forks Pete handed them and nodded their thanks. Pepe put the whole piece of octopus into his mouth and chewed it with gusto. It took Pascal four timid bites to clear his fork.

"What is the occasion?" Pepe asked.

"Gentlemen," said Pete, "as of today, you are looking at Mr.

American Citizen."

"Congratulations, Mr. Pete," said Pepe.

"To Pete Papas, *Mr.* American Citizen," said Steve, and we all clinked our glasses and took a sip.

"Boy-oh-boy," said Pepe, gasping for breath. "This is like liquid fire. It's the strongest ouzo I ever tasted."

"This is homemade ouzo," said Pete. "But if you put a little water in it, it takes some of the fire out."

Carmen stopped filling the saltshakers on the next table and came over. Pete forked a piece of octopus and offered it to her. Then poured some in a glass and added a bit of water to it, which turned it milky white.

"To wash it down with," he said, handing her the glass.

"*Salud,* Mr. Pete." She took a sip and quickly sucked in a lungful of air. "Strong stuff," she managed to say.

Pete offered her another piece of octopus, but she shook her head. "No, *gracias.* I just wanted to see what it tasted like. Now I know." She went back to refilling the saltshakers.

"So, you are an American citizen now, Mr. Pete," I said. My admiration for the man had just tripled. "I will make some more *mezedes* for the celebration. This is an important occasion."

I dashed into the kitchen and returned shortly, carrying two plates loaded with miniature shish kebabs made from cut-up tomatoes, feta cheese, pitted olives, and toasted bread cut into small squares.

"Wow, fancy work," exclaimed Pete. "First-class appetizers."

I assumed Pete was speaking English so Pepe and Pascal wouldn't feel left out, and I tried to do the same. "I worked little time at *ouzeri* in Volos," I said.

"In Greece," Pete explained to Pepe, who looked perplexed, "there are places that specialize in serving only ouzo. They are called *ouzeri.* And since the stuff is pretty strong, as you've noticed, our wise ancestors invented the custom that you should always send some food down there first, to line the bottom of the stomach. That's why they serve appetizers—*mezedes* as the Greeks call them—with the drink."

"And because the ouzo taste same in all *ouzeri*," I said, "what make one *ouzeri* different from other *ouzeri* is the *mezedes*." I pointed to the plates I'd just brought. I was surprised and encouraged at how easy the English words came to me. "*Mezedes* must be different every serving. It is important never to serve same appetizer to same customer two times."

Pete nodded. "Seasoned drinkers of ouzo put great importance on what kind of appetizers a place has. I remember when I lived in Piraeus, there was an *ouzeri* called Kapetan Nickolas. The owner used to bring *mezedes* from all over the world. He had somebody send him *tsitsirava* from Volos and *basturma* from Egypt."

"You can buy *basturma* in New York," Steve said. "I know the guy who sells it. He brings it from Turkey."

"Then it's probably made from old horses," said Peter. "The Egyptian *basturma* is the best. They use camel meat."

I refilled my glass, lit a cigarette, and sat down. All this conversation about ouzo and *ouzeris* had brought in a wave of memories. For a moment I was back at the Ouzeri Zephyros in Volos. I watched my cigarette smoke rise toward the ceiling, and in its grey folds I could almost see the fat, piggish face of the owner, Mister Taso Krasas.

After my military service, the Ouzeri Zephyros was the first place I worked. My job was to prepare the *mezedes*. I put to use what I had learned as the chef's helper at the officers' club in the navy, added some of my mother's recipes, and created appetizers they had never heard of—mushrooms stuffed with feta cheese, tiny peppers stuffed with ham and provolone, and miniature shish kebabs. Every day I came up with new creations.

Word got around about the unique *mezedes* of the Zephyros, and soon the place was packed with the suit-and-tie crowd of the surrounding offices. Mister Taso took the money to the bank by the sack full, but the ungrateful ass never bothered to say even one thank-you to me. During the day he would sit at the table by the serving window to keep an eye on the goings-on in the kitchen. He bragged to his old cronies about his smartness and even had the nerve to name some of the dishes after himself—souvlaki Taso, stuffed mushrooms á la Zephyros.

One day I overheard him tell one of his friends, "These Asia Minor refugees are good workers, but you got to know how to handle them or it'll go to their heads."

I knew he was referring to me, although the old goat knew I was born just a few kilometers from where his fat ass was sitting. It was my father who had been chased from Asia Minor together with a multitude of others and had come to the "mother country," destitute and broken spirited, with nothing but the stigma of a refugee to pass on to his descendants. Fortunately for Taso Krasas, I was fresh out of the service and still had some of the restraint the military had implanted; otherwise I would have flung the ladle I was holding right at his big fat head. Instead, I faked a cough to let him know I could hear him.

Later that afternoon, I asked him for the raise I had been promised. The old goat immediately started poor-mouthing.

"Things aren't as prosperous as they seem to those on the outside," he said. "They don't know all the details. When things get better, I'll give you a raise. I'm a fair and upright man, my boy. Not like some others who try to take advantage of refugees or the less privileged."

The way he had delivered that speech, like a child reciting a poem, I knew this shit-pot of a person had said the same thing to many people who had dared to ask for a raise. It became crystal clear to me that when you are born poor and depend on somebody else's opinion for your worth, your life and what you want to make of it will always be in the hands of the Taso Krasases of the world, unless you yank yourself free from the yoke and get to where your efforts were rewarded.

At the Zephyros, around that time, there were three retired old farts from Chicago who had made the corner table their permanent headquarters. One of them told me that a cook like me could name his price in America. "You would be rich in a year," he said. The other two concurred by nodding and saying, "Thaasfoshur, thaasfoshur."

The very next day after Krasas said he couldn't give me a raise, I applied for my seaman's papers. Three weeks later I was on a plane to Egypt to join the freighter *Poseidon* that was transiting the Suez Canal on her way to Singapore.

"To your health, Diogenes." Steve's voice brought me back from the Ouzeri Zephyros. "Now you can run for governor of Florida."

We wished Pete good health again and emptied our glasses. Then Pepe said he needed to be getting on home to help his youngest with his math homework.

"Congratulations, Mr. Pete," he said as he left. "Thank you for the hospitality, Mr. Steve."

Pascal said, "Yes, congratulations, Monsieur Pete. *Merci beaucoup*." He bowed and went back in the kitchen.

Steve took another piece of the octopus. "So, Diogenes, tell me, did you have to take a test? I might go for mine someday."

"Not bad," said Pete. "A couple of months back, I had to go to the immigration office and answer some questions—"

"What kind of questions, Mister Pete?" I blurted.

Pete grinned as if he'd guessed what had alarmed me. "Simple questions, Kostas. Like who's the president, how many stars on the American flag, what kind of government we have. Stuff like that, nothing serious." He refilled everybody's glasses. "Then I got a notice to show up at the Miami City Hall on this date for the 'naturalization ceremony.' There were people from all over the globe at that hall, at least a couple of hundred. All kinds and all ages. Everyone was dressed in churchgoing clothes. We put our hands over our hearts and pledged allegiance to the American flag and to the American Republic, first in English and then in Spanish. Then we listened to some bureaucrat give a long speech about America that I'm sure most people in there didn't understand. They cut a cake that was made to look like the American flag and gave each of us a piece on little red-and-white paper plates."

Pete refilled everyone's glasses.

"I talked to a man from Andorra who was a college professor," he went on. "And an old Jewish lady from Russia who cried during most of the ceremony. She never thought she would live to see this day, she said. And a couple from Nigeria, and a lot of other people from countries I had never heard of."

"Um-hmm, everybody wants to come to America," said Steve. "Well, cheers again. Now that you're on the inside, tell Johnson I want some of my taxes back. Let somebody else feed the Cubans and the Haitians in Miami."

"You can count on it," said Pete with mock seriousness. "Next time I play backgammon with my buddy Lyndon, it'll be the first thing I tell him."

Most of the appetizers were gone, and the bottle with the potent homemade ouzo from Greece was more than half empty, and we were in the middle of toasting Pete's citizenship for yet another time when a young girl walked into the restaurant. She was tall and slender, with an aristocratic-looking face and glossy black hair that reached her shoulders. She wore a long flowery dress with a slit on the side, like some women I had seen in Shanghai. Her skin was light brown, which could pass as the skin of a European after a month on a Greek beach.

I thought she might be a model or an actress or some rich man's mistress who'd gotten lost and come in to ask for directions. She approached the table and asked us if Pascal had already left. Her voice was soft, like an actress in a French movie.

Steve's drink-holding hand froze in front of his open mouth. After a while he said, "No, he no leave. Pascal still here." He turned and shouted toward the serving window, "Pascal, your girlfriend is here!"

Pascal walked out of the kitchen, wiping his hands on his apron. He said something to the girl that I didn't understand, then went back in the kitchen. The girl walked closer to the poster showing the Parthenon on top of the Acropolis and spent some time looking at it.

Steve stood motionless with the full glass of ouzo in his hand, still staring at her with eyes wide open. After a while, the girl turned and moved further down, as if Steve's eye lasers were burning her thighs. She said something to Pascal in the kitchen and walked outside. I saw her through the glass door, reading a book on the bench.

"Beautiful woman you got there, Pascal," Steve said when Pascal came to clean our table.

"She my . . ." Pascal seemed to search for the word. "She my first child. She twenty-four. Pardon, monsieur." He moved around Steve with a tub load of dirty dishes and went into the kitchen.

"I bet she gets at least a twenty for short time," said Steve in Greek.

"She didn't look like a hooker," I said.

"What else is a good-looking Haitian woman washed up on the beach good for? With almond skin like hers, she can put all those tar-skinned streetwalkers out of business."

"I don't know. I don't think Pascal is the kind to let his daughter be a hooker."

"To people like them, it's a job to brag about," Steve went on. "You've been to Curacao and Aruba, haven't you? All those whores over there are from Colombia and Panama. They might be fucking with every unwashed jack-tar for a five-dollar bill, but when they go back home, all of them become society ladies."

He popped a piece of cheese into his mouth and washed it down with a drink. He belched and went on. "Hell, some years back, I was with a ship that went to Panama every two months. One time in Cristobal, I picked up a sweet young brown-skin like her near the docks. We haggled on the price, and I told her if I had to pay for hotel room, the deal was off, she was getting too expensive. So she said we go to her place. When we got there, an old couple—probably her parents—and three little kids were sitting around the table having supper. The place was a one-room shack with every wall covered with paintings—beaches with palm trees, black kids playing in the street, little yellow frogs in the jungle; weird paintings, all of them. I asked her if one of her kids made them and she said she did. Then started explaining what each one was supposed to be and I told her, 'Chiquita, I pay you five dollars to fuck, not for art lessons.'

"She took me to her bed that was separated from the rest of the room by a blanket hanging from a clothesline less than one meter away from the table. We got going and as I was humping her my foot got hooked on the blanket and knocked it down. Hell, I had just got to the sweet part, so I kept going, didn't miss a stroke. The old woman came over and rehung the blanket on the line, then went back to the table. These people don't care, I'm telling you."

"That's disgusting," I said. "That's doing it like dogs. I would whack my meat before I fucked somebody's daughter in front of them. And the children, they must—"

"There are times, Kostas, when I think God has a cruel sense of humor," said Pete. "He gives you—"

"They got to eat," Steve interrupted. "An empty stomach can change your highfaluting morals in a hurry, Pete."

"That's what I mean," Pete said. "God gives you the desire to do great things, but He won't give you the means to do them, like your Chiquita in Panama. She likes to paint and she might be good at it but can't sell her paintings to make a living."

"I don't know about that, Diogenes," said Steve. "All I know is that if you need the money, you swallow your pride, kiss ass, and let those who got the money play billiards on your back. Like this Jew I met in Baltimore."

"What did he do to you?" I asked.

"Nothing to me," Steve said. "He tried to sell an old coat to the ship's chief steward, the stingiest man who ever lived. It was this long overcoat that God knows what dead person the Jew had gotten it from, big enough to put two more stewards in there. He was skinnier than a billiard stick, you see. The Jew acted like he was adjusting it and gathered all the extra material in the back. Then turned him toward the mirror. 'See? fits you just right,' he tells him, smoothing the front with his left hand while holding the slack with his right. The tightwad steward sniffed the air and said, 'It smells kind of bad.' The Jew wanted that money just as much as the steward wanted to hold on to it, so he says, 'Don't you worry about the smell. The smell is from me, the smell is from me,' and kept on smoothing the front."

"That's an old story," I said. "Some old farts on my ship used to say it happened to them."

Steve refilled his glass and this time didn't put any water in it. "Money changes your thinking pretty damn quick," he said as if he hadn't heard me. "It makes you forgive everything and put up with anything. All of us, and I mean all the people—black, white, red, or yellow—we keep our patriotism and lofty ideals stored in our wallet. Look at the Greeks. There are millions back home who lost family and suffered all kinds of torture by the Germans, but they forgave them and now they wait on them at tables, empty their bed pans, and kiss their ass every day. Why? Because they've got money. The Turks, on the other hand, are just as broke as we are, so we still hate them." He picked up the last of the octopus pieces. In the silence that followed his words, his smacking echoed in the empty dining room.

Pete Papas rose and slowly screwed the cap back onto the empty ouzo bottle. "You may have something there, Steve," he said. "When I was with the President Shipping Lines, we called on Honolulu once a month. That place is crammed with Japanese tourists. All the locals go *yes sir, thank you, sir* and hold the doors for them. They even have signs in the stores and menus in the restaurants that are written in Japanese."

"That's what I'm telling you." Steve grinned triumphantly. "Like the Americans say, money talks. Why you think all the Miami Jews stick those *Se habla Español* signs on their store windows? To get the welfare dollars from all the damn Cubans." He drained his glass. "It's the same all over the world, I know." His voice had the sound of certainty.

Pete did not answer. He gathered up his things and started out. "Good night, everybody," he said.

I felt a pang of envy. There was a man who had all his life's affairs the way he wanted them to be. Would my own life ever be like that?

CHAPTER ELEVEN

A Marriage Proposal

This day, the only customers left after the lunch hour rush were an old man drinking coffee at the far end of the counter and a young couple at the table by the wall, feeding each other a stale piece of apple pie and laughing.

I got busy reloading the soft-drink cooler, and Pascal brought out a tray of clean coffee cups and stacked them under the counter.

Carmen finished wiping the counter and picked up a *Miami Herald* left by a customer and looked at the photograph where the paper was folded. "Another boatload of dead Haitians washed up this week," she said. "It is tragic."

Steve, who had been emptying the cash register, moved over to look at the paper and bumped into Pascal. "Any relatives of you, Pascal?" he asked, pointing to the photograph. His voice had a teasing, sarcastic tone to it.

Pascal glanced at the paper for an instant and whispered something out of which the only words I could decipher sounded like "Gede" and "Agwe Tawoyo," because Pascal kept repeating them.

"Friends of yours?" asked Steve.

Pascal shook his head no and concentrated on emptying the tray with the cups.

"You got to know how to swim if you are coming to America, Pascal," said Steve. "America is a rough ocean. You got to know how to swim and swim good to stay on top." Steve laughed, an annoying, mocking kind of laugh.

Steve was probably trying to say something other than what his words meant, but I couldn't figure out what that might be.

"I'm going to go make a deposit," Steve said and slammed the register drawer shut. "It's not worth opening the last week of the month. All the freeloaders have drunk their last welfare dollar." At the door he paused and said, "After the bank, I've got to go see somebody. I'll be back in the evening."

I went into the kitchen and started scraping the grill with the pumice stone. "The old goat is horny again," I said to Pascal, who was at the sink cleaning the big pot.

He didn't answer and kept on scrubbing and humming a sad-sounding French tune.

"The boss is going to his girlfriend again," I said, a bit louder this time.

"He the boss," answered Pascal, still humming and scrubbing.

I wiped the grill with a dishcloth, then slapped two hamburger patties and a bun on the hot surface.

"You play with Karen too, Monsieur Kostas, no?" Pascal's question startled me.

"Yes, sometimes. When she come to me."

"I think you do it because feels good to get something back from the bad boss, Monsieur Kostas, no?"

I was surprised at how much the quiet Haitian, who seemed not to see or hear anything, was really seeing. Now that Pascal pointed it out, I realized that the feeling of revenge *was* the most satisfying part of having sex with Karen. The knowledge that she was Steve's and I was taking her from him gave me the biggest orgasms I'd ever had.

I flipped the hamburger patties over and put on two slices of cheese, then put them on the bun and piled on tomatoes, pickles, and two slices of onions. I pressed down on the tower to steady it, got a can of orange drink from the cooler, and sat at the counter near the cash register.

At the other end of the counter, the old man sipped coffee and stared blankly at the wall. He had a trimmed white beard and wore a gray suit with a white shirt and a tie, all clean and pressed and past their prime.

Carmen took the coffee pot and went over to him. "More coffee, Professor?" she asked and refilled his cup without waiting for an answer.

"Thank you," he said. "You are a good woman, Carmelita. You are on top of my good-people list."

"I think you are looking at your list upside down," said Carmen.

"I have a very short list, Carmen. And you are on top of it."

"You are a good man too, Professor," Carmen called back as she walked away.

She knows how to hustle the tips. I took another bite of my super double-decker.

Carmen poured herself a cup of coffee, took a cigarette out of the pack in her purse, and settled on the stool next to me.

"*Griego, cómo le gusta* America?" she asked, lighting her cigarette with my matches.

"Is okay." I wiped my mouth and took a long sip of the orange drink while looking at her. Her eyes were big and black, and they always looked tired.

"You must like it," she said. "You are becoming *gordito.*"

"No, I don't think so." I hadn't noticed I was getting fat. I was eating as much as my stomach could hold because that too was part of my pay, and another form of my revenge. "I like it okay," I said after swallowing.

The man at end of the counter got up to leave and Carmen called out to him. "Goodbye, Professor." When he was gone, she spoke to me in a lower voice. "It is lucky the immigration has not come. You're here six months now and have no problem with them."

"I don't care if they come," I said. "Steve took care of all the papers."

"*Hombre,* you are *crédulo.*"

"What am I?"

"You are *crédulo—bobo.*" She searched for the English word. "You are very . . . simple brain," she said with a chuckle. "You really believe that Steve will do something nice for somebody? Steven will only do what is good for Steven." She took a puff of her cigarette. "Did you not talk with the people that live in his apartments? You not see how it was before you came? He only takes their money, never fix nothing. Sometimes he feed some bum leftovers from the restaurant to fix something, but that is all. And if a family has problem and is one day late with the rent, out they go." She took another puff and seemed to concentrate on a stain on the counter.

This was the first time Carmen had said so much about Steve. She was up to something, but I couldn't guess what it might be. Maybe she had found another job and planned to leave, so she was telling me her reasons in a roundabout way since she thought I was Steve's relative.

"Listen," I started to say but stopped and glanced toward the table where the young couple seemed to be licking the ice cream from each other's lips. They were too far away to hear me, but I lowered my voice anyway. "I see some of the damage in the apartments. Maybe Steve has a reason."

"I speak before," Carmen said, still studying the stain on the counter. "A lot of people not like Steve. Not only Jose, the crazy painter. A lot of respectable people who could make problems for him. Maybe somebody goes to the immigration and tell them that he has somebody working here with no papers."

"I don't care if they go. I told you, Steve fixed the papers. He no tell you I am his sister's son."

"*Hombre,* nobody believed that. You seem to be . . . *normal.* Not possible you are relative of Steve, I am sure."

"Well, I *am* his nephew," I said.

"I don't think Steve has human relatives. And I don't think the immigration people will believe that either."

The young couple got up to leave, and I walked around to the cash register to give the man his change. Almost immediately, Pascal came out of the kitchen and cleaned their table.

When I got back to my seat, Carmen said, "You know, the American government has a law called *minimum wage.* It is not legal to pay somebody under that minimum wage, but he has you work in his apartments and in the restaurant for crumbs because he know you cannot go to authorities or get a job in other place."

"But I stay in his apartment for nothing, and I pay nothing for eating," I said. Had Steve put her up to this? Was she spying for him? "Anyway, I know what I am doing. It's nobody's business what arrangement I make with Steve."

She leaned closer and said, "The sonavabiches at the immigration don't give one shit about your arrangements. They will kick you back to where you came from before you know what happened." She ground out her cigarette in the ashtray. "And don't think Steve will do anything to stop them."

I finished the hamburger and took a sip of the drink before repositioning myself on the stool and lighting a cigarette, still wondering what she was up to.

Pascal came out of the kitchen. "Everything is clean, Monsieur Kostas. Is necessary I go home for half hour. Is okay, Monsieur Kostas?"

I said it was okay and took a puff, then turned to face Carmen. "You tell me all this for some reason, right?"

"I am American citizen," she said. "I got the citizenship last year, same place Mr. Pete. If I marry somebody, he stay here with papers, no more problem. We marry, you get the green card and the immigration can kiss your ass."

I tried to look calm. "You know how much Steve pays me. You know I don't have much money."

"We can make arrangement for the money."

"It sounds interesting," I said. "I will think about it, but you—"

I didn't get to finish the sentence. The front door opened, and when I glanced at the man walking in, I jumped off the stool and dashed into the kitchen. I squeezed behind the meat cooler and watched the man walk up to the counter and take a stool right across from the serving window. He seemed to be around thirty years old, wore a dark-grey suit and white shirt with a tie, and he was carrying a new-looking brown leather satchel, like a schoolteacher might own. Or perhaps like an immigration inspector?

My heart raced. I hadn't seen that guy in the restaurant before, and he didn't look like any of the usual type of customers. There were no fancy corporate offices in the neighborhood, nor any schools that I knew of. What was he doing here? He didn't look lost; he'd walked in like here was where he wanted to go. Could Karen have turned me in? Last time we made love she had acted cuddly and said she would like to start a real family, but I pretended I did not understand. Maybe she got angry.

I eased closer to the serving window where I could see and hear without being noticed. I eyed the back door. If the man headed toward the kitchen, I could dash out and run, although that was risky also. When two plainclothes policemen raided the kitchen where Telemahos worked in Savannah, he ran. He tried to climb a wall, but they shot after him. Good thing they only shot off his middle finger.

Maybe this guy was a better shot. He could have a gun under that coat. Why else wear a coat in this heat? And if I outran him, where could I go? Other than the little money I had sent to Mother, everything I had was at the apartment. The immigration was probably already there waiting for me.

Carmen walked behind the counter and set a glass of water in front of the new customer. In English, she asked if he wanted coffee. He nodded agreeably, and she turned to walk toward the coffee urn. Then the man said in Spanish that he would also like a piece of apple pie. I saw Carmen slam the coffee pot down and turn to face the customer.

"Antonio?" she exclaimed. "Is that you? *Dios mio,* you look like a regular Yankee!" She went back to the man and bombarded him with questions in Spanish about how his parents were, where they lived now, and where he worked, all with the informality of having known him for a long time.

"It's Anthony now," he said with a chuckle. "Anthony Gaines. No more Antonio Gonzales." He handed her a card.

Carmen looked at the card for a moment. "Continental Insurance Corporation, Anthony Gaines, Marketing Vice President," she read. I wasn't sure if the tone in her voice was real admiration or made up. She put the card in her purse and stared at him a minute. "You look like a completely different person."

"I had to. I wouldn't get the job if I didn't look like this. When they see you are Cuban, right away it's 'We already have somebody cutting the grass, amigo. No need anything else today, gracias, señor.'" He mimicked an American's voice. "It is a good thing I was young when I went to an American school and I can make my voice not sound Cuban. I can tell them 'I am from down the road a piece, y'all.'" In the last part he mimicked a Southerner's voice, and Carmen burst out laughing. "And I can tell all them pilgrims they better watch their mouth, sister." This time he did a good imitation of John Wayne.

Carmen was holding her stomach and laughing. "*Antonio, tú eres increíble.*" She put a cup of coffee and a piece of apple pie in front of him, then walked around the counter and sat on the next stool. "Tell me about the family. Maria okay? How many children now?"

Antonio pulled out three photographs from his wallet. "Here is Maria holding Rosalina, and this one is our American, Edward, our youngest."

"Oh, *Eduardo, que lindo,*" Carmen exclaimed.

"No, it is Edward. He will be raised as American."

I wiped the perspiration from my forehead and started getting the kitchen ready for the supper. When I peeked through the serving window again, I saw Carmen pointing out someone on a photograph from her wallet, and I had to laugh at myself. That had been a hell of a scare. Almost as bad as some of the scares I'd had on the bus from Hoboken to Miami.

For the rest of the day, I pondered Carmen's proposition. My hands and feet went about the kitchen chores as if on automatic pilot, but my brain busily analyzed everything Carmen had said and done today and every day up to today. Then I tried to recall what I knew about Cuba and the Cubans. By the end of the day, I had not come up with any plausible explanation for why she had suddenly offered to help me. All I had achieved was getting a headache that made my head feel like a boiling cauldron.

On my way home I stopped by the Woolworth's store to get shaving cream and razor blades. It was one of the few stores I felt safe going into when I needed something, because most of the customers were Latinos and I blended in. Today they had put a big table in the middle of the floor near the front door, and on it were piled all sorts of different things—plastic toys, garden tools, screwdrivers, and some things I didn't recognize—all priced at twenty-five cents. A handwritten cardboard sign stuck in the middle said *BARGAIN BIN*. I planned to look up the words when I got to my room, but it was a safe bet it meant "cheap stuff."

I dug in the pile but didn't find any shaving cream or packages of razor blades or anything else I could use. I picked up a plastic toy truck and examined it. It was blue with a yellow hinged back for dumping the load. Karen's kid would love it. I took it and went to look for the shaving stuff. Two steps later, I turned and put the truck back on the pile. If I gave it to the boy, Karen might get ideas, and I didn't want to encourage her kind of ideas.

I found the aisle with the shaving stuff and browsed the other aisles, looking at the myriad of things they made nowadays and wondering how the owner of the store could remember all he had in stock. If only my brother could see these things. Quite often, when I was looking at something awe-inspiring, I caught myself giving my brother an imaginary nudge.

When I ran out of aisles to explore, I started to leave. As I passed by the big table, I paused and read the words again so I could remember them when I looked them up later. *BARGAIN BIN.* I looked over all the toys piled on the table—trucks, guns, and bubble makers.

When I was growing up in the village, all of us played with toys we made ourselves, like small boats we carved out of plane-tree wood that we floated in the community cistern, rifles made out of tree branches for playing "partisans and Germans," but mostly wooden mules for playing muleteers. Pavlos, my brother, used to help me make my mules, and they were the strongest and the best looking. He would bend two chestnut tree sticks into a U-shape for the legs and tie them with the bark of a mulberry tree to a long, thicker stick that was supposed to be the mule's body. He even made saddles that I would load with make-believe cargo. We would pull the wooden mules by a string bridle to imaginary destinations, coaxing and cursing the beasts, just like the big muleteers.

I picked up the yellow-and-blue dump truck and added it to the things I was buying. Poor Joey, he didn't ask to be born.

CHAPTER TWELVE

The Wedding

No matter how many different angles I considered, I couldn't find anything wrong with Carmen's proposition, but I still let it stew in my head for a whole week. During working hours, I studied Carmen through the kitchen window, wishing I could see inside her head. She went about her work the same way she always did, and as hard as I tried to figure out why she was offering to help me, I couldn't come up with a bull's-eye explanation.

The obvious answer for Carmen wanting to become Mrs. Kostas Karaoglou, on paper at least, was that she wanted to make some money, and that was the problem; as every Greek knows, when something seems obvious and logical, there is a catch to it. She had to know I wasn't loaded since she seemed to know how much Steve was paying me. As frugal as I had been, all I had managed to save so far was three hundred dollars, counting my pocket change. Telemahos and some other old-timers who knew more than I did about America had said that the going rate for an "arranged marriage" was around one thousand dollars, and there were no guarantees for a "happy ending." I had known many people who got married and still ended up been kicked out of the country.

Could Carmen have some other shrewder, darker reason?

And then there was the problem of the house. If we got married, we would have to make a show of living together. But where could we stay? Carmen was not going to move in with me—there wasn't enough room in there to add a hamster. And Steve would probably charge me rent anyway, which would squeeze my puny thirty-five dollars a week. Carmen lived in a two-story house about two blocks from the restaurant. Although she didn't talk too much about herself or her family, I was almost sure she did not have a car. Probably that was why she worked at Steve's restaurant, so she could walk to work. Maybe she'd finally had enough of him and needed the money for a car to get another job.

I wished Pete Papas hadn't gone to Nassau. He could give me some good advice, but he wouldn't be back until the end of the week. Pete had said that when the time was right, he would help me. What did he mean by "when the time was right"?

Eventually I would have to do something. I had run the legality problem through my head hundreds of times, and every time the conclusion was the same; in my predicament, there weren't many ways I could stay in the country short of marrying somebody. I couldn't go on dodging policemen and hiding behind the freezer every time somebody in a suit and tie walked into the restaurant. Although it had been some time since the fight with the Cuban painter, I still changed directions when I saw somebody on the street that looked like him.

Quite often when I was daydreaming, I would run through my favored scene. I pictured myself waving my wallet-sized, plastic-enclosed green card in front of Steve's nose and telling him, "From now on you either pay me what I am worth or I am out of here." I had learned enough English to understand parts of the conversations I overheard at the restaurant and could read the want ads of the *Miami Herald*, so I knew that even a sandwich man got fifty dollars a week for just four hours of work at some restaurants. And full-time cooks were getting double that without having to cut the grass, paint the walls, or unclog toilets in some cheapskate's apartment building.

⁘⁘⁘

At last on Friday, Pete Papas showed up at the restaurant. As soon as I saw him, I dashed over and whispered to him about Carmen's proposition.

"Is that so?" he said and started laughing. "I would have never guessed it. Usually it's the man who does the proposing. Did she bring you flowers?" For a moment I thought his jaw-dropped, wide-eyed expression of surprise and his laughter seemed a bit artificial. "I would go ahead and do it then," he said. "Carmen is straight. She won't make trouble for you."

"Why she wait 'til now?" I said. "Why the sudden need for money?"

"I am sure she has her reasons. When she wants you to know, she will tell you," Pete said.

"One thing she did not tell me was how much she wants for this arrangement."

"If I was you, I would say I couldn't afford to pay more than six hundred. I think she'll take it. I think the tuition is about that."

"What's that?"

"Oh, that's something else," he said and quickly added, "You'll have to pay her some rent for the room of course. You'll have to stay with her, you know."

"I don't have that much money. Steve promised me a raise, but God knows when I'll see it."

"I told you I would help you. We'll work something out."

On Monday, at the blood-test place, Carmen acted like a lovestruck teenager. She held my hand and babbled goofy lover's talk the whole time we were there. Then, three days later, I asked

Steve for the day off, saying I needed to spend some time with my cousin whose ship was in port. After releasing a few curses, Steve said I could have half the day off.

"Be back by three," he growled. "I want you here for supper." Since Emilio had quit a week earlier to head a Cuban restaurant in Miami Beach, I had been doing all the cooking.

"I'll try, but I might be late," I said. "My cousin is signing off after this trip and wants me to take him to the shops to buy things to take home."

At the office of the justice of the peace, Carmen again acted lovey-dovey during the wedding ceremony. The justice person was a large man who continuously moved his mouth as if regurgitating that morning's breakfast, and he seemed in a hurry to get the marrying business over with. Carmen wore a brand-new churchgoing kind of dress and looked like a movie star.

She had insisted that I wear a suit and tie also. I tried on about a dozen suits in two different places, but Americans, it seemed, came in giant sizes only. When I complained to Carmen that this make-believe wedding was beginning to cost me a lot of real money, she said I could rent a suit instead of buying. She took me to a place where they rented fancy suits and shirts for dress-up occasions. The salesperson helped me get dressed, and when I looked in the mirror, I wished my brother could see me like that.

"Wow, you look like an English lord!" Carmen had teased.

The bride carried a small bouquet of white gardenias cut from the neighbor's yard. The same neighbor, dressed up in a flowery dress, had come along as the maid of honor.

"Like I said on the phone, it will be forty dollars," the justice of the peace said as soon as he closed his book, indicating the end of the wedding ceremony.

Carmen acted all choked up and told him that she really appreciated him rearranging his schedule so he could marry us this particular day.

"The day of June 3 is a lucky day for my family," she said. "My mother also got married that day, and she had a very happy marriage."

I didn't think the big judge was hearing any of this since all his attention seemed to be focused on searching his wallet and his pockets for change for the fifty-dollar bill I had given him.

Outside city hall, Carmen got into a taxi with the for-hire light on and slid to the far side. I sat on the opposite side and lit a cigarette. The maid of honor sat in front.

"*Ventiocho treinta y dos, Calle Nueve,*" Carmen told the driver.

The driver stopped working his crossword puzzle and turned to face her. "Say again?" He was a youngish-looking fellow with blond hair and an athletic look, like some of the surfers I had seen in Miami Beach.

"Twenty-eight-thirty-two Nine Street." Carmen slid over and snuggled up to me, holding my hand.

Thinking the occasion called for it, I put my other hand over her shoulder. A couple of blocks later, when the cab made a left turn fast, I took advantage of the centrifugal force and let my body press tighter against Carmen's.

I leaned over, squeezed her hand, and whispered, "Maybe you and me go to a hotel for a little celebrate, eh?" I felt her body become rigid, but she didn't pull away from the snuggle.

"We have room at hotel Castaways in Miami Beach, *cerido,*" she said in English, sounding as if she were speaking to a stone-deaf person. "I want to be surprise. First, we go to house to take suitcase—have sexy clothes in it. Maria, *mi prima,* make present sexy night dress, *muy, muy* sexy, *cerido.*" She giggled and acted as if she were about to kiss me.

Although puzzled, I tightened my grip on her shoulder and was aiming for her lips when the taxi jolted to a stop.

"Here you are," said the driver. "It'll be eight bucks."

I gave him a ten-dollar bill and said, "Keep change."

"Thanks," he said. As he drove away, he called out, "Congratulations!"

Carmen held my hand until the taxi turned the corner, then broke loose and faced me.

"Listen what I speak to you," she said, her voice serious, no girly giggling this time. "I say before that we marry for you to get green card and me the money. That is all. There is no sexing, no nothing else. You stay in your room"—she pointed toward the first floor of the building, where earlier I had moved my things into what was going to be "our" bedroom—"and you live your life. Outside, when we are with other people, we make like loving husband and wife. The immigration people are going to be watching all the time. You must be careful when you speak. They are everywhere, and they have snitches everywhere—judges, waiters, taxi drivers, all kinds of people. *Entender*?"

I nodded that I understood.

She turned to go in the house. She started to throw her gardenia bouquet into a garbage bin but changed her mind and said, "I'll put them in the water."

I headed toward Steve's apartment building. All the body-rubbing with Carmen had got my blood flowing. Good thing I'd told Steve the story about taking the cousin shopping. Now I could visit Karen while Steve was stuck at the restaurant. Her kinky brain would really get a kick out of seeing me dressed like I was. "I bet you never done it with a lord," I'd tell her, and that would get us started. I hadn't gone more than ten steps when Carmen called for me to wait.

"And you need to stop going to Karen," she said when she got closer. "That gardenia-smelling tramp can make plenty trouble for you."

The woman thought of everything. "I was taking these clothes back to the shop," I answered, faking annoyance. "I started for the old room by mistake." I wasn't sure she believed me.

In my room I changed into work clothes and put the marriage suit in the bag the rental shop had given me, and I took it back. I started for the restaurant, but one block before I got there, I turned left on Ninth Street and walked toward the waterfront. I wasn't going to work. I would take the rest of the day off to celebrate, and if Steve said anything, I knew how to answer him now.

At the Freedom Tower Square, I sat on a bench and smoked a cigarette. No protesting people and no policemen today, just a couple of German-speaking tourists, newlyweds probably, photographing each other around the tower. They asked me if I could take a picture of both of them and afterward they said, "Tank you" and I said "*Vunderbar*" and everybody smiled.

After a while, I walked toward the harbor. There were no cruise ships today. At the Miami shipyard I watched a group of workers taking the propeller out of a Shell Oil tanker in the dry dock. At the far end of Dodge Island, a freighter was discharging cargo. The men moving on deck and the steam of the winches rose every time they heaved a load, but it was too far to see the ship's name.

Lots of people were in the park next to the harbor, taking advantage of the balmy, late-afternoon temperature—old-timers sitting on benches under the palm trees, women pushing strollers, and young couples in bathing suits sunbathing on spread blankets. At the entrance to the park, I bought a hot dog, then sat on a bench a few yards away and watched the business traffic at the hot dog cart. The vendor was a young American-looking man, tall with long blond hair and a scrawny beard, wearing a flowery shirt, khaki shorts, and sandals. When a customer walked up to him, he would fish out a hot dog from the steaming kettle, grunt a few words about the condiments, hand them the change, then return to his stool and the thick book he was reading. He didn't talk much with anyone, and to those who spoke to him in Spanish, he answered in English.

He looked like one of the tourists. If it were my operation, I would wear a white shirt and white pants and maybe a white cap to keep the hair out, like a vendor I'd seen in a movie once. And this guy didn't say anything to make the customers feel good, like "Good appetite. Enjoy. Have a nice day." It helped to make people feel like they were important when they spent their money, even if it was just half a dollar. Maybe he should decorate his cart with flags or play some music, something to attract attention. And he should have a small grill for onions; you could smell onions on the grill from a block away—the kind of smell that made you hungry even if you'd just eaten. Pete had said that's how Alex Vournaris drew the people to his pushcart and sold hot dogs by the dozens.

I took small bites of the sausage, like a wine taster sampling a new harvest, and I tried to understand what made them so popular. The only thing I could taste was the mustard, the tomato sauce, and the onions I had added. But the Americans seem to like them so much that they made special bread so the sausage would fit just right and be easy to bite into.

If the cart were in the right location, it could be a good moneymaker, no doubt. If the guy in New York could make millions where it rained and snowed and was cold most of the year, it ought to be ten times easier down here. And unlike this guy over here with his nose in the book who didn't even grunt in Spanish, I could carry on a conversation with the Cuban and Colombian customers. I could even find out if there were any Cuban sausages to serve. All it took to get started was a bottle of gas, a kettle, and a little imagination.

Maybe I could come up with some spices that would make these hot *dogs* tastier. Liapouras used to say that Americans had simple tastes when it came to eating.

"The difference between a good American cook and an average one," he used to say, "is that the good cook warms up the food after he takes it out of the can."

He might have been right. Look at the Italians. They had the Americans going crazy about pizza, and it was just dough with canned tomatoes, cheese, and whatever else you wanted to throw on top. The Italians invented it to get rid of their leftovers, but the Americans couldn't get enough of it. Smart people, the Italians. Why didn't some Greek start selling souvlaki? It was a hundred times better tasting and better food.

There were three people lined up by the sausage cart, waiting to be served. There was no disputing it. Convenience was what made the sale. People taking a stroll in the park would eat a plain-tasting hot dog to satisfy a hunger urge if they saw it in front of them. And workers taking thirty minutes for a lunch break didn't have time to go looking for gourmet restaurants. They want something fast and filling.

After a while I walked over and bought another hot dog. It was suppertime anyway, and I also wanted to talk to the vendor.

"Business good?" I asked when he handed me the change.

"Okay," he said and returned to his thick book.

"Must be good book," I said, a little annoyed.

"Got finals tomorrow," he answered and turned the page.

I didn't understand what that meant, so I shrugged and walked away. You couldn't make it in that kind of business if you didn't like talking to people.

When the sun went down, the hot dog vendor rolled his cart away, and I started back to my new home.

On my first night as a married man, I slept very little, but it was not because of the usual first-night newlywed activities. What kept me awake were the ideas gushing out of my brain about things I could do as soon as I had "my papers." So many places I could visit, so many moneymaking ventures I could attempt. I felt weightless and wished daylight would hurry up so I could fly over Miami and Miami Beach and see all the places I was afraid to visit before.

Maybe my first business venture could be selling hot dog sausages out of a pushcart, like Vournaris. If *I* had a cart at the spot where the long-haired man with the "finals" book was today, I would've had the customers lined up three wide for two blocks. I could ask Pete Papas to loan me the money for the cart. He had done the negotiating with Carmen and the lawyer handling the green-card papers. It had come to twelve hundred dollars altogether, and Pete said I could take a year or longer to pay him off. Maybe he could loan me a bit more, enough to start a business, if he saw the possibility of getting paid back sooner. Working with the pushcart for a year, I should be able to save enough to pay off the loan and put a down payment on a restaurant in a good location. That's when the big money would start rolling in.

Yes sir, there was no stopping me now. I was on my way to the *big money*. First I would spend some of that money in a way that would make my name remembered in the village for years after I was gone. Lots of people from Taxiarhes had migrated to Egypt a couple of generations earlier and gotten rich. With the money they brought back, they had built schools and churches and fountains. I'd heard the old-timers telling the youngsters what great men Mr. Kartalis and Mr. Astakos and Mr. Hilopoulos were. People remembered them and talked about them and would for generations to come.

A smart-alecky professor in my high school used to say that those buildings were "the collateral benefits of rich people's ego." I never bothered to ask what he meant by that. What I knew was that those men had managed to lift themselves above the nameless masses who lived and died and nobody knew ever existed. I was going to do something to put my name among those chiseled in marble plaques. And I'd do it while I was young, not wait until I was old and decrepit, when it would look like I was trying to get past sins forgiven. Folks in Taxiarhes used to whisper that Astakos had built the great church Saint Keterini after he couldn't get it up anymore, to atone for taking advantage of a multitude of naïve young girls.

As soon as I had the money saved up, I'd send it to my brother to build a fountain at the spring by the crossroads near our house. It would be like the Korpanaris fountain at the square, only bigger. That should make Mother burst with pride. And it would have stone benches around it so people could sit under the centuries-old plane tree, and it would have a marble spout where the water came out. Above it, in a marble slab, I would have chiseled, *This fountain was erected through the generosity of Konstandinos Karaoglou*, just like the Korpanaris fountain.

And of course, they would change the name from Crossroads Spring to Kostas Karaoglou Fountain. And when people drank the cool, crisp water running out of the marble spout, they would always read my name above it. Children would ask their parents who Kostas Karaoglou was, and their parents would hasten to boast that they knew the man or they knew somebody who knew him.

I drifted off to sleep thinking of what a famous man I would become from all the money I was going to make now that I was *legal.*

⁜⁜⁜

The next morning, I got to the restaurant an hour early. Steve came in just before lunch and went about his usual chores without asking me why I hadn't come in the day before. All day I worked with the surefooted steps of someone who had finally glimpsed the light at the end of the tunnel.

Finally, Pete Papas, as always the last customer, got up and headed for the door. I thought I detected a hint of a wink as he passed.

"How did you do at the track yesterday, Steve?" Pete asked when he paid the bill.

"The fucking horse was ahead by a mile," answered Steve, handing him the change. "But he held it back, I'm sure he did. That faggot jockey held it back. He's done it before, you know. If I could get my hands on that whore's son, I'd beat his fucking ass to a pulp." He pounded his fist on the counter, and the coins almost jumped out of the drawer. "It pisses me off. I was sure I'd make up for a lousy week. Fucking faggot."

"You are a very caring person, Steve," Pete said. "You make sure all God's creatures get fed—His horses, His dogs, His Jai Alai players. Very caring person."

"Diogenes, don't you get me started now," snapped Steve.

While Steve counted the money in the cash register, I tapped him on the shoulder.

"Steve, I want to tell you something."

He slammed the drawer shut and turned all in one quick move.

"Damn it, man! You spooked me sneaking behind me like that. What is it?"

All through the day I had been rehearsing what I was going to tell Steve. I thought of saying, "Steve, I've taken enough of your shit. Now I am *legal,* and from now on things are going to be different. I want a real cook's pay, and if I'm going to run this place, I want a percentage of the profits or I'll go get a job somewhere else. And another thing, I'm not going to be doing the maintenance to your apartments anymore. I'm through unclogging toilets." That would get Steve's head spinning.

Then again, I thought maybe it would be better if I wasn't so confrontational—if I tried to reason with him, appeal to him as one countryman to another. I could say, "Steve, you wouldn't hold it against one of your own if he had a chance to better himself, would you? After all, not much is going to change. I would still work here and only sleep somewhere else, that's all. And since I'll be sleeping somewhere else, it won't be convenient to do the maintenance in the apartments." That way Steve wouldn't get pissed off and try to make trouble for me.

"It's been a bitch of a week," Steve said. "What you want?"

"Carmen and I got married yesterday. I am going to take a few days off to get my papers," I heard myself saying. I reached for my pack, and my fingers seemed to have difficulty getting a cigarette out.

He didn't say anything for a moment. He just looked at me with a blank stare, as if in shock. He took a puff on his cigarette, exhaled; then the words came out in a flood.

"You stupid hick! You dumb, stupid, gullible hick. She's an old whore, you idiot. She'll take you for everything you got and everything you can make, you dumb hick."

"We are going to make a family."

"So that's why she said she had to take her old man to the doctor. And you told me you were going to see some cousin of yours from a ship. I didn't believe either one of you, but I thought you might be fucking the slut. You are going to be sorry, believe me." He put the bag with the money inside his shirt. "You should have asked me, stupid. I could have helped you with your papers if you wanted. How much you paid the slut?"

"I told you, we are going to make a family."

"You are going to be sorry, you'll see. You said you wanted to save your money and go back to the village, otherwise I could have fixed it for you to stay." He took another deep puff and started to walk away. Then he turned and faced me. "And do you know something else, Mister American? From now on the government is going to start clobbering you with taxes. Did you know that?"

I had expected that Steve would get upset and had prepared all kinds of clever answers in my head, but instead I just said, "I took my stuff out of the apartment already. The immigration says it's the law to get out of the country and reenter legally, so tomorrow I'm going to Nassau to wait for my papers. Can I still work here when I get back? They said it will take about two weeks."

"I know, I know but it took me a month, and I had a damn good lawyer pushing it. I might get somebody else to work here," he said.

"That's because your marriage looked suspicious. They know ours is true love." I couldn't resist it.

"Oh, yeah? Like the Americans say, you are full of shit."

"Well, I am one of them now," I said. "See you when I get back." I walked out with a springy stride and headed toward Carmen's house.

I felt invincible.

CHAPTER THIRTEEN

Sailing Again

For an extra hundred-dollar "expediting fee," the green-card lawyer had gotten temporary travel documents for me. So, on Friday afternoon, almost twenty-four hours after the "wedding ceremony," I was aboard the cruise ship *Ariadne.* Carmen knew someone who worked for the cruise line, and they got me a ticket to Nassau, the ship's first stop on a four-day Caribbean cruise. According to Carmen's friend, the cruise line had special rates for people who didn't like to fly and went back and forth to the islands by ship. It so happened that on this trip the ship was only half full, but starting the next week, they would be stuffing passengers even into the cargo holds.

"If I hadn't gotten the fat judge to marry us when he did," Carmen told me, "it would be a long time before my friend could get another free ticket."

Pete Papas drove me to the docks. During the have-a-pleasant-trip handshake, he put a fifty-dollar bill in my palm.

"Have a beer with the guys at the Buccaneer Café on me," he said.

I boarded through a long, sloping gangway that bridged the gap between the dock and the ship's main deck, about fifteen feet above the water. Ahead of me was an old couple who must have been boarding a ship for the first time from the way they were acting. They held the gangway rail with both hands and eased forward an inch at a time, the man behind the woman, continuously whispering encouragement, as if they were crossing a canyon over a raging river on a rickety rope bridge.

At the top of the gangway, a tall man with a gray goatee asked every passenger to pause next to a canvas with the ship's name while he snapped their picture. While posing, the old couple ahead of me raised their hands in a victory salute.

"We made it! We climbed Everest," they cheered.

When it was my turn to pose, I shook my head, but the photographer's young assistant, a blonde in a sailor's outfit two sizes too small with half of her top buttons undone, told me I did not have to buy the picture if I didn't want to.

I gave her my sexiest smile and said, "Okay, if you be next to me."

If the picture didn't cost too much, I would send it to my old shipmates and show them what kind of sailing I was doing nowadays. A few steps farther, a man in a white uniform with gold stripes checked my ticket. He said my cabin was on the Promenade Deck above, on the starboard side. Then he gave me the key to my cabin and wished me a pleasant voyage. My luggage would be there shortly, he said.

I walked in the direction the uniformed man had pointed and started up a wide stairway with fancy balusters and shiny handrails. Without thinking, I rubbed my palms on my pants before grabbing the handrail and proceeded with hesitant steps, half expecting someone to come running any second to tell me I was going the wrong way. The man at the gangway and the man with the gold stripes who'd checked my papers and wished me a pleasant voyage kept addressing me with "sir" every other word, and it made me a bit uncomfortable. I couldn't tell if they were being sarcastic or polite.

Boarding the *Ariadne* was nothing like signing on as a deckhand on the *Aegean Sea*. My life was taking a turn for the better already.

My cabin had carpet on the floor, wood paneling, and modern wooden furniture, nothing like the cabins of the ships I had been in before. I opened an interior door and was shocked to see I had my own toilet and shower. This was fancier than the captain's cabin in the *Aegean Sea*. I pulled back the curtains of the porthole and looked out. A deckhand in khakis was putting cushions on the deck chairs.

I lay on the bed with my hands behind my head and closed my eyes. I heard the faint humming of the turbo-generator and felt the light vibration of the ship's machinery below. For a moment, it was as if I were a seaman again, resting on my bunk after returning from ashore. Soon I was lulled to sleep.

I was awakened by a bump against the hull and jumped out of bed, thinking I was late for my watch. I was almost out the door when I remembered I was a passenger. Out on the deck, I watched the crew getting the ship underway. Deckhands in crisp khakis rushed past me on their way to their stations. Some were hoisting the gangway, some pulling in the lines, and others coiling the ropes in smooth, flat circles, oblivious to the stares of the dazed, awestruck passengers.

The crew's hustle, the whistle blows—first by the tugboats around us, then followed by the ship's replies—the line handlers' shouts asking for more slack, and the clanging of the capstans pulling in the mooring lines, all familiar noises of a ship leaving port, transported me back to my sailing days. Two deckhands by the stern were taking the mooring line off the bit, and I almost joined them. The short guy was going about it all wrong; he could get hurt that way.

For a moment, a wave of uncertainty ran through me. Had I done the right thing? If I'd stayed a few more months on the ship, I would've been considered an experienced deckhand. Some shipping companies paid quite well by Greek standards for experienced deckhands on tankers. And there was the overtime and the extra pay for the cargo-tank washing. In a few years I could have—if I didn't squander it at the "love palaces"—put aside enough to open up a nice restaurant in Taxiarhes and made pretty good money from the hordes of tourists who spread all over the village every summer "like goatherds on the mountainside," as Mother had said. What would have been wrong with that?

I puffed on my cigarette while watching the men below and thought of the pump man of the *Aegean Sea*. "Man is like water," he had said during a discussion of the worthiness of jumping ship in America or in Australia. "He always takes the easiest route. And like water, he gouges himself a groove as he goes about his life. Then after a while, he's afraid to climb out of that groove and abandon the life he's been used to, especially the life on a ship. Here it's like living in a cocoon. Everything is decided and taken care of by somebody else."

I flicked my cigarette overboard and walked toward the bow. *Well, it's done. No use getting nervous now.*

I walked forward as far as I could go until I was stopped by a sign dangling on a chain that read, *NO PASSENGERS BEYOND THIS POINT*. I started to straddle the chain before I realized it meant me also. I stood behind the bulwarks and watched the crew on the bow pulling in the ropes with the windlass as soon as the line handlers on the dock took them off the bitts. On the opposite side, two tugs—one on either end—attached to the ship with braided, four-inch manila ropes, were standing by. Next to me stood a group of three women and two men in flowery outfits, with drinks in their hands.

"George, look how thick that string is," chirped one of the women, pointing to the tug.

"Got to be. It's a big boat," said George, who was wearing an orange baseball cap with *Oklahoma is OK* on the front.

"They call it a hawser," said the other man, his baseball cap adorned with a large-mouth bass on the front.

The pilot gave the ship's whistle a short blast to signal the tugs to start pulling. The blast startled the ladies with the flowery outfits and caused them to spill some of their drinks.

"Oh my. Why in the world did he have to do that for?" exclaimed one, brushing her sleeve.

"He blew the horn to tell the small boat to get out of the way," said Oklahoma George.

I gave them an appraising look. Both men looked to be in their fifties. Maybe they didn't sound so ignorant when they talked about their work in Oklahoma. It's a fact that to those who do a job for a living, everybody outside their profession sounds ignorant. Farmers make fun of the way city people behave around livestock, and carpenters mock the way accountants hold the hammer to drive a nail for a picture on the wall.

I decided to have a look at the stern and zigzagged through clusters of people in flowery outfits who were busy throwing streamers and waving to those on the dock, completely ignorant of all the intricate work taking place one deck below. They probably thought this floating mountain was moving along all by itself.

I reached a spot directly above the ship's capstan, just in time to see a group of men pulling in the last two stern lines. I was standing next to two men who didn't seem to be participating in any of the departure merriment. They kept looking over the side toward the stern and toward the bow and both had the concerned look of someone loaded with responsibilities. Both were short and wiry and old. One wore a blue cap with a gold ship's wheel in the front, and the other had on a brand-new cowboy hat that seemed two sizes too big.

"He'd better ring 'ahead' soon," said the man in the blue cap, looking over the side. "He's going to ram the dock."

"Don't need to," said the other. "He's got bow thrusters."

The ship's whistle gave two short blasts.

"See," said the first one. "He doesn't have bow thrusters. He's signaling the forward tug to pull."

"He's signaling the aft tug to *push*," said the cowboy. "Pulling is one long blast, if you remember."

"It *was* one long blast."

"Will you two stop it?" an elderly woman with grayish-blue hair scolded them. "Somebody else is driving *this* ship. Enjoy the cruise. You're retired now. You promised you'd behave."

One of the men said something, but his words were drowned by the farewell blasts of the ship's whistle. Soon the *Ariadne* was gliding in the middle of the channel with Dodge Island on the starboard and Miami Beach on the port side, slowly drifting by. I glanced toward the bridge and wondered how it would feel to be a helmsman on this ship.

"Show me which one was Al Capone's house," said the woman with the grayish-blue hair.

"It's the pink one with the palm trees in front," said the one with blue cap.

"No, it's the white one by the water," said the cowboy. "The pink is the Vizcaya."

The ship picked up speed, and the propellers' frothy curve told me the helmsman was setting course for Nassau. Standing by the emergency binnacle, I watched the seagulls diving into the wake. The cowboy lit a cigar and came to read the compass next to me.

"He's staying on sixty degrees," he told the one in the blue cap.

Blue Cap pondered it for a few seconds. "He'll make a correction after we raise Great Isaac," he said.

A young couple walked by, and the girl asked her escort to stand by the wheel. The man grabbed the wheel with both hands and grimaced as if he were steering a schooner through a gale. The girl giggled and clicked the camera. I wondered if that wheel and compass were indeed for emergency steering, like they had on the poop deck of merchant ships, or if they were put there for the passengers to have their pictures taken.

I walked toward the bow again, taking deep breaths of the salty sea air as I went, and the feeling of having returned to an old, familiar place came over me. At midship, a group of deckhands secured the gangway on the deck below. They used an electric hoist to pull it up, and when it reached the right level, two men slid it into place and secured it with jacks. It was done effortlessly in five minutes. Nothing like the ball-busting heaving-and-pulling operation of my old ship.

The man who'd checked my ticket, a tall, slender Spaniard with enough gold bars and stripes on his uniform for two admirals, had said that my dinnertime was the second seating, at eight o'clock in the main dining room on the Penelope Deck. I started looking for it a few minutes before eight. I weaved through decks and passageways, determined not to ask any of the white-jacketed stewards how to get there. Wouldn't they have a laugh if I, a seasoned mariner, had to ask them how to get to the mess hall?

I finally stumbled upon it at the end of a long passageway. Outside the dining room, the photographer with the goatee and the curvy assistant were taking pictures of the dressed-up passengers in front of a giant ship's wheel. I walked by them into the dining room. A stuffy-looking head waiter told me he couldn't seat me without a jacket and tie. Looking around, I noticed everybody else was dressed in fancy suits and gowns, as if they were going to a coronation.

I had spent five dollars for a used suitcase for this trip, and put some new pants and shirts in it in case I went to church in Nassau, but I hadn't seen the need to buy a jacket and a tie. Besides, getting all dressed up just to get something to eat seemed too much trouble. And they would probably seat me next to the Oklahoma farmers or the blue-haired women and their nervous old seadog husbands. How can a normal person enjoy his diner sitting amongst people like that? I would really have liked to go to the crew's mess hall and talk to some of the deckhands to find out where they were from, how much they were making, and if they were bedding any of the cargo they were hauling.

I went out on deck, leaned on the bulwarks, and again watched the seagulls following the ship. A couple of minutes later, a young couple holding hands and snuggling like newlyweds went by me, and among the kissing and the cooing I understood the words "go get some dinner." The way they were dressed, in baggy shorts and floppy T-shirts, I didn't think the stuffy head waiter was going to let them "get some dinner" in his fancy dining room.

I followed from a distance, and one deck down and two passageway turns later, I landed in a self-service cafeteria. I was stunned by what I saw. There was enough food there to feed the world. If somebody had told me there were ships giving out food like that, I would have said they were telling tales taller than those from Christos, the Weasel, and Liapouras put together. There was food in trays, in pans, and on platters, under lamps and over ice, on hot tables, cold tables, and plain tables, all arranged in fancy designs that made you feel guilty when you took something and messed it up.

I wondered what the food for the crew looked like. They probably ate what was left from these tables. They wouldn't be throwing it away, that's for sure. I wished the guys from the *Aegean Sea* could see me now.

I got in line and copied the moves of the people ahead of me. I loaded my plate with small quantities of everything, ruining the shapes of a lobster, a turtle, a seahorse, and a few other sea creatures as I scooped up sliced tomatoes, potato salad, and smoked salmon. I spotted an empty table and quickly set my plate on it. I'd never felt comfortable eating next to strangers. When I finished eating, I went for a walk on deck.

The ship seemed to be a floating city. It had restaurants, nightclubs, a movie theater, even a casino, and I wanted to explore everything. I started with the Calypso Nightclub on the Calypso Deck. The place was as big and as fancy as some of the nightclubs I had been to in Amsterdam. I sat at the end of the bar and ordered a rum and Coke. When the waiter set the drink down, I sipped it slowly while looking around.

Calypso and her almost-naked playmates beckoned Odysseus from a large wall mural behind me. Most tables were occupied by couples drinking colorful concoctions with long straws, some of them out of the same tall glass. Three ship's officers in starched white uniforms sat at a center table with four bubbly, middle-aged women in low-cut evening dresses. On the dance floor, four couples were glued together and barely moving to the tune of "Yellow Bird" played by the Jamaican band.

I smoked, sipped on my drink, and watched the couples on the dance floor, all dressed in fancy clothes and all laughing at jokes I couldn't understand. After a while, I felt uncomfortable, as if I shouldn't be here. Like I was intruding on a gathering of a different class of people.

Silently I repeated the words *different class of people.* My mother used to say those words when she spoke of aristocrats from Athens.

In her last letter, Mother had written that among the people the Good Lord had "called to Him" lately was Thanasis Barelas, and there were rumors his wife might sell the big house. *Our village had never been good enough for Lady Julia,* she had written.

I was not born yet when it happened, but I was told the newspapers made a big deal about the Barelas marriage. They called it "a male Cinderella story." In some ways they were right. Thanasis Barelas was the son of a barrel-maker from a mountain village who married a socialite and heiress to the Karystos shipping fortune with roots going all the way back to the Venetians. The kind of love affair that happened in the movies and romance novels.

They had met on the island of Santorini where Thanasis worked as a waiter. They married despite her parents' threats to disown her, and when the socialite gave birth to a cute and cuddly daughter, that was all it took to extract forgiveness from the incensed parents. Thanasis got into politics and was elected to Parliament. He built a huge house in Taxiarhes and used to spend one month there every summer with his wife and two daughters. The family also spent one month in Venice and one month in the Karystos palace in Galaxidi.

In the summer months, when I helped my brother transport fat tourists to the Milopotamos Beach with his mules, Lady Julia was among our regular customers, and the fussiest of passengers. She spoke to her daughters in French and to us, the locals, as if we were slow-witted primates. My brother told me that when Mother heard that our neighbor's son was going to marry Lady Julia Karystos, she told him what she thought about it. "People should stay within their own kind. Wanting to become something the Good Lord didn't mean for you to be only leads to heartache and misery. The Karystos girl is a different class of people, and our Thanasis is sentencing himself to lifelong snubness."

Neither of the Karystos daughters was married when I was there.

"It's hard to find your match when you are that high up," my mother used to scoff.

The younger daughter, Antigone, was close to my age. She had long, silky blond hair that fanned out when we played Ring Around the Roses. She seemed shy and was friendly to everyone, even me. When we were both of elementary school age, she had acted impressed with my tree-climbing skills and my slingshot accuracy, although at first she threatened not to speak to me again until I swore that I would only use the thing to kill scorpions and snakes and would never aim it at birds.

The Jamaican band began playing a fast tune, and I watched a couple waltzing on the dance floor. The woman wore a silver-colored gown, and her long, silky blond hair fanned out as she spun to the music. For an instant, a crazy thought ran through my head. Wouldn't it be something if I went back home a few years from now with a wallet stuffed full of American dollars and found Antigone still looking for her match? And what if I took her out to a fancy place? Wouldn't that make Lady Julia climb the walls? Crazy idea.

I picked up my drink and started for the main deck. On my way out, I paused to look at the photographs mounted on two large boards next to the gift shop door and realize they were the ones the bearded photographer had taken when we were boarding. I found mine near the center next to the old couple that climbed Everest. I didn't look too bad in it, though I wished my hair were combed. The curvy blonde in the tight sailor's suit had snuggled as if she were madly in love with me. Maybe I'd come back later and buy it and send it to Liapouras on the *Aegean Sea*. He'd probably pin it on the bulletin board in the crew's lounge, and everybody's jaw would drop.

I opened a heavy mahogany door and stepped on deck. The sea was calm with a light, warm breeze blowing from the starboard bow. In the sky a full moon was perched about the height of the forward mast. I paused and breathed in the sea air, then walked toward the bridge, pretending not to notice the lovers in every dark corner. When I got to where I couldn't go any farther, I leaned on the rails and stared at the dark distance. The bow sliced silently at right angles through the long, gentle swell. For a moment I felt like I was back on the tanker, standing the night watch.

I looked up toward the bridge, but the wheelhouse was completely dark. All I saw was somebody's cigarette glow at the port bridgewing. I walked a bit farther on deck and sat on a chair with a foamy cushion.

A few minutes later, the AB on watch walked to where I was sitting and said, "Excuse me, sir," then reached behind me to the fire-watch station mounted on the bulkhead. I started to ask him whether they were steering with automatic pilot or there was an AB at the helm, and also if they called the able-bodied seamen "ABs" on passenger ships or if they had a fancier title for them, but at the last moment I decided not.

He punched his fire-watch clock, said, "Sorry to disturb you, sir," and walked off.

He headed toward the bow, the clock slung over his shoulder like a rifle. His uniform was clean and pressed, and his stride was controlled and disciplined, almost as if he were in the navy.

When I sailed on merchant ships, steering was the most important part of an AB's work. Some of the newer ships had automatic pilots, but I had read on a brass plaque when I came on board that this one had been built in Liverpool, England, in 1951.

They must have a helmsman steering her. They probably had to keep changing the course so the waves wouldn't hit the ship from the side and make her roll. With a superstructure as tall as this one, she'd be rolling like a loaded seesaw, and passengers like Oklahoma George and his blue-haired wife would be puking their fancy dinners. And the stewards wouldn't be able to keep all the fancy flower arrangements and ice sculptures standing upright on the dining room tables with the white tablecloths.

I flicked my cigarette over the side and watched it make a long arc until it finally drowned on top of a tall swell. I bet a wave like that would give the ship quite a roll if it hit broadside.

On my previous ships, when we happened to pass a passenger ship at night and saw her all lit up like a small city adrift, everyone talked about how great it would be to work on one of those. It had never occurred to me that there would come a time when I would be on one of those as a passenger and the AB on watch would ask my permission to do his work and apologize for disturbing me. Life sure did take all kinds of peculiar turns. Yes sir, I had done the right thing by jumping ship. Now I was on my way to the good life. I clinked my glass with the ship's metal, toasting myself "to the good life."

Two women with bluish-silver hair, both of them laughing and holding tall, fancy drinks, walked slowly by me. They stopped the AB passing by and pointed toward the starboard bow.

"What is that blinking light far away?" one of them asked.

"That's the Great Isaac Lighthouse, ma'am," he answered.

The giggly women asked him what time the ship would be docking, then asked if the ship did the same cruise all year. The AB said that sometimes they went to other places, like Bermuda and Barbados.

"How lucky to have a job where you are on vacation all the time!" one of the women exclaimed.

"It's a job, ma'am," the AB said and continued walking.

I almost laughed. I had heard the same thing many times

before from the tourists my brother and I carried on the mules to Milopotamos Beach. Only, my brother always said, "Yes ma'am, we're blessed," and I knew he meant it.

For a while I just sat there, smoking and staring out at the water. Soon a middle-aged black couple came walking in my direction. The man held on to the handrail with one hand and had the other wrapped around the woman's waist. They stopped about a meter away from me and watched the Great Isaac Lighthouse blinking to the starboard.

"Ah, beautiful night," said the man.

"Yes, it is," said the woman. "The sky is so clear, and the moonlight in the water is like a golden river. Isn't it, honey?"

"Yes, it is," said the man, and he kissed her. "Happy anniversary." They started back the same way they'd come, the woman humming a song about a moon and a river.

I repositioned myself on the chair and looked up at the stars and the moon and the moonlight reflecting on the water, as if seeing them for the first time.

Yes, I was on my way to the good life.

CHAPTER FOURTEEN

Nassau

The ship was scheduled to dock at seven o'clock in the morning, but I'd been up since five, drinking coffee. It was my first time docking where I was not expected to be doing anything. I watched the deckhands drop the pilot ladder and unlash the gangway and felt I should be with the rest of the men, slacking and heaving lines.

A steward pushing a cart with coffee and tea came along and asked me if I wanted a refill. Instinctively I shook my head no, then remembered I was a passenger and moved my cup forward for a refill. I went up on the next deck where I couldn't be seen by the working crew.

At the entrance to Nassau's harbor, lots of construction was ongoing, and I walked over to the starboard side for a closer look. A giant steam crane fitted with a special grapple hook like a hand with long fingers was picking up huge granite boulders from a barge and gingerly placing them in the water atop a mound of smaller rocks already in place. A man standing on a high spot of the unfinished breakwater directed the crane operator with complicated hand signals.

"We're building a breakwater for the Bahamian government," the man to my right informed his companion. "That there is an American outfit, out of New York." He pointed to a giant steam crane with *FREDERIC SNARE CORPORATION* in large letters on its side.

Farther in, anchored in the middle of the harbor, a freighter unloaded the breakwater material into barges. Two more cranes, one on either side of the ship, hissed and blew steam like dragons fighting over the huge stones stored in the ship's belly. Every time a boulder was lifted from the ship's hold, a loud hissing filled the air, and a cloud of white steam from the crane's engine would hover above the machine for a while, like frozen dragon's breath.

Suddenly the *Ariadne*'s whistle emitted a series of warning blows. I, like everyone else, looked over the side just in time to see a small wooden boat crossing the bow only inches away. She was loaded with conch shells piled high in the center, leaving almost no freeboard. A long time ago the boat must have been painted red and green. In her stern stood a tall black man in tattered pants and a straw hat, sculling at a fast, steady pace. He wore no shirt, and his sweat-drenched torso shone in the morning sun. He broke his rhythm to wave at the photographers and the cheering crowd aboard the *Ariadne*, then kept on going.

The black anniversary couple I had seen the previous night were leaning on the rails to my left. This time they had two boys with them, physically identical and identically dressed. They looked about twelve years old. The woman, dressed in a tropical-looking flowery shirt and shorts like her husband, photographed everything she saw while the man pointed out to the two boys the different landmarks on the island.

"Oh, how cute," the woman said and aimed her camera at the boat with the conch shells.

"One more shell and that little boat would sink," said one of the boys.

"Look how he moves his hands," said the woman, snapping another picture. "He rows like he's keeping time to some music."

"When you row with one oar, it's called sculling," the man explained. "My grandfather was good at it. He used to take me fishing with him all the time. He was the best conch fisherman on the island."

"Are we going to see Grandpa's house?" asked one boy.

"No, it was torn down a long time ago," the man said. "The Halcyon Hotel, the fanciest hotel on the island, is now in its place."

"Isn't that where we're staying, Dad?" asked the other boy.

"Yep, that's where we're staying."

When the ship was within a few yards from the dock, a group of local boys found their way to the upper decks and began diving from the rails, retrieving the coins the passengers kept tossing overboard. All the boys looked to be no more than twelve years old, lean and wiry in raggedy shorts, and experts in hustling the quarters and half dollars from the laughing passengers.

"Wow, Dad, look at that!" said one of the boys. "That's neat. Lucky bums. That's fun."

"That's not why they're doing it, son," said his father.

"Did you do it, Dad?" asked the other boy, but the man had taken out a handkerchief and was blowing his nose and didn't seem to have heard him.

I looked at the two black boys with the flowery shirts, then at the ones diving from the railing of the promenade deck, and I thought of my own youth in the village and of the boys playing baseball in Miami and of those hustling coins in the ports of Surabaya and Port-Au-Prince, and I concluded that the stork was a bird with a perverted sense of humor.

When we docked, I got off the ship as soon as the purser handed me my papers. On Bay Street I turned right and slowly weaved through the straw market, stuck behind a group of gawking passengers inching ahead of me. On both sides of the market's narrow walkway, middle-aged black women, large and loud, stood amidst mountains of baskets, bags, hats, and ugly donkeys made out of straw, trying to coax those walking by into buying them. "A hat for di sun? A souvenir fro Nasso?"

With every step, I grew more and more frustrated because I couldn't maneuver around the gawkers. Tourism was for rich idlers, and to be mistaken for such a one I considered an insult.

I was looking for the Buccaneer Café Pete Papas had told me was only two blocks from where the ships docked.

"It's owned by two Greeks who aren't like the other Greeks," Pete had said. "They'll find you a safe place to stay—cheap. See Niko or his brother Pandelis." After a pause he added, "Tell them I sent you. They know me." That last part he said as if there were a hidden meaning.

I spotted the restaurant as soon as I got out of the straw market. It was a brick building at the end of the block with the *BUCCANEER CAFÉ* sign above a door so massive it could have come from a medieval castle. I maneuvered past a couple shuffling ahead of me and hastened my pace.

Inside the restaurant, when my eyes adjusted to the darkness, I spotted a guy sitting on a tall chair by the cash register, reading a magazine. I asked in Greek if he was Niko or Pandelis. The man took his feet off the counter, closed what looked like a girly magazine, and said he was neither. "Niko is in Greece and Pandelis is in Miami. What do you want them for?"

I told him who I was and what I wanted.

"Oh, yes, Pandelis called yesterday and told me to be looking for you. He went on a trip to Key West with his uncle. He said you were here on your honeymoon." His voice had a teasing note, as if he knew why I was really here.

"Yeah, one-person honeymoon," I agreed with a chuckle. "Maybe I'll get lucky while I'm here. Did Pandelis say anything about a room?"

"He told me to give you the small room upstairs. And he said that if you help in the kitchen in the evenings, he won't charge you for it. With Niko in Greece, we are kind of shorthanded."

"Good," I said. "I wouldn't know what to do if I had a vacation anyway."

"It's not much work, anyway. We aren't very busy right now. You want some coffee? I can make Greek coffee if you want."

"American coffee is fine," I said and sat on a stool. "By the way, my name is Kostas Karaoglou." I extended my hand.

"Mine is Antonis Hassapis. What part of Greece are you from?"

We shook hands and I told him I was from Taxiarhes, a village about eight hours north of Athens. He said he was from Kalymnos.

While Antonis got the coffee, I gave the place a quick appraisal. It was about the size of the Parthenon restaurant, only more elegant. The furniture and the decorations made it look like the inside of an old pirate ship. Some of the tables were refurbished ship's hatch covers, and the others were round like a captain's table. The chairs were wooden, half round, with armrests and black leather seats. The light fixtures were imitations of old-style ship's lanterns, and on the walls were crossed swords and black flags with skulls and crossbones.

I picked up a menu from the rack, leafed through it, and looked at the price column. *They're pirates, all right.*

We drank our coffee and talked about Greece and Taxiarhes and the island of Kalymnos and about the Greeks of Nassau and Miami and of Pete Papas. Antonis was about the same age as I. He was single and said he hadn't been anywhere other than Kalymnos and Nassau.

"Unless you count the airport in London where we changed planes," he said.

I told him that I had sailed with some people from Kalymnos and told him their names, but he said he left young and didn't know any of them.

"How long have you been here?" I asked.

"I came to work for Uncle Pandelis a little over five years ago. He's my uncle from my mother's side. His grandfather came here as a sponge diver and later opened up a store over there." He pointed across the street to a tall building where, near the top, through the faded white paint over the red brick, it was still possible to read, *PAPAS SPONGE EXCHANGE.*

"When the sponge beds died out," he went on, "his son opened a restaurant on the bottom floor. In 1960, Uncle Pandelis moved it over here. That's when he brought me to Nassau."

"Is he related to Pete Papas in Miami?"

"Pandelis is his nephew. Mr. Pete put up most of the money to open this place."

"Are there lots of Greeks in Nassau?"

"About seventy families. And we have a Greek councilor too, and a church with a full-time priest. Want to go on Sunday?"

"Maybe. We'll see."

That seemed to bring us to a lull in information swapping, and Antonis said he would show me the room upstairs. I picked up my suitcase and followed him through the kitchen and up a narrow, creaking stairway.

It was a small room but big enough for a bed and a dresser, and it had a slim window with burglar bars overlooking the harbor. Two white aprons with large brown stains on them hung on a nail behind the door.

"They're Niko's," Antonis said and took them down. "He comes up here to rest when he's working long hours. And sometimes for a quick one when he finds a drunk Canadian or gets the hots for one of the cleaning women." He rolled the aprons into a ball and stood by the door, looking at the folding bed. "I'll tell the woman to bring some clean sheets."

"When is Niko coming back?" I asked.

"He won't be back for a while, the damn fool."

"Why you say that?"

"He went to Greece for a two-week vacation, rented a big car to show off, and crashed it the first day. He's going to be in the hospital for a month, maybe more." He started to leave. "The sink and the toilet are downstairs next to the kitchen. If you want to take a bath, you can come to my house."

"I'll be all right. I brought a bathing suit."

Antonis chuckled. "I'll be in the restaurant."

I lit a cigarette and looked out the window. A narrow concrete wharf stretched between the building and the water. On it, directly under the window, was a cluster of overflowing garbage cans. Two cats dug in them, stopping every so often to growl at each other. In the water a few meters away from the wharf stood a small mountain of conch shells, a loaded dinghy just like the one I'd seen earlier anchored in front of it. At the stern of the dinghy, an old black man in a battered straw hat was chipping the back of each conch shell to take out the meat. He put the meat in a bucket next to him and threw the empty shells onto the mountain.

I tried to open the window. The latch looked like it hadn't been used for a long time, but with some effort I loosened it and slid the pane outward part of the way. Right away, a faint breeze filled the room with the choking stench of restaurant garbage and decaying conch. I threw the cigarette out and slammed the window shut.

Taking the brown envelope that held my papers from the suitcase, I went downstairs. Antonis asked me if I wanted anything to drink, and I said I'd have another cup of coffee while I waited for the American embassy to open.

Just then a series of loud explosions outside made me jump off my stool and run to the window. I got there in time to see an old, blue, patched-up Chevrolet—clanking, backfiring, and burping gray clouds from both ends—hit the curb and come to a stop in front of the window. A tall, thin black man wiggled out from the passenger side in a tangle of limbs.

"That's Luscious, the dishwasher," Antonis said without moving from his spot. He looked at the clock behind the bar. "He's almost an hour early. Damn fool leaves home early because his clunker keeps dying and he doesn't want to be late for work."

A few minutes later, Luscious walked through the door.

"You made it," said Antonis. "Anything fall off this time? Man, when are you going to junk that clunker and get a decent car?"

"Nothing wrong with this one, man," Luscious said. "She's like a woman—all she needs is a little tender loving."

"Start behind the counter," directed Antonis. "They left a mess last night."

Luscious went into the kitchen and came back with a bucket and towels and started cleaning while humming a song about an island woman. He coordinated the moves of his long limbs to the tune as if he were performing a kind of dance. A few minutes later the front door burst open, flooding the place with blinding sunshine. A heavyset black man holding a block of lottery tickets stumped up to Antonis.

"Good morning, *malakas*," the man said. "How many you buy today?"

"No *malakas*, you dummy. I speak to you *malakas* bad. You say to me *magas*, okay? *Magas* mean cool, smart, good-looking man. Okay?"

"Okay, *magas*. How many tickets you buy today?"

"One again. If I win, I buy more."

Luscious took a pause from his cleaning performance and leaned on the counter, looking at the lottery ticket peddler. He let out a sigh and said, "Man, that will be the solution to all my problems. Winning the big ticket—that's what I need."

"Want to half a ticket with me, Luscious?" asked Antonis.

"I would very much like that, boss. But right now, all my funds are invested elsewhere."

"They always are." Antonis shook his head. "I'll pay for it and take it out of your pay."

"That will be fine, sir," Luscious said. "It will be just fine."

Antonis rang the cash register and pulled out the money to pay for the ticket.

"Thank you, Señor Malaka Magas. Thank you," the lottery man said, disappearing into another blast of sunshine.

"When is the drawing, boss?" asked Luscious. The two examined the tickets together.

"It is next week," Antonis said.

Luscious studied them some more. "Man, the first number is ten thousand English pounds, second number five thousand pounds." He paused as if trying to comprehend the magnitude of the numbers. "Ten thousand, split in two, boss. That's five thousand pounds each."

"That's almost fifteen thousand Bahama dollars," Antonis said. "What are you going to do with all that money, Luscious?"

Luscious's face showed heavy concentration. "The first thing I'm going to do is fix the door in my car," he said after a while. "It is most inconvenient getting in and out from the passenger side."

Antonis burst out laughing. "You are some big spender, Luscious. Isn't he a big spender?" He looked at me.

I smiled to show I understood the conversation, but I didn't think it was funny. I had heard almost the same answer from my brother and didn't think it was funny then either. A lottery ticket peddler like this one had come to the Fatolias's coffeehouse in Taxiarhes some years back. My brother and everyone else who happened to be there at the time had chipped in a few drachmas each and bought one ticket. The first number was worth millions of drachmas, and for the rest of the day, while sipping their ouzo, they talked of how they would spend their winnings.

One planned to bank his share and use the interest to live like a pasha in the city. Another planned to give his mule to his brother-in-law, donate his olive grove to the church so the priest would say a prayer for him every now and then, and move to Crete where the winters were warm, the ouzo was twice as strong, and the tourists swam naked.

My brother, after some heavy thinking, said he would buy a new saddle for the mule. The one on the gray mare was still good, but he was getting tired of patching up the one on the mule. He said he'd go to Zagora to buy it.

"It's worth the long trip and the higher price because their saddles are the best," he'd said.

Yep, the damn brain is the same, no matter what color skin is wrapped around it.

I got up. "Which way to the American embassy?" I asked.

"It's the white building to the left, two blocks from here." Antonis pointed out the door. "You can't miss it."

"I'll be back to help with lunch."

"I'm getting off at three," said Antonis. "If you need anything, cousin Tassos will be taking my place. He'll stay till closing."

"I'll be all right," I said. "Can't think of anything I need."

"I'll come around eleven to pick you up and show you the nightlife," Antonis said. "Maybe we hook up with some hot women."

"Now, that'll make it a real vacation," I said and headed out.

I walked at a brisk pace, and I was sweating when I got to the American embassy. After speaking to a young black man with an American accent, I gave him the brown envelope the lawyer in Miami had given to me. He asked for the address and the phone number of where I was staying, so I handed him a brochure for the Buccaneer Café.

"You may give message there," I said.

The embassy clerk said he would call that number as soon as the papers were ready.

"You know how long before ready?" I asked.

"I'm not the one who does the processing," the clerk said, "but matters of this nature are handled rather expeditiously by our office."

I did not understand most of that answer, but I was not going to ask for explanation. If he got the idea that I didn't speak good English, he might tell me to come back when I learned the language.

Instead I said, "Thank you, sir," and turned around.

This time I was not in a hurry, so I took the street along the harbor and enjoyed a pleasant breeze, walking at a leisurely pace, looking at the sights. Nassau didn't look much different from the other Caribbean towns I had been to. Fishing boats were unloading the night's catch at a pier beside a big pink hotel with a regal name, and I paused to watch the weighing of a large grouper that took two men to lift. The water along the pier was clear, and between the cans, condoms, and cigarette packs bobbing on the surface, I saw crabs and small fish at the bottom, darting in and out of barnacled automobile tires.

At the harbor, three white boat launches with wooden benches and colorful curtains along their sides were taking on passengers. Standing on the dock, their captains each tried to coax people into their boats by crying continuously, "Step in for Paradise Island! Leaving for Paradise Island Beach in two minutes! Leaving in two minutes!" During the twenty minutes I lingered in the harbor area, none of the half-filled boats departed.

Just like the carnival criers back home.

CHAPTER FIFTEEN

A Lonesome Honeymoon

I got back to the Buccaneer Café just as the lunch hour started. Cousin Tassos had taken Antonis's place by the cash register. I chatted with him for a while, then went in the kitchen and asked what I could do to help. The cook, a heavyset Bahamian woman, said I could help by staying out of her way.

"Maybe in evening when more busy, you do *some ting*," she said.

"Okay, I go out the way," I said and went to my room to get some rest and be ready for the evening's excursion. I took off my clothes and lay on top of the bed, but after staring at the ceiling for some time, I concluded that I didn't feel tired.

I wore my bathing suit under my clothes and went downstairs.

There was a new bartender behind the counter, a tall, athletic black fellow with his flowery shirt unbuttoned down to his navel and a gold medallion the size of a saucer dangling from a gold chain.

"Where is Mr. Tassos?" I asked.

"He has gone to the bank, sir. Could I be of some assistance?"

I told him I needed a towel, and he went into the kitchen.

"Enjoy your bath, sir," he said, handing me the towel.

"I'm going to the beach," I said.

"Man, it is too hot to be out of doors. The elders used to say that only mad dogs and Englishmen go out in the midday sun."

"I make I'm Englishman then," I said. "This is English colony, no?"

"No, man, we are an independent nation now," he said, sounding a little offended. "As a matter of fact, we've just elected one of our own as prime minister—the honorable Linden Piddling. You must have heard about it." His voice had a large dose of pride in it.

"Don't watch much news," I said. "Where is good place to go swimming not too far from here?"

"On the opposite side of the Royal Victoria Hotel, the large pink structure two blocks from here." He pointed to the right of the exit door.

I thanked him and started in that direction. After a short walk, I saw the hotel sign mounted on one of two massive entrance columns. West of Royal Victoria was a long stretch of beach, the sand powdery soft and blindingly white. The few coconut trees along the beach leaned at angles as if about to tip over. Farther away, out in the middle of the harbor, floated the boulder-carrying freighter, surrounded by cranes and barges like a mother hen.

There weren't many people at the beach. Maybe the intellectual bartender was right about going out in the midday heat. I searched along the beach for a good spot to lay my towel, but all the shady places were already taken. The sun behind me, my shadow ran ahead, tall and slender, and for an instant, I believed it was really me.

On the second sweep, I spotted a lone woman lying on a towel with a Budweiser logo. She was on her stomach with the strings of her bathing suit top untied, reading a book.

I laid my towel a few feet to the right of hers, piled my clothes on it, then sat and lit a cigarette while I examined my neighbor. She looked to be about my age, although she could be younger. American girls seemed to look older than they really were. A straw hat with *Nassau* and colorful flowers stitched on it perched on her head, honey-blond hair cascading down to her shoulders from under it. She had a round, tight-looking rear end, painted toenails, and a bruise on the inside of her right thigh that got me wondering if it was a pinch or a bite.

I studied the evenness of her light tan, noticing the absence of white lines where the bathing suit top usually tied, which meant she had been sunbathing for some time. A narrow sliver of the original milky white skin showed where the bottom part of the bathing suit had slipped back. She kept reading and didn't seem to notice my arrival, my camp-setting noises, or my frequent throat clearing.

After a while I put out my cigarette and went in the water. I dove deep enough to get my hair wet, swam in a small circle for a few minutes, then stood in water up to my chest and looked around, taking inventory of the single women. It had been over a week since I'd had sex with Karen, and the urge for it was becoming painful. I hoped to get some top-grade sex while in Nassau. Hell, this place was famous. They said everybody got laid in Nassau.

I got out of the water and rinsed off at the public shower, then walked to my blanket and dried my hands on my shirt. My neighbor was still absorbed in her book. I tapped a cigarette halfway out of my Winston soft pack.

"Cigarette?" I offered.

She just shook her head no.

I lit one and took a long puff. "Good book?" I asked after a while.

She didn't answer.

"*Habla Español*?" I asked.

She still didn't answer. Instead, she bent the corner of the page and closed her book, then tied the strings of her top and walked to the water. I watched her go and wondered if the way she swayed her butt was natural or if she was doing it for me. She got in the water slowly, staring out at the distant horizon. When the water was up to the level of her nipples, she started to swim, each arm emerging from the water with slow, gentle moves, and her body rolling from side to side like a mermaid teasing a sailor. She swam out a few meters, then turned back, got out, and walked at the edge of the water toward the private section of beach by the Royal Victoria hotel. She talked for a while with one of the black waiters shuttling drinks to people in lounge chairs in front of the hotel, then waved goodbye to him and walked slowly back to her towel.

"Maybe you and me go have drink at hotel?" I said when she got back. "You like?"

Again, she didn't answer. She put on the flowery Nassau hat, dropped the book and the suntan lotion into a matching straw bag, and started folding the Budweiser towel.

"*Parlari Italiano*?" I said.

No response.

"*Sprechen Sie Deutsch*?"

Nothing.

"*Parlez-vous Francais*?" That was all I knew in those languages, but I could mime if she answered. It had worked before. But she folded the towel, picked up the bag, and then, finally, looked at me.

"Bye," she said and walked toward the Flamingo Hotel across the street.

I watched her, half stunned, half pissed off. Maybe she didn't like men.

⁜⁜⁜

The restaurant wasn't very busy that night. I offered to help in the kitchen, and the same heavyset Bahamian cook told me that she had been cooking for Mr. Papas since before his boys were born, and she had been managing just fine without cooks from Miami or anywhere else.

"But since you here," she said with a sigh, "I find a chore for you. Maybe you learn some ting."

She let me chop up some vegetables. After that, with lots of her explicit instructions and close supervision, she let me chop the meat for the conch salad.

When I finished, I washed and shaved in the kitchen bathroom and scrubbed my hands with a cut-up lemon for a long time. Back in my room, I doused my face and body with aftershave. Antonis said he would pick me around eleven, but I was on the bench outside the restaurant at ten. While waiting, I took a census of the couples hugging and kissing as they got in and out of taxis, and the high numbers of that survey boosted my hopes for the evening. There was going to be some wild sex before the night was over for sure.

Shortly after 10:30, Antonis drove up in an Austin convertible with the top down. "Be careful with the leather," he said as I climbed in. "This is Niko's car." We took off and he said, "We'll check out the Big Bamboo first. That's where most single women go, and if—"

"Look out, look out! Turn, turn!" I let out a bloodcurdling scream and hugged my seat.

Antonis started laughing and kept a steady course as a smoke-belching dump truck loaded with gravel came from the opposite direction and roared by us. "They drive on the left side of the road over here. Didn't you know?"

"Oh, hell. I forgot," I said, gasping for breath. "For a moment I thought I was staring Death in the eye."

"That's what put Niko in the hospital," said Antonis when he stopped laughing. "He was used to driving over here. When he went to Greece, he crashed his rented car one kilometer from the airport."

"Fucking English," I said, still breathing hard. "They always do things backwards."

The Big Bamboo nightclub was a large, open room with a stage in one corner where a band of five cocky-looking blacks were playing Beatles songs. The place was almost full. Being optimistic, we tried to get a table for four, but after extensive searching, we had to settle for a table just for two.

On the table to our right, six drunk, noisy Americans were harassing the waitresses. Antonis said they were with the construction company working in the harbor. Most other tables seemed to be occupied by loud tourist couples talking back and forth between groups about the launch ride to Paradise Island and the climb to Blackbeard's Tower and the St. Augustine Monastery, sounding as if they had just gotten back from discovering a new continent.

Two curvy white women in their mid-twenties wearing flimsy, tight clothes, overripe sexuality oozing from every pore of their bodies, danced with two black men who were double their size and looked as if they had just walked out of the jungle. The men were draped over them, kissing and slobbering while barely moving with the music. Antonis said the women were probably Canadians.

"They come down here to get laid by the blacks, you know? We get lots of them from America too. Niko tells me that when they get back home, they won't even eat at the same restaurant as the blacks."

I scanned the entire place with searchlight precision. Other than the waitresses, there were no unescorted women of any size, color, or age. Antonis suggested we finish our drinks, then try Dirty Dick's, the club farther down on Bay Street.

"They have a floorshow there," he said.

Dirty Dick's was crowded, smoky, and smelled of sour beer and horniness. I wanted to sit at a booth, figuring it would be easier to snuggle when we got the women, but there weren't any booths or tables empty, so we got the only two stools available at the bar. I ordered two Beck's beers and paid for them since Antonis had paid for the two at the Big Bamboo.

The floorshow had already started. A black man, lean and limber as an eel, performed the limbo onstage. The horizontal bamboo stick was held in place by two poles with notches in them, and the limber man lowered the stick a notch after each successful pass. He was naked except for a thin cloth with tropical colors wrapped around his waist and between his legs in a way that highlighted the things it was covering. The crowd clapped and whistled and urged him on, and the dancer shook and wiggled and advertised what he had covered with the thin cloth as much as he could get away with. The women were going wild. Every one of them had "Fuck me" written all over her.

I sipped my beer while my gaze probed the room. All I could see through the fog of my erotic intoxication were women and men of all shapes and colors wrapped around each other, and then I spotted her—the beach girl with the Budweiser towel. She sat by herself in a corner, clapping heartily as the dancer slithered under the stick. She saw me, and I was sure she smiled.

Wrapped around her was a dress of tropical colors made from a piece of thin cloth smaller than a bath towel. One side of the dress was open, as if the material couldn't reach all the way around her body, exposing a ribbon of flesh about two inches wide. The dress was held together by a string like a bootlace zigzagging over the tanned skin. As she sat clapping and shaking her hips, I got a better look at the bruise on her right thigh, and now I was sure; it was a bite.

Two Coca-Cola bottles were on her table, one of them empty. She drained the other one into a clear whiskey glass and stirred the ice cubes with her index finger. She licked her finger, moving her tongue up and down and sucking on it with puckered lips while looking seductively in my direction. My erection became painful.

The limbo man had just gone under the last notch of the poles, and the crowd clapped wildly and threw dollar bills on the floor, asking for more. My beach girl was doing most of the clapping. I got off the stool and started toward her; things were finally looking up. I planned to ask her what kind of drink she had and offer to buy her another one. She didn't have a girlfriend with her, and for an instant a feeling of pity for Antonis swept over me, and I turned my head to look at the poor fellow sitting alone at the bar.

When I returned my gaze to her, my heart sank to my toes. The limbo man had beat me to the blonde. He was at her table taking a sip from her glass. When he was done with that, they kissed a long, slobbery, tongue-swallowing kind of kiss. Then he picked up the two empty Coca-Cola bottles and went back onstage.

He rested the limbo stick atop the two bottles, and the music started playing again. Slowly, twisting and wiggling, he leaned back as close to floor as he could get without touching it. By moving his arms and torso and propelling himself with his big toes, he got on the other side without knocking the stick off the bottles. He stood and bowed in a way that showed off his muscles, including those covered by the skimpy cloth. Then he gathered the dollars on the floor and went back to the blonde. Between kissing and groping her, he put on a robe, and the two left the place, glued together and walking as one.

I went back to the bar and ordered two more beers. This was becoming torture. "Are there any whorehouses in this town?" I asked Antonis.

"Yes, there are," he said, "at a place they call Over the Hill, but I don't like going there. I'll wait a couple of days until my girlfriend comes back from New York."

"Maybe we could drive there just to see," I said. "It'll be like when I was sailing."

"Okay, but I hope we don't scratch Niko's car," he said. "He'll kill me."

We finished our drinks and left. After a couple of blocks, we left the city and drove through neighborhoods where most of the houses were wooden shacks with rusty tin roofs. We passed an area with people sitting on front porches, and Antonis steered the car to the center of the road and stepped on the gas.

"Last month Niko was taking Luscious home and around here a kid threw a rock and cracked the windshield," he said.

About thirty minutes later, we arrived at a green frame house with purple shutters and a wide porch. Four men were standing by a taxi, saying good night to some overweight women with smudged makeup. Antonis said he'd wait for me in the car. I started to get out, then heard the four men talking to each other in Greek and stopped, pretending I was checking the contents of my wallet.

I waited until the men were gone before approaching the three plump women with chocolate skin who were sitting on the porch. One of them rose and met me at the steps.

"Hi, handsome. Want a good time?" She rubbed my crotch. "For you, ten dollar."

She led me by the hand into a small room illuminated by a bed lamp with a naked white woman on its shade. There was a dresser with a mirror above it, two dime-store landscape pictures on the walls, and a small statue with the Virgin Mary and Child on a corner shelf.

"My name is Gloria," she said. "What is your name?"

"George," I said.

"Where you from, George?" She unzipped her dress. She wasn't wearing a bra, and her breasts, despite their large size, were not sagging.

"From Turkey," I said, handing her the ten dollars.

The fat around her waist lapped over her black panties. She put the dress on a hanger, took off the panties, then started helping me unbuckle my belt.

"Never had a boyfriend from Two-key before," she said.

I didn't correct her. She was just making conversation, a professional courtesy. I finished undressing by myself.

"Oh, baby, you are big," she said. "Two-key men are big!"

I bet that was her standard opening line even if it was a skinny worm.

"Oh baby, oh baby," she moaned. A practiced, professional moan.

I kept my eyes closed and tried to picture the beach blonde in her place, but then the limbo man sneaked into the vision and it almost killed the erection. It was hot in the little room, and we were both sweating. Eventually, after performing one of the worst imitations of an orgasm I had heard when she felt I was coming, she faked exhaustion and breathlessness.

"Oh baby, oh baby, that was good. Two-key men are really good."

She reached for a paper towel and wiped the sweat off her face and breasts. Then she reached down to the foot of the bed and wet a washcloth from a green plastic pitcher and used it to wipe first my genitals, then hers.

I put on my clothes and went out. Antonis was where I had left him, guarding Niko's car.

"Where shall we go now?" he asked when I got in.

"Let's go home," I said.

"Hey, did I tell you I don't have to work tomorrow?" He must have sensed how I was feeling. "The restaurant is open seven days, so we rotate the weekends off. If they don't need you in the kitchen, want to go fishing?"

"I'm sure your cook will be glad to see me stay out of her kitchen," I said.

"We can take Niko's boat. You do much fishing in Miami?"

"No, I haven't done any. When I was in the village, I fished with a cane pole from the rocks."

"This here is big time. Niko's boat has a radio, a depth finder, a compass, and beds for two."

"Good," I said. "Maybe our luck will get better."

CHAPTER SIXTEEN

A Fishing Trip

The next morning, I sat on the bench by the front door of the Buccaneer Café an hour before Antonis came to pick me up. My early arrival wasn't out of any anxiety about the fishing expedition; when I'm in a new place, I just like getting up early and people-watching.

When a town is waking up, one sees a different type of people, especially in tourist towns like Nassau. Those who've been partying during the night and those planning to party in the coming night are still in bed. At the early hours one sees those who make the partying possible—the restaurant supply men unloading cases of beer and soft drinks, the wholesale food delivery men pushing their dollies loaded with frozen boxes of the "catch of the day," the "custom cut fresh steaks," and the "homemade pies and cakes." The women in maid uniforms getting off at the bus stop in front of the hotel, and the cleaning crews who'll sweep the cigarette butts and mop the beer-soaked floors in the bars and the restaurants from the night's revelry and get them clean and fresh smelling, ready for another day.

I saw a woman around thirty, her blond hair disheveled and her clothes all rumpled, carrying her shoes in her hand as she dashed out of a taxi and ran into the hotel across the street. *Looks like somebody woke up in the wrong bed.*

Two garbage men, one on each side of the street, hurled boxes full of plastic cups and paper plates into an open truck driving in the middle of the road.

Antonis drove up at seven o'clock. He got a pack of squid and a pack of shrimp from the restaurant freezer, put a six-pack of beer and six Cokes in a cooler, filled it with ice, and we were off. We drove east through the still-sleeping town, along the coast and by an empty beach with a cluster of fancy houses behind it.

"This is where the rich people live," Antonis said.

At the Pilot House Marina, Niko's boat was tied up at the end of a pier. Antonis unlocked the cabin and put the padlock in a drawer, cranked the engine, and I cast off. We idled through the marina, then picked up speed. The freighter I'd seen when I was coming in on the *Ariadne* was still in the middle of the harbor, unloading boulders for the breakwater.

"*Giasou, patrioti*!" Antonis yelled to someone who waved from the ship's deck as we were passing by. "It's a Greek ship," he said to me. "They come to the restaurant sometimes. The third mate is from Kalymnos. I bet you the guys we saw at the place Over the Hill last night were from here."

"Good thing they didn't see us," I said.

"Why?"

I didn't want to explain to Antonis why. He wouldn't understand.

"Where are they bringing the rocks from?" I asked instead.

"Some place up in New York."

"They import rocks all the way from up there?" I was not faking my bewilderment.

"Hard to believe, isn't it? For us, I mean. All we have back home is rocks."

He slowed down as we neared the breakwater being built. A group of cranes picked up boulders shaped like giant potatoes from the barges and delicately lowered them in place.

"The manager for this project comes to the restaurant a lot," Antonis said. "He tells me that when building a breakwater, they have to use rocks that are very heavy, otherwise the waves move them out of place. The coral from the islands here is too light for the job. This is the second trip for this ship, and he says they'll need three more."

"Bringing rocks all the way from New York," I muttered. "Unbelievable."

"The manager says the captain of the ship is giving him a hard time. He bitches about the boulders scratching and denting his ship and is threatening to tell the owners to break the charter."

"You know why he's doing that, don't you?" I said.

"Of course I do, but the Americans don't know about these things. Want to steer?" Antonis offered me the wheel. "Head for that island ahead. I know a good fishing spot near there." He pointed to a dot on the horizon and got busy tuning the marine radio.

We got to Antonis's good fishing spot and dropped anchor, then cut up some squid and shrimp on the cutting board mounted in the stern on the outside of the hull. We baited the hand lines and lowered them over the side.

"Let it touch bottom, then bring it up a little so it will be dangling," said Antonis.

"What kind of fish you have here?"

"Grouper, mackerel, snapper, all kinds. Barracudas too, but I don't like them. They're mean looking and have sharp teeth. Sometimes I'll hook a fish and by the time I bring it in, the barracuda gets half of it."

We had anchored at the mouth of a small crescent-shaped cove with a white beach.

"Nice beach," I said.

"Yeah, it is. Usually it's full of couples swimming naked," said

Antonis.

"Maybe that's why it's a good fishing spot." I chuckled.

Antonis tied his line on a cleat before going to the console to fiddle with the radio again.

"Don't you listen to regular music?" I asked.

"I like listening to the marine radio," he said, moving the needle between beeps and buzzes. "You hear all kinds of crazy things." He stopped fiddling and tilted his head toward the radio. The businesslike voice of a man came through loud and clear.

"Miami marine operator, Miami marine operator, this is the charter vessel *Blue Marlin*, charter vessel *Blue Marlin*, requesting traffic. Over."

"I know that man," said Antonis. "He ties up at the Pilot House Marina. Last week a woman got a fishhook caught on her tit and he had to call the hospital to tell him what to do. Let's hear what he's got this time."

I got a bite and pulled my line in. The bait was gone and I re-baited.

Antonis pulled his line in, repaired the bait, and slowly lowered it again while listening to the man from the *Blue Marlin* talk to his stockbroker in Chicago. After a while, I pulled up my line again. The bait was still there. I started whistling a Greek tune, but Antonis signaled me to stop.

"The guy from the *Blue Marlin* is talking to his girlfriend."

"Want a beer or a Coke?" I asked and opened the cooler.

"Either one," said Antonis and leaned closer to the radio. He listened for a few minutes, then burst out laughing. "That guy is something. First he calls his broker. Then he calls his girlfriend and asks her to hurry up and come down. 'Everything is gorgeous here, darling. We'll have ten wonderful days.' Then he calls his wife and tells her he misses them and he's having a lousy time and he went fishing and got seasick and he's ready to give up and come home. She tells him, 'Do like doctor said, darling. Stay the whole ten days, darling. Don't worry about us, darling, we'll manage. You try to get well, darling.' Wonder how much he had to bribe the doctor to write that prescription." Antonis was trying to mimic the people's voices while laughing, and that made it hard to understand him.

"You have an odd taste for amusement," I said.

"Why's that?"

"Because you like to listen to other people's talk instead of music," I said. "That's old people's entertainment. You're a young person."

Eventually I asked Antonis to turn the radio off.

"It's giving me a headache," I said. "It feels like I'm on watch on the ship."

We pulled up the anchor and moved to a spot closer to the rocks of the crescent-shaped cove. The small beach seemed to be deserted.

"Don't see any naked people swimming today," I said.

"Sometimes the whole beach is full of them." Antonis's hand described the arc of the beach. "And over there, on the far side, is where they found the Haitians."

"Were they swimming naked?" I asked.

"No, they were dead. It was about three months ago. Guess you didn't hear it in Miami."

"They wash up all the time," I said. "Nobody pays any attention to that anymore."

"There were three men and a woman," Antonis continued. "The woman had a baby tied to her chest with her scarf. The newspaper here kept writing about it for days. They were in that little skiff—see it over there? They ran into a hurricane and got smashed on those rocks there."

I looked in the direction he pointed. The little skiff lay on jagged rocks at the entrance to the cove. It was a twisted, rusty mass of sheet metal that even in its uncrumpled condition couldn't have been much bigger than a washtub.

During my years as a merchant seaman, my ship had gotten caught in a storm many times. Usually the radio operator would give the captain advance warning, and if it was possible, we would change course to avoid the storm. If it wasn't, we lashed everything down, reduced our speed, pointed the bow into the weather, and waited out the storm. And although I knew the ship was built to take on weather like that and there were also another twenty-five people on board who were each trained at their job, there were still times, as I listened to the wind howling in the rigging and watched the waves swallow the deck on their way to crash in front of me on the bridge bulkhead, that I caught myself promising to send to Mother a couple extra dollars for Sunday's collection plate from the next port. What went through the mind of someone caught in a hurricane, huddled in a tin tub with no control of where the thing was going, being tossed about by the waves, wet and cold, listening to the howling wind and the crying of a hungry baby?

"What makes them so desperate?" I said, almost to myself. "What are they hoping to find where they are going?"

"I guess it depends on how many of the stories you believe from those who make it," said Antonis. "In a way, it's almost like you, I suppose."

"But I didn't get in a dinghy or an inner tube to get to America. And I *did* have some idea where I was going."

We gave up fishing around noon. Antonis scooped up a couple buckets of water and washed off the cutting board.

"See if any bait fell inside the boat," he told me. "Niko brings women on board, and he gets pissed off if it stinks."

⁜⁜⁜

After three days at the Buccaneer Café, I was moving around the kitchen like an old hand. I had undertaken all the dicing of the meat for the conch salad and the chopping of the vegetables, and the cook said her arthritic fingers thanked me for it. She told me I was the "bestest" helper she'd ever had. Once I told her that when I opened my own restaurant in the States, I was going to steal her away from the Buccaneer. She laughed and said, "America is no place for an old woman. Everybody seems to be in so much hurry over there."

During the slow hours, I kept Antonis company. Most of the time he talked sports and politics with the customers, which I suspected he did to show off his mastery of the Bahamian English.

One afternoon when it was pouring down rain, the construction manager for the harbor project walked into the café. He was a big sunburned man around fifty. "Hi, Greek," he said, sitting at the end of the bar. "Bring me the usual."

Antonis said, "Hi, Mr. Snare Corporation. Rain mess you job up?" He gave him a tall mug of beer and pushed a bowl of peanuts closer.

"Yeah, rain mess me job up all right. It'll take forever to finish. I'll be talking like you when I get back." He took a sip of his beer.

"Is the captain angry still with you?" Antonis asked.

"No, I did like you told me. I gave him five hundred dollars *supposedly* to fix the dents and scratches that *supposedly* our cranes made to his ship. I told him it'll be another five on every trip, dents or no dents. Now we are the best of friends. Bosom buddies." He chortled. "He can't wait to make another trip." He took another sip of his beer and scraped the ashes off his cigar. "Hell, for five hundred dollars, a shipyard wouldn't even look at a dent, let alone fix it."

"Where you live in America?" I asked him.

"I live in Fort Liquordale," he answered with a chuckle. "You know where that is?"

"No, I not know," I said.

"It's Lauderdale—Fort Lauderdale," he explained. "We call it Liquordale for the Yankee boozers living there."

"Oh, I know where Fort Lauderdale is," I said. "Is not far from Miami."

"Lots of Greeks live there too," said the Snare man. "There's a Greek restaurant right across from the shipyard. I ate there when we dry-docked the barges before coming here. Good food. An old countryman of yours runs it. He talks like you too."

I stared at the man from the construction company and conjured the perfect picture: a crowd of American shipyard workers at their lunch break, gobbling hamburgers in a hurry and washing them down with draft beer in barrel-sized mugs. And me sitting at the end of the counter, collecting the money, the constant ringing of the cash register a melody to my ears.

It won't be long now.

CHAPTER SEVENTEEN

The CARD!

The clerk called during the lunch hour, exactly fifteen days from the day I came to Nassau. They left a message with the cashier at the restaurant, and when he brought it to me in the kitchen, I dashed over to the embassy. I didn't discover that I still had the kitchen apron on until the lady ahead of me in line asked if I worked at the fish market.

I gave the clerk my name, and moments later I was reaching over his desk with both hands to take hold of a thick brown envelope he handed me. I held on to that package all the way back to the restaurant as if I were walking against hurricane-force winds.

"I've been looking forward to this day for a long, long time," I told Antonis, waving the envelope at him. "I've gone through a lot of anguish to get these papers. Let's go celebrate tonight. Let's have a big dinner at some classy place."

"I know just the place," he said. "We'll go to the Red Lion on Parliament Street. It's the snootiest of all the highbrow places. That's where Simonette, the old prime minister, took Onassis last month. The head cook is from my village. He used to work here before he got the job at the Lion. Now he's changed his name from Manolios to Chef Emanuel and acts as if he never heard of any of us."

"Let's go there and give the help some hell," I said.

"Need to make reservations at least one week ahead," said Antonis. "But I know somebody there who'll get us a table without."

We got to the restaurant at the peak of the dinner hour. Antonis addressed the tuxedoed maître d' by his first name and thanked him for the table. They talked about good fishing spots and barracudas, and the maître d' loaned us two black jackets.

"House rules. Can't seat you without them," he said and escorted us to a round table.

The place was dark. Most of the light came from small spotlights shining on fancy flower arrangements on corner pedestals and small statues set in alcoves. Other spotlights shone on paintings that showed foxhunting in rolling hills of the English countryside.

A woman in a black dress with lots of sparkling stones was playing a soft tune on the piano next to our table. It was the kind of tune that you could neither dance to nor sing along with, so I figured she was making it up as she went. The waiters and the busboys wore tuxedos and bow ties, spoke to the customers in whispers, and shuttled between the tables with small, quiet steps on the carpeted floor.

The waiter who took our order spoke English with a French accent. Antonis said he was probably a Haitian who'd managed to get a work permit. We ordered pre-dinner cocktails and conch fritter appetizers. When the appetizers came, we sent them back, because they were cold in the center.

"He should have taken them out of the freezer earlier and should have cooked them longer and at a lower temperature," we told the waiter.

Later, we sent the steaks back because they were too rare and then back again because they were cooked too much. The last time, the chef himself came out, holding a plate in each hand and looking like he was ready for a fight until he saw who we were.

He slapped the plates on the table and growled at Antonis, "I should have guessed who it was when the waiter said 'It's two queers who talk like you.'" He turned to stomp away, then paused and faced Antonis. "I'm going to get even with you; you just watch."

"Why did the waiter think we were queers?" I asked when the cook was gone. "We didn't hold hands or anything like that."

"Because we don't have any women with us," said Antonis.

"It's not for lack of trying," I lamented.

After dinner, on the way back to my room, we stopped at the jewelry store where Antonis's girlfriend worked. For thirty dollars I bought Carmen a necklace of white pearls. Antonis's girlfriend said even an expert couldn't tell them from the real thing. As we were about to walk out, I thought of something and turned back.

"What is good gift for girl who finish school?" I asked the saleslady.

With some translation help from Antonis, I bought a pearl-looking bracelet for Carmen's niece. She had graduated at the top of her class from her high school in Miami a few weeks earlier.

"She will be starting at the university in the autumn," Carmen had said, her face lit up with pride.

Carmen's niece was a delicate girl who seemed to have her nose stuck in a book every time I saw her. Carmen had introduced her to me as Julie, but I was sure the original name was something different. She probably wanted her niece to be American in everything.

Carmen had specifically told me, "When in the house, you speak English, okay? Only English, even if it is that crazy English of yours."

⁜⁜⁜

Antonis saw me off at the ship the next afternoon. In parting, we promised we would visit each other again.

"Maybe you come over for Junkanoo," said Antonis.

"What is that?"

"It's the local carnival," he said. "It happens the week of Christmas. It is fun."

I smiled and nodded. "Maybe I'll bring a woman with me next time."

While going through immigration in Miami, I watched the people ahead of me show their American driver's license and move on. I didn't have any kind of license and kept looking inside the envelope the man at the embassy had given me, wondering which of the many pieces of paper in there I was supposed to show to the inspector. Did I have the right papers? I should have asked the man at the embassy which document I needed to get back into Miami instead of saying "Thank you, sir, very much" and dashing out.

I counted the people ahead of me. In my line were four couples, tourists returning home loaded with flowery straw bags and goofy hats. Directly in front, an overweight woman of about forty was trying to control three mischievous boys. When she got up to the inspector, she dug for what seemed hours to find her wallet in a bottomless bag, and I started to perspire.

When my turn finally came, I handed the whole envelope to the inspector. The man glanced at every piece of paper in there, stamped one of them, and kept another. Then he tried to put the rest of it back, but it was taking too long and he handed everything back to me in a pile.

"Congratulations," he said.

I felt a surge of relief, elation, pride, and a few other feelings that I couldn't name. There would be no more looking for a hiding place every time I saw someone in a suit or a uniform. No more fearing that somebody might come up and say, "May I see some identification, please?" No more being afraid of looking lost or sticking out in a crowd or being afraid to ask for directions.

I wanted to let out a victory shout like the Indians did in the cowboy movies. This was a great moment—a moment worth shouting and celebrating.

But all I said was "Thank you, sir."

I was heading toward the taxi stand when I remembered Pete Papas's offer and changed direction. He had said he could pick me up if I wanted. It was Sunday morning, and Pete was probably drinking his morning coffee and reading the paper. I called him from a pay phone, and he arrived thirty minutes later. On the way to Carmen's house, we talked about Nassau and about my stay at the Buccaneer Café and about the Papases who owned it.

"You never told me you had business dealings in the Bahamas," I said.

"I guess it never came up," said Pete.

Carmen was on the porch, sitting on a box next to her grandfather's folding chair and feeding him his breakfast. The old man held firmly to the arms of the chair and stared straight ahead, oblivious to what Carmen was doing. She continuously talked to him, and after every second spoonful of rice pudding, she would wipe his mouth with a napkin.

"If she doesn't feed him, he won't eat," I told Pete. "He'll sit there, staring at nothing, and starve to death. He doesn't say a word. Once in a while calls a woman's name; that's all."

"He's been like that since the drowning," said Pete. "He lost two daughters and his wife in one swoop."

"How did it happen?" I asked.

"On the way here from Matanzas, the engine blew up, and soon after, the boat capsized, right in the middle of the Gulf Stream. He never saw his wife or his daughters again. One was Carmen's mother, and the other the mother of that young girl." He nodded toward Carmen's niece, looking very much like an ordinary American girl in blue jeans and oversized T-shirt as she read a book in the folding chair on the other side of her grandfather. "By the time the Coast Guard fished them out, half of that boatload had drowned."

"Carmen didn't tell me anything about it," I said.

"I guess it never came up," said Pete.

⁂

The morning after I returned from the Bahamas, Carmen and I walked together to the Parthenon restaurant. We got there as Steve was putting money in the cash register, and he just grunted when we said good morning. I went about my chores as if I had never left. While I restocked the cold table, I wondered how hard it would be to get fresh conch here. Maybe the Cuban customers would like conch fritters and conch salad.

When the lunch hour rush was over, Steve walked up to me all smiles and asked if I'd had a good time in Nassau. He asked how many women I had bedded and made a goofy joke about me looking darker than Pascal. Then, as if reading my mind, he told me he was raising my pay to fifty dollars a week.

"How about that for a wedding present, eh? That's a hell of a jump from what you were making before."

"Emilio came by the house last night and said I could go to work with him at Chateau Madrid for double that," I answered casually.

I hadn't seen Emilio since he'd left the Parthenon one week before my marriage to Carmen, but I knew he was working at a fancy restaurant in Miami Beach where they had flamenco floorshows, the waiters wore red sashes and tight vests, and people made reservations weeks in advance. I also knew that Steve had been to that place, so he was probably aware that the crumbs he was offering me as a raise didn't compare to even the smallest of tips from one of the Chateau tables.

When Emilio was working at the Parthenon, I'd let him taste my mini shish kebabs made of fried shrimp, feta, tomatoes, and toasted bread. He had decreed that they were just as good *mezedes* for rum as they were for ouzo. In return, he showed me how to doctor leftover pot roast and sell it as *ropa vieja*. Sometimes, when Emilio was late for work, Steve would tease me and say, "I think your friend is in jail again. You might have to take him cigarettes."

"Emilio said I can start right away if I want to," I added.

"Fuck the fucking Milio!" Steve threw his coffee cup against the wall, shattering it into a million pieces. The racket brought Carmen and Isabella running into the kitchen. Steve turned to them and yelled, "Fuck you, too—all of you! You go work with that fucking Cuban. So much for gratitude. *Sto diavolo,* all of you!" He shouted some more Greek curses and stomped out the door. Moments later I heard the tires of the Cadillac screeching out of the parking lot.

He came back just as the dinner hour started. Perched himself on the stool behind the cash register and went about ringing the tickets and giving change as if nothing had happened. At the end of the day, after the last customer left, Steve counted the money in the register, then called me over. He was about to say something when he noticed the waitresses were still there counting their tips, so he motioned for me to follow him outside.

"Listen," he said, resting his left foot on the bench by the front door and turning toward me. "Up to now you have been making thirty-five a week and you did maintenance. Now I'm giving you fifty with no painting and no grass cutting, and you don't like it?"

"Steve, I came in this country to make money," I said. "I didn't come to be a prisoner. I can see what this place makes, and I know what it can afford to pay." I sat on the bench, crossed my legs, and took out a cigarette. "I think one hundred twenty dollars a week is the average pay for a cook. Now that I got my papers, I can work with Emilio or look for another place."

Steve lit a cigarette also and walked to the end of the parking lot with slow, short steps, then turned around and came back the same way.

"Okay," he said finally. "Seventy. Any more and I might as well close the door."

I took a long puff and tilted my head back, watching the smoke rise as I exhaled.

"Okay," I said after a while. "But I will need to leave at six o'clock every Tuesday and on Thursday nights. Pete Papas got me signed up at an English class. I am learning the language the right way now."

"That fucking goofball! He always sticks his nose in other people's business." Steve threw the cigarette on the ground and stepped on it with a vengeance.

"He's going to help me with my driver's license, too," I added.

Steve stopped grinding the cigarette. "You can have the fucking nights off! There isn't that much going on at night anymore anyway." He kicked the spot where the cigarette dust was. "Fucking people, always sticking their nose in other people's business." He started to go inside but paused at the door. "I want you to start opening up again, like before." He reached for the door handle. "And remember, like I told you before, I want you to have your heart in it." He walked back in the restaurant.

Things are going my way. I finished my cigarette and returned to my tasks. Carmen stood by the counter, reading a leftover newspaper, and she winked as I passed by. I secured everything in the kitchen and we left together. We held hands until we rounded the corner out of Steve's sight, then walked side by side, sometimes exchanging a few words.

Carmen lived in a building that in more easygoing days was an average citizen's average four-bedroom house in an average neighborhood. Then, when the Cubans started flooding Miami, somebody hacked out new doors and put up partitions that created more rooms by making everything else smaller. It ended up as a hermaphrodite structure advertised as a "triplex" and rented to as many desperate Cubans as could be stuffed into it.

Everyone in Carmen's building was from around Camarioca, and everyone was in some way related to each other. In the evenings, the men would sit on the porch to drink beer and talk about the good old days, making guesses about how long it would be before Castro got his ass kicked all the way to Russia.

Carmen's unit consisted of two miniature bedrooms, a combination kitchen and dining room that had once been part of a corridor, and a bathroom with a shower stall and a loud, moody toilet that would broadcast its work to the entire building each time someone used it. Carmen and her niece slept in the same bed in one of the two bedrooms, and I had the other, the one closest to the front door, all to myself. That was one of the terms of the marriage agreement—in addition to the six hundred I paid Carmen after the marriage, I would pay sixty-five dollars a month rent for one of the bedrooms. The other terms were that I minded my own business and stayed out of theirs, and that I would always speak English in the house.

Carmen's grandfather slept on a cot wedged between the stove and the kitchen counter. It was the only way the cot would fit, which made a visit to the refrigerator quite an exercise. A person had to climb on the counter and come down on the other side, which required the use of two chairs and always ended up waking up the old man. On the second night of my stay, we moved the cot farther out to give access to the refrigerator, but we discovered that it was blocking the entrance to the bathroom, so we went back to the first option.

One week after I returned from Nassau, as Carmen and I walked home after work, acting conspicuously like a loving husband and wife, I suggested we sit on a bench under the tall banyan tree two blocks away from *our* house.

"Many new-married couples do that," I joked.

"Don't have much time," Carmen said. "Need to check on grandfather."

"That is what I want to speak to you," I said. "I have one idea about the grandfather." We sat on one of the benches among the huge roots of the banyan tree and I lit a cigarette. "About the grandfather—"

She motioned for me to stop and pointed to a man at one of the other benches holding a newspaper in front of him.

She slid closer to me. "Okay, what about Grandfather?"

"You can put his bed in my room," I said. "If you take twenty dollars off my rent."

"What did you say?" Carmen sounded surprised.

"Grandfather can sleep in the same room with me, not the kitchen, and you only collect a few dollars smaller rent. Okay?"

"I will have to do some refiguring," she said. "To see if it will work."

I waited for her to explain. I expected some hardship story so she wouldn't have to discount the rent. Instead she stood and said, "Grandfather will be waiting."

Two nights later when we walked by the banyan tree on the way home, as if the sight of it reminded her of what we had talked about the last time we were at the same spot, Carmen suggested we sit on a bench. We sat and after looking around, she motioned me to get closer.

"Remember, we are loving husband and wife." She took a long puff of the cigarette I offered her. "*Griego*," she said after, "that idea about the grandfather is good but will not work. I must have that much money every month. The school only pays half scholarship."

"Is that what you need the money for?"

"Listen, *Griego*, you speak to Mister Peter to see if there is a school you can go to learn the language. Why? Because you want a better life, right? But you are not the only smart person. This crazy world has made it damn hard for a woman to live her life the way she wants it, especially a woman without education. Julie is going to finish the university, and she will have the life of a lady. No waitressing and no cleaning floors like the rest of us. She has half scholarship at the university, but I have to pay the other half."

"Where's her father?"

"He died in the Bay of Pigs." She was silent for a moment. "Getting here, we lost every relative we had. The only thing both of us have in this world is each other and Grandfather. Julie is a smart girl, but with no education she will have to put up with the Stevens of the world and pretend to like it." Her face had gotten red and her voice louder. "What kind of life is that? I'll find the money for her even if I have to sell my soul to the Devil and I'll—"

"Okay, okay. I will pay the same rent," I said.

We got up and started toward home. A few steps later I stopped and turned to her.

"Listen," I said, "the old man can still sleep in my room. I pay the same rent."

She looked surprised. "Really?"

"Yes, if he doesn't fart too much." What the hell, the old man was as quiet as the appliances I had been sharing the room with at Steve's place.

Carmen looked at me a moment longer, a smile teasing the corners of her mouth. "The other Greek was right. You are an okay person."

"Which other Greek is that?"

"Mister Pete from the restaurant."

"Did he do the matchmaking?"

"He said it was a good way to help each other."

When we were at the corner of Eighth Street and Thirteenth Avenue, Carmen stopped and looked over at an empty lot across the street.

"You see something?" I asked.

"Some people are going to build a monument somewhere around here. I think over there. It's going to be for those killed in the Bay of Pigs."

"That will be nice," I said.

"It will not bring back Julie's father."

"Yes, but his name will be on a plaque for people to read forever," I said.

"What's the good in that? It will be just another name on a stone, and Julie still will have no father."

We walked the rest of the way in silence.

✣✣✣

One Sunday morning exactly six weeks after I moved into Carmen's house, the immigration men—two of them, one black, the other white, both tall and skinny and both about fifty—came calling. Carmen's grandfather sat in his usual spot by the front door, staring at the clouds over Tenth Street. Carmen, in a faded housecoat, prepared the old man's usual breakfast. I had risen only minutes earlier and was still getting dressed. Pete Papas would pick me up soon to practice driving. I hoped this time he would be satisfied with my parallel parking and say I was ready to take the driving test on Monday.

They showed their badges to Carmen. "We happened to be in the neighborhood," said one of the two men. "We thought we'd stop by to see Mr. Kostas Ka-ra-kou-gou-loo." He was trying to read the name from a form.

"It's *Karaoglou*," I said, emerging from the bathroom, still tucking the shirt into my pants. "Kostas Karaoglou. Why you look for him?"

"We just needed to verify residence," said the black immigration man. "It's a formality. We have to do it when we receive a report."

"Who report? What report you speak?" I asked.

"Someone called the office," the white man said. "They reported that Kostas Kaka . . . Kara . . . *this*"—he pointed to the name on the paper—"was not living here. We are obligated to investigate. Can we see some identification?"

"Yes, sir, you can." I reached in my pocket and pulled out my green card. Since I'd gotten the card, I wouldn't even go to the bathroom without it. The first couple of nights I had slept with it under my pillow.

Both men studied it for a minute, then handed it back to me. They asked who else was staying in the apartment and stuck their heads in the bedroom doors.

"I see things are normal here," said the white man. "It looks like *my* house on Sunday morning." He chuckled and tried to turn around but bumped into a chair and almost fell. "Cozy little place you have here," he said, catching his breath.

"We have buy penthouse in Miami Beach," Carmen snapped, "but the furniture from Paris not here yet."

I wanted to laugh at Carmen's spunk but didn't dare.

"Sorry for the intrusion, ma'am," the men said and left.

"I bet it was your little gardenia-smelling whore from Steve's apartments who made the report," Carmen said when they were gone.

"But I have not seen her since we married," I said, but she didn't seem to have heard me.

⁂

Pete picked me up about an hour later, and we drove to our usual practicing place. The area had been in the process of becoming a housing area, but after laying the streets and the foundations of six houses, the developers ran out of money and the project was abandoned. Somebody had moved aside the flimsy barricade blocking what would have been the columned entrance to the subdivision, and since then it had been used for driving practice. With the streets and the curbs installed, the place was ideal for that purpose. Every weekend, parents, friends, and professional driving instructors could be seen teaching would-be drivers by crisscrossing the unpaved streets and parallel parking between make-believe cars.

Later that day, when Pete dropped me off at Carmen's, I asked if we were going for the driving test the next day.

"Don't be in a hurry," said Pete. "We practice a couple more times before we go. I'll come Tuesday to show you how to get to school by bus. Are you ready for your first day at school?"

"I got a brand-new sponge and slate," I said.

Before leaving for Nassau, I had asked Pete if there was a school to learn the language better, and he signed me up for "Adult English" at the Adult Education Center. I hoped that besides learning to speak American, I would meet some hot, unattached foreign women. I was looking forward to the class with the excitement and anticipation of a first grader.

On Tuesday, Pete rode with me on the bus, showed me where to get off, and wished me luck. I was the first one in the classroom, and I picked a seat in the last row so I could observe the others as they entered.

The teacher, a thin, friendly, white-haired lady, was the last to come in. She closed the door and introduced herself, then asked everyone to say their name, the place where they came from, and something about themselves.

I counted twelve people in the group. The first to speak were two brothers, both in their twenties. They were from Albania, and they said they had escaped their "crazy government" by stowing away on an Italian ship. They planned to go to the university here in America and study engineering. The next to speak was a middle-aged woman who had been a French teacher in Port-au-Prince. After her, a man from Syria—who, appearing to be around sixty, was the oldest in the group—said he had come to learn English so he would know when his son and his American wife were talking about him. He said he was keeping his schooling a secret.

A man amongst a family of three said only their names and that they were husband, wife, and a sister from Saigon. After them, an elderly couple from Peru did the same. A hefty Israeli woman who had been dropped off by a man who looked like a wrestler had difficulty explaining what she did and ended up telling the class that she drove a tank in the army and now wanted to learn English to help her husband in his business. The teacher asked what business he was in, and the woman said he was a *pachach*. When everyone looked puzzled she added, "He has a *musach le pachachut*." When that didn't help, she mimicked steering a car.

"Automobeele, eh? Zoom-zoom, then bang-bang!" She moved her hands as if to imitate a crash. "Automobeele no good. Go to *pachach* and automobeele good."

"Is it an automobile repair business?" the teacher asked.

The hefty Israeli woman nodded and blushed.

After her it was my turn. I didn't want to go through what the woman before me had, so I just said, "My name Kostas Karaoglou. I am Greek and I cook to restaurant Parthenon."

A Haitian couple spoke in unison. They said they had come to South Florida two months earlier, both in the same boat. They were married as soon as they got here, and she was going to become a nurse while he worked as a tailor until she finished school; then he would open a men's clothing store. Both beamed with confidence and optimism. They had come to class holding hands and constantly smiled at everybody.

As I sat in the last row looking the group over and bemoaning the lack of nymphomaniac women, once again the opinion I had formed when sailing in the merchant marine was confirmed. People were the same all over the world. They had the same ideas, the same dreams, and the same aspirations, regardless of the color of their skin and in what language they dreamt those dreams.

CHAPTER EIGHTEEN

Extra Income

A few days after my school started, Albert came into the restaurant exactly at six o'clock, just like always. Albert worked for the telephone company and had been coming to the restaurant before I started working there. He was about fifty, short and plump, and he smiled a lot. He always sat at the end of the counter, and Carmen would have a cup of coffee and a slice of apple pie in front of him as soon as he sat down.

"Thank you, but today I would like to order dinner first," he said apologetically.

"No problem," said Carmen. She handed him a menu and took back the apple pie.

I happened to be getting a soft drink from the cooler when Albert ordered. "Wife no cook tonight?" I teased.

"Oh, hi there. Didn't know you can talk," he replied in the same teasing tone. Up until then, I hadn't spoken to him. Without my papers I was choosy about conversation partners. "The kids are out of school and the wife took them to visit her folks in Sarasota for a few days," he said. "I start at the other job at seven and don't have time to fix dinner."

"You have two jobs?" It was the first time I had heard of an American working more than one. "What other job you do?"

"I work as a security guard," he said. "I do that for the vacation money. Last year we took the kids to Yellowstone. For this summer, Miriam has found a cabin in North Carolina that we're going to rent."

"You not tired after work all day?"

"No, the job is easy. I work in the condominiums at the beach. I start at seven and stay 'til ten or eleven at night. It's not hot, and all I do is sit at a guard station and watch who goes in and out of the place. Most of the time I read, drink coffee, and talk to the folks 'til it's time to leave."

"Is that all work you do?"

"Yeah, pretty much. I guess the women there feel safer if there's a guard at the entrance, although some of them can take care of themselves just fine. There are some wild ones there, and I've been propositioned many times, but I'm a family man. Other guys get laid all the time. I've asked the boss to send me to buildings that are under construction because it's quieter and I get to do a lot of reading, but he says the people in the condominiums ask for me. I'm 'trustworthy,' is the way he put it."

From everything Albert said, the words *propositioned* and *get laid* came across louder than cannon blasts. I almost jumped over the counter to grab Albert and run to his boss right then. I had been neither propositioned nor laid since the Nassau fiasco almost a month ago. To make things worse, Carmen and her niece had gotten used to my presence at home and walked around half-dressed, as if I were a real member of their family. The battle between the forces of morality, logic, and carnality had become an unbearable torture.

"I would like to make some more money, too," I said. "I try to collect to buy a car."

"You should talk to my boss. They need people all the time. I could take you to him when you're ready."

Right now, I almost answered, but instead I wiped my hands on the apron and tried to look as if my mind were preoccupied with greater things. "Maybe it is good," I said finally. "You ask the boss first if he want me and then we go together, okay?"

Albert said he'd do it that evening.

My mind shifted into overdrive. Wouldn't it be a thrill to get laid by some of those rich, aristocratic women in those fancy condominiums? The English-language school only took up two evenings a week. All the other nights I got home at ten, and on the weekends the restaurant was closed. It would be a guaranteed way to "have a nice weekend," as the Americans told each other on Friday evenings.

Now that I had my driver's license, there was no stopping me. I could work a few extra days to make the money for a sporty car, a shiny convertible, and drive it with the top down and start exploring some secluded beaches. Maybe go skinny-dipping with some sexy young thing. Women flocked to men with fancy cars.

It had taken me three tries to pass the driving test. I didn't have any problem with the written part. I passed that on the first attempt thanks to the English class and Pete's tutoring, but the driving part was a different story. The first time, the license man told me to turn around and go back a few minutes after we got started.

"Why? What is wrong?" I asked.

"Failure to come to a complete stop at the STOP sign," explained the inspector.

"I no stop because nobody coming from other side," I protested, but that didn't make any difference.

The second time we went a bit farther, but the inspector told me to go back after two turns.

"What problem this time?" I asked.

"Failure to signal proper left turn," the inspector said.

"But nobody behind and nobody in front of me. What use

have making signals if nobody see?" But again the inspector was unreasonable. Maybe he didn't like foreigners.

"Rules are rules," Pete said when I vented my frustration. "There is a reason for having them."

"Don't think I'll ever get used to this lopsided American thinking," I said, but all I got back for an answer was a faint grin.

When I finally got the license, I spent a lot of time examining it. It was not just an ordinary piece of colored paper. It was a ticket to independence, a document of confirmation that I was just as good as all those other people who drove about in the city. On the calendar I had hanging on my wall—the one showing American landscapes that I had brought from my old apartment—I circled the date. Tuesday, August 3. I was going to celebrate the anniversary of that date every year, just like the June 17 date when I got my green card, and May 28, Saint Konstantin's Day, my name day. And it wouldn't be long now before I marked another date on that calendar: the date I bought my first car.

When Albert came in the next day, it took all the restraint I could muster to wait until he had finished eating. Then, as casually as possible, I went to check the soft-drink cooler and pretended I'd just noticed him sitting there.

"Oh, hi, Albert. Still a bachelor?"

"Yeah, I'm still batching it," he said. "I talked to the man and he said to bring you in."

"What man was that?"

"For the security guard job. He said to bring you in anytime."

"Oh, yeah, I forgot all about that. Good, good. When can I start?"

"You can come with me tomorrow if you want. I work afternoons on Saturdays. I can pick you up."

"It is happened that I have no appointment tomorrow." I chuckled. "What time you pick me up?"

"I start at five. How about I pick you up at four? That way the boss can talk to you and have time to fill out the paperwork."

"Okay," I said. "I will be at corner of Nine Street and Twenty Avenue."

"You got it," said Albert.

"What I get?" I asked.

"I will be there," he said with a smile.

I smiled too as I walked away. I should remember to have a couple of condoms in my pocket in case I got propositioned.

⁘⁘⁘

The boss of the security guard company seemed to be somewhere past sixty, short and round, and he spoke like a New Yorker. When Albert and I walked into his little office, he was yelling into a telephone in his right hand while pressing the receiver of another against his stomach with his left.

"You fell off the wagon again, didn't you, Elmer?" he shouted. "Second night this week you don't show up for work! You pulled that stunt last week too." He switched receivers. "I apologize, Mrs. Dean, for the man being rude and intoxicated," he said into the left-hand receiver. "I assure you he is being reprimanded." He put both receivers against his stomach and said to Albert, "You're going to the Ocean View Condominiums tonight."

Back to the right-hand phone. "You were drunk again last night, Elmer. I got a complaint from the Ocean View people. It's the warehouse for you from now on. And you better be here tomorrow or you're finished!" He hung up the phone on the right and spoke into the left. "Yes, ma'am. I'm sending a new man. You'll be very pleased with him. Yes, Mrs. Dean, he's a good Christian and a loyal American. Thank you, ma'am. Anytime, ma'am." He hung up. "Bitch," he said to the receiver.

He stretched behind him to reach a clipboard with a form on it. The right-hand telephone started ringing.

"Fill out this application and bring it back to me." He handed me the clipboard and answered the phone. "Reliable Security Service, how may I help you?"

Albert helped me fill out the application. When I took it back, the fat man glanced at it, put the left phone to his stomach, and said I was hired.

"I like to hire people who just got their green card," he said. "Means they've already checked you out, so I don't have to pay for a criminal report on you."

He started barking into the left phone again. When he hung it up, he told me about the starting pay and what the prospects for advancement were.

"It's like the Army—you start as a private, then you make corporal, then lieutenant and so on. Each time it's a nickel-an-hour raise."

I figured I would have to make ten-star general before I could buy a carton of cigarettes with my pay, but the chance to get laid made me feel better paid than a bank president. I signed one more form, and the boss gave me a Smith & Wesson pistol in a leather holster, six bullets, and lots of advice about being careful with the gun.

"You don't have to worry about him," Albert told the boss. "He's going to be careful. I can vouch for him."

The Reliable Security boss answered the left phone again and put it to his stomach before telling Albert, who was standing next to me, "For the first night we'll start him off with something easy. Drop him off at the Whitecaps in Miami Beach to work with Gomer Pyle. He went there about an hour ago. Introduce your friend to him, then you go on to the Ocean View tonight. Fucking Elmer's got the manners of an English lord when he's sober. Old women love him, but lately he's hitting the bottle too much." He answered the other phone and put his hand over the receiver. "One more thing," he told Albert. "Get him a vest and make a nametag too."

Albert brought me a blue vest with black buttons and a big orange badge on the left side that had *Reliable Security Service* in blue letters.

"Put this on so they'll know you're supposed to be there," he said.

He asked around the office if anyone had seen the Dymo, and when he found it, he said, "Got to make a nametag for you. What name shall I put down?"

"Konstandinos Karaoglou is what's in my papers."

"No way," he said. "That's too many letters."

"Everybody calls me Kostas. You can put that."

He shook his head. "Still too many letters. This damn machine is hard to squeeze. How about Gus? It sounds strong and it's shorter."

"It sounds like a belch," I said.

Albert laughed. "Gus it is then." He glued the letters on a plastic tag, pinned it on my vest, and we left.

"You'll like it at the Whitecaps," Albert said as we drove along the MacArthur Causeway. "It's a condominium under construction. You have the beach on one side and a quiet street with trees on the other. Usually you'd have to watch out for vandals or somebody stealing materials, but this is in a gated area and nobody goes in there." He paused to chuckle. "All you have to watch for is couples coming in from the beach and going in the rooms for a quickie. Don't know why they think they need two guards there. Gomer Pyle would be enough.

"Is Gomer his name?"

"No, everybody calls him that because he's a bit strange, but don't do it to his face."

"Why? What means gomerpyle?"

"Don't you watch any television? He's a funny man on TV." He slowed the car down, trying to read the building numbers. "The Whitecaps is somewhere around here I think."

Suddenly a man popped up next to us with two guns drawn, ordering us to halt. Albert didn't flinch.

"Good evening, Billy Ray," he said. "I was looking for the construction sign. They must've moved it. This here is Gus. He'll be your partner for the night." Billy Ray said he was pleased to meet me. His badge read *BIL*.

I picked up my gun from the seat and got out of the car.

"Strap on your gun. You're on duty now," Billy-Ray said.

I tried to do as he said. Seeing that I was having difficulty with it, Billy-Ray helped me adjust the belt. I took a couple of steps with the gun strapped on my right side, and it felt strange. I had to walk with my arms out, like a rooster going to a fight.

Albert said he was running late for his post and had to go. "I'm jealous of you guys," he said as he was leaving. "It's nice and quiet over here."

The building we were supposed to be guarding was a multistory concrete skeleton with two construction trailers and two yellow Porta Potties on the street side of the parking lot. Billy Ray said the street side should be guarded by the most experienced man. "You never know who might try to come in."

I agreed and walked up to the second-floor balcony and scanned the beach. In the distance a noisy group of teenagers was playing volleyball. Closer by, two older couples walked slowly along the water, holding hands, and farther out a yacht was heading south, its sails painted bright gold by the last rays of the sun.

I sat on a wooden crate, put my feet up on the rails, and lit a cigarette. Doing some "dead-reckoning" navigation, I figured Taxiarhes would be about thirty degrees to starboard of the second coconut tree in front of the balcony. I looked at my watch. It was almost seven. In the village it would be two o'clock Sunday morning. In a few hours my brother would probably start transporting tourists to Milopotamos beach with the mules; summertime was the busiest time for the villagers. In her last letter, my mother had said the new mayor was going back and forth to Athens, trying to convince the government to build an automobile road from the village square all the way down to the beach. She said my brother and lots of other folks in the village were ready to hang the crazy mayor for his cockamamie ideas.

Our new mayor, she'd written, *calls his crazy idea progress.*

> *Who needs this kind of progress, I say. Their monstrous machines making that useless road will destroy a lot of olive trees and tear up good farming land. We'll lose what little we can scrape from this land. And all for what? So some idlers from the city can get to the beach in comfort? "Is this your idea of progress?" we asked him. When the men from the road department came with their measuring sticks last week, a couple of hotheads took their guns and shot at them. The government folk hightailed it back to where they came from in a hurry.*

I guess everybody has problems, I thought as I flicked my cigarette over the rail.

Later, I headed down to the front to use the Porta Potty. The Gomer Pyle fellow walked over and asked how long I've been a security guard.

I told him it was my first night.

"I've been doing it for a while," Billy Ray said, sounding proud. "I've accumulated enough service hours to get promoted to lieutenant." A convertible with two elderly ladies in the front slowed down, and the lady driving was pointing out something on the building to her passenger. Billy Ray started toward them and they sped off. "That's why I said I should take the street side. The senior man should cover the most dangerous post," said Billy Ray when he returned. "I'm from Athens, Georgia. Where do you come from?"

"I'm from the other Athens—in Greece," I said.

He glanced at my gun on my right side. "Don't snap the strap of the holster when you're on duty. It cuts down on your *response* time."

I nodded I understood. I didn't bother to tell him I kept the bullets in my pocket.

Billy Ray moved back a few steps and demonstrated the best way to pull the gun out of the holster when facing a bandit. It reminded me of the cowboy movies.

"And if something goes wrong, I got a backup," he said. "I always come prepared." With his left hand, he pulled a small cannon from behind his back. "This is my personal gun."

He held it in his left hand, and after a momentary hesitation, he gestured in my direction, indicating that I could hold it. It felt as heavy as it looked. It had an ivory-colored handle and a flowery design on the metal part.

"I took it to a jeweler and had him carve my name on it." Billy Ray pointed to the engraving.

I handed the pistol back, holding it in both open palms like something sacred. Billy Ray pulled a red handkerchief with white dots from his pocket and polished it with slow, gentle moves, as if he were massaging a woman's breast, then stored the gun under his vest and the bandana in his back pocket.

"I must be returning to my station," I said. "I have been away too long."

I walked back to my balcony. The rest of the evening was quiet. I spent most of my time looking at the lights of ships passing at a distance, wondering if any of them was the *Aegean Sea*, and wondering where I would be now if I had not jumped ship.

⁂

On my second night as guardian of the Whitecaps, I went through the routine of checking every floor on the beach side of the concrete skeleton, while Billy Ray did the same on the street side. Neither of us found any thieves or copulating couples among the piles of sheetrock and plywood. Assured that our world was safe, we settled in for the night—I on the second-floor balcony, studying the beach crowd and the marine traffic beyond, and Billy Ray pacing back and forth on the street side of the building, like the guards of the Tomb of the Unknown Soldier in Athens.

A few minutes before it got completely dark, a loud, thunderous sound coming from somewhere above jolted me from my seat. I ran inside just in time to see two grey cats falling out of a tin garbage can as it tumbled down the concrete steps from the third floor.

An instant later, Billy Ray came running in with both guns drawn.

"Did you intercept?" he asked.

I told him about the cats, and he seemed disappointed that the culprit was only a galvanized tin can. When he noticed I had my gun in the holster and the strap snapped, he lectured me about the duties and responsibilities of a security guard.

From then on, whenever I went to use the Porta Potty, I would loudly whistle a peppy Greek tune before leaving my post, to let the "guardian of the front" know friendly troops were approaching and to hold his fire.

I had been protecting the Whitecaps from love-hungry couples for over a week when one of the security company supervisors drove up about an hour after the shift started and asked which of us would like to go to the Mai Kai parking lot for the night.

"The regular man couldn't make it tonight," the supervisor said. "His wife is having a baby."

I had been planning to do the schoolwork I brought with me, so I said, "Billy Ray, you go. I've never guarded a parking lot before."

Billy Ray adjusted his gun belt and started toward his car, but he stopped as he was opening the door. "You think the new man will be all right by himself?" he asked the supervisor.

"Glad you thought of that, Billy Ray," said the supervisor, and I thought he sounded relieved. "Best let him go and you guard this place. More responsibility in here." He walked over to me and said, "Hey, Greek, hop in. I'll take you to the Mai Kai."

Fifteen minutes later, we arrived at a restaurant parking lot.

"This is it," said the supervisor. "They've been having some problems lately with kids scratching cars in the parking lot. Just walk around where you'll be seen. It scares the vandals off and makes the customers feel safer."

The Mai Kai was a Polynesian-style restaurant landscaped to give their customers the impression that they were sitting in the middle of a tropical paradise. There were miniature streams and waterfalls and lakes with colorful tropical fish swimming in them. Narrow paths zigzagging among lush greenery led to quaint small bridges illuminated by gas torches on tall poles. Two young couples were walking the paths at the time, holding hands and swapping kisses. The walls of the restaurant were clear glass so everyone had a view of the gardens while having their dinner.

We went inside, and the supervisor introduced me to the restaurant manager. Then we went back to the parking lot. "Like I said before, just walk around where people can see you. Somebody will come to relieve you at eleven," he said before leaving.

On the first leg of my patrol, I walked toward the far end of the parking lot. This was a good time to look over cars since I was going to have one of my own before long. Pete Papas had promised to take me shopping for one soon.

I tried to think of an excuse to peek into the kitchen and see how they cooked in those half-spherical pots I'd heard about. On one of my patrols I saw a ladle under a car parked a few yards away from the kitchen door. I picked it up and went in the kitchen and asked the two guys closest to the door if they had lost it. They burst out laughing and pointed the ladle to a grumpy-looking middle-aged man who was stirring vegetables on one of the half-spherical pots. "He threw it after the pot washer that was running away from him this morning," one of them told me when he stopped laughing. And all this time I'd believed that the Orientals were people with inexhaustible patience. They had a temper just like the Greeks. I got a cold drink from the fountain, and for a while I watched the three cooks stir vegetables and pieces of meat in their funny cooking pots.

Two hours into the shift, as I neared one of the restaurant doors with access to the gardens, a waiter burst out, running after a beat-up Volkswagen that was speeding away.

"Shoot! Shoot!" the waiter shouted.

At the exit, the car slowed for a moment, giving me a good view of the license plate, then darted out and joined the river of cars flowing south on US 1, and soon was out of sight.

"Why you didn't shoot?" The gasping waiter ran up alongside me. "Sonavabitches!"

"What happened?" I asked him as I casually scribbled on my Winston hard pack the numbers and letters I had seen.

"After they ate, the girls said they'll go look at the garden. Then one man said he'll go see what happened to girls. When he was out the door, the other man ran out, got in the car, and they took off. Sonavabitch!" The waiter was squat and plump and drenched in sweat. "Sonavabitch! Their bill is one hundred twenty dollars. Now *I* will have to pay. Sonavabitch! Why you no shoot? Why you have the stupid gun for?"

"I could hurt somebody with the stupid gun," I told him. "Then police cars with sirens will come and people get scared and no come to eat. Bad for business. I write down the number of the car." I held out the Winston hard pack. "You have paper? Write the number and call the police."

"Hey, that's clever." He pulled the order pad from his pocket and started to copy the numbers. "Are these sevens?" he asked, pointing.

"Yes, sevens."

"Are you from Europe?"

"Yes, from Greece."

"I thought so. They write numbers different there."

"You not sound you are from Miami also," I said.

"I'm from the Philippines."

"Really? What town?"

"A small town called Iloilo."

"Is that so?" I said. "I have gone there, with ship."

"When were you there? Do you remember any of the town?"

"That was three years before now. Only remember sugar refinery and Happy Mariner bar."

The waiter laughed. "My father works for the sugar refinery, at the docks. He probably tied up your ship. Small world, no? I go call police."

I pulled a cigarette out of the pack. Yes, it was a small world, and life had all kinds of peculiar twists and turns. Those four smart-alecky freeloaders would never know how close they had come to having Billy Ray on watch. He would have used both pistols and made Swiss cheese out of their little tin can car before they got two meters away from the parking lot.

The regular guard returned to the Mai Kai the next day, and I was back to the unfinished Whitecaps and Billy Ray, which suited me just fine. It could hardly be called work. Most of the strain came from trying to concentrate on my English homework while girls in skimpy bathing suits ran up and down the beach. The only real danger was getting shot by Billy Ray.

Not too bad, except the getting-laid part—the thing I had been looking forward to from the moment I had put on the Reliable Security Service vest with the macho-sounding American name GUS stuck in the middle of my badge—still had not happened.

But I was hopeful. Something Pete Papas had said kept coming back to me: "If it's meant to happen, it will happen."

CHAPTER NINETEEN

A Car of My Own

Monday evening, two weeks after I started the security guard work, I went with Pete Papas to shop for a car. Now that I had my driver's license, I felt like a caged lion, especially during the hours I didn't have to work. I counted every dollar I had saved—except the one hundred that I'd stashed in the light fixture at the old apartment and which was now stored in the lining of my suitcase—and figured I had enough for a down payment on something that would match my aspirations.

At the first car lot we went to, I walked straight up to a red Mustang convertible with the top down and got right in. I ran my palm over the leather seats, held the wheel with my left hand, and grasped the stick shift with my right while looking at imaginary road turns beyond the hood ornament. By the time the salesman walked over, there was no doubt in my mind; this was the car for me.

"Want to take it for a spin?" he asked. "I'll go get the keys."

"We're going to look around some more first," Pete said, coming up behind him.

"Yes, of course," answered the salesman, sounding a bit deflated. "By the way, my name is Jake." He was thin and fast moving and seemed to be around forty. We shook hands. Then he asked what kind of work we did.

"Retired," said Pete.

"I'm a cook," I said.

"A cook, huh?" Jake nodded. "I have just the thing for you. An old friend of mine brought it in yesterday. Come this way."

He ushered us a few yards farther where a Chevy truck with a boxy, stainless steel back was parked. He lifted open the sides and pointed out the shelves, drawers, and hot and cold compartments.

"This is a portable sandwich shop—a lunch wagon," Jake said. "A real money cow. You drive up to a work site at lunchtime, open up, and stand back and let them take what they want. You stand right about here." He hopped sideways to a spot out of the way of the hordes of imaginary customers. "And you collect the money. The man who had it before put two kids through college with this. Now his sons are big-time lawyers and he's retired. He traded the lunch wagon for a Cadillac and taking it easy. He's enjoying life."

I took a few steps back and looked at the silver restaurant on wheels. Driving up to a place and offering more variety than boiled hot dogs might be a good idea, but the "stand back and collect the money" part seemed risky. How could I watch everybody and make sure they didn't stuff their pockets with sandwiches? Then they would come to where I standing, "right about here," pay for just a bag of potato chips, and I'd say "thank you."

"Maybe when I know the Miami better," I said after some thought.

Later, after we left the lot, Pete told me that the men at the construction sites called that kind of truck a "roach coach." After he explained what roach coach meant, we both laughed.

We looked at a few more cars, and finally Pete seemed to favor a blue Valiant hardtop.

"You have an eye for quality," the salesman said. "This is almost new. A rich old lady, a regular customer of ours, owned it. She trades in for a new car every year, but she liked this one so much she kept it for two more years."

When we got back from test-driving it, Pete took me aside and talked to me in Greek. "For three hundred dollars, you can't go wrong with this car. Never mind the rich old lady nonsense. He would say the same thing even if you were buying a dump truck. But this one has a good engine, and you don't need anything expensive for your first car."

We followed the salesman to the office to do the paperwork. Pete loaned me one hundred dollars to make up the shortage. I was to repay him at ten dollars a month.

"And you can buy me a glass of wine for the interest," he said.

"We'll have the shop check it out, and you should be able to pick that baby up tomorrow," Jake said after he finished filling out the forms.

Pete told him we'd call before we came, and we drove off.

"That *Moustang* was some car, wasn't it?" I said when we were on the road.

"No good Greek should drive a Ford," he answered.

"Why's that?"

"Sometime back, there were about a dozen Greeks working at the Ford factory up in Detroit making the Model T. One year, the Greek Easter was a week after the American Easter and they asked for time off. Henry Ford said no. They decided to take off anyway, figuring he couldn't fire all twelve of them. When they went back Henry did fire every one of them."

"You know this for sure, or you just saying it because the *Moustang* was three hundred dollars more?" I asked.

"They told it to me as the truth," answered Pete.

For a few minutes I concentrated on examining the other cars on the road. Then I said, "Have you seen the hot dog guy on Biscayne

Boulevard, by the Bay Front Park? Bet I could make some good money if I had one of those carts in the right place. Where do you think he bought his sausage cart?"

"Be patient, Kostas. You're still a young man," Pete said. "The right deal will come along. When it does, I'll be here, God willing."

"Hope it comes soon," I said. "When I get to your age, I want to be like you are now."

We were stopped at a traffic light, and Pete seemed to be studying a distant cloud. "You should hope to be better," he said after a while. "You should have a family."

"I got plenty of time for that," I answered quickly. "I got to make money first."

Pete kept studying the distant cloud. "Time sneaks up on you," he said and let out a sigh. "You're old before you know it." The light turned and the car behind us gave two short beeps.

I called Pete early the next morning and asked if he had talked to the car salesman.

"Slow down, Kostas," he said, laughing. "Car lots don't open before sunrise. I'll call them later and I'll come to pick you up."

We picked up the car right after the lunch hour rush. On the way back to the restaurant, I drove down Biscayne Boulevard and stopped at the Freedom Tower. I asked a professional photographer stationed there to take a photograph of me standing by the car, with the tower and Miami's tall buildings in the background. I'd include the photograph in the card I was going to send home with birthday wishes for my brother.

Back at the restaurant, I parked the car where I could see it from the kitchen window. Every time I raised my head from the grill, I'd stare at it for at least two minutes. It was light blue—Mediterranean blue, the salesman had called it—with vinyl upholstery and a wooden dashboard, and as many buttons and gauges as the instrument panel of a ship's bridge.

⁜⁜⁜

Exactly three weeks after I started working at the Reliable Security Service, the boss called me into his cubicle.

"You've had enough experience by now to work at the Ocean View condominiums," he said. "Fucking Elmer is drunk again, and Albert's on vacation in the mountains. It's not that hard of a job anyway. All you have to do is stand by the main entrance and deter unauthorized visitors." He must have seen the look on my face because he quickly clarified, "Don't let anybody in who doesn't have a key." He picked up a ringing phone and pressed the receiver to his stomach. "And always be polite and helpful," he added. "Always say 'yes ma'am' and 'yes sir.' You got that?"

"Yes, I can do that," I said. "No problem."

"Okay, here's the address." He handed me a piece of paper with his free hand. "Don't go by way of Venetian Boulevard, too much traffic this hour. Take MacArthur and turn left on Washington. It's faster."

Going east on MacArthur Boulevard, I drove as if I were steering an overloaded tractor trailer. I stayed four car lengths behind the car ahead of me, and from time to time I tapped on my brake to signal the car behind me to back off. I had been the proud owner of this 1961 Valiant for only a few days, and I was treating it as if it were made from fine crystal.

When I got to Ocean View condominiums, I made sure to park away from trees or any other bird perches and walked to the sentry box–looking structure by the entrance. The man I was supposed to relieve was standing by the door.

Three hours into the shift, a woman drove up and parked a few yards away from my post. She got out of her red *Chevroleta* and started unloading bags and packages from the back seat. When she tried to close the door, she dropped one of the boxes and then dropped two others while trying to pick up the first one, letting out a small cry of desperation with each dropped box. She was short, curvy, around thirty, and had windblown red hair.

I remembered the instructions the Reliable Security Service boss had given me: "Be helpful and polite." I dashed over.

"Can I help you, ma'am?" I gathered the dropped boxes and took the others from her hands, offering to carry her load to the elevator.

She seemed pleased with the suggestion. "Thank you very much," she said. "I didn't realize I had so many boxes."

At the elevator, she smilingly asked if I wouldn't mind helping carry them to her door. And when we got there, she asked if I wouldn't mind putting them on the foyer table, and when I had done that, she asked if I cared for something cold.

"It's been such a hot day," she said. The whole effort must have warmed her up, because she unbuttoned the top buttons of her blouse.

When I returned to my post, it was thirty-five minutes later, and one of the Reliable Security supervisors was standing by the elevator door.

"Mrs. Dean called the office," he bellowed. "The old goat was asking why there was no security guard in the building. Where the hell have you been?"

"A woman on the third floor called. She was screaming for help and I run up to see what she wanted." Why did he have to be standing right there?

"What did she want?"

"It was nothing. She thought she saw a mouse."

"And it took you that long?"

"She wanted me to look under the bed and behind the dressers and everywhere."

"Never go inside an apartment alone," he snapped. "We could get sued for that. Didn't they tell you that when you got hired?"

"I work the Whitecaps before. This is first night here. I did not know, sir."

"Well, don't do it again. If it's an emergency and you have to go in, call the office for help."

"I will, sir. I will."

When my shift was over, after some intricate maneuvering to elude the man who relieved me, I revisited the redhead, whose name was Susan. We attacked each other with the hunger of two people long deprived of the thing married life is supposed to offer in abundance. Later, after the initial storm had passed and we lay in bed catching our breath, she said that getting together like this was too risky because she was a married woman and there were lots of old busybodies in the building.

"Don't know what came over me tonight," she said. "Usually I'm a very restrained person. It must've been the two margaritas I had with Charlotte."

"Where is your husband?"

"That's it, my Richard's been gone a long time." She sounded relieved. "It's the first time he's been gone for over two months. Never done that before."

"What job your husband do?"

"He's captain on a big ship. This time the Hess Company has got him going from the Persian Gulf to Europe, back and forth. He's been gone ten weeks now." Again her voice sounded relieved, as if a heavy burden had been lifted. She attacked me with renewed energy. Before I left, she suggested we meet at the Casa Juno from then on.

"It's a motel a few miles north of Miami, in Dania," Susan said. "Charlotte says nobody asks questions there." We agreed to meet there next Monday.

The following evening, I arrived for my shift at the Ocean View fifteen minutes early, a habit that had stayed with me from my merchant seaman days. The man I relieved seemed happy to see me. I got settled in the little sentry box, took out the schoolbook, and started doing the English writing exercise the teacher had assigned. I was filling in the last blank in the last sentence when the phone rang. A woman told me in a bossy tone something about some clamoring somewhere and that I should be doing something about it.

"Yes, ma'am," I said. "Yes, ma'am. Okay."

I hung up and got back to my homework. About a half hour later, I was startled by a knock on the window. I looked up and saw a tall, stout woman getting ready to tap the glass again with the silver handle of her cane. Her lips were moving, and I opened the window to hear what she was trying to tell me.

"Young man," she said, "did you reconnoiter the disturbance I reported to you?"

I stared at her, trying to guess what the words meant. She seemed to be in her late sixties, wore a dark-blue dress that reached down to her ankles, and her hair was rolled back in an old-fashioned way, like the women I had seen in some photographs of my grandmother's era.

"Yes, ma'am," I answered finally, hoping it would suffice for whatever she was asking.

"Well, what was it?"

"What was what, ma'am?"

"The noise I instructed you to investigate."

"Oh, the noise. I go look. Where is the noise?"

"Young man, I will have to report you to your superiors." She shook her cane to emphasize her point. "I was the first occupant of this property, and as such it is my duty to look after the welfare of the other residents. Now come over here." She motioned that I should get out of the sentry box. "I distinctly heard a disturbing noise coming from the direction of the garage, and I suggested that you investigate. Why have you not?"

"My boss said to me not to abandon my post, ma'am."

"You may tell your boss that Mrs. Dean dispatched you to a task. He knows who I am. Now *go*."

"Yes, ma'am," I said and headed toward the garage.

When my shift was over, I went to the boss and asked to be sent to the Whitecaps construction site from then on.

"Too many people ask questions and I have problem understand what they say," I explained. "Maybe I make some big mistake and make trouble for the company."

"I'll be glad to oblige," said the boss. "I'm running out of people willing to work with Billy-Ray anyway."

The Whitecaps post gave me a chance to do the school assignments, look at the women on the beach, fine-tune my money-making plans, or just gaze at the horizon to reminisce and reflect on my life. It seemed that life had rearranged the importance of some things for me. My taste for big, fast cars with convertible tops and tall wings had almost disappeared. Now, when I drove anywhere, I treated the blue Valiant like a prized thoroughbred out for a stroll.

Too bad Mother wouldn't come to visit. My brother would never know what a big city Miami was and how mild the winters of Florida were. Since I'd wrestled the raise from Steve, I had increased the amount in the money order I was sending to Mother every month to twenty-five dollars. I wrote her to go to Volos and buy new dresses and shoes and be the best-dressed woman at church, but she wrote back saying that she had been depositing the money at the Taxiarhes Post Office Savings Bank.

It will be there when you come back, she had written. *You can take it and open a restaurant in the village with it. Now that you have learned all the fancy ways of cooking and serving the foreigners, a restaurant here will be a gold mine.*

That last part of Mother's suggestion occupied my mind quite a bit, especially when there were no bikinis on the beach. It was the second time Mother had mentioned a "gold mine," and I was beginning to think there was some good logic to what she said. Albert and quite a few other customers at the Parthenon restaurant had often spoken about shop owners they knew who had a second shop in some northern place like Chicago or Canada that they operated in the summertime. When the weather turned cold, they would close for the year and come to Florida.

I, too, could do something like that. Only instead of opening a place in New York or Canada, I would open one in Taxiarhes, in Greece. I could have the menu printed in English and Spanish, to work the tourist trade in the summer months; then in the winter I would padlock the place and come to Florida.

In my mind, I walked the cobblestone paths, the ridges, and the scenic spots of the village, searching for a suitable location for my restaurant. Almost always, I came to the same conclusion: the Adrahtases' coffeehouse was the perfect place. Located at the west side of the square, across from the church of Taxiarhes, it was a tall, stone structure built by Mr. Adrahtas many years ago when he'd returned from Egypt with sacks full of money. It had hand-hewn ceiling-beams from the local chestnut forest, wide-plank maple floors, and stucco stone walls with lots of alcoves and niches. The kind of rustic local building that tourists went crazy over.

Old Mr. Adrahtas had died many years ago, and his son seemed to like spending his time cultivating his vineyards and olive groves. He opened the coffeehouse just for a few hours on Sundays for the social hour after church. He had only one child, a daughter, named Rinio. She was in the same grade with me at school.

Yes, that would make a great location for a restaurant, but the younger Mr. Adrahtas was a shrewd man who knew the value of things. If he sold it, I would have to be the Bank of England to afford his price.

But wouldn't it be something if it worked out where I could have businesses on two continents?

CHAPTER TWENTY

The Acropolis Restaurant

Julio was one of Carmen's cousins who lived in the same building. He was in his forties, tall and athletic and widowed. He'd been a history teacher in Cuba, but now he and two of his cousins, also former teachers, worked as welders at a shipyard in Port Everglades. Almost every evening, Julio, the two cousins, and most of the other men in the building sat on the porch, sipping Falstaff beer and reliving the battle of the Bay of Pigs, or rehashing the day's happenings at the places they worked. Sometimes I sat on the porch also, but at the far end of it, immersed in my own thoughts.

That Sunday, while trying to squeeze by them on the way to my usual spot, I happened to hear Julio telling the others that the *pendejo gringo* they had for a foreman on his shift was spending most of the day drinking coffee and telling sea stories with some old farts at a Greek restaurant across the gate from the shipyard. The words *sea stories* and *Greek restaurant* made me pause to hear the rest.

"Goofy old man should have retired long time ago," Julio said.

"Don't know why the shipyard keeps him."

"He's lucky everybody in his crew is Cuban," said one of the cousins. "We do the work without anybody standing over our shoulder. If he had *gringos* for a crew, he'd get nothing done."

"Soon he'll have to find another hole to goof off in." Julio took a long sip from his beer and belched. "The Greek who owned that joint died and the place has gone to hell since. Won't be long before they padlock it."

I turned back and put my hand on Julio's shoulder. "What is the name of the joint, Julio?"

"Pericles or Hercules. Some old Greek name like that," said Julio, sounding slightly annoyed.

"Julio, I want you to do me a favor." I reached for my wallet and pulled out a five-dollar bill. "Tomorrow, go eat lunch in that restaurant—I pay. When you're there, see how many tables they have and how much business they do at lunchtime. And in the evening when you leave work, see how many cars are parked in the front."

Julio nodded and put the five in his pocket, then continued telling the others that yesterday the gringo foreman told a welder to go ahead and weld the heads of the rivets, and now the whole side of the yacht was leaking. They'd have to keep her on dry dock over the weekend, and it was costing the company a ton of money.

"I tell the *idiota* you never weld rivets on a riveted hull, you stop the leak with hammer and special chisel, but gringos think they know everything. Never listen to Cubans."

"How many shifts are working in the shipyard, Julio?" I asked.

"Two now, but when they get a big job, they have three," snapped Julio. "So, I tell the *mama pinga*, 'Remember last month the big problem with the English ship?' But he's too old and doesn't remember."

"How many people are working on each shift, Julio?" I asked.

He turned and looked at me. "I don't know. I'll make complete report *mañana*. Okay, Señor Greco?"

"Okay," I said. "Also look how many other restaurants are near the shipyard, too."

"*Sí, sí, señor*." I could tell Julio was getting annoyed and I walked on.

The next evening, I postponed taking a shower so I'd get to the gathering spot on the porch early. Julio was already there, in the middle of telling the others that the *viejo* gringo foreman had a stroke on his way to work. "He's not coming back to the shipyard anymore"

"Are you the foreman now?" asked one of the men.

"No," said Julio, "the *mama pingas* at the front office gave the job to some relative of the big boss. He knows nothing about shipyard work. Now I have to tell the crew what to do *and* explain what we're doing to the new gringo. I'm really the boss, but he gets the pay." He stopped to take a gulp of his beer, and I rushed to take advantage of the pause.

"Did you eat at the restaurant, Julio?"

"*Sí, patrón.* The name of the restaurant is Acro-polis," he said. He took another sip of his beer.

"Well, how is it, Julio?"

"Okay, listen." He turned his chair away from the group. "At lunchtime I tell the new boss that maybe I'm late coming back from lunch today and he gets scared. He says 'I'll speak to Clemens about raising your pay. You don't have to quit.' Clemens is the big boss of the place." He burst into laughter, then took a sip of his Falstaff.

"How was the restaurant?"

"Oh, yes, your restaurant," mocked Julio. "I go there, I buy lunch, look around, and this is what I see."

He pulled a smudged piece of paper from his shirt pocket and read his notes. When he finished his report, I said, "*Muchas gracias*, Professor. I will buy you a beer."

"You do more than that," he said. "You buy lunch every day." And after a pause he added, "And maybe dinner, if I get a woman."

"Don't worry about the dinner, *Griego*," said another cousin. "He'll never get a woman."

Everybody burst out laughing.

⁂

The next day, I told Steve I needed to get off a little earlier because I had to see somebody in Fort Lauderdale. Steve stopped reading the paper and looked up at me.

"The last time you took off, you went and got married. What is it this time? Another job?"

"If you *must* know," I said, faking annoyance, "I heard there are flocks of college girls up there giving it away right on the beach. I'm going to check it out."

"It would be dumb to go looking for another job," said Steve, as if my answer didn't count. "You got the perfect job right here. You know how many guys wished they had a damn good deal like this?"

"Don't think they're many," I said and got busy putting things away in the kitchen.

There wasn't much traffic heading north on US 1, so I got to Port Everglades shortly after seven o'clock. I spotted the port and the shipyard next to it from four blocks away. *Must be a special magnet inside me that makes me notice the sea and the ships.* I turned right on Eller Drive, and after some zigzagging, I was at the shipyard.

Directly across the street from the main gate of the Port Everglades Shipyard was the restaurant—a gray, stucco, one-story building attached to a gray, stucco, three-story building. On the roof, written on a long sign with cracked paint, I read *Acropolis Restaurant.* Wouldn't it be something if this was the same restaurant the man with the construction company in Nassau had spoken about that rainy day at the Buccaneer Café? Small world.

The way the parking lot was laid out, my car faced the shipyard, and I sat for some time looking at the ships being repaired. The freighter on dry dock looked almost identical to the *Poseidon,* the first ship I had signed on with. My cabin was that third porthole on the aft, starboard side. I'd had some good times on that ship, been to a lot of interesting ports—Surabaya, Colombo, Iloilo. It seemed like that was over a hundred years ago.

I yanked myself out of the reminiscing and walked to the restaurant, but my stride didn't have its usual firmness. *No reason to be getting nervous.* I pushed the door open.

A small bell above the door made a crisp, jingling sound. The dining room was empty. My plan was to have a cup of coffee and make small talk with the help while looking the place over, but all the chairs were flipped over on the tables, and the stools were on the counter upside down. A middle-aged black man was mopping the floor. When he heard the bell, he paused and looked at me.

"Hello," I said, then asked for the owner in Spanish. The man wiped the sweat from his face with a towel from his back pocket and told me in broken English that the boss was in the kitchen.

"You want speak to him?" he asked me.

"Yes," I replied.

He walked to the kitchen door and called, "Monsieur James, a gentleman want speak with you."

"I shall be out in a minute," a clear voice announced from somewhere inside.

I took a stool off the counter and sat, lighting a cigarette and looking around as if I were already the owner of the place. On the dining room walls were framed posters showing blue-domed churches, whitewashed houses mirrored in azure waters, and basket-carrying donkeys on cobblestone paths. The wall itself was rough-textured white plaster. It might look like a Greek whitewashed wall, but it would have to go. I would paint it with a smooth acrylic paint that was easy to clean, and I'd replace those Greek island pictures with beer posters. This was a restaurant for shipyard workers.

I counted the stools at the counter. Fourteen including the one I was sitting on. That souvenir case and postcard rack would also have to go. I'd either extend the counter or put another table in its place. There was no money in selling trinkets in an industrial area. People wanted lots of food, and fast.

I pulled a menu from the holder on the counter and studied

it. This guy must be losing his shirt. He was giving the stuff away. Shipyard workers only got half an hour for lunch, and they weren't going to spend it shopping around for a sandwich. I read both pages of the menu one more time, looking for some Cuban items, and didn't see any. What did the people around here know about mousaka and pastitsio? People didn't come to a neighborhood like this at night for a fancy dinner. I didn't see any beer either. Shipyard people drank more beer than they ate food. This place was neither a diner nor a luncheonette, nor a classy evening place. Whoever was running it didn't know what he was doing.

The black man finished mopping the floor and wheeled his bucket into the kitchen. I got up and pretended to look at the posters while I paced the dining room. It was seventeen paces long and ten wide—not a bad size for a luncheonette.

"May I help you?" A voice from behind startled me.

I turned and saw a tall, thin man across the counter, drying his hands on a towel. He seemed to be about the same age as I, with black hair that hadn't been cut for a while.

"I am looking for the owner," I said.

"I am the owner. What can I do for you?"

"I am Kostas Karas," I said extending my hand.

"I am James."

We had a cordial handshake.

"Somebody said this place might be for sale," I said.

"It might be. Are you interested?"

"I might be."

"Then you'll have to talk to my mother about it," James said. "She will be here in the morning. We open for breakfast at six. I just came to close up."

"I can't be here in the morning. Is there a way I could see her in the evening?'

"She will be at the church in half an hour. You can see her there. Ask for Mrs. Amalia Moskos."

"Can I look around?"

"Go ahead."

I counted the tables, then walked behind the counter and looked at the storage area under it. I checked the drink fountain and saw that it had five dispensers. That was smart of the old man. There was more profit in fountain drinks than cans and bottles. I walked into the kitchen with James behind me acting as a guide.

"This is the grill," he said. "The freezer is over there, that's the oven, and that's the—"

"I know; I am in the business," I said. "I have a restaurant in Miami."

While looking around, I tried to make some small, purposeful conversation, but I couldn't get anywhere with James. Yes, it was hot. No, he didn't watch football. Yes, they were paying rent for the restaurant, but he would have to look up the amount. Business was average. They served breakfast, lunch, and dinner. They closed at eight. He thought the restaurant was over thirty years old. It was started by his father, who'd died four months ago. Yes, they were new menus. He had changed them after his father passed away, "to give the place more character."

At every reply, I nodded as if evaluating the contents of his answer while reminding myself not to show any signs of eagerness. When I finished looking, I tried to speak in a busy businessman's tone. "I need to get back to Miami," I said. "Tell your mother I'll get with her later. I'll call before I come." I asked for the phone number, and James wrote it on an order slip.

After leaving the restaurant, I drove around the neighborhood for a while. There was a McDonald's on a corner three blocks away and a Lum's across from it. Too far for somebody from the shipyard to go on his lunch hour.

The Acropolis Restaurant had potential. I would have to make a lot of changes, but I could do most of the work myself. It all depended on how much the rent was and how much old Mrs. Moskos was asking for the business. I decided to wait a few days before I talked to her. I didn't want to seem too eager.

I spoke to Pete Papas about the restaurant, and he said he would check the place out. Two days later, Pete said he'd had lunch at the Acropolis and thought a man could make a good living from it if he went about it the right way. I called James's mother later that day and asked if I could see her the next evening. She said she would be very glad to talk to somebody *apo tin patrida*, "from the homeland."

When I got to the Acropolis, I asked for Mrs. Amalia Moskos, and the waitress pointed to a frail old woman in a black dress and black kerchief, knitting at a corner table.

I walked over and said in Greek, "Good evening, Mrs. Moskos."

She stopped knitting, folded the needles and put them in the basket with the gray yarn, then looked up at me. "It's going to be a vest for Dimitrakis," she said, although I hadn't asked what she was knitting.

"You have grandson?" I asked.

"No, it's for *my* Dimitrakis. My James," she added with a faint smile. "I keep forgetting he calls himself that now." She took off her glasses and put them in the basket with the needles.

"My name is Kostas Karaoglou," I said and extended my hand.

She took it and held it with both of hers. They were small and veined. Her girlish face and her small bluish eyes brightened as she spoke. "I'm so glad to talk to somebody from home." She pointed to the chair next to her. "What part of the old country you come from?"

She was from Skiathos and spoke Greek with the accent of the island. Yes, she knew where Taxiarhes was. Her father's brother had married a girl from one of the villages around there and used to send them the most delicious apples and the biggest chestnuts she'd ever seen.

"He wrote to my father that the forests over there were so green and the streams so clear. He said he thought he'd found Paradise."

"How long have you had this place?" I asked.

She didn't answer right away. Instead, she looked over the dining room as if she had just arrived.

"This place has been very good to us," she said finally, almost in a whisper. "When my George was alive, God rest his soul"—she crossed herself—"this place used to be a gold mine. We got our house paid off and we put our Dimitrakis through college, all out of this restaurant. God gave us only one child. I prayed for a daughter too, but the Lord didn't decree it, glory be to God." She crossed herself again. "Maybe Dimitrakis will marry a nice girl and she will be my daughter."

She paused and let out a long sigh.

"Yes, this place has been a good provider," she went on. "Got my mother's old house on the island fixed up real nice and even put some money aside. We were planning to spend the summers in Skiathos and the winters here as soon as Dimitrakis got his doctorate. He is going to be a *proffessoras*, my Dimitrakis, you know? That's why he changed his name to James. The Americans don't know how to say Dimitrakis." Again she paused and sighed. "Neither I nor my George had much schooling, but our Dimitrakis took to the letters real easy."

I lit a cigarette and tried to show I was listening. My mother also wore black dresses and black kerchiefs and always crossed herself when mentioning God and the saints. Both women seemed to be the same age, with the same wrinkles on their foreheads, only Mrs. Moskos looked much more delicate and frail than my mother.

She moved the basket with the knitting stuff to the other side of the table and folded her hands in front of her. A moment later, she moved the basket back to where it was before. I inhaled and was about to say something when she spoke again.

"My George, God rest his soul, died here, in the kitchen, over there." She crossed herself three times. "His heart gave out. It was in the middle of the lunch hour. He got a pain in his chest, bent over, and sat down on a box by the grill. We called the ambulance, but by the time they got him to the hospital, he was gone. Never been sick a day in his life, never been to the doctor one time. God rest his soul." She crossed herself again.

While Mrs. Moskos talked, I ran through my opening speech in my head. Before getting to the sale price and the payment terms, I planned to point out that the business had fallen off, and I was going to make a big deal of how hard it would be to bring the customers back.

"In some ways, people are like sheep," I planned to say. "Once they get in the habit of eating at one place, they keep going there without giving it too much thought. It takes a lot of money to turn a losing business around."

And I planned to point out that I knew about it firsthand because that's what I had to do with the restaurant I was already running, only I was working for someone else who was getting rich on my sweat. I would tell her that I'd like a chance to be my own boss, make a decent living, and maybe start a family later. That, plus a lot of similar "poor-mouthing," the main purpose of which is to lower the seller's expectations and bring the price down, was going to be the opening part of my negotiations. I had rehearsed the speech in my head over and over, and I was eager to start delivering it. But Mrs. Amalia kept talking and reminiscing, and I didn't feel right cutting her short.

"We were married on the island, on the Holy day of the Annunciation," she said. "Two days later we took the ocean liner *Olympia* and came to America. I have been working here alongside my George ever since. The last three years my legs have been hurting and I can't stand up for too long, but the medication I take for my arthritis makes me dizzy and I need to sit down. I just hope the Good Lord will keep me 'til I see my Dimitrakis with a good bride. Then I'll close my eyes and go to meet my George." She repositioned herself on the chair. "My Dimitrakis is very smart with the letters." She reached for her knitting basket.

"How much you want for the restaurant?" I took advantage of the pause.

"Oh, the shop," she said. "I forgot. I've been talking as if you were visiting. Whatever is fair. We aren't going to fight about it. My Dimitrakis was going to get some professional people to sell the place, but when he told me a Greek man came to look at it, I said I will wait. Some Cuban fellow was asking about it a couple of days back, but I thought it would be nice if it stayed in the hands of one of our own. I've been praying to the Virgin Mary and to Saint George to make it happen."

"That Cuban fellow was checking it out for me," I said. "He works at the shipyard. He's the one who told me about the place." I thought it would be a good idea to mention that early. The old lady and her son might jack up the price if they thought there were more buyers. All this godliness and saintliness and crossing herself could be a smokescreen.

I told her I would have an appraiser take a look at the place and asked how much they were paying for rent. I got the name and phone number of the building manager and stood to leave. She took my hand in both of hers again, and as she wished for God to be with me and for good luck with the people I had to speak to, it seemed she was about to burst into tears.

I said I would be back to see her soon.

CHAPTER TWENTY-ONE

Meeting a Diplomat

As soon as I left the Acropolis Restaurant, I called the building manager's number from the corner booth. I explained to a woman with an aristocratic accent who I was and, with quite a bit of effort, what I wanted. I wrote down the address she gave me and said, "You speak Mister Manager I come see him in ten minutes, okay?"

Twenty minutes later, I rang the bell on the wrought iron gate of a stucco villa by the canal. Mister Manager appeared on the patio as I was checking the address for a second time. Wearing a green jumpsuit, he seemed to be in his late sixties and was very bottom heavy. As he waddled toward me, a picture of a giant pear with legs came to my mind.

Extending a plump, pinkish hand, he gestured toward a table under a big banyan tree. "My name is Gooderich—Edward Gooderich," he said in a cheerful voice. "A transplanted Bostonian, retired from the diplomatic corps. You can call me Eddy. It's easier."

"My name is Kostas," I said.

"Pleased to meet you." On the table was a bowl of pistachios and a pitcher of something that looked like lemonade. "It's martini time," he said.

He offered me a glass, and I made a tossing gesture with it, then took a small sip. "I am here about the Acropolis Restaurant."

"Oh, yes. I do miss old Mr. Moskos," said Edward with a sigh. "He had been operating that restaurant for quite a few years before I came into the area. I used to tease him about getting such a young bride, but he said he was up to it, the rascal. I was very saddened when I heard he left us. He made the most extraordinary pastitsio and baklava and *cataifi* also." His tongue rolled the names of the pastries in his mouth as if he could taste the flavor, and his voice had the tone of a castaway reminiscing about a scrumptious dinner.

"How much time left on the lease of restaurant?" I asked.

"There are five years left on it. I know because I had to look it up the other day when I heard a Cuban gentleman was inquiring about the place. Are you also thinking of buying the place?"

"*I* am thinking of it; the Cuban gentleman was checking it for me." Julio must have come in his good suit.

"Somebody will end up buying it," said the manager, sipping his martini. "They aren't going to stay open long the way they operate. The boy is a good chap, but he does not have his father's intuition, and his interests are elsewhere. I could have the balance of the lease transferred to you if you are interested in acquiring the business."

"I'm interested in buying it, but I need some help with the rent. It is too much," I said.

"It's in line with other business rentals in the area," said the manager. "As a matter of fact, it's a bit low. You are right across the street from the shipyard—that's at least five hundred available customers. And I hear they will be signing a contract to build a big tanker any day now, so they'll be hiring additional personnel."

"Can't depend on that alone," I answered. "A guy can pull up with a roach coach at lunchtime and take away most of those five hundred *available customers*." I thought emphasizing the words would highlight their uncertainty.

"Pull up in a what?" the manager asked.

"In a lunch wagon. One of those portable restaurants."

"A *roach coach*, eh? That's a good one." Mr. Edward Gooderich burst into hearty laughter that came from deep down in his gut, giving the Jell-O in the green jumpsuit a vigorous shake. "That's the first time I heard it called that," he said. "A roach coach."

For a while we did some verbal seesawing, the manager singing the praises of the location and I trumpeting its faults.

In the end, Mr. Gooderich said, "I'll have to discuss it with my principals before I can give you an answer. I'm not authorized to go any lower than the current amount."

He reached for more nuts, but the bowl was empty, so he called to someone in the house for more. Almost immediately a tall woman in a white maid's uniform appeared with a full bowl.

"Will there be anything else, Mr. Gooderich?" she asked. I recognized the aristocratic voice from the telephone.

"What these people up north know about the Acropolis Restaurant?" I said when the maid had bowed and left. "They probably don't even know where the building is. Is *you* that will have to fight to collect the rent, and is *you* they will blame if something wrong. If I buy the restaurant, you are sure is going to be a good . . ." I tried to think of the word. "Is going to be a good *deal*, like before." The strain of trying to find the right words was giving me a headache. Good thing I had taken those English classes. "And you can have free supply of the best pastitsio and baklava in town. No limit," I added.

"Do you know how to make the . . . *ga-la-to-rico* I think it's called?" I noticed that Mr. Gooderich was looking at me with a sparkle in his eyes. I'd found a crack in the wall!

"*Galactopourico* and honey-drenched *cataifi* with walnuts are my specialty," I said. "And you can have *loukoumades* with honey and cinnamon for breakfast every day."

"I will discuss it with the owners when I meet with them," he said. "I'm flying to Boston tomorrow and will be meeting with my principals over the weekend. I could suggest we work an escalation clause into the lease."

"What you mean *close scales*?" It sounded alarming.

He smiled and explained. "Maybe we can start the rent low and go up a little every year."

"Yes, maybe we can do that."

The manager had some more nuts and poured another martini. "Touch base with me in a couple of days. I'll only be gone for a day."

I wasn't sure what I was supposed to touch. "When I speak to you again?"

"Telephone me two days from today. Today is Friday, and I come back from Boston Monday morning. You can call me then."

"Okay, I call you," I said.

⁘⁘⁘

I called him on Tuesday afternoon instead. It was part of my "show no eagerness strategy," which had resulted in doubling my cigarette consumption. Again, the one who answered the phone was the maid with the aristocratic accent and the fancy words, and I couldn't understand what she was talking about.

"You speak Mr. Eddy I will come to see him this afternoon, okay? You speak to him 'Kostas come this afternoon about the restaurant.' Okay?"

From her answer, all I understood was "okay."

The manager met me at his usual post under the banyan tree, the bowl of nuts and the martini pitcher by his side. "I was expecting to hear from you yesterday," he said. "I thought you had changed your mind."

He said he had spoken to the owners and they had agreed on a rent arrangement that he thought I would like. He handed me a folder with several typed pages in it and read the first page to me.

"The first year you pay this much, the second year you pay a little more, this much, then the third year a little more." He went down the page, underlining each payment amount with a ballpoint pen he held in his meaty fingers. "The rest of the pages are the standard commercial lease gobbledygook. You can keep this copy to study."

I took the folder and got up. "I will show this to my solicitor," I said.

I shook Mr. Eddy's soft hand, told him goodbye, and headed straight for the Acropolis. It was late in the evening and the restaurant was empty. The only customer was an old man sipping a cup of coffee and trying to flirt with Mrs. Amalia, who was knitting behind the counter. When she saw me walk in, she rose to greet me. She asked if I wanted coffee and suggested we sit at a table, gesturing to the one farthest from the counter. She brought the coffee and the knitting basket and sat down with a sigh. The vest she had been knitting had grown by about ten inches.

The flirting man got up from the counter in a disheartened kind of way and said, "See you later, Amy." Mrs. Amalia did not answer him.

"It's breaking my heart to part with this place," she said to me, "but my health is parting with me. I pray the Lord to keep me 'til I go back home one more time before I close my eyes."

"Two thousand up front is all I can come up with," I said. "That's every penny I have in the bank." Maybe the purpose of all that whining was to raise the price.

"My Dimitrakis says you can put something down and sign papers to pay so much a month for the rest."

"That's the only way I can do it. I can put two thousand down," I said. And for most of that I had Pete Papas to thank.

"I was a young girl when I set foot in this place," she said. "George, God rest his soul, brought me straight here after we got married. Never went anywhere after that. One time we went back to the island for two weeks, that's all. I'd love to go and take communion at the old church and to see the old house one more time before the Lord takes me. My sister says she has fixed up the house real nice with the money my George sent her."

I had heard all this before, but I couldn't bring myself to interrupt her.

"When would you like to sign the papers?" I asked when she reached for her knitting basket.

"You talk to my Dimitrakis for that. He knows all about these things." She picked up the needles and, with her thumbnail, counted the threads on the left needle, moving her lips with the numbers. "He is going to be a *proffesoras*. He will be teaching at the university soon."

I lit a cigarette.

"He was born one year after we got married," Mrs. Amalia went on. "I almost had him back there in the kitchen. The black woman washing the pots took me to the hospital. George—God forgive him—couldn't get away because it was in the middle of the lunch hour and we had no cook back then." She stopped and stared out the window. "Ah, how the years ran away." She sighed. "It seems like yesterday. I wanted to have a girl to help me in my old age, but the good Lord—"

"When can I see Dimitrakis?" I had to cut in.

"Oh, Dimitrakis is very busy with his studies and his schooling and his meetings with the book people. He never has time to work in the restaurant. He hardly even comes to church anymore."

"When can I see him?"

"I couldn't tell you for sure," she said. "He comes and goes all the time. I think he told me this afternoon he was going to be at a meeting with some book people at a *cafénio* a few blocks from here. He left me the phone number if I needed to call him."

With a groan, she got to her feet and went to the cash register, rocking from side to side as she walked. She pulled out a calling card and came back.

"This is the place where he goes on Tuesday and Thursday nights." She handed me the card and gave voice to her pain again as she sat down. "He always comes home late from there."

I glanced at the card. The Tenth Muse Coffeehouse. I remembered having a cup of coffee at that place a few days back when I was doing reconnaissance in the area. I'd thought the furniture in the place came from the city dump, and all the customers in there were hippies.

"All I pray is for God to keep me alive to see my island one more time. Just one more time, that's all." She crossed herself three times as she said it.

"I am going to stop by the *cafénio* and see him," I said, and stood to leave.

"You go talk to him and may God guide you—both of you," said Mrs. Amalia, groaning as she rose and walked me to the door.

When I got to the coffeehouse, I saw a chalk-written sign inside the door that read, *Tuesday is Poetry Night—Kavafi, Byron.*

I searched for a regular table and chair, and finding none, I sank into an old lounge chair next to a wooden crate that was supposed to be the table. I ordered coffee and watched Mrs. Amalia's son on a small stage, reading from a book about Ithaca, Cyclopes, and Poseidon. I recognized most of the words, but I couldn't make any sense out of what Dimitrakis was reading. When he finished, the motley audience clapped and congratulated him as if he had done something great. He seemed troubled when I walked up to him and said I was there to talk about the restaurant.

"This is not a good time," he said, almost in a whisper. "Come by the restaurant."

"Your mother say you are in the *cafénio*. Back home, that's where people sit and talk business."

"Come by the restaurant on Sunday. It will be quiet and we can talk."

"Okay, I will see you on Sunday," I said. "What time?"

"Come in the morning. I have a meeting in the afternoon."

"Okay, I come nine o'clock in the morning. I will bring my restaurant appraiser with me to have a look of the place. Okay?"

Dimitrakis said, "Okay."

On the drive back to Miami, I ran through the events of the evening and began to feel sorry for old Mrs. Amalia having raised such a fruitcake of a son. But then quickly I sent that thought away and reminded myself that you don't negotiate business from the heart.

⁜⁜⁜

Time seemed to move slower than stagnant water. I went about my work at the Parthenon in the usual way, but my mind was in Port Everglades inside the Acropolis Restaurant. I'd seen Mrs. Amalia's son at that *cafénio* with the weird customers on Tuesday. Why had he told me to come see him Sunday and not the next day? Was he trying to show that he wasn't in a hurry so he could keep the price high? He hadn't even given me the chance to ask how much they wanted to sell the business for. Was he perhaps talking to somebody else? Mrs. Amalia had said Dimitrakis was planning to get "some professional people" to handle the sale. Had he already done that? How much would these professional people be asking for it? It could be high. The place was clean and the equipment was in good shape. And it was in a damn good location.

All these thoughts ran through my head constantly.

"You are *muy nervioso, Griego*," Carmen said. "And you smoke too much."

"Opportunities like this don't come every day," I said.

While watching her refill the napkin holders, it occurred to me that when the Acropolis Restaurant was finally mine, it would be good to have Carmen with me. I was planning to keep the present crew for a while, but she was somebody I could trust. She could keep an eye on the rest of the help so they wouldn't carry the kitchen supplies home through the back door or pilfer the cash register every time I had to go to the bathroom.

Besides, most of the shipyard workers were Cuban, and she could help bring some of them in. All immigrants preferred to deal with their own kind instead of patronizing places where the help pretended they didn't understand what they said and acted as if they were doing them a favor by taking their money. Cubans had to eat too, and their dollars were just as good as anybody else's. I almost congratulated myself aloud for thinking of it and resolved to use all my persuasive talent to talk Carmen into leaving the Parthenon.

On Saturday morning, after Carmen had fed Grandfather his breakfast, I suggested we go for a long ride in my car.

"It's a nice day and we don't have to go to work," I said. "Good time to see some of Florida. We can take Grandfather and Julie too. It's a big car."

"You're proud of that car, aren't you, *Griego*?" Carmen cracked one of her rare smiles. "Maybe we should go for a little ride," she said. "We supposed to do things together; the immigration could still be watching. I go change." She came back a few minutes later. "It is better we leave Grandfather here," she said. "Julie will look after him. She has to stay and study."

We got in the car.

"How about going to Key West?" I suggested when we got rolling.

"No, no Key West." Carmen's sharp reply startled me.

"No like Key West?" I asked. "I wanted to see the long bridge going over the ocean. When I was on ships, somebody told me it was longer than the bridge across Lake Maracaibo."

"No Key West," she repeated. "The sea brings bad memories. Better we go west."

"Okay," I said and turned left onto Eighth Street. "We go west. Maybe we see some Indians and maybe some crocodiles."

"They call them alligators in America," she said.

"It is same animal, no?"

"I think so."

For a while neither of us spoke. I considered how to ask Carmen to come work for me and decided it would be better if we started talking about it when we were out of the city. There would be no distractions then.

As I drove west on the Tamiami Trail, I wished my brother were there to see the road. It was a perfect straight line, the end disappearing in some distant haze. The car glided so effortlessly and so smoothly along the paved surface that I could hardly tell we were moving. My hand, resting on top of the steering wheel, barely moved.

In Greece, straight stretches longer than a mile were in only a few storied places, and those who had traveled them talked about the experience with the same awe as those who had seen the Taj Mahal. The potholed gravel road connecting my village to the city of Volos was fifty-three twisting kilometers long and took the battered public bus four hours to cover. The longest straight section on that road was about fifty meters. Those who had made the trip before tried to sit by the window for the fresh air and always carried a lemon or an orange to smell along the way as prevention against car sickness. At the halfway point, the bus made a thirty-minute stop by a canteen with a thatched roof. Those whose innards were still in place snacked on fried cod patties, and drank ouzo. Others drank Epsa, the carbonated local lemonade, to settle their stomach, and the rest threw up and pledged candles to the Virgin Mary to spare their lives while promising never to take the trip again.

I lit a cigarette and waited for the right moment to bring up the work subject with Carmen. I believed that timing had everything to do with the success of a proposition. We were passing an area where the sugarcane fields on both sides of the road extended as far as the eye could see, and Carmen gazed out the window.

"Many people from Cuba work in these fields," she said.

Now is the right time.

"You know, Carmen," I said in a soft voice, "if I buy that restaurant in Port Everglades, I would like you to come with me."

She turned to face me but didn't say anything.

"We can ride together, like regular husband and wife," I added.

She still didn't answer and resumed looking out the window.

"Maybe better yet," I went on, "we move to Fort Lauderdale.

Maybe we find bigger apartment."

"*Griego,* you are *un problema grande,*" she said finally, still looking out the window.

I hadn't expected an answer like that, and I stumbled on my well-rehearsed proposition.

"Why I am problem?" I asked.

She faced me. "In Miami I know everybody in the building and everybody in the neighborhood. If I can't run home to check on Grandfather, there are two, three other people who will do it for me. In Port Everglades I know nobody. And Julie—how will she get to school?"

"Yes, I see that could be a problem," I said. "Maybe if we pay some woman in the building, she could watch Grandfather," I said after a while.

Carmen didn't answer.

"Señora Gonzales perhaps," I went on. "Or Señora Nilda from upstairs would be very happy for the extra money. What you think?"

"*Griego,* you no understand nothing." She faced me again. "I must come with you. There is no other choice. What you think *los pendejos* at the immigration will think when *you* buy restaurant in Port Everglades and *I* still work for Steve? And how you think Steve will like? I started work there three years ago because it is two blocks from where I live and because the woman he married was good friends with my family in Cuba. But if you go, I have no choice. I must come."

For a moment I felt deflated.

"But you will like, I'm sure," I said when I recovered.

She didn't reply, and for a while we both watched the road in silence.

"I have an idea," I said about ten miles later. "I pay you ten dollar a week more than Steve, and I give you ten percent of the profit."

Carmen took a cigarette from her purse and lit it. "Ten percent?" she repeated after exhaling.

"Yes. If the bookkeeper say at end of month that we make one thousand dollar profit, I give one hundred to you. We are partners."

I tried to put my arm on her shoulder, but she pulled away.

"Partners, eh?"

"Yes, partners."

"Okay, *partner*," she said and resumed looking ahead.

A few minutes later she tapped my shoulder.

"Partner, you think we can stop at that gas station and get a Coke?"

"Sure, partner," I said.

The sign at the store said *MICCOSUKEE INDIAN VILLAGE GENERAL STORE*. It seemed to be the only building around. I bought two Coca-Colas from a man dressed in blue jeans and a checkered red shirt.

"He no look Indian," I told Carmen as we walked back to the car.

"He is Indian all right. Not everybody wears feathers and paint." As we pulled out of the parking lot, she said, "Maybe we should be starting back. We are gone almost one hour. I forgot I needed to wash clothes today."

"We didn't see any crocodiles yet," I said as I turned toward Miami.

"Maybe next time."

As I drove, I watched her from the corner of my eye. She was a mystery to me. She watched over the old man and her niece as if they were toddlers taking their first steps, but she didn't seem to do anything for herself. It had taken some quite persuasive talking to get her to go out to dinner and a movie a few days back.

"We take Julie with us, okay?" she had finally said. "We tell her this is the reward for good grades, okay?"

The previous week, Julie brought home her report card with all As on it, and Carmen broadcasted it to everybody in the building. I asked what movie she wanted to see, and she suggested *My Fair Lady*.

"Somebody at the restaurant said it was funny," she told me.

That evening she wore the same dress she'd worn at our "wedding ceremony" and put on the pearls I'd bought for her in Nassau. She looked beautiful, elegant, and dignified, and as heads turned to look at us, I basked in her glow. She was nice and sweet during the dinner and laughed a lot during the movie. Occasionally she nudged her niece and said, "Pay attention, you'll learn something."

I suspected that was why she had chosen the film—so Julie would *learn something,* but I couldn't figure out what that could be. The singing was goofy, and I hadn't heard anybody around Miami speak the kind of English they spoke in that movie. At one point, when Carmen's laughter at Eliza's efforts to satisfy Mr. Higgins seemed unrestrained, I got optimistic and wrapped my arm around her shoulder and squeezed her close to me. She gently lifted my arm and placed it on my knee.

"Remember the agreement," she whispered and patted the top of my hand.

"I couldn't resist it," I said. "You look very pretty tonight."

She patted the top of my hand again.

Yes, Carmen was a mystery for sure.

CHAPTER TWENTY-TWO

The Negotiations

When Sunday finally came, I was up and ready to get on the road before sunrise. I didn't know of any business appraisers, and I probably couldn't afford them if I did, so I asked Albert, the man from the telephone company who had gotten me the security job, if he would come with me.

"I'll be glad to," Albert said. "On Sundays the wife likes me to do chores around the house. This sounds more fun than hanging curtains and moving furniture."

On the way to the restaurant, I coached Albert on what a restaurant appraiser should be checking, and when we arrived he went about his tasks like an expert. He turned the meat slicer on and off and frowned at the stickiness of the switch, read the freezer temperature, and counted the heads on the soft-drink dispenser, all the while scribbling on a notepad and maintaining the expression of a bored, hard-to-impress inspector.

At one point he called me over and pointed at the potato peeler.

"What do you call that gizmo?" he whispered, pretending to write something in his notebook.

When the "inspection" was over, Albert and I stepped outside for a whispering, head-nodding "conference"; then Albert said he was going across the street to "look at the big boats at the shipyard." I returned to the restaurant, wondering why Dimitrakis had wanted to meet me on Sunday, almost a whole week since our last meeting. Was it so his "intermediary" would have time to look the place over?

Even if that's the case, Mr. Dimitrakis, you haven't seen price haggling as you're about to see.

Dimitrakis had been sitting at a table reading a book throughout all of this. He raised his head when he heard the bell above the door.

"Could you please lock the door behind you?" he said.

I turned the key, then sat across from him. I lit a cigarette and opened the briefcase I had borrowed from Carmen's niece, pulling out a yellow pad to put next to the "appraiser's" notepad. I was going to "consult his notes" during the negotiations and casually point out the deficiencies that the inspection had uncovered.

I had been running through my head the myriad of imperfections I would bombard the future *proffesoras* with in order to bring the price down to where I could afford it. This was a chance of a lifetime; something like this might never come my way again. For Julio to casually mention to his friends that fateful night on the porch that a restaurant across from the shipyard might be closing soon—when he could have been talking about *cabrón* Fidel like he did on most other nights—and for me to happen to be passing by and overhear him, was an *omen*, a clear signal to me from God that I was still "in the light."

I took a deep puff on my cigarette and started. "From what I saw—"

Two men tried to come in the restaurant. Finding the door locked, they knocked on the glass, and one of them mouthed "*kaffe*" while signaling a drinking motion with his hand.

Dimitrakis stood and walked to the door. "Closed. *Klisto*," he said through the glass and pointed to the *CLOSED* sign hanging from the door handle. The men mumbled something in Greek and walked away. "Merchant seamen," Dimitrakis said as he sat again. "There's a Greek ship at the shipyard."

Another omen. Wouldn't it be something if some of my old shipmates showed up someday?

I cleared my throat and started again with what I hoped was a firm voice. "Well, about the business here, from what I saw—and my people and the appraiser that inspected the place agree—the condition of some of the equipment is not—"

"You say to Mother you put down two thousand dollars and then make payment every one month," Dimitrakis interrupted in Greek. "I received the freedom to sketch one simple agreement of the sale." He put two typed pages in front of me. "You see here, the total sale price of the business is five thousand dollars. If we pull out the two thousand you pay first, will remain balance three thousand. You pay $138.43 every month for two years—that is twenty-four months. It includes interest of ten percent, and the payment totals $3,022.32." As he spoke, his finger pointed out the numbers on each line.

I tried to think of something to say. Dimitrakis had surprised me. He hadn't given me the chance to say even one of the many degrading speeches I had rehearsed in my head all week. It was as if after fussing and agonizing about the right fishing tackle and the right bait, I had rowed to the fishing spot and the fish jumped into the boat before I cast my line.

People in Greece would probably laugh at the way the future *proffesoras* seemed to make the sentences in his head, then translate them into Greek before spitting them out, but there was nothing laughable about what he had put on paper. The numbers were exactly five hundred less than I had estimated it would cost to buy the business. I pulled on my cigarette and pretended to study the pages.

"The fan motor of the walk-in cooler sounds worn out," I said, "and the heating element of the fryer seems—"

"I had been planning to engage a business intermediary for the sale of the restaurant," Dimitrakis interrupted again. "They could bring a price very much more bigger than this." He tapped on the numbers with his finger. "But you appeared and Mother prefers someone from the home country to have it. She cried for hours the past week when she think I possibly make agreement with the Cuban."

I kept doodling on the yellow pad.

Dimitrakis took a sip of his Coca-Cola. "I guess Mother sees in you something I don't have—the desire to stay in the restaurant business," he said, switching to English. "You probably remind her of my father when he was starting out." He took another sip. "I don't really care. All I want is for her to get some comfort in her sunset years. Poor woman hasn't known much leisure or joy in her life. I guess my father went to the island with his pockets full of American dollars, enlisted the services of a busybody matchmaker, then sat back and chose among the matchmaker's inventory of girls desperate to get away from the hard life of the island. He chose the one who seemed of healthy stock and would be grateful and content. I bet that matchmaker got a nice tip for her find."

He took another sip and was silent a few moments before going on.

"I told both my parents a long time ago that I wouldn't be in this business for all the money in the world. Restaurants keep you tethered to the kitchen and slowly suck the life out of you. The way I see it, it's the modern form of human slavery. Ever since I can remember, my old man spoke of longing to visit the island but couldn't do it because he was afraid if he closed the restaurant for a month, he would lose the customers. And look at my mother—she looks like she's a hundred years old. You know she's only sixty-five? Father brought her from the island and put her straight in that kitchen.

"After he died I kept telling her, 'We have enough money now. And besides, I'm going to be getting my teaching certificate soon. Let's sell the place so you can rest a little.' But she worried what my father would say. Now that somebody from the 'old country, like her George' has come along, I finally convinced her to do it."

He stopped as if waiting for me to say something. When I didn't, he stood.

"It would be nice if you promised her you'll be going to church to light a candle on Saint George's day," he said. He pushed the two pages toward me. "Take these papers with you and let . . . *your people* look them over. If I don't hear from you by Wednesday evening, I'll assign it to the business intermediary. Mother might cry some, but after a month on the island I'm sure she will be okay."

He walked to the counter and put the empty Coke bottle in the crate, then went to unlock the front door. I understood the hint and put the yellow pad, the notebook, and the two contract pages in the briefcase and got up.

"I will call you," I said and shook his hand. At the door I paused and added, "I will call sometime this week. Are you going to be here all the time?"

"This is the period of my final examinations," he replied. "I'll only be here in the afternoons after four o'clock. The rest of the day I have classes."

"Okay," I said.

Outside, Albert was standing by the shipyard fence, looking at the ships. I beeped the horn and he came over.

"How did it go?" he asked as he got in the car.

"You did good job," I said.

While waiting for the light to change on Eller Drive, I turned to Albert. "What you say we go home down A1A? Today I no feel fighting the traffic of the interstate."

"You read my mind, Gus," he said. "I like looking at the water. I do it every chance I get."

"I like also," I said. "But I no like you call me Gus. Kostas is same easy and sound better."

He laughed. "You got it, my friend. Kostas it is."

The light changed and I turned left on US 1, then left again toward A1A. While I drove, I ran the meeting with Dimitrakis through my head. Sometimes you think you have figured a person out only to discover you've been way off target. It didn't happen to me often, but this time I had figured the future *proffesoras* completely wrong. He was not a fruitcake at all—quite the opposite, in fact. He knew exactly what he was doing. He didn't want to run the restaurant but kept it open until he sold it because you get more money when you sell a running business instead of a truckload of used restaurant equipment. He was going to list it with a business broker, an "intermediary," and probably would have gotten a lot more from some Canadian or New Yorker with deep pockets who was looking for an excuse to get out of the freezing North, but instead he seemed willing to accept less because his mother liked somebody from the old country. That showed his respect and consideration for her feelings.

Maybe poetry people were not a bunch of goofy stargazers after all. His Greek would make somebody from Greece laugh, but maybe that was a smokescreen too—who knows? Maybe Professor Dimitrakis had figured out that people dropped their guard when they thought they were talking to someone less smart than they were. The way he had said "let your people look them over" when he'd handed me the sales-agreement papers he had "received the freedom to sketch" made me think he had seen through me and knew that "my people" didn't exist.

But there was one thing the poetic *proffesoras* had all wrong. He'd said restaurant work was a modern form of human slavery. The way I saw it, anybody could read books and learn from them to become a lawyer or an engineer, but to be a good cook took God-given talent.

No other profession offered the gratification that cooking did. When a man who ran a jackhammer all day came to your place for a half-hour lunch, ate the food you put in front of him, and belched loud enough to crack the ceiling plaster, and you heard him tell the waitress that it was the best chili he'd ever eaten, that, Mr. Future

Proffessoras, was real gratification. It made the customer happy, and he would go back to work and do a better job, which would make his boss happy. It made the waitress glad for the extra quarter tip and made the cook feel good inside because they knew they'd done something good for mankind. It was a fine, satisfying feeling, much more satisfying than the polite clapping of an audience when they heard you read about "voyaging to Ithaka." On the scale of life's priorities, in my opinion, cooking was at the very top of the list, right up there with doctoring and farming. After all, nobody's life was threatened because the lines of a poem didn't rhyme or the Miami Dolphins lost the game or because the good guy didn't get to marry the pretty girl in some movie.

"There's a good spot up ahead where we can pull over and look at the water," Albert said, snapping me from my thoughts. When we reached the place, I parked the car and Albert got out.

"I'll go get us a Coke," he said.

I lit a cigarette and stared at a distant ship heading south. Was I doing the right thing? I had spent all the money I'd saved—and some borrowed money on top of that—for a used car that I didn't know how long would last, even if it had been owned by a rich old lady. Now I was about to borrow more to give to somebody I had never met before, and I was going to sign papers promising to make payments for years to come in order to buy his business. I had no way of knowing if it would turn out all right.

The distant ship was a tanker, similar to the one I had been on not too long ago. I thought of my old shipmates and the life as a merchant seaman and wondered what I would be doing now if I hadn't jumped ship. Probably I'd be like most people who lived secure, predictable lives on ships and then retired to draw meager pensions, frittering away their days at coffeehouses, twirling their worry beads, and telling embellished stories of their lives over and over.

Was going against the tide of ordinary people's expectations wrong? I had known many men who had migrated elsewhere and tried to make it and failed. They'd returned home poor and dispirited and the source of endless jokes. I always felt admiration for those men and anger for the ones doing the taunting—the ones who didn't have the balls to climb out of their rut.

Knowing you're a failure has to be the most cruel punishment. I flicked my cigarette toward the water. In some ways, the Cubans and the Haitians were lucky. They had been forced to leave their homes.

"They didn't have it in cans," Albert said, handing me a bottle of Coke. "Drink it and I'll take them back inside to get my deposit."

"Cheers," I said, and we clinked our bottles.

"Good luck with your deal." Albert took a long sip. "Ah, that sure hits the spot. That's a big boat out there." He pointed to the tanker with his bottle. "Was the one you were on that big?"

"Yep, maybe bigger."

As soon as I got home, I sat down and wrote a check for one thousand dollars. After looking up the spelling of the words in the dictionary, I wrote *buy restaurant Acropolis* next to the word *For* on the bottom left corner. It was the second check I had written out of my brand-new checkbook. Four weeks earlier, Pete Papas had gone with me to Miami Federal and helped me open an account.

"You be nice to this man," Pete had told the stiff, middle-aged woman behind the desk. "This man will be putting plenty of money in your bank."

"We value all our customers, large as well as small depositors," she said, and looking at Pete over her glasses, she asked, "How does he want his name to appear in the checks?"

I handed her a slip of paper on which I had written my name and Carmen's house address. From the samples the old-maidish bank lady showed me, I picked the plain light blue with a white curvy line around the border that looked like the Grecian key. It seemed more serious, more businesslike than the ones showing sunsets and palm trees and beaches with seashells and starfish.

When the checkbooks arrived, I spent a long time examining

them. *KOSTAS KARAS* appeared on the upper left-hand corner in bold, dark-blue letters. A feeling I didn't know came over me, but it made me feel that I was somebody.

In my next letter home, I had enclosed the first check—thirty dollars made out in Mother's name. *Since you have an account with the Post Office Bank, they shouldn't have any trouble cashing it,* I wrote. *I've been very busy lately and didn't have time to get a money order.*

As I sealed the envelope, I pictured Thimios—my gossipy old schoolmate who, through some political connections, had finagled the position of post office clerk—reading aloud my name and the amount in English. My mother would be beaming as she explained to him that I had changed my name because the Americans had difficulty saying Konstandinos Karaoglou. And she would probably go on to describe how her smart son was prospering in the country of the not-as-smart-as-him Americans.

⁂

On Monday morning, I telephoned Dimitrakis and said I would bring him the check on Tuesday. I skipped the adult English class Tuesday evening and drove to Port Everglades. In the parking lot of the Acropolis, I took a final look at the check, then got out of the car and went inside.

Dimitrakis was reading a book by the cash register. I handed him the check, saying I would give him the other thousand when we signed the papers. He wrote out a receipt and said he would call me sometime the next week, when the lawyer had the contract ready.

"Call me between two and four," I said. "It's quieter then." Actually, those were the hours Steve was away from the Parthenon.

Outside, before cranking the car, I read the receipt again. Dimitrakis had written *For purchase of restaurant business* on the blank line. I tried to imagine Steve's face when I told him tomorrow that I was not going to work at his place anymore, and I burst out laughing. I started the car and searched for music on the radio, but none of the songs felt right, so I turned it off and sang an old Greek folk song. The lyrics had nothing to do with restaurants or business or feelings of elation, but it was a fast-moving tune supposedly sung by brave freedom fighters. Soon I was singing at the top of my voice. At the traffic light, I noticed an elderly woman staring at me as I belted out a high note. I didn't care.

I was the king of the world.

Dimitrakis called me the next afternoon. "Would it be possible to meet at two o'clock at the lawyer's office this approaching Friday?"

I said it would, and he gave me the address.

On Thursday, after the restaurant closed and all the help had left, I approached Steve as he emptied the cash register and told him that Carmen and I were quitting. He looked stunned and stared at me a moment, as if trying to see inside my head—then unleashed a torrent of threats and cuss words. I told him I didn't blame him for being upset and I regretted the short notice, but it was an opportunity I couldn't pass up.

⁂

I left Miami soon after breakfast, just in case there was too much traffic on the road to Fort Lauderdale, and I was parked at my destination almost an hour before the appointment. Mrs. Amalia cried the whole time we were at the lawyer's office. It was a quiet, barely audible cry, and she kept drying her eyes with a handkerchief. She had worn her "church clothes" for the occasion—a two-piece black dress, a black kerchief, and a shiny black purse. After the papers were signed, she kissed me on both cheeks. With tears running down her face, she wished me success and happiness. Her hands were shaking as she gave me the two sets of keys for the place.

"The lock of the back door sticks sometimes," she said and quickly dried her eyes.

It was Friday afternoon, the twenty-fifth of February, 1967. One year and four months from the day I had jumped ship in Hoboken.

CHAPTER TWENTY-THREE

We Are Open for Business!

I went to bed early on Friday, the same time Carmen's grandfather went to lie on his cot, because I planned to start working early at *my* restaurant the next day. After lots of tossing and turning, I finally gave up on sleeping, put my clothes on, and tiptoed out of the room.

I sat in the old man's chair under the porch light and lit a cigarette. The magnitude of what I was getting into was dawning on me. Maybe I should have waited a little longer. I was only twenty-six, so waiting another year wouldn't matter that much. I would have saved more money by then, and I would know the language better.

I went in the kitchen and looked for paper and pencil. I found a pen that probably belonged to Carmen's niece, but the only paper I saw was a McDonald's bag in the trash can. I went back out to the old man's chair, smoothed out the McDonald's bag, and started to write.

Payment to Dimitrakis for restaurant: $138.43 every month
Payment to Pete for loan for car, for restaurant and for wedding: $130.00 every month
Payment for rent of restaurant: $145.50 every month
Payment to Carmen for rent: $65.00 every month
Total of payments: $478.93 every month

I stared at the total. Almost five hundred dollars I had to pay every month, and that didn't include lights, gas, water, supplies, and a whole lot of other expenses that went with the operation of a restaurant. Maybe life in the cocoon of the ship was not that bad. *What was I thinking?* Of course, the loan payments to Dimitrakis and Pete were going to be finished in two years, but would I be able to last that long?

Well, it's done, I said to myself. Second-guessing it would only make the job harder.

I got in the car and drove to Port Everglades. Daybreak found me at the Acropolis Restaurant, moving chairs and rearranging tables in the dining room. Around ten o'clock, I stood back, wiped the perspiration from my face with a dishtowel, and appraised the new look.

Yes, that was much better. I had repositioned the tables and created a corridor so the waitresses wouldn't have to zigzag all over the dining room to get to the customers. The new arrangement also opened room to put two more tables, three if I moved the gift case out of the way. I lit a cigarette and after a couple of puffs remembered that I hadn't had any coffee yet. Searching under the counter, I found the coffee packets and got a pot going, then took inventory of the water glasses and the coffee cups on the shelf.

I poured myself a cup of coffee and sat at the end of the counter. I scanned the entire area, reveling in the fact that all of this was mine now—even if I was in debt up to my ears. Before I came to America, I hadn't owned anything bigger than a suitcase. Now I had my own car and was the proprietor of a restaurant. I was a businessman. I was like Steve and the cheapskate Taso Krasas, the owner of the Zephyros Tavern in Volos. And in some ways I was like Mr. Klapsis, the owner of the *Aegean Sea*. Now I had earned the right to participate in conversations about things like the high taxes, the unreliable help, and the government meddling in a person's business.

Right then I had less than thirty dollars in my pocket, but I felt like I could hug the world. I was on my way up—the master of my destiny.

I finished my coffee and went back to the kitchen to find ingredients for *arroz con pollo*, which was going to be Monday's main dish. I planned to stretch the existing food inventory and use whatever money the cash register collected during the day to buy the supplies I needed from the Food Fair until I opened accounts with the restaurant vendors. Most of the large-volume buying would be done after I got to know my customers anyway.

For now, a good cleaning from top to bottom would have to do. I drained the oil and cleaned the inside of the fryer. There were at least four inches of leftover food in the bottom of it—dried and blackened bits of shrimp, fish, fried potatoes, and everything else that went through the fryer of a restaurant. Whoever did the cooking needed a good talking-to. It must've been months since the thing had been cleaned.

I was about to start refilling the fryer with new lard when I heard tapping on the glass of the front door. It was Carmen in her housecleaning clothes.

"The shipyard called Julio to work overtime, so I got a ride with him," she said. "I thought you could use the help if you plan to open Monday."

"But on Saturdays you do the housework," I said.

"It can wait."

"How about the grandfather?"

"Julie will look after him." She came in and got busy filling the mop bucket with water.

I watched her with admiration. She was not obligated to do any of this.

"Carmen, you are an okay woman." I tried to think of something that expressed better what I meant, but that was the best I could come up with.

"I know it," she answered.

"When I finish in kitchen, I'll come to help you," I said and returned to checking the supplies.

In the bottom of a box with ten cans of green beans, I found a half-empty bottle of McCormick vodka. If it had belonged to the dishwasher, it would've been hidden among the cleaning supplies. This was the cook's territory. I held it up and marked the level of the liquid on the label with my thumbnail before putting it back.

We worked, totally absorbed in what we were doing, hardly exchanging any words between us. When Julio tapped at the door to ask if Carmen wanted a ride home, I was surprised to realize the day was almost over. I heard Carmen tell Julio she would be riding with me.

"We will be leaving soon also," I called from the kitchen.

By the time we were ready to leave, Carmen had mopped the dining room, and she'd cleaned and rearranged to her liking the storage area behind the counter. I had organized the kitchen, boiled a pot of potatoes to be used Monday as "home fries" with the breakfast instead of the frozen kind, and I'd made a trial batch of rice pudding. After tasting it and judging it *almost* as good as Mother's, I poured it into five 24-ounce bowls and placed them in the refrigerator.

On the return drive to Miami, I took the coastal road. Halfway home I turned to Carmen and said, "We did plenty work today. Want to stop for Coca-Cola at place by the water?"

She chuckled. "*Griego*, you are big spender, but I'm too dirty and too tired for that."

"Okay, you tired. What you like to eat tonight?"

"Anything," she said. "Let's get some Kentucky Fried Chicken. It's on the way home."

⁜⁜⁜

On Sunday I was up early again. Carmen offered to join me if I could wait for her to finish feeding her grandfather, but I said she didn't need to.

"You worked enough for two days yesterday," I said.

I spent most of the day cleaning the freezer and the refrigerator and rearranging things in the kitchen. At the end of the day, I took two bowls of the rice pudding I'd made the day before, dusted some cinnamon in the shape of a smiley face over them, and put each in a box. I stopped at the building manager's house and gave him one of the boxes and the rent check for March. After peeking inside the box, the jolly manager poured out the thank-yous in a torrent.

I gave the other bowl of pudding to Carmen. "I saw you feeding the old man pudding. See if he likes this one," I said.

I tried to get some sleep because I would need my strength the next day, but I couldn't. Questions pounded my head, demanding answers. Would there be enough customers to cover the expenses? Would I collect enough cash to buy what I needed until I got credit from the suppliers? Would anybody order the *arroz con pollo* special? Would the help show up? Was the help any good? Was the half bottle of vodka hidden among the bean cans really the cook's? What would happen if I had three bad days in a row? Even a dead person couldn't get to sleep with so many cares in his head.

On Monday, I was on the road again before daybreak. The plan was for Carmen to get a ride with Julio in the mornings and return with me in the evenings, but this morning she was waiting for me by the car.

"I figured you'll need the extra help the first day," she said.

I told her I appreciated her offer.

At the restaurant, we got busy preparing for the breakfast rush. I lit the grill, then took the potatoes I had boiled on Sunday out of the refrigerator and sliced them.

"Where you keep the English muffins?" Carmen was in the kitchen looking for them.

"Damn, I forgot, we don't have any," I said. "I was going to get some on the way here."

"Someone might ask for it; lots of people like them for breakfast. I'll go to the store and get a small box," she said.

"I'm glad you came," I said and handed her the keys and my only ten-dollar bill.

"I'll get a box of donuts too, then," she said and left.

I checked the temperature of the grill and adjusted the gas, then laid six strips of bacon on it and put the steak weight on top of them. Soon the sizzling sound filled the kitchen. I took a couple of deep breaths. To me, the breakfasty smell of a restaurant was like smelling spring flowers. I moved the crate with the eggs closer to the grill and the loaves of sliced bread closer to the toaster so they would be easier to reach. I turned on the dining room lights and checked the coffee, then stood behind the counter and looked out.

Through the entrance-door glass, I could see almost to the end of Twenty-Second Street. I counted five cars going toward the port. Two freighters were in the harbor, and some of the stevedores unloading them might stop for breakfast. Julio had said that besides the Greek freighter in for repairs, the shipyard received an order to build a tanker for Shell Oil and had hired a bunch of new people.

Things are going to work out. No need to worry.

I wondered who my first customer would be. Would it be someone who would bring good fortune, or a goat-footed one? In our village on New Year's Day, every household was anxious about who their first visitor would be. If it was someone they considered the bearer of good luck, the home would have good luck the rest of the year. As a rule, persons with good looks, good health, and those well-to-do were considered good-luck bearers. Poor, crippled, and squalid-looking persons were considered bad luck and were called "goat-footed."

In the superstition-saturated culture of our village, everything that happened first—the first person one saw in the morning, the first basket of harvested crop, the first sale, the first customer—was taken as the forecast of what would follow.

I went back in the kitchen and moved the cooked bacon to the coolest corner of the grill, then placed five more strips on it. I spread the bacon grease on the hot surface and scattered the sliced potato pieces on it.

"Hello, hello! Anybody here?"

A hoarse voice, barely understandable, almost made me drop the spatula. I wiped my hands on the apron and went to look. When I glanced at the door, I froze at the sight of my first customer.

What did I do to deserve this?

Curses of the most robust kind, collected through years of waterfront experience, sped upward, eager to jump out of my mouth. *So much for good luck.* Standing in front of me was a scruffy middle-aged woman wearing a hat that looked like an upturned flowerpot with plastic cherries pinned to one side. Her dress, a tattered piece of cloth with faded, large red roses on it, seemed to be held together by a million safety pins. A shopping cart from the Food Fair rested against the entrance door, loaded with what looked like blankets and cardboard boxes.

"The kitchen not yet open," I shouted through the glass, but it seemed she couldn't hear me. I opened the door and said it again.

"Young man, you don't know to whom you are talking. I am the Grand Duchess Nikolaevna Romanov," she said, raising her right hand as if to emphasize her point. I took a step back, out of range of the saliva bombardment launched through the gaps of her missing teeth. She looked frail and swayed slightly back and forth as she held on to the shopping cart. A pair of tired eyes sunken deep in her skull stared back at me with a plain, matter-of-fact stare—none of the sparkle that betrayed mischief or the fake seriousness of a hustler.

She believes it. She really believes she is a duchess.

I said, "I give you some food and you go eat in park, okay?"

I went in the kitchen and cracked two eggs on the grill and put two slices of bread in the toaster. As I scrambled the eggs with the spatula, I told myself that at least this was a good chance to check how everything worked. I put the eggs in a carryout plate with the toast, two pieces of bacon, and a scoop of the home-fried potatoes. On the way out of the kitchen, I filled a Styrofoam cup with coffee.

"Now push your house to the park, okay, Duchess?" I wedged the plate and the cup between a hairy coat and a trash bag in her shopping cart. "Sit on bench, look at water, and eat breakfast like first-class tourist, okay?"

"Thank you, young man. My butler will settle the account later."

Carmen pulled up as I watched the grand duchess push her cart down the road. "Who was that?"

"Our first customer, the Grand Duchess Romanov. Damn." I kicked an imaginary pebble.

"That's good. In Cuba that means good luck," said Carmen.

"Is it really or you just say it?"

"Does it make any difference?"

I didn't answer. I straightened the cardboard sign taped to the door announcing *NEW MANAGEMENT* and went back inside.

Mrs. Amalia walked in ten minutes later. "It wasn't until after I paid the taxi that I remembered I didn't need to come anymore," she said and started crying. Dressed in black as she was, slightly bent and advancing in short steps, I thought for an instant I was seeing my mother walking across the dining room.

"I was hoping you would come," I said. "Can I get you some coffee?" I pulled a chair for her at the table nearest to the counter, and Carmen brought her a cup of coffee.

Mrs. Amalia reached for the cup but started crying and pulled out her handkerchief instead. "I feel awkward just sitting here and being waited on like a stranger."

"I like for you to try my home fries and tell me what you think," I said. "Maybe I fix some eggs to go with them?"

She looked toward the kitchen. "I see the cook has not come in yet."

"I'll cook them for you," I said. "How you like your eggs?"

"Just one egg, scrambled," she said, almost in a whisper, as if embarrassed.

"You didn't tell anyone about the restaurant changing hands?" I asked from the kitchen.

"No, and I told Dimitrakis not to say anything either. You said you didn't want the help to know."

"Yes, I'll tell them when they come in today."

I put the egg and fries in a plate with two triangles of toast and two packets of jelly and set it on the serving window, then walked around and sat next to Mrs. Amalia.

"It feels strange sitting here and being served," she said again when Carmen set the plate in front of her. After Carmen was gone, Mrs. Amalia said, "Nice girl. Is she Greek?"

"Almost," I said.

I told her about my first customer. "I'm glad you gave her some food. She's been coming here for years," she said. "It's a sad story."

Mrs. Amalia started on her food with small, exploratory bites. Every time I looked in her direction, she tried to smile and nod approval of the meal.

"These potatoes taste just like my George's," she said.

"What did he put in them?" I hurried to ask, seeing that she was about to cry again.

"He used to slice an onion real thin and mix it in with the potatoes." She seemed uncomfortable in her chair and put down her coffee cup. "It doesn't feel right just sitting here doing nothing."

"You have done plenty, *Kyra* Amalia," I heard myself saying. "Not many mothers in Skiathos have a *proffessoras* for a son."

"I guess now I'll have the time to help the church with the cooking for the bazaar," she said as she stood. "I'll call Dimitrakis to pick me up. He should be awake by now." She took a coin from her purse and walked to the pay phone. On the way back to her table, she paused and scanned the dining area. "You made the place look bigger."

"I'm going to put in two more tables," I said. "Maybe three if I take out the souvenir case."

Mrs. Amalia looked at the display case. "It would be just right for the gift shop at the church," she said after some thought.

"They can have it if they haul it off," I said.

"That's very nice of you. I'll tell them. I'm sure they'll be glad to have it," she said. "The bazaar is next week. You should come. We have lots of nice Greek girls in our church."

A few minutes later, a car horn beeped outside—two short double beeps.

"That's Dimitrakis." Mrs. Amalia got up. At the door she paused and scanned the dining room one more time, and I thought I saw her lips move. In a choking voice, she wished me prosperous business and walked out.

The first food-ordering, money-paying customer came in soon after Mrs. Amalia left. It was a grumpy, bald man around fifty who sat at the counter and ordered coffee and an English muffin with jelly.

"Make it dark but don't burn it," he said. "And hurry it up. I'm running late."

I set the coffee in front of him and soon brought the muffin with one packet of butter and two packets of jelly.

"Give me some grape jelly," the man called a minute later. "I don't like this strawberry junk."

I brought him the jelly and he spread it on his muffin with hurried moves. He was finished within minutes. He put a one-dollar bill and a dime next to his plate and left.

I cleared the counter and rang up the sale. I held the dollar with both hands: it was crisp, almost new. George Washington looked at me straight in the eyes, and there seemed to be a hint of a smile on him. *A good omen*. The first dollar of my first day in business in America. I was going to frame this one.

Sebastian, the Haitian dishwasher, came in a few minutes before seven o'clock.

The cook came around nine. “Morning, Seb,” she said to the dishwasher. “My fucking alarm didn’t go off again.” I was flipping potatoes on the grill and she stared at me. “Who are you?”

“I’m Kostas Karaoglou,” I said. “I’m the new owner.”

She smirked like she thought I was joking. “Yeah, sure. Where’s Amalia?”

“She was here earlier but went home,” I said. “I asked her not to say anything about the sale. We signed the papers last Friday.”

“Don’t feel like playing games,” she said. “I’m getting to the bottom of this shit.”

She tramped out of the kitchen toward the pay phone and came back a few minutes later, smoking a cigarette and looking deflated.

“That’s gratitude for you,” she said to no one in particular. “Been cooking for this place for over a year, and none of them said a word about it to me.” She looked at me. “Want me to stay?”

“Yes,” I said. “What’s your name?”

“It’s Gianni.”

“I have a nephew named Gianni,” I said. “He’s my brother’s oldest.”

“Mine is short for Giannoula. I’m George’s second cousin. Is there anything you want me to do different?”

“No,” I said. “Just do your usual. I’ve started chicken with rice. Keep an eye on it.”

Gianni was a tall, stout woman of about forty-five, with short black hair, heavily tanned skin, a Mediterranean mustache, and a big nose. She wore blue jeans and a corduroy shirt with rolled-up sleeves. She bombarded the Haitian dishwasher with orders and moved around the kitchen with the air of someone who had the run of the place.

There had been only three breakfast customers so far, and all they had ordered was coffee with toast with jelly. I had begun to think I would have to eat the cooked bacon and the potatoes myself when the little bell above the door started ringing. Four shipyard workers walked in and ordered breakfast.

"Bacon and eggs over easy, with the works," said the biggest of the four, and the other three nodded agreeably.

I loaded their plates with extra scoops of my version of home-fried potatoes, and everyone raved about them.

When he paid his bill, the one who had done the ordering said, "Now that's what I call a working man's breakfast."

"Thank you," I said. "You speak your friends also. Okay, buddy?" I had heard that word often before and surmised that Americans use "buddy" in place of "good friend."

As the men got to the door, a light rain began to fall. "Think it's going to last?" the shortest one asked the biggest.

"Nah, it won't even keep the dust down. It's clearing already—look." He pointed to a blue hole in the sky.

The lunch hour crowd was sparse, too. Carmen worked the dining room area, and I took care of the counter and the cash register and keeping an eye on the activity in the kitchen. Most of the orders were for hamburgers, shrimp, and fish that could be cooked in the fryer. The pan of pastitsio I had taken out of the freezer went untouched. I guessed I'd be sharing that one with the grand duchess. I also noticed that most of the customers had not touched the dehydrated mashed potatoes we served as a side dish.

"From tomorrow, we make real mashed potatoes," I told Gianni, who stood by the worktable, sipping on a glass of orange juice.

"I've been making mashed potatoes this way ever since I've been here and nobody has known the difference. They taste the same and it's a lot less fuss." She put the glass on the table with a little too much force, as if she had misjudged the distance. "It's just slow because of the rain. Everybody goes home when it rains—shipyard workers, stevedores, everybody."

She seemed to have trouble rolling her tongue around words with *R*s in them. When she turned and marched to the bathroom, I peeked at the vodka bottle among the bean cans. The level was about two fingers below my thumbnail mark.

At the end of the day, I counted the money in the cash register, then got a Coke and sat at a table across from Carmen. "Not bad for the first day, hey?"

"Mister Partner," she said, "we have to make some changes and make them quick if you're going to pay back what you borrowed."

I readjusted myself on the seat. "What changes are you thinking?"

"First we need to change some of the dishes," she said. "The customers here don't know anything about Athenian beans, pastitsio, and mousaka." She pointed to the items on the menu. "What they want is some filling food and a couple of beers, which we don't sell."

I felt a smile coming on and turned my head, pretending I didn't want to blow the smoke in her face. She was thinking exactly what I'd been thinking. I knew she would be all right. At that moment, I felt like jumping up and giving her a bear-style hug and a cheek-swallowing kiss, but I mustered enough restraint to stay in my seat.

"I'll think about it," I said.

"Good, and while you're thinking, think about a new name," she said. "Need to let people know that things are different now. Acropolis is hard to pronounce and hard to remember. Some even say it sounds sissyish."

"How about Taxiarhes? It's the name of my village."

"*Madre mia*, you got to be kidding. Nobody would be able to pronounce that. You need something simple, easy to remember."

"How about El Greko? He was a famous Greek who lived in Spain."

"Then the Americans will think it's a Cuban restaurant and will stay away. Americans are even dumber than Cubans." She got up and headed toward the bathroom, then stopped and turned. "How about Gus's? It's simple, easy to say, and it's how the Americans say Kostas."

"No, that's what they call me at the security guard company," I said. "I don't like it. It sounds like a belch."

She turned for the bathroom again. "How about Kostas then?"

"I'll think about it." The answer jumped out of my mouth as an instinctive reflex.

A few minutes later she was back. "How about Costas with a C, no K. Sounds like an Italian place."

"I'm thinking about it."

I liked the name as soon as she said it. It had a manly sound to it, and it was also *my* name—I was somebody! Also, there was a big Italian shipping company named the Costa Line. I had seen one of their luxury cruise ships in Nassau. The name had prestige.

"Name of a business is important," I said. "I need to think some more."

⁘⁘⁘

Word that the Acropolis Restaurant had changed hands seemed to spread through the restaurant suppliers overnight. On Tuesday, we entertained a constant parade of salesmen for fresh goods, dry goods, and goods of any kind. The Pepsi Cola representative said he could put in a brand-new soft-drink dispenser with twice as many heads if Coca-Cola took their antiquated machine out of there.

"Sounds good," I said. "I check to see if Coca-Cola Company has contract with the owner before me. You can leave a few cases free samples, to see how customers like it. Come back next week and I have answer for you." By then I would know what kind of a deal I could squeeze out of the Coca-Cola people.

The two men from the laundry company were not happy when I told them I didn't need the white tablecloths anymore.

"Linen tablecloths make the place look classy, *patrioti*," said one of the men. "And we are people with class. *Entaxi, patrioti*?" He pointed to the name on his calling card. "I am Greek too—from Sparta—but I was born here and don't speak much Greek. *Entaxi, patrioti?*"

The Spartan kept repeating "okay, countryman?" at the end of every sentence as if saying it would seal the deal. He was a short, nervous kind of person, bald and around fifty, whom the driver of the laundry truck had introduced as his supervisor. I wondered if he used the same line with the Cuban and the Italian restaurant owners, or if the office had a different man for each occasion.

"These tabletops are Formica, easy to clean," I said. "It's a working-class restaurant. White tablecloths make it look expensive and scare the customers away. Besides, they get dirty easy and you charge dollar fifty each to wash them."

"Oh, well . . ." The bald man from Sparta seemed to concentrate on crushing his cigarette in the ashtray. When there was nothing left of it, he lit another one. "I'll tell you what, *patrioti.* We have some nice dark-blue tablecloths that go for half a dollar less. They don't show stains and will make your place look classy just as good. *Entaxi, patrioti*?"

"I will remember that," I said. "Maybe later I'll get some. For now, I'll keep the same number of aprons and towels but no tablecloths. Okay?"

"I guess it'll have to be," the Spartan said, letting out a sigh.

Later in the evening, while I was struggling with a clogged drainpipe under the kitchen sink, Gianni approached me.

"I looked for you earlier and couldn't find you," she said. "I wanted to ask what you got in mind for tomorrow's menu."

"I went to the store to get bread rolls. We ran out," I said. "Tomorrow we're going to have pot roast for special. And next time if I'm not around, ask Carmen for anything you need."

Just then the drainpipe broke and I got drenched. I grabbed a towel and tried to wipe the stinky gunk from my face.

"I'll quit before I take orders from a Cuban," Gianni snapped. "I'll surely do."

"Then I guess you just *quitted*," I said.

She stared at me for a moment to see if I was joking.

"You bet I did," she finally said and yanked her apron off, throwing it against the wall.

She grabbed her little purse and went in the dining room and stood by the cash register. I finished cleaning my face and followed.

"It never fails," she said when I handed her the pay for two days. "It's always your own kind that'll stab you in the back. I'll tell everybody at the church what kind of Judas you are." She shook her finger as she headed toward the door. "Nobody will set foot in here. You're not going to last till the end of the month. You'll see."

CHAPTER TWENTY-FOUR

The Kostas Restaurant

After some thought I decided to open the restaurant five days a week and be closed on Saturday and Sunday. Later, if it was worth it, I would open on Saturday also, but for now I used the weekends to take care of the maintenance.

Just as when I worked for Steve, I set up a routine and stuck to it. Every morning I got up at four, drove to the restaurant, and was ready for business by five. Around 5:30, the stevedores and shipyard workers would start coming in for coffee and breakfast. I cooked a full breakfast plate—ham, sausage, thick bacon strips, grits, and my homemade home fries. And everything was served in generous portions. I needed to get the people coming back and would worry about profit margins later.

I had found a hole under the kitchen sink where a pickle jar fit snugly. At the end of each business day, I tried to put at least forty dollars in that jar—my "piggy bank," as I called it—to cover the loans and the rents I had to pay at the end of each month. If I had an extra-good day, I would put in a few dollars more for a cushion against a bad day.

Heeding Carmen's advice, I replaced the handwritten cardboard sign with a long banner from the paper goods supplier and hung it above the entrance door. In big, bright-red letters it broadcast *NOW UNDER NEW MANAGEMENT*.

The first Saturday, before I did anything else, I climbed on the roof and took down the old sign. The man from the sign shop had said it would cost one hundred dollars extra for removal and installation, so I thought I could do it myself. The sign was awkward and heavy—the painter had said it was a standard three-quarter-inch four-by-eight plywood—and it turned out to be quite a challenge. I loaded it on top of the Valiant and drove to the painter's shop. When I first stepped on the gas, the car felt like it was about to go airborne, so I drove very slowly. By the time I got to the painter's, I had a tail eight cars long with every one of them probably volleying curses at me.

I spent the rest of the day painting the bathrooms. When I got home I went straight to bed and didn't wake up until almost noon on Sunday.

During the week I called the sign painter three times to check on the progress until finally, on Friday afternoon, the man said my sign was finished. I was at the painter's shop on Saturday morning half an hour before he opened. The painter propped the sign against the wall and let me examine it: *Kostas Restaurant* appeared in dark-blue letters on a white background on both sides of the plywood.

The word *Kostas* was centered at the top of the sign in bold letters, slightly leaning forward as if written freehand. I had changed my mind about using the letter *C* instead of *K* because I didn't want people in Greece to think I was working for an Italian. The word *Restaurant* was in square, machinelike letters below my name. For the same price, the painter had also drawn the Grecian key around the edges, which I thought made the sign look classy and was very nice of him. The painter brought some rugs and helped me wrap the sign for the transport back, and I thought I would reciprocate the niceness.

"You and your woman come to the restaurant for dinner," I told him. "You select any item on the menu, dessert too, and no pay nothing."

The man smiled. "Thank you, Kostas. We will come for dinner one night when 'my woman' doesn't feel like cooking."

I spent most of the day installing the sign back in its old location. As soon as it got dark, I turned on the two spotlights and trotted across the street to look at it. Then from the corner, farther down the block. It looked great. I was sure it could be seen from two blocks away.

I wanted to clap and shout and tell everybody walking by that it was *my* name up there. *I* was *that* Kostas, and it was *my* restaurant.

I leaned on the telephone pole and smoked a cigarette while I admired it. As I went back inside, I wished I could go somewhere to celebrate, and that I had somebody to celebrate with. I didn't think I could talk Carmen into going to a nightclub with me, and even if I did, then what? Seeing everybody around me kissing and rubbing each other and knowing that most of those people were going home to finish what they'd started at the club, while I was dancing at arm's length with my partner and then going home to sleep alone, sharing the room with an old man who talked in his sleep, didn't seem like fun.

Neither could I go to a nightclub with Susan, the captain's wife. She was too worried about her reputation. At the thought of Susan, I realized I hadn't been with her since I'd first looked at the Acropolis. Somehow she had slipped from my mind. I called her from the restaurant pay phone. She said she was about to call me because she had a surprise for me.

On my way to Casa Juno, I stopped and bought a box of chocolates. On a whim, I also bought a small bottle of Madeira. I'd heard women liked that kind of drink. When I got to the hotel, I registered as "Onassis," our code name. It was Susan's idea not to use our real names. At first I'd tried Smith, but the nosy old man behind the desk had sneered at me.

"You don't sound like a Smith," he said. "Besides, I got four of them registered today already."

"Okay, my real name is Gonzales," I said.

"Sounds more like it," said the man.

We registered as Mr. and Mrs. Gonzales for a while until one time when Susan came twenty minutes after I did and a new receptionist sent her to a room with another Mr. Gonzales in it who came to the door stark naked. After that, we settled on Onassis. It was very unlikely the real Onassis would bring any of his mistresses to this place.

This time the man at the front desk was someone who had seen me before. When he noticed the five-dollar tip included in the payment, he winked at me and said, "I'll send your guest right up when she comes, sir."

I had just finished showering when I heard the door open. She was getting later every time. I dried and stepped out of the bathroom with the towel over my shoulder, then quickly stepped back when I saw that Susan had company. The two women laughed, and Susan walked into the bathroom.

"Come on out, Kostas. No need to cover up. She knows all about you."

I wrapped the towel around my waist and stepped out.

"This is my friend Charlotte," she said. "She'll be taking my place. Richard is coming home tonight, so we won't be getting together for a while."

As she spoke she held Charlotte's shoulders with both hands, turning her front and back as if she were a dress I was inspecting.

"I told Charlotte all about you. I'm sure you two are going to love your . . . getting together." She sounded like she'd had a few drinks. When she spotted the bottle on the table, she said, "You brought sherry and chocolates! How nice. If I'd known you'd do that, we wouldn't have stopped at the lounge downstairs for Charlotte to build her nerve up."

Susan yanked the towel away from me.

"See? What did I tell you, Charlotte?" she said, laughing.

Charlotte took my hand and put it on her shoulder. Then she pulled me close to her and kissed me long and passionately on the mouth.

"You can join in if you want," she told Susan when she stopped for air.

"No, I'm going to stay hungry. I'll wait for Richard in my bathrobe and rip his clothes off as soon as he's inside the door."

She inspected the contents of the chocolate box, then picked one piece and popped it into her mouth.

"Oh, oh, this is delicious," she moaned. "I better go before it's too late." She resolutely walked to the door. Before she went out, she turned to look at us. "Have fun, my children."

During the brief intermission of our first session, Charlotte told me a bit about herself. She also told me that her husband was impotent.

"What kind of important?" I asked. "Big shot with government? Maybe immigration? I no want trouble with them."

She burst out laughing. "Susan said you were funny. The husband is important—that's funny." Her hands got busy massaging a sensitive area of my body. "See?" she said triumphantly moments later. "*Impotent* means he cannot make this come to life."

From then on, every time we met my opening line would be something like, "How's your *important* husband?" or "Your *important* husband didn't follow you here, did he?" It got her laughing and seemed to get her extra passionate.

⁂

On the way to work the following morning, I scanned the horizon for my sign as I got close to Port Everglades and spotted it as soon as I turned left from Sixth Avenue onto Twenty-Second Street. I slowed to admire it. The spotlight was a bit too low; it should be adjusted to shine more on *Kostas.* The driver of the car behind me leaned on his horn, and as he went around me, I saw his mouth moving. Probably some flunky worried about getting his ass chewed by his supervisor for being late. *Nothing like being your own boss.* I whistled a peppy tune the rest of the drive to *my* restaurant.

At ten minutes after six, as he had done every morning since I'd opened, the burly man rushed in and sat at the first stool by the counter. Today he had cameras and tripods dangling from his shoulders. It had started to rain a few minutes earlier, and he spent some time shaking the rain off his hat.

"Get me the coffee and the muffin, not too dark. And make it quick. I'm running late," he said, using the same words as yesterday and every day before.

I brought him the muffin and nodded toward the cameras. "You tourist here?" I felt the one week of acquaintance allowed me to say more than *yes sir*.

"Hell no," he answered. "These are my tools. I'm a children's photographer for a studio in Boca." He stirred spoonfuls of sugar in his coffee. "I fight this miserable traffic every day." He paused to take a sip. "I guess it's going to rain all day. Miserable weather."

His moves were sharp and he sounded irritated. He seemed the kind of man who—as my mother used to say—would pick a fight with his own clothes if there wasn't anybody around to argue with.

"The rain only last a little time," I said, thinking that it would be hilarious to watch him try to get a kid to relax and pose right. "Maybe one day you take a picture of the restaurant?"

"Sure, if the damn sky ever clears," he growled. "Sunshine State, my ass."

The sky did clear the next day, and the grumpy children's photographer coached me on where to stand in front of the restaurant and how to face the camera.

Three mornings later, when he rushed in and took his usual place by the counter, he handed me an envelope with the photographs. For a moment I silently scolded myself for not having asked him for the price first, like I had been doing with everything I bought.

"How much it cost?" I asked, bracing for the pain.

"It doesn't cost anything," he said. "My gift to you. Good luck in your business. It's a jungle out there."

"Thank you, sir. Thank you. I buy you breakfast. Want breakfast *deluxe*, like this?" I pointed to the two plates loaded with three eggs, four strips of bacon, three links of sausage, and a mountain of home-fried potatoes that Carmen was carrying to the shipyard workers.

The photographer glanced at them as they went by. "If I decide to kill myself, I'll let you know," he said. "Just give me the usual. And hurry it up. I'm running late for work today." He tried to pour sugar in his coffee. Not satisfied with the way it was pouring, he banged the glass shaker on the counter and cursed "the stupid thing."

I propped one of the photographs against the cash register and glanced at it every time I came near it. The photographer had asked me to stand by the front door and look at the camera.

"Look at it like you're looking at your girlfriend," he said.

I had thought of Karen and Charlotte, even of Consuela at the "love palace" in Aruba, but my look didn't seem to satisfy the fussy photographer. Only when Carmen popped into my mind did the man behind the camera say, "That's it! Now you got it."

In the center of the picture, behind me on the rooftop, was the sign with my name and the Grecian key around it. The first rays of the morning sun emerging behind the beach condominiums reflected on the white paint, giving the building and my smiling face an ethereal glow, as if in a divine blessing.

I enclosed two of those photographs in the next letter to my mother. In the same letter, I asked her to send me her recipe for *galactopourico. To show the Americans what the real sweets taste like,* I wrote. I imagined Mother bragging to the women in the village that the Americans were raving about her desserts.

With Carmen's help and the collaboration of the paper goods salesman, I spent many hours redesigning the old Acropolis menu. I did away with the four-page leather-bound bifold thing that looked like a church book and replaced it with a one-sheet job with large writing on both sides of the paper.

"I want simple words that are easy to read," I said. "And I want some covered in plastic to keep in the restaurant and some in simple paper to give to people."

"I get you, Mr. Kostas." The salesman nodded. "You want some laminated and a bunch on plain paper to hand out and maybe put on the windshields, like the folks are doing from Chicken-on-the-Run over by Las Ollas Boulevard. Pretty smart. Let me see . . ."

He stood and counted the tables. "One, two, three—you need twelve for the tables. And one, two, three—about that many more for the counter, and a few extra if some get cigarette burns. Let's say about forty laminated and a couple hundred plain. Let's make it fifty laminated and two-fifty plain; that way we get a price break in the printing cost. It's the setup that's expensive. The paper is cheap."

He quickly scribbled the numbers in his order book. "Now, how about the placemats? We can make them look the same as your sign." He pointed toward the roof. "And maybe at the bottom we put *Kostas Karas, Proprietor*." He smiled at me and added, "It means owner. If I throw in the placemats with the menu order, we get another price break. It'll save us more money that way, Kostas."

I thought about it a few moments. The idea of my name in bold print telling everybody that I was the owner of the business sounded good. The Greeks in Fort Lauderdale would see it, and if some crew members from the Greek ships happened to come there, they would see it too. Not a bad way to tell everybody whose place this was.

"No, not right now," I finally told the salesman. "The way you save me money, I think I will go broke soon."

"Kostas, Kostas, my friend," said the salesman with a smile that took up half his face. "In business you have to spend money to make money."

"All salespeople say that. I was brought up to believe it was the other way around," I said. "Maybe I buy the special placemats later. For now I use the plain ones. Only I no want white. You have light blue? I like the blue color."

"I'll check with the warehouse," he said.

A few days later, when the paper goods man brought the new menus, I knocked on the doors of every apartment in the three-story building the restaurant was glued to. To those who answered, I handed paper copies of the new menus and gave them a brief sales pitch.

"I bring to you good dinner cheap when no feel cooking."

On that short expedition, I discovered I had more oddball neighbors in that one building than in the whole village of Taxiarhes. On the second floor, a man in a tight undershirt with very broad shoulders and big muscles came to the door cradling a tiny white poodle like a baby. He pet it and baby-talked to it the whole time I was pointing out the items on the menu. On the third floor, a guy with a shaved head jogged in place while I spoke with him. And farther down, a very plump woman in a loose flowery housecoat kept turning back and telling a dog with a squeaky bark, "Hush, Eugenia! It's not Oscar." I wondered if Oscar was a man or a dog.

There was also an old man who introduced himself as Professor Hannagen. He asked what the accent was, and when I told him I was Greek, he started reciting parts from the Odyssey in old Greek. At another apartment, two middle-aged women, one with hair down to her waist and the other with hair shorter than mine, came to the door holding hands. On the last floor, the man who had come to the door slammed it shut as soon as I started to speak.

"Fucking Cubans everywhere!" I heard him mumble.

A dollar is a dollar, no matter which screwball it came from. I kept knocking on doors.

On his next visit, the paper goods salesman told me about a new gimmick some restaurants had started.

"They call them Senior Citizen Dinner Coupons," he said. "They come thirty-one coupons in a book. The old folks buy them when their social security check comes in. That way they know they are going to eat for the month. It's good for them because it gives them a discount for the meal, and it's good for the restaurant because you get the money up front. We just delivered a big batch to a restaurant in Miami Beach. When I saw the order, right away I thought of you, Kostas. I'm always thinking of you, Kostas."

"Why? You not have girlfriend?" I said.

The answer lingered in the air for a second. Then he burst into a hearty laughter. "That's a good one, Kostas. 'You have no girlfriend?' That's a good one."

I knew that everything salesmen said was meant to sell more of their stuff. The first thing they learned was to always make the customer feel good—to never say his ideas were stupid or that he was screwing up, and to always laugh at his jokes no matter how corny. Just like Bill, the salesman from Integrity Meats in Miami who called on the Parthenon restaurant. He used to laugh his head off at Steve's stupid jokes, and Steve thought Bill was the most loyal friend in the world. He paid top dollar for the freezer-burned rib eyes and T-bones but wouldn't buy from anyone else because he thought they were crooks selling horse meat.

I always ran everyone's suggestions—especially those coming from salesmen—through the fine sieve of my mind, looking for weevils in the flour.

"This is working people's restaurant," I told the salesman. "And this neighborhood around here is no retirement community."

"You're surrounded by condos, Kostas," he said. "And you're next to a bus stop. When word gets around about the Senior Citizen Coupons and your good food, the old folks will be flocking here. You're sitting on a gold mine, Kostas. Didn't you know that?"

"The damn gold must be buried real deep," I said. "I'm digging harder and harder every day but have not seen any of it yet. What is littlest number coupon books you sell?"

"I'll write you up for a dozen books, and I'll throw in a couple of signs for free."

"What kind of signs? What they say?"

The salesman chuckled. "Always suspicious. Relax, Kostas. They don't say you're giving anything away. They're small cardboard signs you can stick on the window or by the cash register. They say, *SENIOR CITIZEN DINNER COUPONS AVAILABLE HERE*."

"Okay," I said. "You can write up one dozen for me. It looks like the harder I try to get out of debt, the deeper I get."

"Kostas, my friend, you have to spend money to make money."

I sighed again. "Everybody who sells say that."

CHAPTER TWENTY-FIVE

George Matzeos

I poured myself a cup of coffee and sat by the counter for a few moments of recharging before unlocking the doors for the breakfast rush. I looked over the dining area. It was Friday, my fifth week in business, and the place was shaping up the way I wanted it. I had managed to make all the loan payments the past month, although when I'd called Pete he said he would come by the restaurant to get his. New customers came in every day, and word was that the shipyard would be starting another shift soon. The restaurant supply man was going to bring me three more dining tables to match the ones I already had.

The previous Monday, I held a grand opening. The supplier of paper goods loaned me two big banners with the words *GRAND OPENING* in huge, multicolored letters. All day I sold two-for-one hamburgers, Cuban sandwiches, and half-price arroz con pollo.

And the idea for Senior Citizen Coupon Books had turned out to be a pretty good one. The money was paid in advance, and most of them ate only small portions of plain steamed vegetables. The first one to buy a coupon book was George Matzeos, one of the men working in the shipyard who had become a regular. George was about fifty-five, short, and round, with a light-gray fuzz on top of his head and shifty eyes. He said he had sailed as chief engineer on some of the freighters that used to shuttle between Florida and Cuba in the "good old days, before Castro and the Americans screwed things up." Now he was the maintenance man at the Port Everglades Shipyard. George came from Skyros, an island in the Aegean about fifty miles straight east from my village.

"We are almost neighbors," he said.

It was probably that proximity that George considered bonding enough to let me in on some of the secrets of his success. In order to get his papers, he said he had married some American birdbrain. When the time was right, he'd made her run off.

"She had more ass than sense," George said. "She wanted to eat at restaurants every day and go dancing every night and shop for new clothes all the time. One year and one month after we got married, I told her I wasn't having any of that anymore. She didn't like it and asked for a divorce. It worked out just as I had planned it."

George lived alone in a pigeonhole in an apartment complex west of US-1. His biggest entertainment was watching the exchange rate of the dollar with the drachma and talking about how he planned to live like a millionaire on the interest of his investments, back on the island when he retired a year from now.

"You have relatives in Greece?" I asked.

"None that I want to claim," he said. "There's a cousin on the island, but we haven't spoken in years. He might be dead for all I know."

"It's a shame," I said.

"No it isn't. Relatives means moochers. They're after your money. I don't need them."

"Maybe you have something there," I said. You didn't disagree with your customers, no matter how screwy.

George bought the coupon book and had his dinners at my place every evening after work while dispensing advice on how to make it big in America.

I thought he put a bit too high of a price on his advice. Quite a few times, after dispensing some great Matzeoan success formula, he would forget to pay his bill and I'd have to ask him for his coupon. He would always act as if I were ungrateful.

I glanced at the Coca-Cola clock on the wall. Julio should be dropping off Carmen any minute now. Besides Carmen, the other help was Sebastian, the Haitian dishwasher who had worked for Mrs. Amalia for three years and whom she said she trusted even with the keys to the cash register, and Tracy, a skinny waitress in her forties who had been working there for a long time and knew most of the customers by their first names. Since business had fallen off after Mr. Moskos died, she had been coming in only for three hours during lunchtime, until last week when I asked her to work full time.

"God bless you, Mr. Kostas," she had said. "Now I can quit slinging hash at the truck stop." For a second, I thought she was about to kiss me.

To help Sebastian with the lunch hour rush, I also hired Ernesto, a young man from Guatemala who was a student at the Broward County Junior College.

I was about to return to the kitchen when Grand Duchess Anastasia tapped on the glass door. She too had become one of my regulars.

I went and unlocked the door. "I am not open yet, Duchess, but you wait here. I bring your breakfast."

"Young man," she snapped. "You must learn to be punctual. Punctuality and promptness are of utmost importance in any enterprise."

"I no understand fancy words," I said. "I open six o'clock, one quarter more."

She reached in her shopping cart and moved a fuzzy housecoat aside to uncover a clock the size of a dinner plate. "My chronometer indicates twenty-one minutes after six o'clock," she said. "It has never erred."

"You wait here," I repeated. "I bring you breakfast."

She took a folding chair from her cart and sat by the door. When I came back, she put the coffee and the bag with the food in her cart, then folded her chair and slung it over her shoulder with a sigh. "It is becoming ever so much harder to obtain decent service in this uncultured society."

I watched her lean on the shopping cart and waddle toward the port. She must have been an educated woman at some time in the past—maybe a professor, for knowing all those fancy words. What made her lose her mind?

In Taxiarhes, there used to be a woman we called Crazy Franga. She walked around the village, always in a fancy churchgoing dress, carrying a parasol with faded lacing and talking constantly to herself in a steady monologue full of fancy words.

Some of us, when we were no older than eleven, would run up to her and say, "Your Zak is waiting at the church," or "We saw Zak with another girl on the beach." Then we would watch as Franga ran crying to the church or the beach or whatever place our meanness had inspired us to send her. The grown-ups would scold us, and quite a few times I got a taste of the switch from my mother because of those pranks.

"God looks after people like that and frowns upon those who are unkind to them," my mother would say. "When you grow up, you'll learn that the mind is a very fragile thing."

I didn't learn Franga's story until many years later. When she was a young girl, her mother had sent her to work as a maid in a rich Jewish man's house in Thessaloniki. That was where she had learned the fancy ways of talking, dressing, and behaving.

The man's son and Franga fell in love and got married just a few days before the Germans invaded Thessaloniki. Thinking it was safer in our village, they came to stay with Franga's mother. Unfortunately, during one of their sweeps through the area, the Germans had rounded up twelve men, my father and Franga's husband of two weeks among them, and as many mules as they could find to transport their loot to another village where there were trucks waiting.

When they got there and the mules were unloaded, they lined the men up against a wall and said they had information there was a Jew in the group. If they would point him out, the rest could leave. Nobody moved, which pissed the Germans off, so they machine-gunned all twelve of them. Franga and some others had followed the Germans from a distance, and when she saw her Isaac—Zak, as she called him—ripped to pieces by the bullets, her mind had flipped.

After that, she would sit for days on a boulder at the Platanakia overlook, watching the road along the distant mountainside, sure that her Zak would come around the bend any minute. Somebody nailed a piece of tin on two poles and made a roof over the boulder to shelter it from the sun and the rain. They called it Franga's Tower, and when the townsfolk saw her perched there, some mother would send her child with a bit of food and some water.

A light rain began to fall, and the Grand Duchess opened a blue umbrella with *Pan-American Airlines* on it. I stared at her until she turned the corner, then went back in the kitchen.

The rain lasted almost the whole day. It was slow and steady, and some of the customers griped about it and some others were glad for it. About 11:30, the bell above the door gave its nervous jingle, and I looked up from the cash register to see two men from the shipyard walk in.

"What do you say there, Easy Money?" said Charlie, the bigger of the two. He was about six feet tall and thick all around, with a big belly. He pulled a chair and sat down by the table closest to the counter. The other guy, named Joe, sat across from him. He seemed to have been made out of the same mold, only a third smaller.

"Hi, Charlie. Hi, Joe," I said.

As if they had rehearsed it, both of them pushed their yellow hard hats back at the same time, and with duplicate moves, they each lit a cigar. Tracy started toward the cooler, but I motioned to her that I'd take care of them. I liked talking to people who worked on ships.

"Bring us two Schlitzes, Greek," Charlie said.

"In bottles, and with two mugs," added Joe.

The distributor of Schlitz beer had helped me navigate the complex bureaucracy of the liquor licensing commission, so for the last two weeks I had been selling beer. I was also allowed to sell wine, but I didn't think anybody would ask for it and didn't keep any in stock. The salesman had acted as an interpreter for me to the county clerk at the license office, and it was a good thing he did. The wimpish little clerk, after reading my full name, had turned to the man at the next desk and said, "Every damn Cuban that washes up on the beach wants to open a bar."

I was about to do something that probably wouldn't have helped my case, but the Schlitz salesman pressed my hand and winked at me. When I got the licenses, I stocked up on everything the Schlitz man was selling, since he was the only one who would sell to me on credit.

Ernesto, the Guatemalan student I'd hired to help, volunteered to draw a sign announcing our new addition to the menu. On white poster board, he wrote with a blue marker *COLD BEER SOLD HERE,* in both English and Spanish. Each letter had snow piled on top of it and icicles hanging from the bottom. It made you feel cold just looking at it.

I taped the sign high on the wall behind the counter. The little cooler strained to chill the cans and bottles of beer running through its belly. The Schlitz supply man had also given me a dozen beer mugs, which I kept in the meat cooler for those who didn't like to drink their beer straight out of the bottle.

The salesman had also tried to talk me into putting in a draft beer machine. "In beer, it's double the profit, Kostas," he said. "I know where I can get you one that's almost new, for a song."

“I don’t sing very good,” I said, “but I will think about it. When I get a couple of loan payments ahead, we can talk about it.”

When I brought the beers to the two shipyard men, I said, “You got rained out today?”

“Yep, only got in half a day,” said Charlie. “We were working on the anchor windlass on the German ship and the rain messed us up. You know what an anchor windlass is, Greek?”

I nodded. “It’s the machine at the pointy end of the ship that lifts the anchor. Right?”

“Right. You’re a smart Glik Plik.” Charlie chuckled as he filled his mug and waited for the head to settle. He took a long sip and belched. “You know the joke about the Glik Plik?”

“I not know that one,” I said.

“When you bring the lunch, I’ll tell you.”

“The usual?” I asked.

“Yep, the usual.”

“And another beer,” said both in unison.

A few minutes later, I put a plate in front of each of them and said, “There you go, gentlemen. Two hamburgers with extra onions.”

“Thanks, Glik Plik,” said Charlie. “Now I’ll tell you the joke.”

“Maybe next time,” I said. “Right now I have a pot on the stove.”

Their jokes were always hard to understand, but they were good-paying regular customers, so I always played along. In the mornings they came in for breakfast, always the same—three eggs over easy, with bacon and sausage and my special home-fried potatoes. At lunchtime they would wash down a hamburger with three beers, and after work they stopped by to take three beers each “for the road” while they drove home to a town called Jupiter, forty-five minutes north on I-95.

A few minutes later, two more men from the shipyard entered. They nodded to Charlie and his sidekick, then sat at the counter. Carmen wrote down their order and clipped the green slip over the serving window. I picked up the two empty beer bottles from Joe and Charlie and started to walk away.

"Glad to see some of our crew coming to eat here now, even if you're a Glik Plik," Charlie said. "Most of them went over to Lum's before. They ate hot dogs with sauerkraut for lunch, and you couldn't get near them after that."

"Get near them?" Joe said. "Try welding with one of them inside those tiny tanks of the new construction. When they started farting, I was scared that I'd either choke to death or get blown to kingdom come."

Later that evening, George Matzeos walked in and sat at his usual place, the corner booth by the window.

"You didn't get rained out?" I asked while filling his water glass.

George preferred to be waited on by me because he said the waitresses didn't understand him and always messed up his orders. It took me a while, but I finally figured out the real reason he wanted me to wait on him. In some parts of Greece, it's considered an insult to tip the owner of the establishment, so George claimed he respected the customs of the motherland.

"I never miss any time," he said when I brought him his dinner. "And I work more overtime than anybody in the yard."

"I saw some guys leaving earlier," I said. "I thought they might have sent you home too."

"You got to know how to control your skill so you can sell it expensive," said George. "From years back, I've made it a practice to get something out of whack that only I know how to fix, so they'll call me in on overtime." He started eating and I left.

"Why you think they called me in last Saturday?" he said when I checked on him a bit later. "The sandblasters couldn't get enough air pressure to blast the ship on the dry dock and had to call me to fix the air compressor. It cost them three hours of time and a half for me to come and close all the drain valves I had cracked open on Friday night." He emptied his water glass. "Like I said, you got to be able to see the big picture. Got to be able to think for the long run." He moved his coffee cup toward me, signaling he was ready for a refill.

"And I bet you they'll call me to come in tomorrow. They'll have a hell of a time starting the big crane. I never told them about the new switch I put under the seat."

"That's like someone I knew in Greece," I said.

"What did he do?"

"He was a mechanic in a big garage in Volos. He told me whenever he was adjusting the timing of an engine, he would cover it with a sheet so the helpers couldn't see how he did it."

"Well, they used to say back home, 'Teaching apprentices is pocking your eyes out,'" said George.

After draining his third cup of coffee, he got up.

"See you Monday," he said and started to leave.

He was almost at the door when I reminded him he hadn't left his food coupon.

CHAPTER TWENTY-SIX

Expanding the Menu

Patrick Fahey had been coming to the restaurant since I opened, sitting alone at the end of the counter, sipping on a cup of decaffeinated coffee. He was tall, slender, and bald and seemed to be in his late sixties. I started talking to him, and he mentioned he was surprised there weren't many places selling pizza. "It has a good profit margin and it's easy to make," he said. He offered to teach me how and help me get set up.

I was always suspicious of offers for help that came uninvited, and I asked him what was in it for him. "I'm retired, got too much time on my hands, and I don't have the stomach for painting classes," he said.

I told him I'd think it over, and on Saturday afternoon I made a trip to County Line Pizza, the closest restaurant of the kind, about fifteen miles north from my place. It was my first time there. Usually when I ate in other people's places, it was for spying purposes, and until Patrick's visit, I hadn't remotely thought of selling pizza.

It took me a while to find an empty parking spot. Cars darted in and out of the lot like bees in a beehive. Inside, the place was filled with the buzz of chatter, and the air carried the Mediterranean smell of oregano and garlic and freshly baked bread. Customers ate their pizza slices on paper plates, sitting on wooden benches around ten primitive and tortured-looking tables. The owner didn't spend much on furniture.

A fat man with shifty eyes in a white undershirt with sweat stains on it sat by the cash register, collecting the money and answering the phone. I recognized him right away. He had come to my grand opening. He'd ordered the breakfast special, soft-scrambled eggs with bacon and home fries, and he'd sat at a corner table, nursing a cup of coffee for over an hour.

I got in line behind a couple in their forties who were trying to decide what to order.

"You're busy tonight, Mr. Murphy," said the woman when she finally placed her order.

"Hell, we're busy and shorthanded every night. Can't find any decent help anymore," muttered the fat man while writing down the order. "Here or to go?"

"We'll eat it here," said the man. "And a pitcher of beer." He handed a bill to Mr. Murphy.

"Here you go. Number forty-five," Mr. Murphy said, handing the man his change and half of the order ticket. He clipped the other half on a wire behind him and called out, "One large sausage for here."

I stepped forward and ordered a small pepperoni "for here" and a Budweiser.

Mr. Murphy rang it up and gave me the change. "Not eating your own cooking tonight, eh?"

The damn guy recognizes me.

"Closed tonight," I said. "I thought I'll try some of yours."

"You're number forty-six," he said. "Enjoy it."

I sat on the end of the bench at the table closest to the kitchen and watched the three surfer-looking guys behind the counter filling out the orders, assembly-line style. The first one got the dough from the cooler and kneaded it on the table with his fingers. Then he picked it up and twirled it with his knuckles to the right size before placing it on a peel. The middle guy spread the tomato sauce, added the cheese and the sausage topping, then pushed the peel to the third man, who picked it up and put it in the oven. The oven guy unloaded it, checked on a couple of other pizzas in there, then pulled one out and put it on an aluminum tray. After cutting it into triangular slices, he placed it on the counter and rang the bell.

A tall, skinny waitress in a white dress and yellow apron looked at the order ticket and turned to call out, "Number forty-one!" Somebody shouted, "Here!" and she took the tray and some paper plates over to the table. Meanwhile, the first guy behind the counter was already stretching the dough for another order.

"Do it in the air, Ronnie," some girls at a front table, called out. "Throw it in the air."

Ronnie obliged them. With a slow upward movement of both hands, he had the dough spinning over his head for a few seconds like a hovering flying saucer before it gently landed on the back side of his hands. He repeated the feat a couple more times. The high school girls cheered and clapped, and quite a few other customers shouted, "Bravo!"

The telephone rang almost constantly. The fat man would write down the phone orders, shout them out in the direction of the kitchen, then clip the slip on a spinning wheel-like thing.

When my pizza was ready, just as I did with my first hot dog, I ate it with slow, exploratory bites, trying to identify the ingredients. Maybe a bit more garlic and oregano would give it a stronger Italian flavor. I wondered how Mr. Murphy got into the pizza business, since his name didn't sound Italian. Probably another transplant from New York.

By the time I finished the last piece, I had concluded that the pizza addition would be a good move. It would take up the slack hours of the evening, and I was far enough from County Line Pizza that I didn't have to worry about competition from Mr. Murphy. The hardest part would be talking on the telephone to take the orders, but I could find a way to solve that problem.

When Patrick came on Monday evening, I told him I had decided to take the plunge. "Smart decision," he said. "I'll help you pick the oven and the pans. All the suppliers around here are transplants from up north. All of them owe me favors."

The pizza oven, a massive, black, iron contraption with brass handles and yellowish firebrick, arrived two weeks later. It took the guys from Broward Kitchen Supply half a day to install it. They had to move the potato-peeling machine and take the back doorframe off to get it into the kitchen. They hooked up the gas, lit the pilot light, and showed me how to turn the fancy brass knobs to regulate the temperature. Then they asked me to sign the delivery ticket, wished me good luck, and left.

So much for hoping to put something extra in the piggy bank. I sighed as I watched the delivery truck drive off.

⁜⁜⁜

Patrick Fahey came in after the lunch hour rush the next day. He inspected the pizza oven and hummed approvingly.

"This is a good brand," he said. "Same one I had in my place in Long Island. The firebrick keeps an even temperature and gives you the best crust."

"You do plenty pizza business in the Long Island?" I asked.

"More than I cared for," Patrick said. "I got into it as something to do after I sold my restaurant supply business. I'd been in it for thirty-five years. It was hard to get used to doing nothing all of a sudden, almost went nuts. Did I tell you my first sale was to a Greek?"

"No, you not. Want some coffee?"

"Yeah, I'll take a cup, decaf."

He sat by the counter, and I put the cup in front of him.

"His name was Stavros Papa . . . Papa-something," said Patrick. "I was fresh out of the Army. I had been with the Plymouth Restaurant Supply Company for one whole week and hadn't sold even a bottle opener yet. I was thinking of hanging it up. I stopped at Stavros's place for a cup of coffee and got to talking with him. He was from the old country too. Next thing I know, he buys three ladles, one 22-quart colander, and three 20-quart pots. I felt on top of the world. Went out and made two more sales that day."

He paused to take another sip of coffee.

"For some months after that," he went on, "every time I stopped at Stavros's place, I'd see my stuff hanging on the hooks, some with the original labels still on them. I asked him why he'd bought them if he didn't need them, and he said I looked like I needed the sale." He stared silently into his coffee cup. "Yep," he said, as if coming back from somewhere, "who knows what I'd be doing if Stavros Papa-something hadn't given me a leg up."

"What was he give you?" I asked.

He smiled. "If he hadn't bought the pots he didn't need."

Patrick showed me how to stretch the dough with my fingertips and my knuckles instead of the rolling pin, and he showed me how to spread the sauce and the cheese on the pie. He said the tossing-in-the-air part could be learned later.

"It's only for show anyway," he said.

We made three of the small pies and loaded them with the tomato sauce, the grated cheese mixture, and the pepperoni. Patrick put the first one in the oven, and I did the other two. When I tried to unload them, they stuck on the peel and ended up oblong-shaped, and I ended up cursing.

"You must put some corn flour on the peel," Patrick said. "It makes the dough slide off easy."

When I took the pies out, I started to throw away the two deformed ones, but Patrick stopped me.

"No, don't do that," he said. "We'll cut them up in small squares and give them as free samples. Tell your customers you'll be selling pizza in the evenings from now on. And you can give them as appetizers to the beer drinkers instead of peanuts."

From the man who printed the menus, I ordered flyers announcing the pizza addition. When he brought them a week later, I looked in the box and told him to take them back.

"I speak to you when I order that I want three color," I almost yelled at him. "First red, white in middle, and green in the end. I ask you 'You understand?' You say to me 'Okay.'"

"That's how we pack them, Gus," he said, looking puzzled. "You saw them—three separate bundles. The top one is the red paper, the middle is white paper, and the last is green. They're all stacked on top of each other, are they not?"

"Bullshit! This no look like Italian flag."

"Oh, is that what you wanted? I'm sorry, Gus. I misunderstood you."

"That seems to be happening a lot to me," I muttered.

The man ran his hand through his hair and seemed to be thinking. "I'll tell you what, Gus," he said finally. "I'll let you have them for half price."

I lit a cigarette and thought for a while. "No," I said finally. "I no keep it. Is not what I ordered."

Slowly, looking depressed, the man reached over and picked up the box with the flyers and started to walk out. Before he reached the door, he turned and dropped the box on the table by the door.

"Just pay me for the paper, if you can," he said, pointing to the box. "I'll eat the labor." He looked like he was about to cry.

"How much cost, the paper?" I asked.

The fellow did some computing on the box top and told me the amount. I took the money out of the cash register and started to hand it to him, then I stopped and pulled out another ten dollars.

"I will divide the loss with you," I said. Right then, I was not sure if what I felt was sorrow for the salesman or anger at myself for not being able to communicate like all other people.

Ernesto wrote with red marker on white poster board the three sizes of pizza we offered: small (ten inches), medium (twelve inches), and large (sixteen inches). Under each size was the choice of toppings and the price. Then with a green marker he made a two-inch border and stapled it to the wall, next to the board with the day's specials from the regular menu.

That display arrangement lasted only one day. My first pizza customers were two women about forty, both round and fluffy. They spent a long time studying the menu on the wall. Finally, one of them asked, "How big is your twelve-inch pizza?"

I got the tray from under the counter and showed it to her.

"How big is your sixteen-inch?" asked the other.

I showed the large pan.

"You think we can eat a large one?" they asked each other.

They wanted to see the medium pan again and then the small one.

"Maybe we should order two small," suggested one. "Could you hold up all three at the same time?"

I began to perspire. It was the first pizza I would be making for a paying customer, and since Patrick had to be out of town, I was on my own.

At the end of the day, I took three trays, one of each size, wrote what they were in the center, and nailed them to the wall below the pizza price list.

CHAPTER TWENTY-SEVEN

The Glik Plik and a Visit from Pete

At lunchtime the next day, Joe and Charlie, the shipyard welders, came in promptly at 11:30. I had a hamburger and a bottle of Schlitz in front of them the moment they sat down.

"Thanks, Glik Plik," said Charlie.

A few minutes later, I took their second beer to them.

"You're on the ball, Glik Plik," said Charlie. "Did I ever tell you the Glik Plik joke?"

"No, you not tell me." I folded my hands in front of me and stood by their table, ready to listen. Might as well get it over with.

"There was this Greek fellow up in New York, you see," Charlie said. "He spoke no English. He used to eat at a dime-store cafeteria every day, and all he knew how to say was 'ham 'n eggs.' It got to where when the little Chinaman behind the counter saw him coming, he would start cooking. By the time the Greek sat down, he'd set the plate in front of him. Well, the Greek fellow had a cousin who tried to school him in the language. 'You can't be eating the same thing all the time,' the cousin told him. 'You're Greek. You don't want that Chinese prick thinking you're dumb.' So, he taught him how to say *hamburger with French fries*. The next time the Greek goes to eat, he orders 'One hamburger with French fries.' The Chinaman stares at him for a sec, looks down at the plate of ham and eggs he's holding, and says, 'What?' The Greek repeats, 'Hamburger with French fries,' and the Chinaman says, 'Fuck you, Glik Plik!'"

Charlie started laughing hard and loud with his mouth wide open, his front teeth, brown and crooked, standing like an old fence in a cave entrance.

"Fuck you, Glik Plik," repeated Joe, keeping up his part of the laughter.

"Funny," I said, although I didn't think it was.

"Oh, by the way," Charlie said as I started to walk away. "Did you hear what happened to that other Glik Plik friend of yours?"

I turned around. "Who you speaking about?"

"We call him Mr. Fixit," Charlie said. "Your friend who always sat at that corner booth by the window."

"Oh, you speak about George Matzeos." I wasn't sure if I considered myself a friend of his, any more than George probably considered me *his* friend. "I no see him for many days. I think maybe he go to Greece."

"They found him dead last week," Charlie said like it was a piece of ordinary news.

"What happened?" I asked.

"One of the crane operators who lives in the same building said the landlord went to get the rent and found him dead. They said he had been dead for a few days. Heart attack."

"That is bad," I said. "He speak of going to Greece and live like rich man."

"Now the government will take all his money," Charlie said. "They couldn't find any relatives, and he didn't leave a will. The landlord's bitching because he owed him three month's rent and he's got to file all kinds of papers to get it."

"That's bad," I said again. It was all I could think of to say.

"It's sad, that's what it is," said Charlie. "It's a hell of a way for a man to finish his life, even if he was a real prick."

"Yes, it is sad," I repeated and walked away.

⁘⁘⁘

I had been running the restaurant for over two months before Pete Papas came to visit. He came in around three o'clock one afternoon and walked over to where Carmen was refilling the napkin holders. He spoke to her for a few minutes, then went and sat at the end of the counter.

I put a glass of water and a cup of coffee in front of him. "What took you so long to visit us?"

"I wanted to wait until you got settled." He sniffed the air in the direction of the kitchen. "I bet that's the stuffed tomatoes à la Kostas."

"Tomatoes and stuffed peppers," I said. "I make it every other week, mostly for the dinner customers. There's good profit in it, and people seem to like it. I just took a pan out of the oven. Want some?"

"Just a small portion," said Pete.

I brought him a plate with one stuffed tomato in the center, with pieces of steamed carrots and zucchini sliced lengthwise and arranged around the tomato like sunrays.

Pete took small bites and chewed slowly. "This is good, the best I've tasted," he said finally.

"I pick the tomatoes myself," I said. I had started doing that when I found out there were tomato farms nearby where you could go and do your own picking. It was like being back in the village, only here they measured the garden size in acres instead of rows. I was even thinking that after I got things running smoothly at the restaurant, I could get my mother's recipe and start making my own tomato sauce.

Pete scanned the dining area while he ate. "I like the way you arranged the seating. Makes the place feel cozy."

When he finished eating and pushed his plate away, I went over with the money. "Here it is—two hundred sixty dollars. Payment for two months." I counted the money in front of him.

"I can wait a little longer," he said. "You're just starting. Some emergency might come up."

"An emergency comes up every day," I said. "But I don't like owing money."

"Some people say it's better to owe than to be owed," said Pete with a chuckle and put the money in his pocket.

A customer got up to leave and I went to the cash register. "Tell me some news from the old neighborhood," I called from the other end of the counter. "It's night when I leave and night when I get home. It's like I don't live there anymore."

"Come closer," Pete said, "so I won't have to shout."

I refilled Pete's cup and put the pot back on the burner. "I'm listening."

He took a sip of coffee. "For starters, Steve sold the restaurant."

"He did?" I was surprised.

"He sold it to two Cuban brothers. They are renovating it and say it's going to be a classy restaurant in the style of Old Havana."

I shook my head. "And Steve was saying there was no hope for the neighborhood."

"They seem to think otherwise. They are spending a lot of money in that place."

"I guess now you found another place to eat supper," I said.

"I eat at the Versailles, down the street from where the Parthenon was. Remember it?"

"Yeah, I remember it. What's Steve doing now?"

"Nobody seems to know. I hear a young woman who was living in his apartments is suing him."

"Would her name be Karen?" I asked.

"Yes, I think that's it. She married a man from Argentina who's studying to become a lawyer, and they're suing him for child support."

"I can't say I'm surprised. Does she still live in the apartments?"

"No, a group of investors from Chicago bought the building,

and they're tearing it down. There is a rumor that they will put up a motel in its place."

I thought about Karen and her little Joey. Probably the Argentinean student married her for the green card.

"Did you know a man named George Matzeos?" I asked.

"No, I don't recognize the name."

"He worked in the shipyard across the street and used to eat here every evening. Always hustling overtime, never spending a penny."

"What about him?"

"They found him dead a week ago," I said.

"Is that so? That's too bad." I expected to hear some of his usual philosophizing about life, but all he did was sip his coffee.

"He didn't have a wife or any relatives or even any friends," I added.

"Very sad," said Pete. He seemed to be studying the coffee in his cup. "You see, whether we want it or not, life goes on. Then one day some of us look back, longing for the old days, and feel sorry for not using our days better instead of wasting them by letting some things that now don't seem important interfere. But by then it's too late."

Okay, this is the Pete I know.

"Are you speaking for yourself or George Matzeos?" I asked.

"Like the Book says, 'Those who have ears to hear, let them hear.'" He took a sip of his coffee and remained silent.

"Let me show you my new toy," I said. "I'm selling pizza now."

"That's a smart move."

I ushered him into the kitchen.

"It's almost brand new," I said, pointing to the pizza oven.

We chatted some more; then Pete said he had to go to work and left, promising not to wait two months for another visit.

Mrs. Amalia came into the restaurant soon after Pete left.

"We're going to Greece," she announced before I said anything.

Her face was radiant and younger looking, and she walked with short but steady steps. I pulled out a chair for her, but she said she wouldn't be staying.

"Dimitrakis is waiting for me in the car. I just stopped by to wish you a good summer. Dimitrakis got his professorial diploma, and he is taking me to the island before he starts teaching in the fall. Can't wait to see Skiathos again."

"You'll be the envy of every mother on the island," I said.

She turned and started toward the door, then looked at me again. "Good business and good summer."

I escorted her to the door and wished her a pleasant trip and an enjoyable stay. She paused and leaned toward me.

"I pray to Panagia to find a nice Greek girl for my Dimitrakis while we're there," she said, almost in a whisper.

As the car pulled away, she waved at me with her white handkerchief.

CHAPTER TWENTY-EIGHT

A Letter from Mother

Every day, the last chore at the restaurant was to do the "office work," as I called it. It consisted of adding up all the waitresses' tickets stuck on the spike next to the cash register, then making the money in the drawers match the register tape, after subtracting the opening money and supplies I'd paid for in cash. I sealed the whole mess of tickets and the register tape in an envelope and wrote the day's date on it.

At the end of the month, I put all the envelopes in a bigger envelope and took it to the accountant. It was the same one Mrs. Amalia had used. He had a closet of an office in a Fort Lauderdale business building, stuffed to the ceiling with cardboard boxes and brown envelopes. On the glass door was written *James Pappas and Associates, CPA*. Every time I went there, it was only Mr. Jim hunched over an adding machine behind mountains of paper. I never saw any of the associates. He was charging me a small fortune for writing a few numbers in a book, but I had no choice. At the end of the year, I had to make a report to the tax people, and the accountant was the only one who knew how to do it.

"We will be leaving in five minutes," I called out to Carmen.

"I'm almost ready," she answered from the kitchen. "I'm getting some rice pudding for Grandfather. He will eat nothing else for breakfast now. You got him spoiled."

I smiled. "He has good taste."

I was down to the last chore of my office work—checking the day's mail. As he had every day for the past four months that I'd owned the restaurant, the mailman walked in at two o'clock, and as always, I opened a bottle of Schlitz when I saw him pull into the parking lot. He handed me the mail and I handed him the bottle.

"Bitch of a day," he said, as always, when he set the bottle down after draining it. "A bitch of a day." Wiping the sweat from his forehead with a white towel, he walked out.

I picked up the mail bundle from under the counter and leafed through it without bothering to remove the rubber band. My mail was usually bills and advertisements. I would put the bills in an envelope marked *BILLS* to be paid at the end of the month, and I would throw away the advertising flyers, invitations to free dinners by condominium builders, and the almost permanent congratulatory letters saying I had been nominated for inclusion in the upcoming publication of *Who's Who in American Business* if I only hurried up and sent a check for twenty-five dollars.

I didn't see any bills today and started to throw the whole bundle in the trash can when I noticed the familiar blue-and-white border of a Greek envelope wedged in the folds of a flyer for a pizza oven. It was a letter and a postcard from my mother. The postcard showed the flagstone-covered square of Agios Taxiarhes, with the big marble fountain in the center and the church's bell tower farther away.

On the back she had written birthday wishes. June 2, four days earlier, had been my birthday, and I had forgotten all about it. When I was at home, my mother would make loukoumades, bite-size, delicious honey puffs. She would pour honey and sprinkle cinnamon over them and serve them with my coffee on the morning of my birthday.

I wondered how serving loukoumades for breakfast would go over in this restaurant. I had been getting two dozen donuts every day from Dunkin Donuts. The customers seemed to like them, but they were always asking me for something Greek. Loukoumades could be the Greek version of donuts.

But I would have to buy another fryer just for that. In every city in Greece, pastry shops made good money serving loukoumades for breakfast. They also served homemade butter and honey on hot toast for breakfast. There was good money in that too, but that was another world. Maybe I could do that when I opened a restaurant in Greece. I had been thinking a lot about that idea lately.

Besides the postcard, there were four full pages of the lined "letter paper." In her unique handwriting, with little regard to punctuation and spelling, Mother told me whom the Good Lord had called to him lately, who'd married whom and what dowry the bride's family gave, and who had turned their barn into another guest house.

> *Yesterday, Garoufalia took me aside after church and told me that Nikos Demeritis is giving his oldest daughter Maria the chestnut grove in Profitis Elias and the vineyard in Fakistra for a dowry.*

I grinned when I read that. Old busybody Garoufalia was the village newspaper and the self-appointed matchmaker.

> *She also told me that Mister Adrahtas told her that if the right man came along, he's willing to give the building by the square for a dowry to his daughter Rinio. Remember Rinio? Garoufalia says you would be a perfect match for either one of these girls. She would be glad to make the proxenio for you, she said.*

There were a couple more names of nice girls with respectable dowries and, as always, the letter ended with the same sentence: *When are you coming home? Will I see any grandchildren before I close my eyes?*

I looked again at the postcard. The photograph was taken from an angle that highlighted the fountain with the four bronze lion heads spewing water, and the church at the edge of the square with the outline of the distant mountain behind it. My attention was focused on the Adrahtases' building at the right side of the card—three stories tall, light-blue stucco, and large windows facing the square. On Sundays, Rinio's father would operate a coffeehouse for the social hour after church, and I had been inside it many times. Was it a coincidence, or had my mother purposely picked this card?

Carmen emerged from the kitchen carrying two bags. "I'm ready."

"Me, too." I put the card and the letter in my shirt pocket and walked out with her.

We didn't talk for a while. My mind was in Taxiarhes, pacing the square, looking at Mr. Adrahtas's building from a distance, then walking through the massive wooden door and surveying the interior—the tall ceilings, the alcoves and built-in shelves, and the hand-hewn chestnut beams. The perfect building for a restaurant.

"Julio told me the shipyard signed the contract to build the tanker for Shell Oil," Carmen said after we had driven for some time.

I didn't answer, still lost in my thoughts.

"He said they will be hiring about a hundred more people," Carmen went on.

I just nodded and kept staring ahead. I wondered what Rinio looked like now. She had been a skinny, airheaded, giggly thing when we were at school. I glanced at Carmen, who was looking at a restaurant supply magazine.

"You go blind reading in the dark," I told her.

"There's plenty of light. They have some nice coffee urns in here and we need a new one. The one we have can't keep up at breakfast time."

"And I bet they want some nice dollars for them too," I mused, not really paying attention.

"If the right man came along," the busybody matchmaker had said. In their way of thinking, that meant a man having money or having a job that made money. Eligible bachelors, as they were called, got the best dowries in Greece. It was the rule: the better job the groom had, the bigger the dowry. When I was sailing, I had heard the third and second mates say many times that they would wait to get the captain's license before they got married because it meant double the dowry.

Well, damn it, I too was an eligible bachelor, and not a bad-looking one. I was an established businessman now with a respectable income. When the accountant had finished tallying up all the receipts I took to him, he told me that for the first quarter of business, the Kostas Restaurant had made two thousand dollars profit.

"Not bad for a beginning," he had said.

I told him about the 10 percent I had promised Carmen, and he wrote in bold, red letters a check for two hundred dollars with his check-writing machine. At the bottom, on the blank line with the *For* in front of it, he had written, *Profit Distribution.*

When I handed the check to Carmen and she saw the amount, she had given me a rib-crushing hug and a kiss on the cheek. It seemed a spontaneous and sincere reaction, and it brought me more satisfaction than all the kisses I had gotten up to then.

"We're married half a year and this is the first kiss," I said. "Some funny wife I have."

She started walking away and turned to say, "Here is another one—catch." She blew me an air kiss.

"Maybe next time, if we make more profit, I get a kiss on two cheeks, eh?"

"Maybe," she said, and it had taken all the restraint I could muster to keep from grasping her smiling face in both of my palms and covering it with kisses.

The traffic light turned red and I stopped.

"Whether you want it or not, life goes on," Pete Papas had said. I hadn't quite understood the rest of his philosophizing, but I was certain of one thing: I didn't want to end up like George Matzeos. All the scheming and hustling he'd done, for what? He had died alone, and now it was as if he'd never existed.

The driver of the car behind me blew the horn.

"Your mind is traveling," said Carmen.

"Oh, sorry," I said. I turned toward her. She was a good woman, a very good woman indeed. And she was a beautiful one, even if she never seemed to spend time in front of a mirror. She had a good heart and a good head for business. For a man to live a satisfying life, he needed the kind of partner that would feel the same way he did about things. Someone who would share the load, feel his pain when he was hurting, and rejoice with him when he was rejoicing.

I ground the cigarette out in the ashtray with firm moves. Those who had the balls and were sure of themselves didn't depend on dowries or inheritances to make it in life.

When I wrote the next letter to Mother, I would send her some of the money to start the work on the fountain at the crossroads by her house. That would make my brother green with envy, and maybe it would ease some of her disappointment for the other things I was going to write.

Carmen cut short my thinking. "*Griego*, you passed our street."

"Oh, okay."

I turned around and pulled into our parking spot. Carmen started to get out but I stopped her.

"Wait one minute. Don't go yet." I lit another cigarette and kept staring ahead.

"What's the matter?" she asked.

"Carmen," I said without looking at her, "I've been thinking. We're already married on paper. Why not make it real?"

"What are you saying?"

I turned and faced her. Her left hand was on the armrest dividing the two seats, and I put my hand on top of it.

"Why not be real husband and wife? We can get the Greek priest in Fort Lauderdale to marry us."

She didn't say anything.

"Or we marry here, in Miami. What do you think?"

She moved her hand and seemed to attempt to laugh. "*Griego,* is that a real marriage proposal?"

"Yes, it is."

She turned her head away and started sobbing quietly.

"*Griego,*" she said after a while, "you are too romantic." The tone of her voice was somewhere between sad and sarcastic. I tried to think of something appropriate to say.

"We can be real family. We will be good together." She didn't answer. "Okay then?" I said.

"I will think about it," she said.

"Okay, you think about it. And from now you call me Kosta, okay?"

"I'll think about that too," she said, and this time there was a brief laugh.

She opened the car door and stepped out, then turned and blew me a kiss.

"Good night, *Griego* . . . Kosta."

THE END

ACKNOWLEDGMENTS

In the course of writing the various drafts of this book, I've received important guidance and advice from a multitude of people who, if their names were to be listed, would greatly increase the number of pages. From the bottom of my heart I thank all of them; those who said they hated it, for it prodded me to make it better, and those who loved it, for it encouraged me to keep on writing. (I'm still friends with both sides.)

However, I would like to offer special thanks to Alexandra Christle for her editing help and to Charles Morris for helping me navigate through the computer minefield.

Also heartfelt thanks to the team of Koehler Books for their help, encouragement, and outstanding work.

CPSIA information can be obtained
at www.ICGtesting.com
Printed in the USA
FSHW011722111121
86157FS